The Hoard of Mhorrer

Also by M. F. W. Curran

The Secret War

M. F. W. CURRAN

The Hoard of Mhorrer

Book Two of the Secret War

Macmillan New Writing

First published 2009 by Macmillan New Writing
an imprint of Pan Macmillan Ltd
Pan Macmillan, 20 New Wharf Road, London N1 9RR
Basingstoke and Oxford
Associated companies throughout the world
www.panmacmillan.com

ISBN 978-0-230-70980-5

A CIP catalogue record for this book is available from
the British Library.

Typeset by Intype Libra Ltd
Printed and bound in the UK by
CPI Mackays, Chatham ME5 8TD

For Sarah

CHAPTER ONE

The Hunt

△ I △ Prague, 26 March 1822

The interloper sat calmly amid the smog of pipe and candle smoke that curdled the air of the inn. Dressed in a simple grey jacket with matching breeches, he appeared prematurely aged, his crown of light grey hair and black beard flecked with silver contrasting with a younger face.

Throughout the inn, the clientele of aristocrats in their sumptuous coats, fine shawls and top hats ignored the stranger, wrapped up in their own little worlds of vanity and gossip. And if they did raise their eyes towards him, alighting disdainfully on this gentleman, they may have been curious as to why such a fellow would find himself in this inn of all places.

The clientele here were no different to those the interloper had discovered in other inns, be they in Paris, Madrid or Rome. They still told jokes in a tongue he did not understand, they conducted business with sly expressions and secret bargains disguised in their patter, and there was still the petty gossip (the gossip that was the same in any language).

In such a place, austere appearances were easily forgotten; the gossips soon returned to their conversations, and the vain continued to admire themselves without giving the interloper a second glance. Yet it might have amused them to learn that this innocuous man was an assassin, and that to date his sword had claimed more than thirty lives.

1

His name was Peruzo.

Laughter and tobacco smoke continued to spill from the tables, the bar counter and booths, lifting and swirling to curl about the drinkers and the gossips, as Peruzo sat silently with his back to the main stairs that twisted up to the eaves and the balcony high above. Not once did he look up from the tankard in front of him, nor did his eyes dart elsewhere in the room, even when a second man, dressed in similar fashion to Peruzo, appeared between the locals crowding at the counter.

The second man, however, was quite different in other ways. He carried himself confidently, at ease amongst the patrons of the bar; a few women looked his way appraisingly. His jacket was unbuttoned at the top and a bright white collar stood out. He was clean-shaven and immaculate, and much younger than Peruzo.

The second man strolled over to take a seat opposite him, a tankard in his hand.

'You seem uncomfortable,' he remarked.

'Amongst the decadent, flagrant peoples of this city, I am,' Peruzo told him. 'Are you not?'

'You forget my heritage, Peruzo. I've known such decadence before,' the man opposite remarked casually.

'Yet now you appear so plain,' Peruzo teased. 'In this place, there is no austerity. It almost feels unnatural. Like that harlot in the corner.'

The man looked over Peruzo's shoulder and found a young woman, not much older than twenty years, with a red shawl draped about her shoulders, a gentleman beside her draped over that. Peruzo's companion laughed. 'Every man or woman should have their pleasures, Peruzo. You were always a tyrant to the fairer sex.'

Peruzo grunted. 'If I live twice without meeting a fiend in a dress, then I can count myself a lucky man. Should a woman ever weep in my company again, I would scarce believe her. If she professes love to me . . . Again, *never* would I believe it.'

'*All* women?' the man asked.

Peruzo glanced up at him, his sharp blue eyes gleaming. Realizing that he'd stepped over the mark, he held up a hand. 'My apologies, William . . . I did not mean Adriana . . . She is the fairest of all . . .'

The man called William laughed again, drawing a slender pipe from inside his jacket. 'No apology needed, my friend. You are too cynical to be bested by any woman.'

Peruzo nodded soberly. 'My captain knows me well.'

'I am only surprised that you can abide a man who has so willingly fallen in love,' William said fondly.

'You are my captain. It can be overlooked,' Peruzo replied.

Peruzo had first met William seven years ago. At first he thought little of him, the son of an English aristocrat and an officer of the British army. At the time William had found himself caught up in a war most people were completely ignorant of; a war of infernal damnations and infinite horrors. That such a man should still be alive seven years later, and moreover still fighting this clandestine conflict, was a miracle in itself. But that this man, William Saxon, would be responsible for most of their victories during that time was beyond a miracle in Peruzo's eyes. Captain Saxon had brought the war between Heaven and Hell back to the balance during the last seven years of servitude, and Lieutenant Peruzo would have happily given his life for him.

Then there was the matter of the angels. That the captain was believed to have made allies of Seraphim and Cherubim, and that Archangels themselves had come down to aid him during a time of great peril, was a potent rumour, substantiated by surviving accounts. But Peruzo, who was a pragmatic man, believed only what he saw and experienced. And in that he shared a trait with his captain . . .

William looked at Peruzo with dismay. 'How can you drink *that*?' he said, gesturing with his pipe at Peruzo's tankard.

Peruzo glanced down into the contents that lapped against

the side of the pewter rim; the dark and cloudy liquid smelt like earth and dung. He shrugged. 'I have drunk worse.'

William looked down at his own tankard and pushed it aside, quickly losing his taste for it.

During the time it took for two courtiers to conclude business and a bearded gentleman to tell his lady friend a particularly lewd joke (judging by her shocked expression and his gruff laughter), a man arrived at the door to the inn, pushing it slowly open. He was dressed in a black jacket and breeches that appeared a little worn. His face was drawn and pale, and his eyes darted about the room as he entered, not settling on anyone in particular. He was agitated; his fingers scratching against the short hairs of his beard as he walked over to the bar.

Peruzo saw him at once and his pupils widened.

'He's here?' William said, noting the Italian's tension.

Peruzo nodded.

The nervous gentleman tapped the top of the counter restlessly as he waited for the barman to walk over. Muttering a few words in German, the barman nodded and poured a glass of something bronze-coloured which the nervous man picked up with a trembling hand. He put the glass to his lips, seeming to take for ever to lift it, until he finally sipped and turned around to the rest of the inn.

His eyes met Peruzo's. They were tired, and they were terrified.

The gentleman knocked back the rest of the spirit and gave a curt nod towards the stairs behind Peruzo. He then placed the glass on the counter and walked out of the inn without looking back.

Peruzo bowed his head and locked his hands in front of his tankard of ale. 'My suspicions were correct,' he murmured.

William stared at him silently.

'Those we seek are above us,' Peruzo said just loud enough for William to hear.

'*Those* we seek?' William repeated. 'There's more than one?'

Peruzo nodded. 'Last night he said there could be two.'

'Two. I see. And you trust him?' William asked.

'He is the Law here,' Peruzo imparted. 'Four nights ago he lost one of his militia chasing our quarry to this district. It had killed a twelve-year-old girl and almost slew her mother when they found it. It fled and they followed, but one militiaman was separated from the others . . .'

'And was slain,' William finished, knowing too well what their quarry was capable of.

'How should we deal with them?' Peruzo asked as William disappeared for a moment within a cloud of tobacco smoke.

'I do have a plan,' William said, tapping the side of his head, 'but one that is hastily conceived.'

'A hasty plan is better than no plan at all.'

'How do you think these pleasant folk would react should our quarry find itself pursued down here?' William asked.

'With dismay, Captain,' Peruzo replied. 'What do you think?'

William laughed gently. 'I was terrified the first time I saw a vampyre and yet I was a soldier. These socialites would be scared out of their wits!'

'That will only aid our quarry's cause,' Peruzo lamented.

'Not if we deal with it up there,' William suggested, and emptied his pipe on the table, the contents smoking still. 'If we stop the vampyre at the balcony, it has but one route of escape.'

'The window,' Peruzo suggested.

'The window,' William agreed, and slipped the pipe back in his jacket pocket. 'Cover the stairs and Marresca will do the rest.'

'You are letting Marresca loose?' Peruzo asked incredulously.

William smiled grimly. 'Wouldn't you?'

'He's still very young . . .' Peruzo began.

'Young or not, he's accounted for two vampyres and three daemons in five months,' William pointed out. 'He is the most formidable soldier I have had the pleasure of leading. He is young, yes, and a monk for only six months. But it is a risk worth taking.'

Peruzo gave way, and for a moment wished he had a full tankard of ale. Some courage wrapped in pewter would have warmed the cold feeling in his stomach. Tonight there would be killing. *Much* killing.

William rose, his fingers absently stroking the engraved hilt of the sword hidden under his grey jacket. 'Take the stairs and be ready in case they fly from the balcony,' he said. 'Use your wits, my friend. And do not hesitate.'

'For they will not,' Peruzo added. He got up from his chair and looked up the stairs.

'Good luck, Lieutenant,' William said to him.

'Good hunting, Captain,' Peruzo replied.

△ II △

In the chill of the early spring evening, Jericho and Anthony were tending to the horses in an alley adjacent to the inn. Brother Jericho, a fervent young monk, looked expectantly over his shoulder, noting the assortment of courtiers and local people wandering down the cobbled streets from the carousel of businesses that sat at the foot of the hill. Brother Anthony coughed gently, alerting his companion to a man strolling through a pool of light cast onto the street by the candles burning in the window of the inn.

'Captain,' Brother Jericho greeted.

William acknowledged them silently and blew against his cold hands.

'Have we found our quarry?' Brother Anthony asked.

William eyed them over his cupped hands, noting both monks' eagerness. He pointed silently up to a window on the first floor of the inn high above them. It was lit by a dull glow and there were shadows betraying movement within.

William lifted the hem of his jacket, freeing the hilt of his sword. He put his hand around the cold metal, feeling the

6

smooth leather grip against fingers and palm. 'Be certain that if the creature tries to escape from those windows, it will come down here. You know how sly the vampyre is; you know how dangerous . . . I do not wish a repeat of Vienna, understood?'

The brothers nodded nervously, anxious to give a good account of themselves.

William turned to the shadows. 'Marresca,' he said.

There was movement in the darkness beside them and an athletic figure emerged. His short blond hair and youthful face made him seem too young to be involved in the savagery of their secret war, but the experience in his eyes was that of a man twice his age and with a lifetime of killing. Marresca was, as Engrin Meerwall had once remarked, 'a killing machine . . . A weapon of the Order . . .'

He stepped forward boldly and swept his sword free in the dim light of the alley. 'What are your orders?' Marresca asked, straight to the point as usual.

William gestured to the window. 'I don't want to chance the vampyre escaping from the inn,' he said, and pondered for a short moment, chewing his bottom lip. He regarded the wall of the building, the imperfections in the brickwork, the unfinished beams jutting out sporadically like a house that had been cut in half. 'Can you climb up there?' he asked the young monk.

Marresca's eyes danced up the wall as though mentally climbing it already, deciding where to put each foot and hand. He nodded.

'Do it,' William said, 'and be careful.'

Marresca pulled his scabbard away and tied it across his shoulders. He slipped his sword, just a shortsword but razor-sharp, into the scabbard and began to climb.

'Be ready in case,' William murmured to the brothers.

As they watched Marresca climb, William saw a bright flash from the window above. It looked like a blaze of gunpowder, but after the initial glare, something glowed and crackled within. William stepped back to get a better view. From where he was standing he could not be sure what he was seeing.

Suddenly there was a howl, like a terrible animal bellowing in pain, that shook the outer wall of the inn.

William at once knew the source.

How could I have been so wrong?

'Marresca!' William shouted. 'A daemon!!'

Marresca looked upwards at the same time as the window above him shattered. Shards of glass rained down and for a moment the young monk was obscured by the debris as it tumbled to the street. Behind it plummeted a creature of immense size cloaked in smoke and fire.

William saw the daemon coming and flung himself out of the way, rolling against the ground. Brother Jericho stumbled and lay rigid with fright on the cobbles, sprawled in full sight of the daemon as it landed with a crunch of bone and sizzling flesh, a spray of orange embers dancing on the ground. The creature raised itself upon its distended haunches and stretched above the frozen monk with long arms and giant claws breaching their ends. The daemon stared out from two burning eye-slits torn in its ruptured blackened skull, relentlessly crackling with sparks. As it opened a mouth the length of a carving plate and riddled with several rows of broken and jagged teeth, a terrible smell of sulphur and burning flesh poured forth, causing Brother Jericho to gag. Shaking, he pushed himself up, expecting nothing but death.

And then Brother Anthony swung his double-handed axe into the beast's side.

The daemon howled as it felt the head tear through the armour of fused flesh and bone. It roared down at Anthony and swung its arm as the brother used all his weight to tug the weapon from its hide, unable to pull the axe-head free. As Anthony put both hands on the handle in desperation, the swollen claw of the beast caught him. It hurled the monk from his feet, throwing him several yards away to the cobbled floor.

William flinched at the sound of breaking bones as Brother Anthony landed hard on the road. Cursing, he launched himself at the daemon, raining down a barrage of blows upon the creature. The first and second clanged uselessly off the plating of the daemon's arms, the third tore a wound through the daemon's left wrist, and the next severed it in a flash of fire and ash.

The daemon howled again. Yet instead of turning to attack, it batted William aside and fled, its hulking body pounding down the cobbles, trailing smoke and embers. William swore loudly as he watched the misshapen beast disappear down a nearby street.

'Anthony!' Brother Jericho cried as he stared at the figure lying still in the road.

William faltered. His instincts were to pursue the daemon, but Brother Anthony could still be alive and would require assistance.

Above them, Marresca clung to the wall, having ducked much of the debris. He too had seen the beast flee and was determined to follow it. He pushed off from his position on the wall, and landed directly on the back of a horse tethered below. Before the animal had time to realize what was happening, Marresca had cut the tether and urged it into a gallop, leaving William no chance to utter a word of encouragement or warning as the young monk rode in pursuit of the daemon.

△ III △

The very moment the daemon was let loose, Peruzo reached the second door along the balcony. He stepped back quickly from the cacophony of discordant howls and shrieks. How many times had he heard such sounds, and how many times faced the creatures that uttered them? Usually his instincts were sharp enough to confront anything that came through the door, yet tonight he was not prepared for a daemon. He retreated to the top of the stairs, his heart pounding so hard he felt it resonate inside his skull.

There was a sudden crash, like a wall collapsing within, followed by shattering glass and the fall of masonry. Realizing that at any moment the slavering beast could break through the door towards him, Peruzo raised the sword to shoulder height, oblivious to the fact that all chatter had ceased inside the inn. All attention was now focused on the noises issuing from the room at the top of the stairs.

There followed another sound, of shouting from the street and more falling debris, and Peruzo feared for his captain as he recognized the cries of desperation and battle. The daemon was loose outside, and his comrades, *his friends*, were facing it without him.

Making a swift decision more out of urgency than strategy, Peruzo reached for the second door. Tiny threads of smoke leaked from its edges and around the hinges, while freshly shivered cracks upon the wood groaned and widened. He was within an inch of the handle when the door flew aside suddenly and a white-faced man with bright yellow eyes hurtled out of the room. His hair was shoulder-length and black, seeming to writhe about his neck as he stormed out of the room and almost ran straight into Peruzo. As the man faltered, Peruzo noticed something shimmer in his left hand: a pyramid made of stone that crackled faintly with cyan light.

Instantly Peruzo knew who this stranger was and what he bore in his hand: a vampyre, and holding a Scarimadaen.

The lieutenant stepped back as the creature came to his senses, shoving the pyramid inside his long ebony cloak with one hand as he pulled out a short black sword with the other. The transfer occurred frighteningly fast, yet Peruzo's instincts were just as swift and he lunged at the vampyre with his blade.

The creature bent backwards, the lieutenant's weapon raking nothing but air.

Under another swing of Peruzo's weapon, the vampyre dived to his knees before raking his black sword across Peruzo's leg. He cried out, swiping his shortsword across in blind defiance. The vampyre, not expecting such a wild attack, rose to retreat and Peruzo's sword tore through the creature's throat more by chance than skill. The vampyre staggered as fluorescent bile began to belch from the gash in his neck, his arms flailing wildly in disarray. He lurched against the balcony with a force that bent him over and flung his head back hard enough to tear loose what flesh and skin it was clinging to.

Peruzo watched the head fall into the drinking hall below to the screams of those nearby as bright light consumed the body, the ebony cloak around it smouldering. Aflame, the torso tottered for a moment and then plummeted stiffly over the balcony rail like a fiery statue. It hit the benches below and shattered, exploding ash and embers in every direction.

△ IV △

William knelt by Brother Anthony. He put his hands on the monk's chest and lowered his cheek to his mouth. He felt breathing against the skin.

He lived.

William turned over his body slowly, noticing the damage done to the side of his head. The left cheek looked caved in, utterly shattered, with a large wound by his ear. His left eye was engulfed by a swollen pulp of bloody flesh and tissue, and his right arm twisted out in the wrong direction. William seethed. If these were the injuries he could see, how bad were the injuries he could not?

Brother Jericho stood over them both, shaking. He was terrified and ashamed that he had frozen in front of the daemon.

11

William knew this, but it wasn't the time to counsel the young monk.

'Is he . . .?' Brother Jericho began.

'He lives,' William replied. 'Help me.'

The monk knelt down and they began to lift Brother Anthony slowly and carry him into the shadows. Now William heard screams as crowds of people began to flee the inn.

'Captain!' Jericho alerted as the panicked mob spilled past them.

'Oh lord . . . *Peruzo*,' William gasped distractedly. 'Stay with Anthony!' he ordered Brother Jericho and headed back to the inn.

△ V △

Peruzo slumped on his side, the pain of his wound reverberating through his body with bouts of nausea. He could not tell how deep it was, though he'd suffered enough injuries in his career to know it was not a mortal wound. Despite this, the pain was enough to cause him to lose his grip on his sword, which clattered to the floor and skittered across the balcony boards. Before he could reach out for it, it slipped over the top step and rattled down the stairs.

The second door opened again. Another vampyre appeared.

Peruzo wiped his eyes and his heart pounded at the sight of this more formidable creature. The second vampyre was taller than the first by a couple of feet. His ears were pierced many times with thick golden hoops, his long white face spattered with blood, the crimson drops appearing quite black. His eyes flashed and crackled with light, radiating out from their black pupils to the yellow irises. But it was the hair that Peruzo recognized, hair the colour of flame, streaked with black. It was unmistakable, as it had been when he pursued this same creature through the grounds of the Schönbrunn. Peruzo had no intention of letting the vampyre escape this time, yet the pain in his leg was overwhelming and his sword was lost.

The vampyre looked down at Peruzo, hate causing his eyes to burn brighter. '*You!*' the creature hissed, remembering Peruzo instantly. '*You will pay for Ferdinand's destruction!*' He reached under his cloak and pulled out a broadsword of black, edged with barbs. He raised it to his face, the metal glistening as though wet, and the creature smiled coldly, sharpened teeth emerging from between his white lips.

Peruzo gripped his wounded leg as he scrambled back towards the steps.

'I will enjoy this, as I enjoyed killing your friends in Vienna,' the vampyre teased as he stood over Peruzo, dancing the tip of the broadsword a few inches from the lieutenant's chest.

Peruzo's hand was inside his jacket. 'To hell with you!' he growled and pulled it out. He raised it towards the vampire, who realized too late that it held a firearm. Peruzo pulled the trigger, there was a flash and smoke spurted from the pistol. From within the fire the lead ball burst towards the creature, striking him in the hand and taking off three fingers at the knuckles. The vampyre shrieked and stumbled backward, his black sword falling tip-first into the balcony floor just inches from where Peruzo sat.

The creature cursed in agony, ash spitting from the severed digits. Peruzo took his opportunity and kicked the black sword away so that it clattered over the balcony and through the gap in the hand-rail to the floor below, much to the vampyre's fury. The lieutenant began to reload the pistol.

'I will feed your balls to my dogs! Son of a whore!' the vampyre cursed, cradling his obliterated hand.

'Not before I shoot *your* balls off!' Peruzo spat back as he fumbled with the shot and powder. The vampyre hissed again, considering his chances, before a voice bellowed from below. The vampyre looked down and found a second man pointing up at him with his sword.

'You!' William shouted defiantly. '*You are mine!*'

The vampyre uttered a cry; that he should be bettered by these two fools was unthinkable! Spitting at Peruzo, he leapt onto the balcony rail and then into the air, casting a vast shadow over William below, who lanced out his sword expecting the vampyre to swoop straight at him. But the creature had only one thought: to escape. The remaining barmaid behind the counter screamed, as the vampyre hurtled through the air and straight through the nearest window, shattering it utterly.

William ran to the door to see their enemy escaping up the hill towards the castle, evaporating into the night.

'Captain?'

William turned back and found Peruzo attempting to descend the stairs. He stumbled on one step, the part-loaded pistol falling from his bloody fingers.

'Well, at least you're alive,' William said as he jogged over.

'Just,' Peruzo replied weakly. His face was pale and his leg was drenched in blood up to the groin.

William put his arm under Peruzo's, sheathing his sword as he supported the stumbling monk from the steps.

'There's a daemon . . .' Peruzo groaned.

'Marresca's in pursuit,' William told him.

'And the vampyre . . .? I killed one, but the other fled . . .' Peruzo began.

'I know, I know,' William said as he helped him to cross the room to the door.

The inn was very different to how William had left it minutes before. Stools and tables were turned over; belongings had been left in haste with their drinks: a fancy hat lay next to a glass of red wine, an expensive coat was spread across the floor, a red shawl underneath that. There was even a purse discarded on one table which was now covered by a thin layer of ash.

'Captain,' Peruzo managed and nodded over to a pile of charcoal and clothes. 'There . . .'

'The vampyre?' William ventured.

'Inside the cloak,' Peruzo continued, pointing to the ash-smeared garment, 'is the Scarimadaen.'

William's eyes widened. He sat Peruzo down on a nearby bench and scrambled over to the black rubble, the smell of sulphur and rot intensifying. With a mixture of elation and disgust, he rummaged through the remains of the vampyre and pulled out the cloak. The Scarimadaen toppled out and rolled along the wooden boards of the floor. William held his breath, and with the ebony cloak in his hand, he swooped down and plucked the pyramid from the ground, careful not to touch it with his naked flesh.

Returning to Peruzo, he put his arm under the lieutenant's again and pulled him to his feet.

'Can you walk?'

'I think so . . .' Peruzo groaned.

William half-carried the lieutenant into the night air, feeling the Scarimadaen throb faintly in his covered hand.

Outside it was strangely quiet. The locals had long since fled, and only Brothers Jericho and Anthony were in the street, the horses standing nearby.

William beckoned Brother Jericho over to take Peruzo's weight. 'Look after them both,' he began. 'Peruzo is hurt, so dress the wound.'

Brother Jericho nodded.

William pulled off his jacket. 'I am not going to let that bastard creature escape a second time. The hunt is not over.'

At that very moment from the shadows at the far end of the street streamed a dozen men-at-arms, soldiers and deputies. They surrounded William and his companions, their muskets and pistols levelled at the men in grey. William stared back with incredulity, considering whether to fight their way out.

'Wait!' Peruzo shouted and waved his bloodied hand at William. 'Captain, those are the sheriff's men! They'll shoot us for sure!'

William met Peruzo's deploring eyes and understood: the hunt was over.

Air billowed through Marresca's hair, lashing it into his face as he galloped down the lane. The horse was one of their finest, yet it struggled to keep up with the monk's demands. Marresca pushed the beast harder and harder as the daemon appeared at the top of one street before fleeing down the next.

As Marresca galloped after it, almost trampling a local in his haste, he pulled his mount about and directed it down a side alley. It was a risk, but Marresca believed it a shortcut to his quarry, a quarry that was fleeing towards the river. Marresca had to intercept the creature before it reached the bridge and whatever haven might lie there.

Above the sound of pounding hoofs, Marresca heard screams as he galloped out of the lane and into the street beyond. It was a marketplace by day, and there were still traders present packing away their wares as Marresca charged out, crashing through an empty stall. The monk paid no heed to the cries of anger from the stall's owner as he saw the daemon's smouldering outline lumbering away from a group of traumatized locals who had been unlucky to stray into its path. Two were slain, the others were cowering, screaming and sobbing in its wake.

The daemon clattered into a wheelbarrow full of pots, and it turned over, shattering the earthenware against the ground. It paused only to hear the horse galloping towards it before it ran on, gracelessly charging down another street on its swollen legs with a sound like hollow tree-trunks pounding on stone.

Marresca could smell the sulphur on the daemon's breath, the smoke of its smouldering skin and burning flesh. Driving his horse on, he drew the sword from his back and stood up in the saddle. The daemon seemed to mock Marresca's pursuit with a high-pitched whine, before diving into a nearby building, an elegant hall fronted with two oak doors that shattered when it crashed through. Marresca didn't falter but followed inside, carried by his mount through the ruined entrance.

The hall beyond might have held a peaceful function moments before, but it now lay in chaos. Food and wine were splashed to the four winds, and several diners were torn apart by the monster's elongated claw as it panicked and struck down those who blocked its path.

Amongst the wreckage and hysterical guests, Marresca called out to it, catching the daemon's attention again. It glowered at Marresca venomously, as though aware who this young monk was. It stepped back and howled despairingly towards him, waving its claw and severed arm with anger. It then lurched about and leapt on a table at the head of the hall, which instantly split in two. Unbalanced, the daemon slipped to the floor with a stone-shaking thud, before rising again. Over the detritus and debris, it swayed and collided ungainly into a free-standing candelabrum which toppled over against the nearest tapestry. The age-old material was ablaze in moments, and soon the next caught fire, and the next.

Marresca refused his terrified horse the opportunity to retreat, even as the flames began shooting up the walls, igniting the beams above them. In the centre of the fire the daemon was blind, desperate to find an escape. A veil of flame fell between it and Marresca, and behind the glare and the haze of intense heat, the monk watched as the beast pounded its way along the wall, flames beginning to cascade upon its howling form. It was heading for the largest stained-glass window at the far end of the room.

Marresca spurred his horse on and charged back to the shattered entrance. Behind him, the fragile timber roof collapsed, the sound of its destruction muffling the daemon's escape as it burst through the ornate window.

As Marresca closed the distance between them, he held on to the reins with one hand, drawing his sword again with the other. He balanced effortlessly as the horse swung from side to side, cornering buildings within inches of walls, Marresca ducking swinging shop-signs that the daemon had clattered into.

Ahead loomed the river, a black void gushing between the

two halves of the city. Against the night sky stood the giant gateway to Charles Bridge, oil lamps lit on either side. Marresca was not far behind the daemon and he urged his exhausted mount to greater efforts. The daemon did not falter as it hauled its burning body under the arch, its outline streaking in and out of the lamps across the bridge. Marresca held his sword out to his left, waiting to swing the arc that would take the monster's head. His cold eyes looked to the daemon's neck, already rehearsing how he would wield the blade and at what point it would enter the monster's body.

In his mind, Marresca had already killed the daemon.

The monster's bulging feet broke flagstones as it clunked towards the middle of the bridge, sometimes lurching to the side, disorientated and bewildered, knocking lamps into the river below or tearing off the face of one of the bridge-statues as it stumbled on.

Hearing the horse gallop closer, the daemon halted abruptly and turned about. Marresca had not expected the sudden stop; he pulled back on his horse's reins as the daemon turned and hurled a section of a statue in his direction. The chunk came within inches of crushing Marresca's left foot in the saddle.

When Marresca recovered, pulling the horse about as it reared, the daemon had run on, clearing the bridge before heading into the heart of the city.

△ VII △

By now Marresca's charger was near to collapse, and even Marresca was beginning to tire. Ahead, the daemon lumbered into the main town square. It juddered across the great open space in front of the Tyn church while the Orloj was in mid-chime. The astronomical clock's rings were lost on his prey as it charged towards the enormous Gothic basilica and the clergy who were filing out of it.

Marresca burst forth from the side street and hurtled after

the daemon's shadow as it thudded across the flagstones. The daemon was nearly upon the clergy, who panicked and ran for their lives, dividing in two like the Red Sea as the monster broke through them and into the church. One priest was caught up in front and ran before it. He fled down the aisle, praying in spluttered sobs. The smoking daemon lurched after him, knocking pews aside with its apelike arms.

The priest reached the altar and sought sanctuary, terrified and muttering prayers. 'Demons in the streets! Demons in the streets!' he cried.

The creature halted, its burning eyes glowing with hatred. It would have been the end of the priest, as it had been for many others that night, but Marresca did not pause as he charged into the church. The priest barely registered the sound of hoof beats echoing high into the roof, and never saw Marresca ride down the daemon. The monster looked up too late, just in time to see Marresca swing his sword down upon it. The shortsword, made by the finest smith in Italy, sliced through the brittle black bone of the daemon's neck plate and into the rotting tissue beneath. The steel carried on unhindered, and the daemon's head was ripped like a cork from a bottle, an eruption of ash and bright blue light spewing out from the wound.

The decapitated body fell sideways against the ranks of wooden pews, sapphire flame consuming it completely as tremors filled the church. The body was soon engulfed by mote-clouds and racked by hideous shrieks that rose in waves of voices. A hundred. A thousand. A cacophonous wave of sound that drove the gibbering priest into a foetal position.

When the worst of the inferno had abated, the radiance from the decapitated body imploded, drawing all its brilliance into a tremendous sphere of light, before it hurtled out of the church, bursting through one of the great windows. Marresca was buffeted by the blast and was almost torn from his horse, hanging on to the bridle as the animal reared up and staggered. The priest felt the ungodly power gust through his hair and he prayed for deliverance in a voice that could not be heard above the shrieking expulsion of the daemon's spirit . . .

. . . And then it was over.

The sobbing priest peered up between his fingers at the blond-haired warrior astride the horse in the aisle.

'*Who are you?*' he pleaded.

The young man did not answer but stared at the smouldering carcass prostrate across a row of shattered pews. Beneath the smoke the raw tinge of skin could already be made out as the host's decapitated body returned to its original form, less a head which was lying elsewhere, having rolled under the wreckage of the aisle.

The priest gathered his composure and got to his feet, leaning against the altar to face this mute saviour. He tried again, this time in Latin.

'Who *are* you, my son?' he asked.

The young man cast his eyes down at him. 'I am Marresca,' he replied.

'Marresca? A saint, an emissary . . . An angel?' the priest asked.

Marresca smiled. 'None of those. But pray for me, Father, and I will become one,' he replied as he pulled his horse about to trot wearily out of the church, leaving behind the fading smell of sulphur.

△ VIII △

'Peruzo, tell them we are not hostile,' William said as he placed his sword slowly on the ground and raised his hands. The point of one musket was a little too close for comfort, and the owner was young and nervous. Accidents often occurred with the young and nervous, so William backed away carefully.

Brother Jericho had dropped his weapon also. At his feet, Peruzo seemed to slip in and out of consciousness, while Brother Anthony was deathly silent.

One of the uniformed men began shouting at them, which rattled the nervous young musketeer even further.

'What is he saying?' Brother Jericho implored, but Peruzo, one of the few who understood German, did not answer. He had blacked out.

William felt the urge to protect the Scarimadaen, throbbing inside his jacket pocket. City militias were officious, but they were also superstitious. With the daemon released, the pyramid could not possess a second soul, but it was also far from harmless. When there was any sign of devilry or vampyres, witches were always to blame. Often it was William and the men he led who were accused of being in league with the witches themselves, and the Scarimadaen was truly a sign of 'witchcraft'.

The militia grew aggressive, and William was faintly aware that his pocket was beginning to glow. He looked down, eyes wide, just as the accusations started. 'Witch!'

'We are not witches!' William shouted back. He gestured at himself and the other monks, shaking his head furiously. 'We are from Rome. The Vatican. *Pope Pius!*'

The well-dressed leader glowered at William and began shouting again. He then pointed down to the ground, and William followed the tip of the sword to where the daemon had lost its claw. On the floor was the severed hand of some unfortunate, its bones ripped from the flesh and terribly askew. The manifestation had reverted to human form, which could only mean that Marresca had succeeded.

Yet this did not help their cause, as the militia looked up murderously at William and his men.

He was about to protest their innocence when there was a sudden and terrible scream and a streaking flash of light tore down the street towards them. It was the daemon's spirit, hurtling back to the one thing that had released it: the Scarimadaen. It brought shock-waves that shattered the windows of the buildings a few yards away, and William watched in horror as the blue light dived straight for him, dragging with it an inhuman chorus of cries and shrieks that were quite deafening.

21

The light hit William head-on, tearing through the ebony cloak in his hand and causing it to burst into flames, while the force of the energy jolted him off his feet and flung him back against the wall of the inn.

William was surrounded by a blinding flash, a pall of smoke, accompanied by searing pain . . . and then he too lost consciousness.

CHAPTER TWO

Consequences

△ I △

William put a hand to his head and groaned. His skull was throbbing and beneath his hair, matted with coagulated blood, he touched a large lump where he'd struck the wall of the inn.

At least the sounds of shrieking had ceased.

He felt cold; a gnawing cold that chewed through the skin and into his bones. A perpetual dripping ran down the wall from a window high above in one corner of the room. It had been dripping for years judging by the long lime trails down the crusted stone, and there were marks where previous guests had been forced to lick the moisture from the wall.

Even in his drowsy state William had an idea of where he was. The conditions and the gentle cascading of water in the corner were enough to tell him his liberty had been removed. There was nothing to eat or drink, just a wall of bars separating him from freedom.

'Are you awake?' came a voice from the gloom.

William made to answer, but his throat was too dry. He coughed harshly, drawing moisture to his parched throat. He looked about and found his cell was occupied by another, hunkered silently in the shadows. But it was not that figure who had stirred.

'Captain, is that you?' asked a shadow from the adjacent cell.

'Jericho?' William croaked, finding his voice.

'I'm here,' Jericho replied, and some fingers appeared at the other end of the cell, through the wall of bars that separated each cell from the next.

William crawled over and took Jericho's hands, his skin cold.

'I was worried, Captain,' Jericho said.

'I'm fine,' William replied, and looked in the direction of the second prisoner, still all but hidden. He wanted to ask who his cellmate was, but coughing nearby reminded William of another. 'Peruzo? Are you in there, my friend?'

'Good morning . . . Or evening . . .' Peruzo said near Jericho. He tapped the metal bars with his fingers to show his whereabouts and then sighed painfully.

William felt his way across the bars until he reached the source of the harsh breathing. 'How's the leg?' he asked.

'It's stopped bleeding,' Peruzo murmured weakly.

'We can be thankful for that at least. What happened back there?' William said as he rubbed his sore head.

'The daemon's spirit returned to the Scarimadaen,' Peruzo told him. 'It knocked you out.'

'They think we're witches,' Jericho said.

'Where would they get that idea?' William laughed bitterly. It was a hollow, echoing sound in their dank cells. 'At least we know Marresca destroyed the daemon's host, right?' he added and then frowned. 'Where *is* Marresca, by the way?'

'Here,' said William's cellmate from the shadows.

William turned about. 'Come into the light,' he ordered.

Marresca shuffled into the centre of the cell where some of the torchlight managed to filter in.

'Are you harmed?' Marresca shook his head. 'That is something at least,' William sighed. He blew out his cheeks and looked to the ceiling. 'Where is Anthony?'

'They took him,' Jericho groaned.

'Where?' William insisted.

'I saw him, Captain,' Peruzo murmured. 'When they attended to me, they looked at Brother Anthony. He wasn't well.'

William put his head in his hands. 'Is he dead?' he murmured.

24

'None of us knows,' Peruzo replied.

'Does anyone have an idea where we might be?' William asked despairingly after a few minutes of silence.

Jericho told William of their passage to the cells. On arrival it had been night and their journey into the dark heart of the gaol was long, down several flights of stairs, each colder and darker than the last, until they arrived in a place that rattled with a subterranean sound. Jericho finished the account with the arrival of Marresca, how the lieutenant had been arrested trying to cross back over Charles Bridge but was surrounded by militia and then thrown into gaol.

As William listened he concluded they were surely somewhere underground, and that window high above them was more likely a portal to the outside world up there, rather than an inaccessible view of the grounds of their prison. Peruzo added that if they were to escape, a bloody struggle with the militia would ensue. And that was no easy task if there was a garrison above them (which was likely). It would mean fighting innocents, and in a desperate breakout slaying them would be inescapable, an inexcusable crime in the Order.

What made matters worse was their fate if they *didn't* escape. They would be burnt alive, as all witches were, as soon as the sheriff saw fit. And if not burnt, then hanged as murderers.

'What did they do with the Scarimadaen?' William asked.

'Who knows?' Peruzo murmured.

'Will they use it?' Jericho whispered.

'If they do, then we don't have to worry about escaping,' William replied. 'If a daemon is summoned, the militia and every prisoner in this gaol are as good as dead.'

∆ II ∆

William spent an almost indefinable time in their cell thinking about their choices, the lack of natural light making the passing

25

of time incalculable. It could have been day or night for all he knew.

He had not slept since regaining consciousness, though through the bars in the adjacent chamber he could see that Brother Jericho had fallen into a restless sleep, while Peruzo was sleeping out of exhaustion. To their gaolers' credit, Peruzo's shallow wound had been attended to, though hastily, so that already the dressing was coming away and a rusty stain was visible on the bandage. William's first lieutenant needed attention. He was certain that he could save Peruzo's leg with the proper ointments, but he had seen lesser wounds than that turn gangrenous, simple wounds that had not been cleaned after a day's battle and left to fester in the rain and cold. Those legs were taken by the surgeon soon after.

William's other lieutenant, Marresca, was resting, though it was difficult to discern whether the young monk was asleep or just sitting with his eyes closed. Even though Marresca added little to the debate of their escape or fate, it was comforting to know that the lieutenant was fit and ready in case they did try something.

Brother Anthony was another matter. A hollow feeling deep inside William doubted that the brother's treatment would be any better than their own. In his heart, William already knew the monk was dead, but he couldn't accept that quite yet, not until his body proved it.

William heard Marresca stir. He looked up and found the young lieutenant staring back at him, his eyes gleaming from the dark.

'Can you not sleep?' William said.

'Can you?' Marresca replied coldly.

'I've been thinking of a way out of here,' William replied.

'You have a plan?'

'Not as yet,' he admitted, and sighed.

During past missions to Spain, to France and the snowy mountains of the North, there had been at least some hope that allies would aid them, once caught in similar situations. This was not the first time William had spent a night or three in gaol. But it was the first time there was no one to come to their rescue. Even in a crowded city, they were very much alone.

In the adjacent cell, Peruzo woke and tapped on the bars with his hand.

'Still there, old friend?' William asked.

'*Still*, Captain,' Peruzo breathed in the shadows and William sensed a wry smile as he said it.

'You should all be sleeping,' William insisted.

'There is plenty of time to sleep after our visit to the gallows, Captain,' Marresca answered bluntly.

William glared at Marresca and shook his head. 'I swear to you all, we are not finished yet,' he announced. 'We will not be hanged, and we will not rot in this prison.'

'We know, Captain,' Brother Jericho said confidently. 'You will save us.'

William hesitated, surprised that his bravado should encourage his men so quickly. 'Get some sleep. All of you,' he said eventually. He had yet to formulate a flawless plan, but at least he had the backing of his men.

Peruzo groaned again and William hunkered down next to the bars to look at the wound. 'You're in a bad way, my friend,' he said, looking at the stained bandage.

'I'll live if we can escape this place,' Peruzo replied.

William smiled and looked past him to Jericho's outline against the far wall.

'What was that about?' he whispered to Peruzo.

'What, Captain?'

'What Jericho said about me saving us,' William said, secretly pleased that the young monk had such belief in his abilities.

'Don't be too hard on his trust,' Peruzo joked, uttering a gentle chuckle that soon turned to a harsh coughing. 'He is just naïve. And . . .'

'And?'

'Well there are rumours, Captain.'

'Rumours about what?'

'About your friends. Your allies.'

William looked bewildered.

'The angels, Captain,' Peruzo said as quietly as possible.

William was staggered. 'What are you talking about, Peruzo?'

'All the brothers in the Order think it, Captain,' he explained. 'They believe angels watch over you, *and* the men under your command. They've listened to the rumours about what happened in Aosta. That angels came to your aid. That they've aided you other times as well.'

'*Other times?*' William gasped. He shook his head. 'This is one story that has been embellished, Peruzo. There have been *no* other times.'

'Then it is true. Angels did aid you?' he asked.

William fell silent. He was aware that Marresca and possibly Jericho were listening. He pressed his face against the cold bars of the cell.

'Just the once. In Aosta,' he whispered. 'But that was years ago, and they haven't come since.' He tried to hide the dismay in his voice.

'But what of your friend, Lieutenant Harte? Wasn't he taken by angels?' Peruzo whispered.

'He was,' William said distantly. 'But that was a long time ago. I haven't seen him or those angels for almost seven years.'

Peruzo sighed.

'Lieutenant,' William began, 'everything we have achieved, *every* victory has been our own. We have never needed the help of angels.'

'Not even now?' Peruzo asked.

William chewed his bottom lip. He put his hand through the bars and clasped Peruzo's shoulder gently. 'No. Not even now.' He got to his feet.

'It is time for us to leave, gentlemen.'

'You have a plan?' Jericho asked hopefully.

William put his hands inside his shirt and pulled out a chain that was always hung about his neck. On the end of the chain was a silver medallion, with several words in Latin engraved on one side, and on the other an image of Pope Pius. He displayed it for them all to see.

'The Papal seal,' Peruzo whispered.

Jericho grew suddenly hopeful.

'We cannot bring the Papacy into our troubles . . .' Peruzo said.

William frowned. 'Why not? It is not often we ask the Church for help, yet we have done much for her over the years. The Papacy *owes* us,' he whispered, and slipped the pendant back inside his shirt.

'Of that I have no doubt, sir,' Peruzo replied, 'but we are bound by our orders to be as anonymous as possible . . .'

'Our anonymity was gone the moment the vampyres released a daemon in this city,' William replied curtly, addressing them all. 'Anonymity is meaningless once war is being waged in the streets. The Count's men grow more daring. Our victories have driven him into the open, and that is where we fight. I am tired of serving under cloak and dagger. We are not secret agents. We are soldiers, aren't we?'

No one replied, but Peruzo gave a low and painful moan. It was enough for William to reach out for his lieutenant again.

'My leg hurts, that is all,' he groaned.

'Blast it, Peruzo! I will not rest here under anonymity while my first lieutenant sits wounded in a cell! While a brother lies somewhere in this prison dying from his wounds! Damn the Church! I will use everything we can to get us out of here!'

'I know, Captain, I know,' Peruzo murmured dutifully. 'But what would Cardinal Devirus say?'

William touched the silver disc around his neck, fingering it as he considered the effect of its use. Even if their captors should listen, to invoke the Papal authorities would almost certainly be the end of their service in the Order of Saint Sallian, and perhaps the end of that clandestine brotherhood altogether. The Order only existed covertly. The Church would have it no other way.

Burdened by this charge and the need to escape, William felt tired and leant heavily against the bars. In the adjacent cell, Jericho crawled over to sit next to Peruzo, checking on the lieutenant's leg in what little light there was.

'I think the wound has opened again, Captain,' he said after a careful examination.

'We've waited enough.' William pushed himself away from the bars of the cell. 'I'm using what aid we have left. Let us see these men cower in the face of the Church. Guards! Guards!'

At first there was nothing, not a single reply, as though they were the only prisoners in this dank level of the gaol. William called again. Still there was nothing.

'Have they abandoned us down here?' Jericho asked.

William stood silently, staring up to the hole in the ceiling. What would it take for their hosts to answer him? Could they risk trying to climb out?

The sound of footsteps rang down a flight of stairs nearby. *Many* footsteps. The Papal seal he wore seemed precarious now. William began to doubt they would listen. Would they believe him? After all, how many Papal delegates run around decapitating the local citizens?

'Marresca . . .' William said under his breath, hearing them come. 'Be ready.'

'What about the Papal seal?' Peruzo whispered.

'I've decided not to use it,' William said desperately.

'We're fighting our way out?' Jericho said, his voice shaking.

'If we have to,' William replied. 'Ready, Marresca?'

'Ready,' the young monk replied quietly.

'*Only* on my signal,' William urged him, 'not before. And try not to kill anyone.' He knew Marresca's skills. The blond monk could break a man's neck with his bare hands and could disarm several men before any drew breath. Marresca would be their one chance of escaping, if it came down to it.

From the direction of the footsteps appeared a light, a gentle glow that grew and grew. When it emerged from the flight of stairs at the far side of the cells, it was joined by voices, some low, some excited.

William stepped back from the bars and joined Marresca in the shadows as men approached.

'Can you stand, Peruzo?' William whispered.

Peruzo pulled himself up from the floor with a series of groans. 'Barely . . .' he said.

The voices were now at the cells, led by one gaoler holding a brand that lit up both chambers, stinging William's eyes with its bright fiery glare.

There came a flurry of excited words again, as if an argument had begun between two of their hosts.

'What are they saying?' William asked.

Peruzo listened but did not reply. The men were not only speaking in German, but another language the lieutenant did not understand.

With a series of muddied movements, one of the gaolers unlocked Peruzo and Jericho's cell.

'*Stand by me, Marresca,*' William murmured and heard the young lieutenant step forward shoulder to shoulder. 'Peruzo, what are they saying?'

'They're apologizing I think,' he said gleefully.

'They're *what?*'

One of the men came into the cells, a man William found familiar. It was the same man they had seen in the tavern. The contact who had gestured to the stairs at the inn; the lawman. He began shouting at the gaolers, one scurrying away while the other stood dumbstruck in the doorway, the torchlight flickering shadows about them.

'He apologizes for our treatment, Captain,' Peruzo translated. 'If he'd known earlier, he would have ordered our release.'

'Well, a late apology is better than none at all,' Jericho said gladly.

With a click and banging of chains on metal, William's cell was opened and they were led out by a wary gaoler who kept his distance from him. Peruzo, supported by Jericho, was already in the corridor with the sorry-looking official who kept apologizing before abusing the gaolers some more.

'Peruzo, tell them I demand to see Brother Anthony,' William said wearily. But he knew in his gut that the brother's fate would be worse than theirs.

△ III △

The outside air was pungent with the odour of smoke and drizzle, the musty smell that marked so many cities across the Continent. For William, it brought memories of London when he was just a boy, when tall chimneys of factories had only just started growing from the city's skyline, gushing great clouds of rolling grey across the sky.

The faint drizzle dampened their clothes, their hair and their skin; an insidious downpour they could see but barely feel until water dripped over their brows and down their cheeks. When they eventually crossed the river, the drizzle had ceased and all that lingered was a sweet spring aroma mixed with the industrial tang of burning wood and coal.

William's mood had barely lightened since their release from prison. At his request, they had been led to Brother Anthony, finding the monk half naked and cold on a butcher's slab in the gaol mortuary, his eyes staring out blankly into whatever realm his soul had been sent to. He had evidently been neglected.

William was furious and he delivered his demands abruptly and without negotiation: the gaolers were to wrap Brother Anthony's body in a shroud and return the Scarimadaen to them immediately. A cart would be provided at the sheriff's expense to take Brother Anthony away, returning also their weapons and their horses.

On their part, the gaolers wanted William and his men out of the gaol as soon as possible. They were still convinced these strangers were warlocks or sorcerers of some kind, and their presence was unsettling. The official who had served as Peruzo's contact and now as their liberator ensured that all demands were met, in repayment for the retribution William and his men had dealt out on those responsible for killing one of his militia. As long as they promised to leave Prague immediately, all parties would be satisfied.

Within an hour, everything was prepared and William led them away to their only safe haven in the city.

The chapel in Stare Mesto was older than much of Prague, and smaller than most of the buildings surrounding it, so small that it was barely noticeable, with only its ivy-covered façade to show that it existed at all. But its parishioners knew it, as did the four figures now arriving at its doors, appearing like outcasts or beggars in their dishevelled state, each man's clothes either grubby or torn. But it was the cart on the road with the bound body laid upon it that people marked as they strolled past on that Sunday afternoon. Curiosity was pricked to wonder who lay within the white linen, some loitering to gossip in that strange mix of German and something else.

William might have spoken, but he was too exhausted and could only rap his knuckles on the thick wood of the chapel door several times impatiently. When he met with no reply, each rap grew more frustrated and insistent. He wanted to get inside, out of the melancholy cold, to put his fallen man in the shelter of the chapel.

Eventually the door was pushed ajar.

'Father Gessille?' William barked.

The door opened wider. 'Captain,' the man greeted. 'You have come back so late . . . What has happened?'

William pushed past him. He was beyond courtesy; the city's charm had worn as thin as his patience. Father Gessille looked to the other three men: Peruzo hobbling inside supported by Jericho, Marresca following after, calm as ever. Then the Father's eyes fell on the cart.

'Who is that?' he asked.

'Brother Anthony,' William replied, cupping his hands in the font. He lifted them to his lips and drank. It was an ungodly thing to do, but he was thirsty and he thought God owed him.

Shaking the drops from his hands, he marched back to the Father's side. 'I need help carrying him.'

'Of course,' Father Gessille replied.

They walked out through the slowly growing crowd of folk around the cart and Father Gessille climbed into the back and began to drag the linen-wrapped body across the boards to where William stood at the rear. William took hold of the ankles and pulled Brother Anthony along, before letting the weight of the body fall on his arms and shoulders.

The Father climbed out of the cart and took part of the weight as they stumbled back to the chapel, the shrouded body carried between them.

When they entered, Brother Jericho closed the door firmly behind them and William lowered the body onto a bank of pews, breathing hard and heavy as the burden was lifted.

'May I see?' Father Gessille asked.

'Please,' William offered, 'after all, you will be reading his prayers at the burial.'

'Burial?' Father Gessille looked up. '*Here?*'

'We should take him back home, Captain,' Jericho said, 'to be buried at Villeda.'

'There's no time,' Lieutenant Peruzo said behind them. He sat drooping and exhausted on some benches a couple of rows in front of Brother Anthony's body. 'The body will rot before we can return.'

Jericho frowned and looked back at his captain, who agreed. 'He will be buried here, Jericho. With all the dignity we can muster.'

'When do you wish this?' Father Gessille asked as he began to unravel the shroud.

'Tonight. We leave at first light in the morning,' William said, stretching wearily. Head bowed, he trudged down the rank of pews and out of a side entrance to where they were lodged.

William ate his broth in silence. He could not sleep while the others dozed, and Peruzo snored like a drunkard or an old man. Peruzo was ageing, and the wound had brought his frailties to the fore. William trusted his experience and his skill with a sword, but there were only a few more years left in Peruzo. The War had taken its toll on him, as it had on them all.

William finished the broth and took a mouthful of wine. It was thick and oily, but slid down his throat, taking the tang of the broth with it. The food was as bad as the drink, but he had barely eaten in two days and was famished. Throughout the repast, he watched Father Gessille as he redressed Peruzo's wound and made arrangements for Brother Anthony's burial.

Finally, as the sun was setting, the priest came up to William. Father Gessille looked down at him hesitantly.

'Something troubling you, Father?'

'I examined Brother Anthony's wounds. There was a mark upon his body. A burn mark. Did the militia do that to him?'

'No,' William replied abruptly, not wishing to engage in conversation about Anthony's death.

'Then what?'

'Do you really wish to know, Father? Many men who have succumbed to curiosity about our ways have wished they hadn't.'

'Had these same men seen similar violations?'

'Some had seen worse.'

Father Gessille looked appalled. He shook his head in despair and took several steps away, as though William was a danger. A threat to the flesh and the soul. 'I would have said such marks came from torture or . . .'

'. . . Or they were diabolical?'

Father Gessille stared at William and nodded slowly, understanding him better. 'Then it is true. You *are* the ones they speak about. The hunters of the Infernal.'

William nodded, satisfied that word of their heroics had reached even this corner of the Continent. 'We are they.'

'And your prey was diabolical?'

'It was. We tracked it down to a tavern just over the river.'

Gessille looked over his shoulder to the shrouded corpse with an expression of sorrow. 'Was your discovery worth his death?' the priest asked.

'Just Brother Anthony's?' William considered this for a moment. 'Had it cost just one life for every Scarimadaen, we would have finished this War years ago. I lost eight men in Vienna, Father. *Eight*. Even before we came here.'

'Then I hope your mission has been a success,' Father Gessille said, bewildered as he walked away, 'for there is no drive to compel me to sacrifice so many.'

William got to his feet, staring at Father Gessille with rebuke. 'Are you questioning my motives, Father?' he called after him, stopping the priest in mid-step.

'No,' Father Gessille called back, the word echoing in the confines of the chapel. 'But think, my son. Should a man who professes to serve the Church be so ready to make such desperate sacrifices? Does such a man truly understand his own reasons to serve?'

'This is a war, Father. I am a soldier. My reasons are *only* to serve, and are grounded in honour.'

'There is no honour in war, my son. None at all.'

William wanted to protest, but his readiness to argue had waned. 'An exile has little choice, Father,' he said finally as he pulled a pipe from his jacket and began packing it with tobacco. He reached to take a light from a nearby candle, putting it to the weed in his pipe.

The pipe had been a gift from a man he often thought of on cold nights such as these, a lieutenant of the Order who had been killed during William's first mission several years ago. That man – his name was Cazotte – had started out as William's antagonist, but they had ended their time together as friends. A friendship that was cut short by a bloody battle.

William pulled the chapel door ajar and slipped outside. Wrapping his jacket about him, he stood on the top step in the shadows of the ivy and listened to the quiet of the night as he smoked the pipe.

Lieutenant Cazotte had survived many of the rigours of William's first mission, escaping death a number of times, saving William's life on more than one occasion, before the final battle in the mountains of Aosta. William had not seen the lieutenant fall, but heard from first-hand accounts that it had been a 'good death' – if there was such a thing. A hero's death.

But heroic deaths seemed not to matter when there was no one to talk to, or share a joke with on cold nights while you stood in the dark and smoked pipe-weed.

Above him the sky was clear, with a crescent moon high above and many stars. There were no clouds, yet there came a rumble in the air, like thunder. Perhaps it was a cannonade being practised far away on a drill field. Maybe it was a storm, lying too far from sight but loud enough to hear.

A gentle breeze suddenly caressed his skin. It quickly grew stronger, lifting William's unruly hair. At the other end of the street he saw several men and women fleeing towards the church. One woman was in tears, while another simply turned in horror and pointed skyward, mouthing something that could have been a prayer. William followed her wavering hand and saw the sky suddenly swamped by oily clouds that rolled in fast to smother stars and moon.

Squinting against the gale that now swept by him, he put a hand over his brow and watched as lightning crackled violently across the burgeoning underbellies of the clouds. There was a blinding flash, and for a heartbeat a streak of light seared William's sight, as it crashed down behind a row of houses in the distance. A second strike hit the same spot and William was dumbstruck. Dumbstruck that the night could be so quickly overturned, so changed by a storm that had appeared in moments . . .

But more astounded by the memory the pyrotechnics had

awoken in him. A memory of seven years ago when lightning struck the frigate *Iberian*, which was under attack from their enemies. That strike of lightning had saved their skins that night. A night of vampyres.

A night of angels.

'Can it be . . . ?' William murmured to himself. He grew eager, half stumbling down the steps in his haste.

The battle on the *Iberian* was the first time he had seen an angel ride the lightning. The last time was when his closest friend, a brother in every respect save blood, was taken by them. That he hadn't seen Kieran Harte in so many years was reason enough to be overjoyed; that he should bring these holy terrors with him – the Dar'uka – was a greater reason to temper that enthusiasm with trepidation.

William felt his mouth grow dry with anticipation. At the end of the street, the shadows seemed to fracture. Where they should have been long and thin, they jumped and flickered as two figures emerged. In the middle distance, dogs cowered and whined, afraid of the night's new guests.

William froze, elated yet anxious as he watched them march down the road towards him. The figures shimmered with a sapphire light that crackled about their feet and arms. As they grew closer, the light curled about their faces and hair. It was the same light that snaked about daemons as they were summoned, or across the eyes of vampyres and their wounds. But the two who approached him were not of Hell, but fought on the side of some *other* cause.

For these were Dar'uka. The Plainsmen. To everyone else, they were simply angels, seraphim incarnate, but beyond visions of winged babes and angelic presentations.

Despite his brave countenance, they disturbed William. Feeling clumsy, like a child, and thoroughly humbled, he frantically tapped the pipe clear against the side of his hand as they approached. The first was a tall albino with long hair and dressed in a wolfskin cloak. A two-handed broadsword showed beneath the gown of fur and flickered with that same ethereal light, trembling up and down its edge.

The second figure had short black hair. He was shorter than the albino, but he too had a large broadsword that hung at his hip under a long black coat. While the albino was dressed like a barbarian of old, the second man was dressed in more modern attire; he might have even passed for normal in polite society.

William did not know this first man. The second, however, was familiar.

'After all these years!' William gasped. He began to grin, his heart pounding harder. He was suddenly overcome with joy and stepped forward to embrace the second man. 'Kieran! I knew you would return!' But as William approached, he faltered and his smile dropped. The Kieran Harte William once knew had changed. His face was white and gaunt, his skin the colour of ivory. The entire surface of his eyes was black, and within them flickered a smaller version of the storm that swirled overhead, lightning spilling over the lids, like tears of light sparkling down his cheeks. His hands were scarred, ruined with symbols and lines that were incomprehensible to William. And these scars flickered with that azure light, sometimes seeping from the grooves across finger and thumb, rasping the air with bright tendrils that quickly melted into oblivion only to rise again a moment later.

'My God, Kieran,' William murmured as he watched the lightning dance over him, 'what have they done to you?'

'We have come for Marresca,' the albino said, and as soon as he opened his mouth, the words drowned William, flooding his ears with a cacophony of fractured voices that parted before him, and then merged again discordantly inside his skull.

William retreated, not even understanding what had been uttered. 'I don't understand,' he groaned, wincing against the sensation.

Kieran stepped forward. 'We have come for Marresca, William Saxon.'

William stared at his friend. A man he had known all his life.

Yet this man was *not* Kieran. This man was not the one who had left him seven years ago. The Kieran he knew would never have been so bold and discourteous.

'Seven years, Kieran,' William said finally. '*Seven bloody years?* And those are the first words you greet me with?'

Kieran stared at him.

'I haven't seen you since you said goodbye in Villeda. I thought you were dead. Sometimes I even hoped you were. It hurt less to believe so. And now I see you . . .' William fought his emotions, the despair and incredulity. 'How dare you come to me and say this! How dare you greet me in this manner! After all our years of friendship!'

'We are only here for Marresca, William,' Kieran said and looked past him to the church.

William turned about and shook his head. 'Why?'

'One of us has fallen,' the albino replied.

'David,' Kieran added, 'was destroyed at the Gates of Hell. We need a replacement.'

'A replacement?' William said, aghast. 'Just as *you* replaced that Dar'uka in Aosta?'

Kieran inclined his head slightly.

'*Always five we are. The five Dar'uka. No fewer, no more, to fight this war,*' the albino said.

William shook his head again, this time firmly. 'No.'

'*No?*' the albino angel said. The word seemed to attack William, driving against his temple and crashing against his ears.

He stepped back again. 'No,' William replied, his hands at his head. 'He is too young.'

'Age matters little, William Saxon,' the albino angel said.

'Marresca is strong enough to be Dar'uka,' Kieran said. 'We have seen what he has become. We have seen what he has done.'

'And he has done all this without you,' William retorted. '*Everything* we have succeeded in doing has been done without you. We don't need you.' He turned to Kieran. '*I* don't need you.'

Kieran stared back, his expression unflinching. 'This is not your choice.'

William felt his rage rising. 'To hell with you!' he shouted. 'He is under *my* command!'

'But this is his choice, not yours,' the albino angel replied calmly.

'Just as it was mine, William,' Kieran said, his voice almost serene, and for a moment the old Kieran returned. It disarmed William, who seemed to give in with a sob.

'But I've *lost* you,' William implored. 'You willingly destroyed our friendship, Kieran. Can't you see that? You abandoned me.'

'Friendships do not matter,' Kieran replied coldly. 'All that matters is the War.'

'I wait seven years for you to come back, and when you return, you don't even know me,' William moaned.

'We know you, William,' Kieran assured him. 'We know everything.'

'You *don't* know me,' William protested. 'Much has happened in seven years.'

'I know you are a man of honour, Captain William Saxon,' Kieran replied. 'And I know you will tell Marresca. It is not your decision, but Marresca's alone. Only he can choose whether to become Dar'uka or not.'

'And become like you? To become less than human, Kieran?' William taunted. He hoped for something, just a sign of anger or indignation to crack that terribly calm and cold façade.

'You will tell him, William,' Kieran continued, 'that we must have his answer by the third full moon. And then we will come to him.'

'In all conscience, I cannot,' William seethed.

'Do you wish us to confront him now?' Kieran asked.

William considered what this might do. To reveal the Dar'uka to his men in the church, and to Father Gessille, would only make matters worse. 'No,' he conceded.

'Then tell him,' Kieran said and turned away, the giant albino by his side. William watched them returning to those fractured shadows at the end of the street, back to obscurity, and in spite of himself he was still in awe. In awe of how someone could so suddenly disrupt his life, and make him question his feelings and beliefs.

There came another rumble, the world appeared to shake, and light blazed from the ground beyond the houses before the tremor subsided. As the Dar'uka disappeared, the storm above abated and the starry skies returned. Soon afterward came a chorus of barking as the dogs in the distance found their courage again to howl at the tempest that had left as quickly as it had arrived.

William didn't return to the chapel immediately, but considered the turn of events that had brought him such heartbreak from his encounter with the Dar'uka. For a fleeting moment, William hated Kieran. Not just what he'd become, but Kieran Harte himself; he who had betrayed their friendship so easily. He looked down at his hands and opened his balled fists. Indents were in his palms where he'd squeezed his fingernails into the skin.

Inside the chapel, Father Gessille was brewing tea for Lieutenant Peruzo. He poured a mug for William, who took it gratefully yet silently.

'I heard voices,' Peruzo said. 'Who was it?'

'No one,' William lied, his hands trembling.

'There was thunder . . .' Peruzo added.

'The storm has passed us by,' William said between sips, unable to look Peruzo in the eyes. He managed to look up for a moment to Marresca, who lay sleeping on one of the benches. His hands shook harder with fury.

Father Gessille noted the shaking and peered down at him. 'Is there something still troubling you, my son?'

'No. Thank you, Father. Everything is quite, quite clear to me now,' he said as he sipped again from the cup, unable to stop his hands from trembling.

CHAPTER THREE

Another Homecoming

△ I △

The burial of Brother Anthony of Turin was a muted affair. Peruzo elected to speak independently, having known Brother Anthony since initiation eight years before. During the burial, William's thoughts strayed to the Scarimadaen they had captured, and he fought to master his frustration that their quarry, the flame-haired vampyre of Vienna, had escaped yet again. He was not accustomed to failing. But it was not just this disappointment that gnawed at his mind.

William had once harboured some hope that Kieran would return and the angels would fight alongside them in a common war. That this hadn't happened, and worse, that Kieran would make such demands of him on his first appearance in seven years, caused William disbelief. If the Dar'uka felt so little towards what the Church was doing, then why were they doing it? Why take the risks? Why all the sacrifices, Brother Anthony's for one?

It was these thoughts that haunted William during their long journey home from Prague, a journey that took longer than expected. Their passage across the Alps was beset by bad weather and for two weeks they were marooned in Innsbruck, a tiny place just inside Austria where the streets were often quiet and the evenings icy cold. During their reluctant stay, William cultivated a beard. He spent long hours sitting inside their simple lodgings while he reviewed his motives.

This internal debate was a distraction he did not need. In the past his reasons had been simple. William fought for the glimmer of hope that Count Ordrane of Draak, that hated creature who commanded the vampyres and kafalas, would one day be defeated and William's exile ended. He had not seen his mother, father, or sister in over seven years, yet his last words to them had been of a swift return. In light of what followed, the promise had been futile, but then William could not have foreseen the circumstances that would eventually drive both him and his lost friend Kieran out of England and across the Continent to Rome, where his exile began.

In the intervening years, William had written home often, if only to reassure his family, fashioning a fiction by telling them he was on business for the British army and would return when best he could.

He had once toyed with telling them that Kieran was now dead, but wasn't sure how badly his sister would have taken the news. Elizabeth had loved Kieran dearly, and had designs to marry him, something that could never happen now.

Now that Kieran had become Dar'uka.

So William kept up the pretence that Kieran was serving alongside him, making up stories until it became too much to endure. Finally he stopped, unable to write anything but meandering lies about transactions and travel, trite observations of places he had never visited. William had not written home to England for almost a year now.

After a mission to Spain, his motivations for fighting the War had begun to change. Victories had come, but they were costly. Yet as the war with the agents of Count Ordrane moved from the shadows and into the streets of cities such as Paris, Vienna and Prague, William greeted the open battles with relish. What mattered was destroying the enemy, not the issue of anonymity, and as the veil of secrecy over their clandestine war began to slip, notoriety and rumour grew.

The Vatican fought hard to keep the war quiet, fearing that the monarchs and governments of this fragile Continent would turn against the Church if it were revealed that the Vatican was warring with devils in their own territory. The Church feared the repercussions of doctrine clashing with disbelief. But it feared most the return of the Inquisition, an arm of the Church that had not been entirely quashed over the past hundred years. It would take little for the Inquisitors to return, especially if the heads of State demanded it.

Yet despite the Vatican's attempts at controlling rumour, William had become a whispered legend even in the Church, one that bishops and cardinals spoke of in hushed voices, inventing wild stories sometimes to the point where they spread to the populace of Rome. In the brothels and the courts, people spoke of an Englishman who battled dragons, or a priest who faced the 'Devil' – and 'for the first time, the Devil was frightened of his enemy'.

These stories travelled abroad upon merchant ships or buried in the columns of newspapers. Once *The Times* had run an article on the legend, hinting that several murders in Blackfriars had been the work of some diabolical creature that this so-called 'warrior priest of Rome' had vanquished. How ironic if Lord Saxon of Fairway Hall had read such a story, not suspecting that its source was nothing less than his own son.

William's absence had been long. He knew nothing of the story *The Times* carried, but was aware of other legends and myths, rarely true, and even then inaccurate. His sudden reputation had brought him a respect he had never imagined before, and soon, if unconsciously, he'd craved it. It was like opium, alluring and captivating.

And if fame and adulation were not motivation enough to continue fighting, then Adriana was. She was everything he wanted, and William believed it was his heroics that kept their love alive. Each time he returned it was like seeing her anew again.

Yet there was a price. How many times had he considered

marrying her? How many times been ready to propose, only to find himself thwarted by another mission, another leave-taking? He was sure that Adriana was in love with him, and hoped it would stay that way, but would her adoration fade if he left the Order?

If William was honest, he had everything he could possibly want right now: adventure, excitement, fame, and a beautiful woman he had never in his wildest dreams hoped to find. If fighting the War meant keeping all this, then wasn't that reason enough?

At Innsbruck, after toiling with motive and doubt, he realized that he was not fighting this war for the Dar'uka or the Church.

He fought it for himself.

After the weather cleared, the four men left Innsbruck and travelled through bleak mountain passes, emerging days later into green fields and hills. A few nights in Verona sharpened the spirits again, and Brother Jericho recovered his confidence, much dented following the burial of Brother Anthony in Prague.

William approached him on the matter of his moment's hesitation, and they spoke at length about the fear that the enemy projected. Vienna and Prague had been Jericho's initial missions since enrolling as a monk, yet he thought himself a failure after Prague. William told him the truth of survival: 'The enemy uses fear as its weapon. Disarm that fear, and the enemy is weak. This is a war of the mysterious. Believe, then, in everything you see, but do not fear the uncanny and grotesque.'

As the days of contemplation worked on him, the young monk began speaking of his eagerness to sign for another mission, to test himself. Before they left Verona, William agreed to send him on the next available assignment for the Secretariat and the Order.

Brother Jericho was not his only concern as they returned. It was during the final stage from Verona to Rome that William approached Marresca on the subject of recruitment as Dar'uka.

The response was suitably calm. After a few minutes of serious conversation, when William spoke his mind and Marresca listened, the monk promised to consider what he'd said, and then the matter was closed.

From that moment on William felt exposed, with no control over Marresca's fate. Marresca said nothing of his decision, not even confiding in Peruzo, and William found himself on several occasions wishing to broach the subject. But this was Marresca, and conversation with the lieutenant was difficult at the best of times.

△ II △

Villeda was a welcome sight, even with the faint rain on the hills. Nothing could diminish their enthusiasm at finally returning home. The green fields and slender slopes were alive with lush spring grass. The trees were in blossom, yet already shedding a vivid carpet of pink and white along the road to town.

In the years since William had first arrived in Villeda, the place had thrived. Families had flourished, farmers had bought new lands and accrued wealth in the wake of the wars with France and Napoleon. At times the mystery of Villeda threatened to reveal itself to the region (how it prospered when much of the country was still suffering), but the people of Villeda were protective, and close-mouthed with strangers. To an outsider, the town was subdued, a place not obviously extraordinary. Opulence was never worn on the shirtsleeve, and reputation was often discounted, kept secret within this furtive society. Like the Order of Saint Sallian that made its home in the monastery just outside of town, Villeda craved anonymity.

But it never forgot to hail its heroes, and the people of Villeda knew how to celebrate. Street parties were not uncommon, especially for the returning monks, and they sometimes threatened to overshadow the mission.

Celebrations for Captain William Saxon were usually the grandest, if only to attract Adriana into the town (being deemed its fairest woman). At first the attention was overwhelming, but over the years it had ripened into custom, a welcomed way of life in Villeda and the Order.

On the day William and his men returned from Prague, it was quiet. They saw only one farmer attending to his fields as they rode to the outskirts of town.

Then as they stood talking, several locals appeared and began gesturing towards them, their faces alive with smiles and cheers.

'They've returned! They've returned!' shouted one beaming woman, the wife of the local baker.

William waved back. 'So much for the quiet entrance!' he grinned.

'She'll tell the entire town,' Jericho laughed.

'I reckon so,' William agreed. 'What do you think, Peruzo? A little merriment is in order, at least?'

Peruzo sighed. 'Very well.'

'And you *will* be attending?' William pressed, making it sound like an order.

'I don't have much choice, do I?' Peruzo replied.

They waved as more people turned out of their homes and shops to greet the surprise return of their heroes. Even Marresca managed a half-hearted salute.

At the junction just outside the piazza, they halted and parted ways. The monks trotted up the road to the monastery of St Laurence, while William turned right and headed towards the open fields at the edge of town. And home.

On the way he passed more locals who waved to him through the rain. The drizzle had grown fainter until only the occasional drop could be seen falling from the terracotta roofs of the homes he rode by. Very soon, the clouds melted away and the sun lit the road before him, warming the back of his neck as he rode his horse up the path to where the fields divided.

There, nestling in a dip and looking out across the hills of Rome, was William's house. He closed his eyes and drank in the smells of spring. He hadn't been home since midwinter, and seeing the villa now made his heart ache with happiness. He kicked in his heels and as he galloped down the road his mind was already passing through the vine-entwined archway. As he rode under that, his thought was on leaping off his horse to find Adriana, a thought that progressed to kissing, as he pulled the horse up and dismounted, leaving the animal to stand and rest in the courtyard.

William tugged off his belt and scabbard and tossed them onto the porch at the front door. Then he jogged around the front and down the side of the villa, his heart beating fast, his face breaking into a grin, eager to see his lover.

Past the water pump he moved quickly and silently, through the garden and its banks of ivory and gold spring flowers that only Adriana knew the names of. At the rear corner of the villa he stopped and listened. Someone was humming an off-key tune, and he knew at once that it was Adriana. She had no ear for song, though when she hummed it was different. There was always a whimsical melody in that sound, and it lightened his mood whenever he heard it.

He stayed at the wall and smiled, waiting for as long as his heart could give him as it filled up suddenly with love. His first thought was to surprise her, to creep up and wrap his arms about her, but his desire was too great to wait. William marched from the corner of the villa and into the open, careless of how much noise he would make or whether she would see him coming.

Adriana was hanging out a sheet and undergarments to dry in the first sunshine of the season, and her back was towards him. Her long dark hair cascaded off her shoulders as she reached down to pick up another sheet and then paused, hearing footsteps. Turning quickly, she seemed to know it was William and she let out a joyous cry, dropping the clothes in the mud at her feet. He caught her in his arms and held her tightly. 'Oh, I've missed you so much,' he whispered into her ear. '*So much.*'

49

'I can't believe you're here!' she purred, kissing him time and time again on his neck and face.

William broke their embrace just to look upon her again, into her deep brown eyes, her graceful face. He kissed her soft lips once and then again, and then harder, his longing strong and passionate.

They broke the kiss, and William put his forehead to hers, breathing heavily. It would have been easy to lose himself in her, but he wanted to make it last. He wanted to savour every moment now.

'I missed you,' Adriana whispered, 'every day.'

William sighed and replied with a gentle kiss.

'You have no idea what it feels like to see you again,' she said as she parted from his lips and nuzzled her face under his chin. She slipped her hand under his coat, laying it on his chest. 'It grows more difficult every time,' she continued sadly.

'I know, my love.' He kissed her again. 'I need to wash and change. I'm carrying many days of dust and sweat.'

'I can see,' Adriana smiled slyly.

William grinned. 'I'll take a bath,' he said and ran his hand down her back.

'You should shave as well,' she said, and put a hand to his face.

◬ III ◬

William crossed the bedroom as the light outside began to fade. The room was rustic, with simple furniture arranged at the corners. Their only extravagance was a large four-poster bed William had purchased in Rome from a Greek carpenter. Above it to the right was a small mirror fixed to the wall.

He pulled on a loose-fitting cotton gown and laid his clothes on the chair by the mirror.

'You look much younger after you shave,' Adriana remarked from the doorway.

William looked over his shoulder fondly. She was smiling

lovingly across to him, an intense expression in her eyes; she was dressed in a pale skirt and a blouse that was as rustic as the room.

'Do you think?' he replied and rubbed his face, the days of stubble having been removed by Adriana's gentle hands and a sharp blade.

She nodded, and her eyes stayed on him longingly.

William looked into the mirror and saw she was right. He had undergone a transformation in a matter of hours. His skin was clean-shaven, and in the light of the candles nearby he looked youthful; almost as young as when they'd first met in Aosta.

Their glances were full of desire. Adriana wandered over to the other side of the bed. Her hands ran slowly over the posts as she moved to the opposite side. She wanted him, and William had wanted her for the last two hundred miles. He was wholly in love with her, and in those moments knew nothing but Adriana.

He watched as she unbuttoned her blouse, tracing her every movement as the buttons undid one by one. She then slipped off the blouse, revealing her breasts until she was naked at the waist.

William felt his breath quicken, mesmerized as she now untied her hair, the long dark curls falling down her shoulders, spilling over to lie on her bosom. He found it was the hair he looked at the most, not the dark rings of her nipples, the curve of the breasts as she bent to unbutton her skirt. It slipped off slowly with her undergarments until she stood naked before him.

He made love to Adriana tenderly, a far cry from when they were first intimate seven years before. William had been clumsy then, oafish and inexperienced, but Adriana had taught him progressively, not embarrassing him but encouraging his affection, requesting the lightest of touches, the fullest embraces and finally the act of *gradual* love, which that evening was a feat even for William. He was sure he'd explode from her very touch, but

51

stayed the course until he felt her peak with ecstasy and then came himself, pleasure and relief in equal waves.

Afterwards they lay in bed, the sheets draped over their cooling bodies, her head resting on his chest, and he ran his fingers through her thick black hair.

'Will there be celebrations?' Adriana asked.

'Aren't there always?' William replied, his eyes on the ceiling. Adriana had dusted recently, and the winter cobwebs had been brushed away.

'I thought you might have returned quietly,' she said.

'I did my best,' William lied. 'Lucio's wife saw us.'

'Ah,' Adriana laughed without much humour. 'A baker's gossip for certain. Everyone must know by now you have returned. They'll be expecting you.' She raised her head from his chest to look up at him with sadness, then lowered her chin on his breast. 'Won't they?'

'They'll be expecting *both* of us,' William replied. 'Who am I, without you?'

'You're the hero of Villeda,' she replied, but it was rueful.

'I thought I was the hero of Llerena?' William teased.

'That was last time,' Adriana replied coldly and sat up, pulling up the sheets to cover herself.

'What's wrong?' William asked, but knew straight away.

'I have barely seen you, and now I must share you again,' she complained.

'For a small part of the night only, my beautiful Adriana,' William said, reaching for her.

Adriana slapped the hand away playfully. 'Just another night? And then when do you leave again?'

William laughed. 'There are no missions yet,' he told her. 'I am here in Villeda, with you. *I am home.*'

She regarded him for a moment and then dived under his arms, wrapping her own around his torso. 'That pleases me,' she whispered.

William kissed her forehead. 'I thought you liked the celebrations,' he said.

52

'Not as much as I like having you to myself,' she replied.

After a while, when the first of the crickets began chirping in the crops, William hugged Adriana again and then relaxed his grip to rise from the bed. Adriana leaned against one of the bed-posts, the sheet about her.

William stood up and stretched, glancing back at her, and then again as he began to pull on his shirt.

'Do we have to go so soon?' she asked.

'The sooner we leave, the sooner we can return,' he said, but-toning his shirt. At the last button he paused and listened intently. 'The villa is quieter than usual. Where is Marco?'

'Staying at the Maldinis',' she replied.

'Oh?' William said, secretly pleased. Since he had rescued both Adriana and her nephew from Count Ordrane's followers in Aosta, the boy had grown unruly, and was often in trouble, haunted by the memories of his parents' violent deaths. Adriana did her best, but what he needed was a father-figure.

Despite wanting the best for Marco, William was realistic. How could *he* be such a figure to Marco when he spent most of his time on hazardous missions for the Church? Nor was he *ready* to be a father to Marco. He had only just got used to living with Adriana, and parenthood worried him, so the idea that someone else might try to drive a little discipline into Marco's thick skull was appealing.

'He's farming for Tustio, so I thought it was right he should live there . . . To rise when they do, work when they do.'

'How is he finding it?'

Adriana looked at William for a few moments and then slowly shook her head.

William frowned. 'What is the matter?'

'He wishes to be a soldier like his "Uncle" William,' Adriana mocked.

'Stubborn child,' William growled under his breath.

'He idolizes you.' Adriana slipped from under the sheet to pad naked across the room. She pulled on a gown. 'He still wishes to join the Order.'

'I've been through this with him several times,' William reminded her, pulling on a pair of trousers.

Adriana sighed. 'He is an obstinate boy.'

'Like his aunt.'

Adriana was not impressed. 'Obstinate, am I?'

'Incredibly,' William replied.

'Do you like that about me?' she flounced as William walked over to her.

'I adore it,' he grinned and seized her arms.

She pushed herself away for a moment. 'You are *so* arrogant!'

'I know,' William grinned. 'But you like that.'

'Are you sure?' she said and pulled him close, her tongue entering his mouth to seek out his as her hands went about his body.

William's fingers parted the gown and found her breasts, then moved down to her hips and at last between her legs, so warm and inviting. This touch made her draw a sharp breath, and she seemed to fold into his arms.

'We don't have time for this,' she sighed, kissing his neck.

'I'm sure they won't mind if we're late,' he whispered, and carried her back to the bed.

△ IV △

The tavern in Villeda was overflowing, the townspeople spilling out into the streets armed with smoking pipes and tankards. William and Adriana's arrival was greeted with clapping and cheering. It was like a procession, and William soon broke into gregarious laughter, shaking the many hands that were offered.

Even Adriana, who had been quite silent during the walk into town, began beaming and absorbing the attention. Lucio's wife wrapped her arms around her, expressing relief at William's safe return. Adriana did not have to pretend her response. Her expression was earnest as she told the local gossip she intended to cage him before he ran away on 'another foolish mission for the Church'.

William was still greeting the townsfolk. There was Edward the blacksmith, Tustio Maldini, who employed Marco, and Antonio, recently elected mayor of Villeda, who laughed heartily, one hand on his barrel of a stomach, the other gripping a large pot of ale. Before William could resist, the mayor was hugging him like a bear.

'Welcome back, Captain Saxon!' he shouted, announcing it to everyone.

'Thank you,' William replied humbly.

'We are pleased you returned,' Antonio continued.

'I am pleased to be home,' William said, like the mayor addressing all within earshot.

At the bar, Peruzo was watching with Jericho and several other monks. He lifted a cup of wine and smiled. It was an excuse for William to forge forward towards them, away from the gathering circle of locals who were surrounding him to wish him well.

'Captain,' Peruzo greeted and raised his cup.

'Good evening, Lieutenant,' he replied and glanced at the monks. 'And gentlemen.'

The monks were sipping water, looking a little vexed that they couldn't drink.

'No wine today?' William said.

The elder lieutenant raised an eyebrow. 'Today they fast,' Peruzo said.

'I see,' William mused. 'You must be glad you're not a monk.'

'That I am, Captain,' Peruzo grinned.

'For my part, I am glad you were not feeling sour enough to keep away from tonight's proceedings, old friend,' William said.

'A man can rot at St Laurence if he isn't careful,' Peruzo conceded slyly.

'Well said,' William replied as a pot of ale was shoved into his hands by the landlord.

'A toast! A toast!' yelled a farmer from one side of the bar, gesticulating with his tankard at William, which then escalated into a louder request from others crammed into the tavern.

William held up his hand, gesturing for some quiet. He glanced to Adriana, who stood nearby with her arms folded, feigning a look of exasperation. He laughed weakly and addressed the crowd.

'My thanks to you all,' he began, and coughed to clear his voice. 'These celebrations mean much to me and my men. There is time for celebration just as there is time for remembrance. We lost nine brave men on our journey, and a gathering like this should be about their mourning, as well as our success. So please, I ask you to raise your glasses to our fallen friends.'

'*Fallen friends*,' the tavern said as one, and then grew silent.

'To Captain William Saxon!' shouted someone from the back, breaking the silence before William could. The crowd repeated it, this time louder than before, and the sound overwhelmed him.

As the calls subsided, William turned to Peruzo apologetically. 'No offence is taken,' Peruzo said. 'You are a hero in Villeda.'

'There are four heroes in Villeda this day,' William replied, 'not just . . .' He trailed off and looked about. 'Where is Marresca?'

'At the monastery,' Peruzo sighed. 'He was not persuaded to join us.'

'Hardly a surprise,' William replied distantly, thinking about the decision the young lieutenant had to make.

The smoke of the tavern grew heavy, and after a while William turned from the bar, pausing to kiss Adriana, before slipping outside. The evening air was cool and he felt a faint breeze brush his cheek with the smell of cut grass. Around the courtyard people were chatting in the shadows while others occupied benches and stools. The courtyard backed up against several cottages and two-storey buildings. There was no music to speak of, though instruments leaned against a fig tree in the corner. The courtyard itself was awash with light. A string of lanterns hung from the same tree's branches, and more lanterns hung from posts and balconies.

It was under a string of lanterns that William noticed someone sitting on a bench by himself, quietly enjoying the evening. William sauntered over with his tankard of ale, pausing now and then to exchange greetings. He walked the gauntlet courteously yet swiftly. At one point he thought he might be drawn into an argument about the Church by a farmer he knew as a local troublemaker, but he left the group to argue among themselves.

Under the lanterns, the sitting figure smiled and stared back at William, amused by all the attention.

At last William was free of them, until a boy stepped into his path. His expression was a little different from the rest. Here there was no adulation. William looked down at him. 'Marco,' he said, and raised an eyebrow.

'Uncle,' Marco replied.

There was a moment or two of uncomfortable silence, and then William said: 'I understand you are working for the Maldinis?'

Marco shrugged. He was now almost fifteen years of age and had grown into an agile young man. He shared the family's dark eyes, but unlike Adriana, his hair was fair.

'Farming is not to your liking?'

'I would rather be doing something else,' Marco replied stubbornly.

'Farming is a respectable profession. And if you didn't wish to farm, you could have continued with your study,' William chided.

'I do not wish to be a farmer. I do not wish to be a student, Uncle!' Marco seethed.

'I know exactly what you wish for,' William said and put a hand on the boy's shoulder. 'The answer is still no.'

Marco shrugged off his grip. 'Why is it you have the final say? Others can join the Order, so why can't I?'

'Because I am your guardian,' William replied.

'I wish you weren't,' Marco grumbled.

It was surprising, but this hurt William. He'd looked after the boy for seven years since Aosta, teaching him where he could, allowing others to do so in his absence. The title of 'Uncle' was an adopted one, but he thought of Marco as family. If it had not been for William, both Marco and Adriana would have been penniless refugees in Rome.

'That could be arranged, Marco. Adriana could look after you in my stead, and I would have nothing to do with you,' William suggested, trying to sound calm. 'Is that what you wish?'

Marco looked up and shook his head. Despite his sulking, he didn't wish that. 'I just want to join the Order, Uncle. Nothing more.'

William sighed and rubbed his eyes. He was tired. 'We'll talk about this later,' he said.

'Then there won't be much talking at all,' Marco sulked, crossing his arms.

'*Later*, Marco!' William growled at him and walked away, angry with himself, as much as with the boy.

Under the lanterns the sitting figure shook his head and watched Marco slip out of the courtyard.

'He is wilful.'

'Like his aunt,' William replied.

'Like his uncle,' the man teased.

'You think *I'm* stubborn?'

The man moved closer into the light to reach for his cup. His hair was grey and fell about an old face that was still bright, though the eyes were fading.

'Not stubborn, but perhaps headstrong,' the old man said.

William laughed. 'You always say pleasant things about me, Engrin.'

Engrin laughed with him.

'What is that you're drinking?' William asked after a few minutes of relaxed silence.

Engrin looked embarrassed. 'Just water.'

William raised his eyebrows. 'Water? You? Surely not! I don't think I've ever seen you drinking water before.'

Engrin smiled, though there was regret. 'I'm not as young as I was, William,' he replied. 'Nor as healthy.'

William marked how frail his old friend appeared. 'Is something wrong? Are you not well?'

'Damned influenza,' Engrin replied. 'Ever since the turn of winter, I haven't shaken it.'

William tried not to study his old mentor's expression too closely. 'You look . . .' he began, and then couldn't finish the sentence.

'I look terrible, William,' Engrin told him bitterly, 'so don't humour this old devil. I am ill, and old. Too old to be teased.'

William held up his hands as he opened his mouth to say 'Sorry.'

'And too old to be apologized to,' Engrin added before he could.

William closed his mouth and nodded. 'Very well.'

'How were your adventures in Vienna?' Engrin asked.

'They were hectic. I lost some men. We took one vampyre head and a daemon. Not to mention a Scarimadaen.' William was tempted to speak of Kieran's reappearance, but this wound was still raw.

'It sounds like a successful mission,' Engrin remarked.

'One got away. But he won't next time,' William replied confidently. 'I expect I'll be sent after him soon enough. Hopefully to the Carpathians. If only I could launch an attack on Count Ordrane, then this war would be over.'

'The Carpathians? Ah, so the rumours haven't reached you yet?' Engrin said, delighted that he could surprise William once more.

'Rumours?'

Engrin nodded and bent close. 'A company of monks was dispatched to Rashid several days ago, and the rumours say something has happened in Egypt.'

William frowned. 'What's in Egypt?'

'I don't know. These are but rumours after all, but the Secretariat is *very* much excited.'

'And you can't tell me more?'

Engrin shook his head.

'Always the same Engrin,' William replied. 'So full of riddles. I suppose only you and the Secretariat know the truth.'

Engrin looked into his cup and coughed slightly. 'I no longer visit Rome these days. I leave such things to greater men than I.'

'Greater than you? Who in the Secretariat stands so high?' William scoffed, and took a mouthful of ale.

'Cardinal Devirus for one.' Engrin shook his head.

'Devirus?' William repeated. 'He of all people should realize the necessity of your wisdom and . . .'

'The cardinal only recognizes I am old,' Engrin interrupted.

'Nonsense.'

'William, I *am* old. Too old for adventure. Too old to offer an opinion.'

'*I* value your opinions,' William told him squarely, 'and if the Secretariat does not, well then, we'll see what they say once I've . . .'

'Do nothing, William.' Engrin held up a weary hand. 'Some part of me is glad that I'm no longer at their beckoning. No longer part of their politics.'

'This is not the same Engrin Meerwall I know,' William remarked.

'Perhaps not. But the Engrin I too used to know is long since gone, before we even met. I lack the strength to argue my corner. I have disagreed with the Secretariat, and they no longer listen. There's nothing you can do. Just as a captain cannot argue with his general, you cannot argue with the cardinal.'

'Really?' William jeered. 'Well, I like to think I carry *some* weight with the Secretariat.'

Engrin reached over and patted William's arm. 'Your respect and friendship is touching, but quite unnecessary,' he said. 'You should concentrate on what is to come.'

'You mean these "rumours"?'

Engrin nodded. 'When the Secretariat sends an entire company of monks to a country outside Europe, you'd best take notice.'

CHAPTER FOUR

The Greatest Mission

△ I △

William rose early and rode out of Villeda, taking the long and well-worn road down the valley to Rome. He passed fields waking with cattle and goats, orchards alive with birds beginning their chorus. The first rays of morning sunshine filtered through burgeoning clouds as he entered the suburbs of Rome hours later. Soon he was trotting past the courtesans and courtiers who prowled the streets even this early in the morning. Some woke with the dawn, and dressed up in pomp and ceremony to impress not only the other sex but anyone of note who happened by. The people of Rome were all rivals, it seemed, whether for affection, wealth or status. William was glad not to be a part of it.

Past a bridge over the Tiber, the main road to San Pietro appeared through the throng of journeymen and priests streaming from one side to the other. William guided his horse through them, tailing an elaborate carriage that cut a path straight over the bridge and into the street beyond. In the distance stood the ashen dome of San Pietro, the mid-morning sun casting long shadows upon it and the piazza at its feet.

The road was flanked by great pale buildings, their balconies filled with flowers and with courtiers already busy watching the great and the good travel up and down the promenade. William likened it to watching a circus; aspiring individuals from all over the Continent seemed to find their way to the steps of the Vatican through their own self-importance or because they were seeking something else. Sometimes it was spiritual. But often it was financial.

William could see what kept Engrin away. In the seven years since his first visit to the Vatican and its surrounds, the area had flourished from its battered state into a thriving yet greedy community. It was something William had noticed in each of the countries he had visited since, that smell of corruption. The Church was in decline, a steady one that might have started hundreds of years ago, but it was obvious now as he passed the final ranks of great houses on the street and appeared at the Piazza San Pietro. A new age was coming, the age of the proletariat and insurrection.

The piazza was as busy as the promenade, priests and bishops walking to and fro. Monks stood in discussion with others, and sisters communed together, gesticulating to the great dome or a saint far above on the baroque arches surrounding the square.

Even after so many visits to the Vatican, William was always impressed by its magnificence. But the weight in his saddlebag, the Scarimadaen from Prague, seemed to dull all this into insignificance.

He trotted his horse around the piazza, under the arches and then down the adjacent and crowded street of buildings and traders, before he followed the high wall around Vatican City to a rear entrance where several Papal guards stood in their blue and yellow uniforms. Recognizing William's uniform, they let him through the gates to the stables.

He stabled his mount and walked through the gardens to several small buildings hidden under ivy, known as the Chambers of Deconstruction. These were the furnaces of the Secretariat, the buildings populated by a scant number of monks tutored in a specific area of exorcism and destruction: the perfect men to dispose of the instruments of the Devil.

At the entrance to the building was a single plain door

belying what lay within. William felt a certain satisfaction as he hoisted the Scarimadaen in the bag. No longer would this instrument be used; no longer would its daemon be let loose upon mankind.

With a slight swagger, William pulled open the door and marched boldly inside.

He didn't stay long. After seeing the Scarimadaen destroyed by the rituals of the Order, William left quickly and entered San Pietro via the rooms under the Sistine Chapel. The doors opened onto a small courtyard and then a second door led through into the basilica itself.

St Peter's was hushed, but William marched on, unabashed by the sounds of his sturdy boots thudding across the stone floor, which caused several priests to glance his way forbiddingly. William marched on under the marble-stares of great saints and martyrs, not pausing to look at the paintings adorning the walls, the gold filigree in the decorations nor any of the art that made most visitors to St Peter's weep.

For what was a painting by Raphael compared with the slaughter of innocents by a rampaging daemon?

From the basilica, he made his way down a flight of steps to the grottoes, the tunnel before him adorned with more elaborate paintings curving under the ceiling and gilding the walls. Turning left, he came to a large oak door flanked by two papal guards who let him pass as soon as they saw him.

He put his head down and made the long cool journey underground, past the tombs of saints and popes, along rows of alcoves lit by candles that were tended to dutifully every morning and every evening by novices and clergy.

The number of alcoves dwindled. The descent to the next level brought a chill, and William wrapped his jacket about him. Ahead the tunnel sloped downwards, lit sporadically by lamps. Occasionally there would be the scrit-scrit of a rat or some other creature scurrying away.

Eventually he came to a set of thick doors. On either side stood not the papal guards, but monks of the Order.

'Captain,' they greeted and William nodded to them.

'Another victory, sir?' asked one as he passed between them, his hands pressing on the door.

'You may give thanks, gentlemen,' William replied.

The brothers of the Order smiled and looked pleased, perhaps dreaming of the day they might follow Captain Saxon on a mission against the Count.

William felt his step lighten as he pushed open the doors and strode into the room beyond, a small reception room that housed the records of the Secretariat on tall oak shelves. Between two of the imposing shelves of books hung a crimson curtain that swayed from a subterranean breeze. William pulled it aside and crept down the dark passageway behind it. The tunnel ceiling was low, yet after frequent visits he knew by instinct when to lower his head.

At the end of the passage was another room, brightly lit by candles and lamps. It was decorated elaborately, though a visitor might have noted how it eschewed the themes of the basilica and the rest of the Vatican. Instead were paintings and objects of another kind: of men struggling with a menagerie of mythical beasts, creatures with wings of flame, cloven-hoofed monstrosities, bulbous and bloated beings with many eyes, columns of flame and those who cowered before them.

There were also the instruments of war: the sword of Saint Sallian still gleaming in its glass case, and by that a pyramid, not unlike the one William had delivered for destruction. This one was made of gold, and William looked upon it for a moment, as he often did, listening to the slight hum beneath the glass that housed it. He had once marvelled why the Secretariat had not destroyed this Scarimadaen: its danger was unparalleled. Yet over the years he came to understand its purpose, and for every visit he found himself meditating on it, a reminder of what the pyramid represented. And what they all fought for.

For this was terror unlimited. The eye to Hell itself.

William was stirred by voices beyond the stairs and the circular wall. He walked past the Scarimadaen, past more collections of books and drawings, before ducking through a low doorway and into the dazzling light beyond.

Here was the map room, a wide circular room overlooked by a gallery high above. On its floor was a map of the known world fashioned completely from gold, perhaps the only excess in the Secretariat but one that rivalled most of the art in the Vatican. It was said the wealth of that room might have been that of a small state, yet to all those who worked at the Secretariat, the map was worth so much more.

On the surface were candles of many colours: blues, greens, reds, and golds. By Prague stood a single candle, its flame a bright green as it crackled and fizzed, newly placed upon the map. Not so far away was a larger candle, a red flame that burned atop a bulbous mass of cream-coloured wax that had built up over many years. It was the oldest of the candles, and one that had been replaced time and time again.

'Every visit, you look upon that flame, Captain Saxon,' someone said from the far side of the circular room.

William smiled faintly. 'For I wish to be the one who snuffs it out for ever, Your Eminence.'

'I look forward to that,' came the reply, 'though your confrontation with Count Ordrane of Draak must wait a while longer.'

Half in the shadows was a lectern that sat just north of the Continent in the icy regions of the world; from this Cardinal Devirus emerged, his feet crossing over Scandinavia until his toes stopped on the edge of Bohemia. He was dressed in immaculate scarlet robes, his face quite plain save for a beard like an arrowhead upon his chin.

He looked down at the green flame flickering over Prague. 'I do hope this marker is not presumptuous and indeed there *was* a victory?' he asked, his hands clasped inside his robes. He attempted to smile, though every effort seemed like a strain to the cardinal's naturally sour expression.

William nodded. 'I delivered the Scarimadaen to the Chambers before coming here,' he said.

'Excellent news, Captain,' Cardinal Devirus applauded. 'One more Scarimadaen destroyed. Your tally is impressive. Perhaps the greatest there has ever been.'

The cardinal walked around the Continent of Europe, negotiating the various markers that flickered over cities and towns, until he reached the Atlantic Ocean and stood on its empty expanse. 'What news from Vienna and Prague?'

William told Cardinal Devirus everything: from hunting the red-haired vampyre in Vienna, losing several men in the process, to the encounter in Prague and their imprisonment.

At the end, Cardinal Devirus was stroking his beard. 'Your imprisonment was unfortunate.'

William felt chastised. 'It was unlucky, Your Eminence,' he replied.

Cardinal Devirus revealed his hands and wrung them together in deep thought. 'I will send a delegate to Prague to tidy up this mess that you left,' he said grumpily, 'though perhaps it is already too late. I would have hoped that such interference had been negotiated.'

'As would I, Your Eminence,' William said boldly, 'but the tactics of the War have changed.'

Cardinal Devirus stared across at him.

'The War is no longer a secret,' William clarified.

'Perhaps that is true. It was inevitable that one who is cornered will soon disregard all rules. The Count is wounded and understands his precarious position. Even now he watches the politics of the Continent and wonders if he can survive unmolested,' Cardinal Devirus mused.

'You're talking of forces aligning *against* Ordrane?' William asked, eager for news.

'Count Ordrane's influence in the north is weakening. Those he could once frighten into submission are becoming more daring. Even confrontational. Ordrane's downfall may come sooner than expected. All of which *will* take time, Captain, so we must be patient.' Devirus held up his hand to placate William. 'Now, what of Marresca?'

William frowned. 'What of him?'

'You have told me nothing of this request from the Dar'uka. To recruit him,' Cardinal Devirus rebuked.

William's cheeks reddened. 'How did you know?'

Cardinal Devirus crossed his arms again and walked around William. 'Lieutenant Marresca came to me last night to deliver the news. I am his sponsor. He sought my advice.'

William bowed. 'I apologize, Your Eminence. I have had little opportunity to ask him myself.'

'His decision must be made tonight, Captain,' Devirus reminded him. 'I would have hoped you would speak with me sooner.'

'Again, I apologize,' William said with difficulty. 'I wished Marresca to stay. But the Dar'uka left me with no choice but to approach the lieutenant with the bargain.'

'Not much of a bargain,' Devirus replied. 'They offer nothing in return.'

'Quite so, Your Eminence,' William replied quickly, sensing an ally in this cause. 'We lose the finest soldier this Order has ever known. Any mortal could be a Dar'uka, in my opinion. Marresca is . . .'

'Is what, Captain?'

'He is almost Dar'uka *now*, Your Eminence. He may not be immortal, but he fights with all the strength, courage and instinct that I have seen from any Dar'uka. If we lose Marresca to allies that we cannot call upon, then we lose a powerful weapon . . . in my opinion, Your Eminence.'

'I agree,' Devirus replied. 'But it is not our decision.'

'No, Your Eminence.'

Cardinal Devirus shook his head. 'I have advised Marresca, and he knows my mind. Should he agree to the request, we may yet profit. Two former soldiers of the Order in the Dar'uka may benefit us.'

'I disagree, Your Eminence. From experience,' William said bitterly, thinking of Kieran, 'friendship and loyalty are lost to them. They care not for our desires.'

Devirus waved his scrawny hand in the air dismissively. 'Regardless of Marresca's decision we have other matters that concern us.' The cardinal stepped down the side of Africa, planting his feet in the centre of the continent. He pointed down at the section where Africa met the Mediterranean Sea.

'Egypt,' William said.

'Yes. Egypt.'

'You have sent a company there, I understand.'

'Not just one, but the remnants of another from Spain,' Cardinal Devirus corrected him. 'In all, over thirty men with provisions and weapons. And they require a captain.'

William had an inkling this was coming. 'I am at your service, Your Eminence. Of course I will lead them.'

'You must leave soon. Tomorrow morning at the latest.'

William nodded with difficulty, remembering Adriana. 'So soon?' he asked.

'There isn't a moment to spare,' Cardinal Devirus replied as he took a seat by the lectern. 'Does the term "The Hoard of Mhorrer" mean anything to you?'

William nodded quickly. 'Of course. The fabled collection of Scarimadaen lost for thousands of years. Perhaps the greatest concentration of Scarimadaen ever assembled. Two hundred pyramids as I understand it.'

'Two hundred and fifty, Captain Saxon,' echoed a voice high above them. William looked up into the shadows and saw someone looking down from the gallery.

'Father Antonio, please join us,' Cardinal Devirus called up.

The father made his way down the steps and under the arch into the map room, his glasses perched upon his bony nose, unruly strands of hair straggling from his top lip and chin. He was slightly bent, and although not much older than William, he was gaunt and his eyes looked tired.

'Father Antonio,' William greeted, having met him several times during his visits to the Secretariat.

'Captain, I am delighted to meet you again,' he said with his high-pitched voice. He looked with nervous excitement over to Cardinal Devirus, who beckoned the priest forward. Under his arm was a large thick book, bound in a material that shimmered like silver. He rested it on the lectern, which creaked under its weight.

'Father Antonio is the most learned man in the Church on matters of Mhorrer,' Cardinal Devirus said. 'Please tell Captain Saxon more about the Hoard.'

Father Antonio's eyes lit up as he balanced the sizeable tome and opened it at a marked section. 'As written down in the *Book of Man*, the history of the Hoard was chronicled in the passages of *Gran-Man on Hu-Terra*. From what was translated by Nostradamus and Heracles, we know that in the last centuries of Revelation the one we call Mhorrer was entrusted with preparing the world for the coming of our Lord. However, Mhorrer was secretly working with Hell and designed the Scarimadaen, the individual gateways between our world and Hell, from which the spirit of the daemon can return time and time again through a host. It was Mhorrer, the architect of this instrument, who led a sect known as the Eyes of Fire, or Rassis Cult. Their sole cause was to undermine belief in God and to lure Humanity to the Traitor, the prince who governs Hell.

'One of the Cult's members was a man called Ordrane . . .'

William raised his eyebrows. '*Count* Ordrane?'

Father Antonio nodded. 'He was a student under Mhorrer; a gifted student according to the text. But Mhorrer saw ambition in the man as well. An ambition to rule rather than follow. It is said that Ordrane desired to imprison hundreds of men and women as hosts and through them release the daemons upon the world and conquer it for himself. Fearing that such a plan would rouse the suspicion of the Dar'uka, Mhorrer refused and hid the Scarimadaen from him. Most were scattered across the lands, hidden or lost, while Mhorrer concealed the greatest number of Scarimadaen in an unknown place to ensure that Ordrane would never find them.'

'But isn't the goal of Hell to conquer Man and drive us to our knees?' William said, confused by the revelation.

'Hell's ambition differs from Ordrane's,' Devirus told him. 'The Prince of Hell wants to punish Man for what has happened in the past. Only the destruction of Humanity will appease him. To achieve this, he must use more than the Scarimadaen. You see, the Scarimadaen are a tool, Captain Saxon. Like a scalpel. And the Rassis are the surgeons. They will unleash the Scarimadaen only at the right time.'

'When?' William said.

The cardinal shrugged. 'No one knows. Whatever plans the Prince of Hell has to achieve his aim have never been recorded. They can only be wondered at. Or feared. We may have time, but how much time is not known.

'Count Ordrane's ambition is much simpler. He wants the kingdom of the entire world as *his*, and Humanity in servitude. To Ordrane, the Scarimadaen is the ultimate threat, the means to force obedience. He cannot control it, but he can dangle it before heads of State and make examples of cities. With the Hoard in his hands, he could control countries. Continents. The world would fear him for eternity. And in this aim he is impatient. He will not wait for some unspecified time. Count Ordrane wishes our enslavement *now*.'

William nodded thoughtfully. 'His ambition contradicts the will of his masters.'

'Correct,' Devirus replied. 'He serves only himself.'

William blew out his cheeks, feeling a little bewildered. 'These Rassis . . . How will they react to Count Ordrane's followers?'

'We think aggressively, Captain,' Father Antonio replied. 'As far as the Rassis are concerned, Count Ordrane is an enemy. If they still guard the Hoard, the Rassis will no doubt know of the vampyres and the kafalas. They should be quite as hostile to them as they are to you.'

'Me?'

Cardinal Devirus nodded again, his smile broadening.

'The Hoard of Mhorrer has been found?' William surmised, only whispering it in case it was untrue.

'Yes! It dwells somewhere in the Sinai peninsula!' Father Antonio said animatedly, leaning over the lectern with a wild expression. 'Which is significant! For the Hoard to lie so close to Giza, where the *Book of Man* was discovered, must be no coincidence.'

'Is there a connection between Giza and the Hoard?' William asked.

'None that we know of,' Father Antonio admitted. 'The site around Egypt's pyramids was scoured by people from the Vatican, and nothing else was found. As for the Great Pyramids themselves, if there is a connection with the Scarimadaen, no scholar in history has discovered it.'

'Gentlemen,' Cardinal Devirus interrupted, 'these are matters for philosophers and academics. For the sake of urgency, shall we return to the matter at hand?'

Father Antonio bowed apologetically.

William stared down at the map again. 'I trust the information is reliable?'

'We have a good man in Egypt by the name of Charles Greynell. He is well travelled and has risked much to come by such information. He is your contact in Rashid and will guide you to the Hoard,' Cardinal Devirus said. 'Your mission is simple, Captain. You must locate the Hoard by any means and bring it back to Rome.'

'Return it *here*?'

'The Scarimadaen will be properly destroyed in the Chambers of Deconstruction, Captain,' Father Antonio explained.

'I understand,' William replied, but was concerned. 'You do of course see that there is a very real chance that Count Ordrane will ambush us on our way back from the Sinai. For such a prize he would send an army of kafalas against us.'

'We will send reinforcements to Rashid when we can,'

Cardinal Devirus said. 'We are stretched thin as it is and this news has caught us unawares. To wait any further for our people to return from their various missions might cost us dear.'

'Then you believe Count Ordrane knows the Hoard's location?'

'A distinct possibility, Captain Saxon,' Devirus confessed. 'Count Ordrane has many spies, as we do. And he has been searching for the Hoard of Mhorrer longer than there has been a Christian Church.'

'What of this Rassis Cult?' William asked.

Father Antonio leafed through the tome. 'According to the *Book of Man*, only Mhorrer was apprehended and tried for treason, not the cult. The Rassis might still exist.'

'Mhorrer died without passing on the hiding place of his Hoard,' Devirus added, his fingers locked together. 'His followers, if they survived, would have ensured utter secrecy on this matter. We are fortunate that we have found it after centuries of searching. Further time must not be wasted. You must gather your wits and prepare.'

'I would like Lieutenant Peruzo with me,' William said.

'There is already a lieutenant waiting in Rashid,' Cardinal Devirus replied.

'And I am sure he's able enough, but I trust Peruzo with my life,' William explained. 'Who else in the Order, apart from Engrin, has as much experience? This mission is a dangerous one, perhaps the greatest in the annals of the Order. I want the right men with me.'

Cardinal Devirus nodded. 'Very well. Peruzo travels with you.'

'And what of Marresca?' William said suddenly. 'We could use his help on such a mission.'

Devirus narrowed his eyes. 'Brother Marresca has made his decision, Captain. He will *not* be coming to the Sinai.'

William bit his lip, realizing that all talk of persuasion had been a screen to placate him. Marresca had already agreed. He would be a Dar'uka by morning.

Devirus rose and motioned to Father Antonio at the lectern. 'Antonio will furnish instructions, Captain. Study them well and then destroy them. There can be no record of the mission.'

Father Antonio took several letters from the lectern and passed them to William, his expression hopeful. William took them from his hands, while trying to hide his concern.

△ II △

For two dark hours in the subterranean surrounds of the grottoes, William pored over the letters, reading them three times before burning what he'd memorized. The final letter was a message from Charles Greynell, which William read but kept with him:

To my sponsors,

This is a letter of some importance, yet written in haste as I believe I am being followed by the agents of malevolence. Note that while I cannot say too much, I will tell more when I meet your representatives in the city.

For your pleasure, as I am certain you will share this news with vigorous joy, the secret of the architect has now been discovered. In my possession is its whereabouts and we must not delay in locating and dispatching a treasure that is worth more than any currency of this world.

Again, I must advise haste. The secret I refer to may relocate if any inkling of discovery has been aroused. The Rassis are not indolent. If they find me I will be dead and the enigma will relocate elsewhere. I will guard all such matters with my life, but be swift. Other agents are here and may learn my secret. A riddle of fire that could be unlocked by wanderers in the desert.

Your faithful servant,
Charles Greynell

William had read the letter several times and found there were more riddles contained in its brevity than in a whole evening of conversation with Engrin Meerwall.

He slipped the letter into his jacket and left the gallery quietly, Father Antonio's voice echoing with Devirus's in the map room.

The rooms were suddenly colder now, and William shivered as he made his way through the passage and the thick wooden doors to the grottoes beyond. Pausing first to take leave of the guards, he walked down the tunnel, the faint trickling of water resonating from some hidden place in the vast catacombs.

Only at the stables and in the outside air did the full implications of what had passed begin to dawn on him. Humanity and its nemesis had been searching for the Hoard for thousands of years. None had been successful, not even Count Ordrane, for all his power and influence. The mission might well promise failure and death. But it also offered the greatest victory ever known, a victory unparalleled. The victors would be immortalized, perhaps even as Saints.

William didn't consider what consequence it would have on Adriana until he was trotting down the thoroughfare towards the bridge over the Tiber. She would surely baulk at his leaving again, and if she learned that this mission was so perilous, she would not easily let him go. Would she understand?

Through the thronging midday streets of the city, a colourful, bountiful medley of sights, smells and sounds, William could have been distracted, but they seemed colourless compared with the burden he had agreed to bear. All those he passed, from the beggar bowed in shame as he murmured pitiful requests for money, to the noble and his peacock-feathered hat, resplendent in jacket and breeches, flouncing down the main street with an entourage close behind in paid respect – all meant nothing beside this new quest.

Yet to fail would destroy all of it.

As he reached the suburbs, the weather took a different turn. The once fathomless blue skies were now smothered by quickly forming clouds, at first brilliant white, then bulging into grey and black, with rain in store.

It was a cold, bitter downpour that followed and William might have considered waiting for an hour or so before taking the journey back to Villeda, perhaps even frequenting a tavern nearby. But the matter at hand allowed him no choice.

He must return, and quickly.

△ III △

Hours later he arrived in Villeda, soaked through and miserable. After a while, he dismounted and led his horse on foot through the streets of the town. Most of Villeda's folk had retired inside save for a few dashing under cover with their hands full of food, drink or clothes. None noticed William, too preoccupied with staying dry. He let the water run from his scalp, his hair bedraggled and hanging over his eyes and down his neck.

As he turned down the next street, the rain was falling so hard he could only see a few yards in front and was up to his ankles in water. Grumbling, William patted his sodden horse and considered remounting him. But there was a sound nearby, of crashing feet in water, and William turned just as something lunged towards him through the rain. He reacted at once and ducked the thrust, reaching for his sword. The accuracy was poor and would not have killed him, but the intention was there and he swung his own sword towards the assailant, his blade slicing through the downpour. The attacker bent to his right, parried and covered up as William fought him. Again he swung low, but this time the attacker feinted left, brought his sword up and connected with William's just above the hilt. With the water wetting his grip, the sword slipped from William's fingers and flew through the air to skid through a puddle by his horse.

William stood breathless and defeated in the rain. The figure in front, a foot or two smaller and just as wet through, pointed his sword towards him for a few moments. He then walked steadily over to the puddle and retrieved William's sword. Sheathing his own, he surprised William by presenting his weapon back to him, almost nonchalantly.

As he did so, William saw his assailant clearly.

'By all that is holy!' William cursed. 'Marco?'

Marco grinned back at him.

'What the hell are you doing?' William ranted.

'Hello, Uncle,' he greeted gently.

'I could have killed you!' William shouted.

Marco laughed. 'Today you *wouldn't* have.'

'You think this is a game?!' William said incredulously.

Marco shrugged. 'Not really. I felt I needed to prove myself.'

William lunged forward and took Marco's arm roughly, yanking him over to the horse. 'Prove yourself?' he yelled. 'Prove yourself by being killed? I would have run you through!'

'I can handle myself!' Marco protested.

'You can handle *nothing*,' William shouted. 'And you've proved only that you are irresponsible.'

'I need to join the Order! To serve with you!'

'How many times must we talk about this?' William growled. 'This is not your destiny! You are *not* to become a soldier of the Order. Never!'

'I can make my own decisions,' Marco retorted.

'You are only fourteen years old . . .'

'Fifteen in the summer.'

'. . . And far too young!' William shouted back.

'Marresca is only three years older than I,' Marco replied.

'Marresca is a genius. You are not!' William replied sternly, but fell quiet when he noted the change in the boy's expression. Marco looked down at the ground, almost humiliated. William had hurt his pride. He relaxed and let go of his arm. 'You are fine with a sword, Marco,' he conceded, 'but not good enough for the Order.'

'I disarmed *you*,' he said petulantly.

William did not reply, but mounted his horse. 'Are you

coming home with me? Or back to the Maldinis'? Either way, get inside before you catch a cold.'

Marco stayed silent, skulking away through the rain.

'Bloody fool,' William murmured, but was secretly worried. Marco had indeed disarmed him, and disarmed him well. He put it down to a lack of concentration more than anything. Yes, that was it. He was thinking about the mission ahead of him, and wasn't prepared for an attack in Villeda itself. I mean, who would attack him in Villeda?

'Plenty of people,' William murmured to himself, thinking about Count Ordrane among so many enemies. He realized he had been complacent. The William of several years ago would not have been so relaxed.

And he could not afford to drop his guard in Egypt.

△ IV △

Adriana sat in the porch combing her hair as the rain abated and the sun dared to return, the smell of fresh rain on the grass and the plants scenting the air. She put down the comb and sighed, waiting for her lover to return.

William rode up, his expression troubled. At first sight of her, he tried a dazzling smile that came out awkward under his sodden state, and could only make a half-hearted wave.

'You're soaked to the skin!' she exclaimed as she stayed on the porch.

'I think maybe to the bone,' he corrected, wiping the rain from his face. He dismounted and led his horse to the stable before jogging over to the house.

Adriana towelled him down and helped undress him. She could see he was preoccupied, yet felt playful as she unbuttoned his shirt and pulled it away. Then she pulled down his breeches, towelling his chest, his stomach and then groin. There was instant arousal there, replacing his distraction. It was what she needed. She wanted him now, concentrating on *her*.

William made love to her, though his thoughts were else-where.

Lying in bed, the outside world growing dark all too soon, William was drowsy and his mouth felt parched, tasting only Adriana. The smell of sex hung in the air as he sat up and swung his feet over the edge of the bed. He stood up and stretched, the chill of April causing him to gooseflesh.

William donned his gown and walked down the hall and into the kitchen for some water. He helped himself to a slice of bread from the work-table, and looked through the half-shuttered window to the world outside. The sky was clear and the stars seemed to shine brighter than they had in months. He found himself staring at them as he did most nights, staring in case he saw a shooting star, and that shooting star might be Kieran. In the past he had hoped the shooting star would visit him, but tonight he hoped it didn't.

'Are you restless, my love?' Adriana said behind him. William turned, surprised by her appearance.

'You should be in bed,' he said to her.

'So should you,' she replied.

William looked at the bread in his hand. 'I was hungry,' he said, 'and thirsty.'

'So am I,' Adriana replied plainly as she crossed over to him. She reached up to his hand and William expected she would take some of the bread, but instead her hands ran down his arms and across his chest, slipping beneath the gown. She leaned up to him and his lips met hers twice, and then stronger. Putting down the bread and water, he held her close again, tasting her sweet lips and tongue, feeling himself grow harder against her body. He couldn't believe how much desire one person could rouse in him, and he felt his reserves of energy being tapped again. Her hands moved over his body, pulling the gown apart. They ran lower to his groin and William gasped. She smiled and kissed him again before nuzzling close.

'You put a fire in me, Adriana.'

'The fire was already there, my love,' she whispered back playfully. 'I only feed it.'

William kissed the top of her head and sighed. 'I wish it could last for ever.'

'Then why shouldn't it?'

'*Because* . . .' he confessed. 'Because of who I am.'

'I love you, William,' she said. 'And I will love you whatever you are.'

'I know,' William said. 'Marco attacked me today.'

'He attacked you? Where?' she said, surprised and then pleased.

'Just outside the square,' William murmured. 'The bloody fool jumped me.'

She laughed.

'It's not amusing, Adriana!' William grunted, still bewildered by it.

'With a sword?' she asked.

'Yes!' William said, thinking she didn't believe him.

'He was just trying to impress you,' she said calmly.

'Impress me? I almost bloody killed him!'

'Really?'

He shrugged. 'Well, maybe not . . .' he conceded, 'but it was a damned foolish thing to do.'

'He has been practising for a while now,' Adriana admitted.

'With the sword?' William said. 'Who's been teaching him?'

'Well . . .' she said and lifted her head, 'don't be angry, Will, but I've taught him a little . . .'

'*You?*' William barked. He was angry. Adriana knew how to use a sword; she had been taught by her father in Tresta before the town was destroyed by Count Ordrane's men. But even she was a novice with respect to William and the monks of the Order.

'And Peruzo,' she added and smiled coyly.

William's eyes grew wide. 'Peruzo as well?! Behind my back . . . I don't believe this!'

'You said you wouldn't be angry,' Adriana protested.

80

'I said nothing of the sort!' William replied and untangled her arms from around his body. He stormed to the other side of the kitchen.

'Marco is strong-willed and would find trouble with or without your blessing,' Adriana called after him. 'Peruzo taught him tricks in case he put himself in harm's way. He didn't want him defenceless.'

'He encouraged him!' William growled.

'No, he didn't,' Adriana rebuked. 'He tried to teach him to resolve conflict peacefully. As a monk is taught. But Marco would not accept that. You know him, Will . . . You *know* what kind of boy he has become. He is surrounded by death. His family was murdered by the same evil you fight against. You are a hero that everyone looks up to. And Marco feels no differently. He loves you. But worse, he wants to *be* you.'

William looked haunted. 'I didn't ask for his adoration, Adriana,' he said.

'But you have it all the same,' she replied and walked over to him. 'Whether you like it or not. Don't be hard on Marco. Remember it was you who told him he could not be part of the Order. Perhaps if you had let him, he would have learned himself that there is a choice between fighting and not fighting.'

'Do you think a boy of Marco's age could learn the words of Sun Tzu? Do you think a boy like Marco could hold his nerve in sight of the horrors I witness on every mission? I very much doubt it.'

'You have never given him that chance.'

'I won't let him be killed,' William said. 'Just once I'd like the people I care for not to be involved in whatever terrible things *I* have to endure.' He bowed his head and closed his eyes. 'You have both been through so much, you should not have to endure any more.'

'Marco thinks differently. Maybe you should let him join the Order,' Adriana cooed, and stroked his chest with her long fingers.

William shook his head. 'If Marco joins, he will wish to serve under me. I could never lead Marco and be myself as well. It would be folly. Do you wish for that?'

'No,' Adriana admitted after a few moments.

'Marco must be content with his apprenticeship at the farm, and that is the last word on the matter,' William said. 'No more training with the sword. I will speak with Peruzo tomorrow.'

'Don't be hard on him, Will,' Adriana urged. 'Peruzo has only done what he thought best in my nephew's interests.'

'As do I,' William reiterated. He looked to the horizon and his brow knitted together, causing long lines of worry to age his face by years.

'Is that everything?' she asked.

'Everything?' he echoed.

'There's more, isn't there?' Adriana remarked. 'I know you too well. Something else is wrong.'

William fidgeted, but Adriana would not let it go.

'Do you remember my friend Kieran?'

Adriana smiled. 'The handsome one?'

William looked indignant.

Adriana laughed and cuddled him. 'I'm only teasing. Yes, I remember Kieran. How could I not? You were inseparable until that night in Villeda.'

William rested his cheek against the top of her head and held her tighter. 'I saw him in Prague a few weeks ago.'

Adriana pulled away from him and looked up into his eyes. 'He came to you?'

William nodded, his expression grave.

'You've waited seven years for his return, so why so sad?' she asked, judging his expression.

'Kieran is dead,' he said, and checked his remark after Adriana looked horrified. 'What I mean is, the Kieran I knew is dead, since he became Dar'uka . . . One of those "angels". Oh, he has changed so much, Adriana. He looks at me as a stranger might, not as a brother. He was so pale, and those eyes . . . He . . .'

Adriana put a hand to his cheek. 'What is it?'

'He put *fear* in me,' William said, despairingly. 'I loved him, but now he is this *abomination*. His power is unimaginable. And he is *so* cold. Before, he would have given his life for me, and I for him. Now I fear that he would take my life if it helped his cause. I mean nothing to him.'

'But you are both fighting the same war, aren't you?'

'On different terms,' William corrected. 'And he wants to take Marresca on those terms.'

'But Marresca is just a boy,' Adriana said in disbelief. 'They cannot seriously . . .'

'They can,' William interrupted. 'And Marresca has told them he will. Just when I need him more than ever.'

'*You* need Marresca?'

William looked down at her, realizing what he'd said.

Adriana fell silent. 'You're going away, aren't you?' she said finally, pulling away from him.

'Yes,' he murmured.

She walked over to the doorway of the kitchen and glanced back. 'When?'

'Tomorrow morning,' he said, feeling guilty.

Adriana looked distant and sad. 'I see.'

'Adriana . . .' William began, trying to think of something to say that would explain why.

'I know you have little choice, William,' she interrupted. 'We'll just have to make the most of our time together.'

William nodded but she left the kitchen in silence. He looked down at the bread but had lost his appetite. Drinking the water in two gulps he followed Adriana to the bedroom and stayed at the door as he watched her slip back beneath the blanket.

'What if you were to leave?' she said quietly, barely daring to say it.

'What was that, my love?'

'What if you left the Secretariat and the Order? What if you stayed here with me?'

William smiled. 'You know I cannot.'

'I know. But if you could?'

William strolled over and stroked away the hair from her brow. 'If I could, I would, my sweet, sweet Adriana,' he purred, but there was hesitation too.

'I think you would not,' she said as she pulled away.

William lowered his hand sheepishly. 'Life is good right now,' he confessed. 'I have everything I want. I don't want it to change.'

'Life is good because you are alive,' she told him. 'Would you be thinking the same if you were dead?'

'Foolish words,' William scoffed, though his fragile laughter hid his understanding. He knew she was right.

'Do you think I will wait for you to die? Do you think it is so easy for me to see you leave, thinking I may never see you again?' she said angrily.

William laughed and took hold of her, Adriana squirming in his grip. 'But I always do! I always come back!'

She wriggled out of his arms and sat on the edge of the bed. 'One day you might not.'

The seriousness of her voice was enough for William. He didn't want to part on such bad terms. 'Maybe some day it can change,' he whispered to her. 'We will live a simple life, and I will become a farmer.'

'You would?' she asked hopefully.

He kissed her forehead. 'I would do anything for you. Just be patient with me.'

Adriana rolled over onto her side. 'Of course I will,' she admitted. 'I will wait for you until Judgement Day. You know I will.'

William did know, and that hurt more.

'Lie with me,' she said.

'Later,' he answered, now stroking her bare shoulder. 'I am too awake with thoughts.'

'I will stay awake with you,' Adriana murmured drowsily, her words growing quieter and quieter. 'If it bothers you so much . . .

you should try to convince young Marresca not to join Kieran. If it bothers you so much, you should talk him out of it . . .'

'I could try, though would he listen to me?' William whispered back.

There was no reply. Adriana was already asleep.

CHAPTER FIVE

Dar'uka

△ I △

There were few ties to bind Marresca to his life. When he left the monastery at Saint Laurence he had no need to say good-bye to the other monks, no need to pause at the places where he had spent most of his childhood training, the armoury where he'd been given his first sword, and where he'd begun to master most of the Order's range of weaponry. He simply mounted his horse and urged it under the ivy-covered arch to the front gates, pausing by the two guards standing outside in the cold, the long mists of that spring evening settling about them.

'Lieutenant,' they greeted him.

Marresca nodded.

The first guard glanced at his comrade with suspicion. 'It is past midnight. Where are you going at such an hour, sir?' he asked.

Marresca stared down at him long and hard. He had not counted on there being some resistance to him venturing out so late.

'He is here to see me,' came a voice from across the road.

The guards looked over and saw a solitary rider, his head covered by a grey hood against the chill of night. The rider stepped his horse forward and pulled away the cowl.

'Captain Saxon,' said the guard. 'My apologies . . .'

'Not needed,' William assured him. 'It is indeed a strange

86

night for a ride, but these are strange times. Are they not, Lieutenant?'

Marresca looked over at him and gave a curt nod.

'Good night gentlemen,' William said, and pulled his horse to the side to let Marresca trot past. William turned his mount about and rode alongside the lieutenant.

'I hope you don't mind,' William said, 'I thought I would join you.'

'If you wish, Captain,' Marresca said, 'but I doubt you will be going where I will.'

'Quite,' William agreed. 'But if it's all the same to you, I'd like to accompany you part of the way at least.'

The sky was almost clear except for a thin veil of mist hanging below it. There was a full moon that seemed to light the mist from one edge of the horizon to the next, the light extending to the fogbanks that clawed their way over field and ditch, rose against stone walls, and crept around tree and bush. The road from Villeda was thick with it, and the air was cold.

William pulled up his collar and breathed out a sigh. They had ridden two miles already and Marresca had not uttered a further word.

'Why didn't you come to me, Marresca? Why haven't you spoken about your decision to anyone other than Cardinal Devirus?' William said finally, the silence between them growing irksome.

'What would you have me say, Captain?' Marresca asked, either not seeing the problem or unwilling to discuss it.

'I expected you to ask me about the Dar'uka,' William complained. 'I expected you to seek the truth about what you are letting yourself in for. My association with them is not a secret within the Order, is it? So why not come to me before now?'

Marresca shrugged. 'It had not entered my mind, Captain,' he confessed. 'Being asked to join the Dar'uka is the greatest honour any man can ask for. It felt impertinent to question their reasons.'

'It is not *their* reasons I speak of, Lieutenant,' William griped.

'I have seen what happens to men who trade in their mortal lives for this so-called gift. You remember my friend?'

'Kieran Harte,' Marresca said.

'The same,' William replied. 'When he came to me outside the church in Prague, I saw what they had done to him. They *ruined* him, Marresca. They cut out his soul and left him dead.'

When Marresca glanced at him, William couldn't tell whether the lieutenant was impressed by what he said. There was just this cold, flawless expression of indifference. Marresca shrugged again. 'So you came tonight to convince me *not* to become Dar'uka?' he accused.

William felt defensive and made noises of denial.

'I understand why, Captain,' Marresca said.

'You do?' William said hopefully.

'You are looking after my welfare, as you always have,' Marresca said, turning to look straight ahead towards the road that rose up one of the steepest of hills.

William felt relieved. 'That's right. Your welfare.'

'So it has nothing to do with the Hoard of Mhorrer?' Marresca said bluntly.

'Naturally I would prefer you to join the mission,' William replied. 'You are the finest soldier in the Order. You will be greatly missed.'

The young lieutenant glanced at William again, and there was the faintest of smiles. 'Thank you, Captain.'

'My concern is your fate, Lieutenant,' William said, hunching his shoulders.

'My fate?' Marresca stopped his horse abruptly. He turned in his saddle and studied William. 'Or the fate of Kieran Harte, Captain?'

William stared at Marresca, stunned both by the accusation and by Marresca's intuition.

'This is not about Kieran . . .'

'I believe it is, Captain,' Marresca said. 'He has changed and you do not like what he has changed into. It is only natural. He was like a brother to you, Captain.'

William nodded. 'Yes. He was.'

'Why did he become Dar'uka?'

William breathed out, a cloud that quickly melted. 'For a deadly sin, Lieutenant,' he said and brooded in the saddle. 'Seven years ago, neither Kieran nor I believed in daemons or vampyres. We were just soldiers. We knew little or cared little for the affairs of the Church.

'When we faced our first daemon, we barely escaped with our lives. But many didn't. One of those killed was a woman called Katherine. She and Kieran were very much in love at the time. He blamed himself for her death. And when he stopped blaming himself, he blamed the daemon that killed her.

'I resigned myself to what happened that night, but Kieran could not. His fury possessed him, and he sought revenge. That is why he became Dar'uka. For the sake of vengeance. To satisfy his own anger. He would murder all of Hell, if he was able.'

Marresca listened closely, nodding at every pause, and although at times it seemed as though his attention was elsewhere, William could tell by the intensity in his expression that the young lieutenant was taking in every detail.

'I remember when I first met you, Captain,' he said after William had finished. 'You were sparring against Lieutenant Cazotte in the courtyard. When the sparring was done, Master Yu gestured for us to leave. I watched from afar as you spoke to Lieutenant Harte. I saw you were close. As close as brothers.'

William felt choked up and he blinked rapidly to stop the tears from welling up in his eyes. He hadn't expected Marresca to remember, and the mention of Kieran, then Cazotte, overwhelmed him. He looked away. 'You have a good memory,' he said, his words caught in his throat. 'You were an initiate. Just a boy, as I recall.'

'Now I am a man,' Marresca reminded him. William looked back and saw clearly that he was. He was more of a man than many he knew. Courageous. Strong. A warrior without equal. 'And I have made my choice, Captain. I have never had a brother. Never a sister. I never knew my mother, and my father . . . he was just a travelling man who gave my mother a son. I never knew him either. My only family has been the Order. And now my family will be the Dar'uka.'

William nodded. 'Don't expect your new family to be as compassionate, Lieutenant.'

'I won't,' Marresca said and started to ride again. 'But I am not Kieran Harte. My reasons are not governed by vengeance. They are quite straightforward. I am a weapon. And becoming Dar'uka will make me the most powerful weapon there is against Hell. That is my reason – the *only* reason.'

As Marresca rode ahead, William hung back to think about this. The lad had certainly thought it through, and some of it made sense. He *was* a strong warrior, and would become stronger as Dar'uka. A warrior of little equal, even among the angels. Would such a warrior drive fear into the heart of Hell? Would such a warrior bring a swift end to this eternal war?

But there was also the matter of the mission to the Sinai.

'What if you delayed your decision?' William called after him, and trotted up the hill to be at his side again. 'What if you came to Egypt first?'

'To fight the Rassis Cult and take the prize?'

William, again, was surprised. 'How much do you know about my mission?'

'Cardinal Devirus told me everything,' Marresca said. 'I have known about the Rassis for some time. It was part of the cardinal's teachings. I also know of the Hoard of Mhorrer. It will be a dangerous adventure.'

'All the more reason for you to delay your decision and come with me to Egypt,' William replied cannily. He smiled at him, but it was not reciprocated.

'The Dar'uka wish for an answer by the third full moon,' Marresca said, gesturing to the bright glow behind the mist.

'They can wait surely?' William said.

Marresca did not reply.

★

After half a mile, the road began to level off. The conversation rarely turned from the Dar'uka, but Marresca sidestepped William's wish for a delay by asking questions about the angels. After a brief description of the battle in Aosta, Marresca told William what *he* knew, and again revelations were abundant, as William soon discovered he knew less than Marresca.

'The *Book of Man* speaks only of the first five Dar'uka,' Marresca told him, 'not of those who replaced the fallen. Did you know, for instance, that one of the first Dar'uka, a man called Mykael, was killed by Ordrane?'

William shook his head, bewildered and stunned into silence. He had been silent for the last quarter of an hour.

'Count Ordrane has accounted for two Dar'uka as I understand it. One was documented in the *Book of Man*, the other is folklore. You can learn both from Father Antonio.'

'I know,' William conceded, echoing the words of Cardinal Devirus. 'Father Antonio is the most learned man in the Church on matters of Mhorrer.'

'Not just Mhorrer, but all of the *Book of Man*,' Marresca marvelled. 'There is little in that book that he does not know.'

'So you know enough to come to a decision, ill-judged as it is,' William begrudged.

'Ill-judged to you maybe, Captain. You have only your friend as a gauge,' Marresca replied as they arrived at a clearing which marked the top of the hill. He paused to look to the sky; the mists were fading above them. Behind them were clouds, gathering as they had in Prague.

'A storm?' Marresca ventured.

'Not so natural,' William remarked, and led them over to a nearby tree. He dismounted and tethered his horse to the trunk. Marresca did the same, wrapping the reins around a thick branch.

The clouds seemed to bulge outwards, spreading like ashen dough from the sky above them, radiating outwards. Their undersides began to crackle. A single flash tore the rolling formation in two, but then it merged again as the first drops of rain fell.

William put out his hand and felt the first drop hit his palm, and then the second. 'They're coming,' he said.

Marresca stepped away from the tree, his face upturned to the clouds as the rain fell harder. Soon his face was awash, the rain running over his cheeks and down his chin. His long, blond hair straggled down over his eyes and slapped haphazardly across his forehead.

William elected to stay under the tree, where raindrops were few, but large. He felt them striking his head and shoulders and he pulled the jacket's collar up as far as it could go.

There was a deep rumble and a bright flash lit up the clearing. Marresca smiled into the storm and raised his arms to the sky. William marvelled at how calm the young warrior was. Was he too naïve to understand his peril, or did he understand it better than William could?

Another rumble, this time louder and deeper, sent a tremor through the air and it appeared as though the cascading rains were shunted to the east. They reset themselves a moment later with a greater downpour that soaked Marresca through.

'Can't you feel it, Captain?' Marresca shouted.

William shivered. He could, but would not admit it.

'The power! Can't you feel the power?'

Another thunderous groan pounded the air, but this time the sound was incredible. The whole hill shook and the horses panicked. William grabbed hold of his reins just as the animal reared, almost kicking William to the ground. But Marresca's horse broke free and galloped away into the night.

William turned to warn Marresca what had happened, just as the entire clearing was lit up by a blinding and searingly bright glare. William threw his hand to his eyes as the world around him was rent apart by a deafening explosion of sound. The power shook William to the bones, bones that he could almost see through his closed eyes from the bursts of light landing nearby.

He cowered, painfully aware that he was doing so, and swore at the top of his voice, also aware that no one would hear him under the tremendous boom of thunder.

'. . . stards!' he finished as all fell quiet again.

His horse, once stunned, began to struggle again, causing the trunk to groan as it pulled and pulled. William did not fear the crazed animal would tear down the whole tree, more that it would break its own neck if it pulled any harder.

William looked over to Marresca and found him kneeling in the mud. There was a pool of water around him, and he knelt like the defeated and the humbled, his head bowed, the rain falling over him.

He was not alone.

To his left stood the albino warrior William had seen in Prague. To the right there was a man as tall as the albino, but more slender, his long arms tattooed with great black symbols. He was barely clothed apart from a loincloth and a flag draped around his shoulders that appeared to be Hispanic.

A third warrior appeared from a few yards away. He was oriental, with long black hair tied back against a white scalp. All three shared a common trait: they ignored William completely, interested only in Marresca.

Apart from Kieran, that is, who was staring across at William. 'Why are you here, William Saxon?' he asked. His voice seemed to fracture into many. They darted through the misty air, swirling about to where William stood, the intonations breaking upon his ears like driven rain.

William held his ground. 'To talk. To talk to you,' he replied. After the quite blunt and one-sided argument with Marresca so far that night, he half-expected Kieran to tell him there was nothing to talk about.

'Very well,' Kieran agreed.

Yes, the night was *full* of surprises, William thought as he walked out from the cover of the tree. He was soaked through in moments, but it was worth it.

They walked from the tree to a small brook that ran from

the hills above them to the town in the valley below. Despite the darkness and rain, they could see the valley laid out before them.

'What do you want, William?' Kieran said, his voices parting and merging in an unsettling weave of words. William hoped he would talk less and would just listen (he wasn't sure how much he could take of this unfamiliar and uncomfortable sensation).

'It's about your decision to recruit Marresca,' William said. 'I'm asking you again to reconsider. I will be honest with you, Kieran, for the sake of old times . . . I've tried to persuade Marresca *not* to join you.'

Kieran looked at William with those full black eyes, azure light crackling about their surface. 'Why would you do that?'

'Because I need him more than you do,' William lied.

'Explain yourself.'

William smiled coyly. 'I thought you knew everything,' he teased, but Kieran's expression was unsettling. 'Fine. As you do not know . . . I've been given a mission. A mission of great importance.'

There was still no change in Kieran's expression.

'They've found the Hoard of Mhorrer,' William said finally.

'*Mhorrer's Hoard . . .*' came a flurry of voices, not just from Kieran but from the other three Dar'uka nearby.

'*Can it be true?*'

'*The Hoard has been found?*'

'*By whom?*'

'*And the Rassis?*'

All the words seem to jumble together into a maelstrom of nonsense and William flinched under the onslaught. 'Enough!' he shouted. 'I can bear just one of you talking at once . . . My head feels ready to explode!'

Kieran held up a hand. 'Is this true, William Saxon? Has the Hoard been found?'

'Yes,' William confirmed. 'It is somewhere in the Sinai. I need

94

Marresca's help to retrieve it. He is a great soldier, and we will surely miss him, Kieran. Can you not see that?'

'We have searched for the Hoard of Mhorrer for thousands of years,' Kieran said.

William brightened. 'Really? So Marresca *can* stay?'

'No,' Kieran replied. 'He cannot. He must become Dar'uka.'

'*Always five there are, the five Dar'uka. No less, no more, to fight the war,*' said the Dar'uka in a jarring chorus.

'I've heard this before,' William said, raising his voice, 'but you have just said that you've been searching for the Hoard for thousands of years . . .'

'We have,' Kieran conceded, 'but there is more at stake than the Hoard of Mhorrer.'

'What could be more important?' William said, completely baffled.

'The battle for the Gates of Hell,' Kieran told him. 'It was there that David perished, there that we almost lost the war, and it is there that we must prevail. All five Dar'uka must fight to secure the Gates.'

'The Gates?' William said. 'Where are these Gates?'

'You would not understand,' Kieran told him. 'They are beyond this world. And beyond your comprehension. We will take Marresca to the Gates of Hell. As Dar'uka, he will help us seal the Gates for ever.'

William was feeling nauseous, either from the effect of Kieran's fractured voices, or the bombardment of revelation upon revelation until everything grew meaningless. He staggered away and leant against the tree, stroking his horse's neck to calm the beast as much as it provided an anchor to the familiar. His conversation with his best friend was requiring great leaps in a faith he did not possess, nor did he understand. 'Look . . .' he said, 'you want the Hoard as well, don't you?'

Kieran looked blank.

'Then at least promise me you will come to our aid when we find it,' William implored.

95

'We cannot . . .' Kieran said.

'Goddammit, Kieran!' William cried out. 'I have never, *ever*, asked for your help before now. I've hoped for it, even prayed that you or your friends would come to our aid at the worst of times, but you never have. Now I am asking you . . . *Please help me*. I don't want to beg.'

'You do not have to, William,' Kieran replied. 'Begging will not change anything. There is no swift return from where we are going. For the time it takes to travel to the Gates of Hell, many weeks will have elapsed here on *this* world. And the battle at the Gates will not be short, believe me.'

'Then you will not?' William said angrily, teetering between fury and despair.

'We *cannot*,' Kieran said and then faltered. 'But we will *try*.'

'You will?' William asked hopefully.

Kieran nodded just the once.

'That is all I ask for,' William said with relief. He wanted to shake Kieran's hand to seal the pact, or to embrace his friend, believing that the impasse had been overcome. But the light that stroked Kieran's eyes, crackling over his hands, repelled him. He kept his distance and his fear of Kieran returned.

William retreated to his horse and untethered it. It bucked, but steadied, and he whispered calming words. He walked the animal through the rain to where Marresca knelt. Crouching down, he put out a hand to him.

'Good luck, Lieutenant,' he said. 'It was a pleasure to have you under my command.'

Marresca looked up beneath his straggly wet fringe, his face drenched. He smiled and shook William's hand. 'Thank you, Captain.'

William mounted his horse and turned about to look on the eerie and washed-out scene before him. The rains had not relented and the Dar'uka stood dispassionately under the downpour, steam rising and hissing from the power coursing over their bodies.

'William,' Kieran called out. It surprised him, and also

William's horse, which stirred and pulled. 'Do not underestimate the cult of the Rassis. They are cunning. They are strong. They have been fighting this war longer than you. In our absence, you should find allies where you can.'

William stared over at Kieran and gave a short nod. He wanted to say something, maybe even thank him, though he did not know what for.

Kieran had made no promises. Kieran had offered nothing, but took much. All William could do was ride away through the rain and let Marresca's fate be decided for him.

△ II △

The villa was quiet. Even the crickets had been silenced, and only a few brave dogs in the yards of Villeda were barking, roused by the distant storm that had since faded with the midnight mist.

William stood in the gloom of the bedroom and undressed, pulling away his sodden shirt. He dried himself with a towel and slipped under the sheets to lie next to Adriana, her warm, soft body bringing comfort after a hopeless cause.

The ride back to the villa was dominated by thoughts of the mission to the Sinai. There was much to do, and much to prepare for, now that his most valued soldier was gone – blazing away through the storm with the four other lights that erupted from the top of that hill.

William had watched them leave, and watched some measure of hope leave with them. But his own words to Kieran came back to him: '*Everything* we have succeeded in doing has been done without you. We don't need you . . .'

He had made that claim all those weeks ago in Prague, through rage and frustration. But now its clarity and truth was irrefutable. And *inevitable*.

'Will?' Adriana murmured, stirring by him.

'I'm here, my love,' he whispered and kissed her neck.

'Is it done?' she asked sleepily.

William knew what she meant: was everything resolved? He kissed her neck again and smiled, holding her close. 'Yes, my love. I know what I must do now.'

Chapter Six

Leaving Again

△ I △

William disliked prolonged partings, so it was with a muted farewell that he left Adriana after breakfast. He leaned down from the saddle and kissed her on the lips, cupping her cheek with one hand while holding the reins with the other.

'I will return. I promise,' he said to her, more in hope than certainty.

Adriana was strong; she did not cry, and bit her lip against the desire. She knew William hated seeing her upset, and she would do right by him. But once he had ridden out of sight, the tears would fall without control. Every time she watched him leave it felt painfully final.

As he cantered down the path under the arch, she cried out, unable to contain herself any longer: '*I love you!*'

William half-turned and waved back, gathering his composure as he rode away.

Villeda was already awake with the news that Captain William Saxon was leaving again. As he rode to St Laurence, a farmer and several children waved over to him, and William returned the gesture, but awkwardly. Like Adriana, it all felt strangely climatic.

'You're being foolish,' he muttered to himself as he galloped up the mile or so of road to the monastery. Under the arches of trees and ivy, his horse took William proudly to the gates of Saint Laurence, where a handful of monks were waiting. He greeted each in turn, dismounting quickly.

The brothers jostled forward, eager to take his horse, leaving William to march under the big stone arch towards the courtyard inside the monastery.

How quiet it was.

He walked around the edge of the quad and looked about the stone benches, pots of white flowers at each corner, the chimes ringing gently from the gallery. He closed his eyes for several minutes and drew in a deep lungful of air, smelling the primroses close by.

William relaxed and his doubts lost their potency. How many times had he trained in this courtyard? Many, he recalled, since Lieutenant Cazotte had tried to make an example of him in front of the other initiates years ago. It was a strangely fond memory.

'My friend . . .' he murmured. 'What would you have made of me now?'

An initiate – shaven-headed and younger than Marco – appeared at the gallery.

'Boy,' William called, 'bring me Lieutenant Peruzo.'

The initiate bowed and William sat down on one of the benches, resting in the sun. The morning remained calm, and William made the time to relax. If they were to leave soon, there would be little time to rest until they left Naples.

Peruzo appeared at the steps to the courtyard, looking guarded. William sensed him nearby and turned to him, smiling. 'Ah, my friend,' he said.

The lieutenant came over, his hands behind his back. 'Is it true?'

'That the Hoard of Mhorrer has been found? Yes, it's true,' William confirmed.

Peruzo blew out his cheeks and looked skyward in thought. 'All those years, and finally . . .'

'Yes, *finally*,' William said impatiently. 'Lieutenant Vittore is already in Rashid with one full company and one half company from Spain. Regardless, I want you with me.'

Peruzo smiled slyly. 'Me? But with Lieutenant Vittore . . .'

'Vittore is a good officer, but I want someone I can trust and who thinks as I do. I won't be the first captain to have two lieutenants under his command. Unless you refuse, of course.'

'I will not,' Peruzo replied boldly, barely hiding his enthusiasm. 'This will truly be a mission for the ages.'

'I hope so,' William said quietly. 'And your leg?'

The elder lieutenant shrugged, slightly self-conscious. 'It is almost healed. Healed enough to ride with you.'

'I promised Brother Jericho he would be sent on the next available mission to recover his courage,' William said.

'And you think this one would be appropriate for him?' Peruzo said doubtfully.

'Brother Jericho is a good man,' William reminded him, 'if a little young. If Jericho survives then it can only make him stronger.'

Peruzo nodded. 'I will tell him to pack. And I'll raise Marresca . . .'

'There's no need,' William interrupted.

'But Captain . . .'

'Marresca is not coming,' William said. 'He has already been sent out on a mission.'

Peruzo appeared puzzled. He looked over to William with an expression that begged for an explanation.

William wasn't about to provide one. 'Be quick, Peruzo. We must leave within the hour. The *Iberian* is waiting at Naples and will sail the evening after next,' he said instead. 'We have much ground to cover between now and then.'

Peruzo frowned, but bowed again, leaving swiftly after.

William considered calling on the armoury before Engrin Meerwall appeared at the arch to the courtyard. The old man huffed and puffed over to him before settling down on one of the benches, breathing heavily.

William went over, his face grave. He had never seen Engrin so frail.

'I can get you a drink if you wish,' he fretted.

Engrin shook his head. 'I am not a child, nor am I at death's door!' he scowled. 'Do not treat me as such.'

'My apologies,' William said, looking down at him for a moment.

Engrin sighed. 'If you must know, I feel better than I have in days. I am recovering, so I kindly request you keep your pity to yourself.'

'That hurt, old man,' William replied curtly. 'You are my friend. I am only concerned.'

'You needn't be,' Engrin dismissed, and patted the bench next to him. 'Now sit and speak to me.'

William did as he was asked, and for a few moments there was silence between them.

'Why didn't you tell me about Mhorrer's Hoard?' William said finally, trying to disguise the reproachful tone in his voice.

Engrin turned with a cunning expression. 'News such as that should not be given second-hand. I wanted you to know everything before you made your own decision.'

'My decision on what?' William said, puzzled.

'On the mission, of course,' Engrin replied. 'What do you think of Cardinal Devirus's glorious vision of ending this war prematurely?'

William looked long and hard at Engrin. 'By your tone, I see you are sceptical.'

Engrin now shrugged. 'I have my reasons.'

'If you must know, I think it is dangerous. Perhaps the most dangerous mission the Secretariat has undertaken. If you're asking whether or not I can succeed . . .'

Engrin raised his eyebrows. 'Do you think you will?'

William nodded. 'It *can* be done.'

'But not without great cost?'

'Of course. I expect I will lose most of the company,' William confessed.

'And what of Devirus's orders to return the Scarimadaen to the Vatican?'

William shifted on the bench uncomfortably. 'I can't say I was delighted about the prospect of bringing them back to Rome.'

'I see,' said Engrin, now content.

'You always were one for riddles. What are you trying to say to me, old man?'

'Cardinal Devirus visited me before the brothers were sent to Rashid,' Engrin replied. 'He wanted to discuss the particulars of the mission. While I was overjoyed at the prospect of finding the Hoard of Mhorrer, still we argued.'

'Argued?' William said, surprised.

'Strongly,' Engrin added sadly. 'Quite the shouting match as it happens. I disagreed with his plans to bring the Hoard back to Rome. I thought it was rash. Too much risk.'

'Rome is the safest place to destroy the Scarimadaen,' William remarked.

'There are other ways of ensuring the Hoard can no longer be used, William,' Engrin told him. 'From what we know, the Rassis Cult will be formidable.'

William agreed. 'They have kept the Hoard intact for all these years, so they must have strengths. I don't expect them to be easy opponents.'

Engrin coughed and then cleared his throat, breathing heavily. 'No, *no*. They won't be. It is unfortunate the *Book of Man* ends before the New Testament. Of their strength we know only that there is one Rassis for each Scarimadaen.'

'Two hundred and fifty men,' William surmised. 'They would have been easier to fight with Marresca at my side.'

'Ah yes. *Marresca* . . . Keep him out of mind, William,' Engrin advised.

'That is easy for you to say, old man,' William replied. 'Our enemies are very strong. Stronger than the Secretariat believe. If the Dar'uka believe the Rassis are cunning and powerful, then their reputation is justified.'

103

'The Dar'uka think this?'

'I saw Kieran last night,' William admitted. 'I tried to convince him to leave Marresca alone. He didn't, obviously. But he warned me about the Rassis. He also told me to find allies whenever I could.'

'That's good advice,' Engrin remarked.

'It is also contrary to the code of the Secretariat.'

'Whose advice would you rather listen to, William? Kieran's or the Secretariat's?'

'Neither,' William said churlishly, and then screwed up his face. 'Both, I suppose. But one defies the other.'

'You know, as well as I, this war cannot be kept a secret any longer,' Engrin told him. 'People must take sides to avert calamity.'

'That will involve them in the fight,' William reminded him.

Engrin stamped the ground with his foot. 'William, everyone is involved in the fight now. *Everyone*. Because everyone stands to lose if we lose. The time for secrecy is over. Both of us know it. Our enemies are no longer concealed, but are numerous; it is an open war now. Count Ordrane is losing, so he will take greater risks. He cannot afford not to.'

William nodded. 'He is certain to find out about the Hoard.'

'If he hasn't already,' Engrin said.

William looked at him earnestly. 'Surely not?'

'Our agents in the north, Mallinder and Staley, believe they have. A coven left Castle Draak not long after the Secretariat received Charles Greynell's letter. Nothing is a secret, William. Remember that,' Engrin said. 'But not to worry, I have sent something with the brothers in Rashid, to ensure that you *do* succeed.'

William went to ask what that was, but Engrin held up his hand. 'Wait until you get there . . .' he whispered, a devilish glint in his eyes. '. . . It goes against Devirus's orders and there may be recreant tongues even here.'

'I understand,' William said, though he was decidedly curious about Engrin's contingency.

'I wish I could do more,' Engrin replied, and looked tired again. 'There will be other perils than just vampyres and the Rassis to contend with. Egypt is in turmoil, William. They distrust foreigners, especially pale-skinned foreigners. The viceroy of the country is fighting wars against anyone he wishes, and I've heard stories of massacres. Beware of the ambitions of others. Beware of the chaos you wade through. Simple misunderstandings could mean calamity.'

'I will keep my eyes open,' William said.

'I'm sure you will.' Engrin slipped his hand inside his greatcoat. He pulled out a long velvet bag drawn together by gold-tasselled strings. These he pulled apart with shaking fingers, revealing the metallic handle of something within.

William knew at once what it was. 'Engrin, I can't . . .'

'But you *must*, William,' Engrin said as he pulled out the sword, the blade shining like new in the morning light. 'It is mine to give to whom I wish.'

William took hold of the sword's handle and lifted it. It felt light as always, as light as the first time he had wielded the sword years ago on the *Iberian*. The blade was as sharp as ever, and the few nicks that had marred it over the years had been rubbed down to nothing. It was the finest sword William had ever known, owned by the finest swordsman.

'I am too old to use it,' Engrin confessed. 'My last duty for the Secretariat was to bring you to Rome. I achieved that, but since then I have not been used on any other mission. I will never fight again.'

'If you feel you're being neglected, I can speak to Cardinal Devirus,' William began.

'You misunderstand me, William. I don't want another mission. I am not as strong, nor as quick.' Engrin began coughing again. The illness that had taken hold of him that winter had clearly not let go.

As the coughing abated, he caught his breath and slumped a

little. 'The battle on the *Iberian* was my last,' he admitted slowly. 'I was bested that night by a vampyre I should have easily defeated, yet I weakened. If it hadn't been for your intervention, I would have certainly been killed.'

'He would have bested anyone,' William objected.

Engrin lifted his hand. 'No, no,' he replied, 'not me. Once I would have taken that contest in my stride. *Once*. Not now. Fighting this war is a game for the young, not for someone whose joints are inflamed and whose lungs are choked with this wretched illness.'

William tried not to express any pity or sadness. Instead he rested his eyes on the sword.

'As long as you wield that weapon, then part of me fights on with you,' Engrin said hopefully, nodding once towards the sword in William's hands.

William smiled. 'Thank you,' he said. 'I promise I'll return it.'

'I'm certain you will,' Engrin said warmly. He pushed himself up from the pew and reached out to shake William's hand. William looked down at it, grinned and put his arms around the old man, embracing him firmly.

'You are my good friend,' William said.

They were the last words between them before he and the monks left the monastery, and the journey to Egypt began.

△ II △

Adriana was one of the first to line the road out of Villeda. She stood outside the tavern in the town square, a heavy shawl wrapped about her shoulders against a cold breeze. On occasion it blustered into something stronger, tugging at her curled dark hair. She was not alone, and many of the townsfolk waited to watch their heroes set out again. Nearby was Mary from the tavern, Isabel from the apothecary's, and finally Tustio's wife, Katrina Maldini.

'It's a cold day,' Isabel remarked.

'The coldest for some time,' Adriana replied bleakly.

'They say they won't be back for a while,' Mary remarked.

Adriana stiffened. Mary meant no offence, but she could be quite indiscreet. 'They *will* return,' Adriana assured them. The words were more for her personally, and she muttered a prayer as cheers broke out from the road ahead. Children began to dash along the road, some ahead of the horses that trotted down the path towards the square.

Adriana heard the horses grow closer and she gathered herself, murmuring quietly: '*Don't cry. Don't let him see you cry.*'

Katrina must have heard her and she put an arm around Adriana's shoulders, lifting her head. 'Here they come, Adriana.'

She straightened up, her brown eyes stinging with effort as the three men rounded the side of the tavern and came into view. At the head was William, trotting proudly on his horse. Behind sat Lieutenant Peruzo and another monk, young, proud and excited. William appeared to share their enthusiasm, appearing as heroic as ever. He looked so brave as he waved to them all, the confidence in his smile, in his eyes and posture.

At once the cheering locals grew tumultuous and from one corner tree blossom was scattered from a window of a cottage, the pink and white petals cascading like rain.

She stared up at William and smiled lovingly as he rode past. William looked down just briefly and his smile faltered. For a moment the expression was full of doubt. Of regret. It was too much for Adriana, who simply wept. She prayed he hadn't seen her, prayed he had left with just an image of her gaily waving to him, smiling hopefully.

But what of William? He looked lost for a moment. He looked so . . .

'He'll return,' Adriana sobbed. '*He has to.*'

'He will, I'm sure,' Katrina said and hugged her close. It was no good. Adriana had never felt so alone. Something was telling her this was the moment, their final time together. Despite any assurances to the contrary, despite Katrina's reassurance, deep down Adriana *knew* that William wasn't coming back.

William fixed his thoughts on the horizon and the road leading down across the hills, yet despite his efforts he could only think about Adriana. He had seen her weep, and it had been his fault. His intention had been to play the hero, invincible, completely free of doubt. But on seeing Adriana, it seemed futile. William had to face the stark truth that this mission could end in grief for all involved. This was not about adulation, nor about excitement, there was too much at stake. All thought of reunions had to be locked away. All that mattered was the mission, its success, and if possible, surviving it.

'We have a long journey ahead of us,' he said to his men as they left the suburbs of Villeda. 'Are you both ready for a little exercise?'

Peruzo nodded, looking to Jericho, who lifted his reins in readiness. William drew in a deep breath of Villeda air and then kicked in his heels to gallop away down the road that carved the rape-seed field ahead in two. Peruzo and Jericho followed close behind.

△ III △

Adriana was led away by Katrina, who wiped her eyes with a delicate handkerchief.

'I'm sorry,' Adriana sniffed, trying to seem brighter.

'Nonsense, you're upset!' Katrina replied. 'I don't know how you do it. Watching them leave like that.'

Adriana sniffed again, another tear running down her blushing cheeks. 'I know. And this isn't over for me. Not until I see him again.'

'You're a braver woman than I. I couldn't let Tustio do such a thing. I know exactly where he is, every day and every morning.'

'I envy you,' Adriana admitted, but in a way she didn't. She hated seeing William leave, but he was the bravest and most honoured man in the town. He had the respect of all, and that wasn't because he toiled in the fields or brewed ale, but because he risked his life to serve others.

Adriana brightened up and thought of him riding down the mountain road to Naples, the wind in his hair, his face upturned to the sun. He always looked free and happy in that vision, and Adriana did her best to keep it in mind.

But as the crowd dispersed and Katrina led her to the tavern for something to calm her, something struck Adriana as unusual and she lowered the handkerchief, craning her neck around to view the town square. She scanned the small crowd in the road, looking at the children, young and older, who were returning to their games.

'Katrina?' she said, distracted. 'Have you seen Marco? *Have you?*'

Katrina looked surprised and then realized she hadn't.

'Marco has never been absent when William's left for a mission,' Adriana said, her frown deepening. 'Did Tustio make him work early?'

'No,' Katrina replied. 'He gave him leave.'

Adriana looked worried. 'Then he should be here.'

'Maybe he was and we missed him,' Katrina suggested.

That's right, Adriana thought, maybe they had. But that felt wrong too. Marco was not here, and never had been.

'They had an argument,' Adriana conceded. 'William was angry with him.'

'He's been angry with him before,' Katrina reminded her, 'and that has never stopped him adoring him.'

Adriana looked bewildered.

Katrina put her arm around her again. 'I'll send my husband to look for Marco,' she calmed her. 'He'll find him. I'm sure he hasn't gone too far.'

Adriana nodded silently and allowed Katrina to lead her away.

The days were short, and the three men of the Order spent little time resting on the way to Naples. The first night they slept for two hours and then rose early to ride on through the darkness. They dozed in their saddles where they could and forged on against fatigue, knowing there would be time enough to sleep during the voyage to Rashid.

On the ride from Villeda, Peruzo asked about the decision to send Marresca elsewhere. William put off the discussion until the early morning while Jericho was still asleep in his saddle.

'He is the finest soldier in the Order, Captain,' Peruzo said. 'He should be here. I find it difficult to understand why the Secretariat sent him elsewhere. Is there a mission more important . . .?'

'The Secretariat did not send him anywhere, my friend,' William said quietly.

Peruzo pulled a face.

'He has joined the Dar'uka,' William explained.

At the mention of their name, Peruzo's eyes grew wide. '*The angels?*'

William nodded, glancing at Jericho ahead of them, slumped in the saddle, swaying as the horse walked along the mountain track.

'When?' Peruzo asked, but there were clearly more questions behind that.

'Last night,' William said. 'He is no longer part of the Order.'

'Did you see them?' Peruzo asked him.

What if he hadn't? William thought. Would that matter? Perhaps he should have lied, but he couldn't. Peruzo had known him far too long, and William was not a convincing liar to his friends.

'I did. Briefly,' William added, hoping to stop more questions. It didn't work.

'How many were there?' Peruzo asked. 'Are they going to help us?'

William held up a hand. 'I met them *briefly*, Peruzo. They hardly said a word to me. I was just there to talk to Marresca before . . . Before he left with them. I mentioned the Hoard of Mhorrer . . .'

'What did they say?'

'There were no promises,' William replied.

'But they said they would come?'

William shrugged. 'If they can.'

Peruzo grinned and he looked to the sky. 'Then we have nothing to worry about.'

'I didn't expect my best lieutenant to be that foolish,' William chided.

Peruzo looked apologetic. 'I am sorry, Captain. It is difficult not to be carried away by the idea that angels are watching over us.'

'They are not, Lieutenant,' William said, and there came a snort from ahead as Jericho stirred in his saddle. 'You can't tell the brothers about this.'

Peruzo frowned.

'It will give them false hope and distract them,' William explained. 'They already think I'm in league with angels, this would confirm it.'

'But you are, Captain,' Peruzo said plaintively.

William shook his head. 'No, Lieutenant,' he said gravely. 'Be assured that I am not.'

When they reached Naples, William guided them to the docklands and the row of tall ships anchored along the quay. About them, the port was chaotic: each corner, each refuge along the quays and about the roads, was alive with merchants, travellers, seamen, stevedores. William, Peruzo and Jericho rode through the crowds until they halted and dismounted alongside the sixth-rated frigate *Iberian* to see Captain Gerard peering over the handrail of the quarterdeck down to the quayside.

'You weren't expected until this afternoon, Captain Saxon,' he boomed down to them.

William smiled slightly. 'I thought we'd surprise you, Captain. Permission to come aboard?'

Gerard broke into laughter. 'Granted, sir. Granted indeed!' he said. 'It is good to see you again. You look well.'

'Thank you, Captain.' William climbed the steps to the quarterdeck. 'As do you.'

Gerard looked over William's shoulder at Peruzo, who was amused at them both. 'And what is an old dog like Peruzo doing here?'

'Captain,' Peruzo greeted, but his cool expression belied a friendship that reached back before William had known him.

Gerard straightened his jacket and looked proud as usual. 'If I'd had prior warning, you would have taken the guest cabin, Captain,' he smirked. 'Alas, it was not to be.'

'We don't have a cabin?' William said, trying not to show his displeasure.

'I'm afraid not. Another notable has that honour, and I'm sure you would not wish to turn out a fellow companion of the Secretariat?'

William frowned.

'The Papal messenger, Andreas.' Captain Gerard gestured over to a short gentleman in fine clothes standing at the prow of the ship, one foot resting on the rail.

'Andreas?' Peruzo said under his breath to William. 'What is he doing here?'

'I don't know,' William conceded. He knew Andreas from his visits to Rome. A Papal messenger used much by the Secretariat, he had been employed to take letters to William's family at Fairway Hall in England on more than one occasion. Andreas had been missing of late, sent to treat with princes and statesmen around Europe no doubt. His absence suited William, as he liked to expound about such matters, often to the point of irritation.

'Where might *we* be staying, Captain?' William asked, not taking his eyes from Andreas as the messenger stepped away from the rail and began to walk aft. His eyes alighted on them, and he waved.

William waved back.

'You'll be sleeping below deck,' Gerard told him. 'The space will be a little cramped, what with the pigs . . .'

'*Pigs?*' William frowned.

'Prize-winning pigs. The best on the Continent, they tell me.'

'Pigs are going to a largely Islamic country?' William said, surprised.

'They're not for the people, but an English ambassador to Alexandria. Some gentry fellow. He loves pork, so he's being sent pigs.' Gerard struggled to hide his indignation. William guessed that transporting pigs was a dent to his pride. 'It's quite a squeeze in there. I've even had to remove the cannon.'

'No guns?' William said, concerned.

Gerard shook his head.

'But if we're attacked . . .?' William said seriously, remembering his previous journey on the *Iberian* several years before.

'Aye, it is a risk, Captain Saxon,' Gerard added, 'but I'm being paid well for it. And we'll have the escort of the *Sussex*. She lies just outside of Naples and will run with us halfway before making a patrol west.'

'Well, if you are not uneasy, then who am I to argue with the captain of the *Iberian*?'

△ V △

Jericho hung his thick leather bag over the rail and walked down to the gangplank past two of the sailors who were walking Peruzo's horse on board. One of them brushed by him, and Jericho halted for a moment to look back. The sailor was only a young man, about fourteen, with shoulder-length hair, but he was someone Jericho seemed to recognize, though he wasn't sure from where. Was it Rome, or maybe Naples? It certainly wasn't the *Iberian*.

Dismissing the suspicion, Jericho walked up to the deck, leaving the young sailor to take William's horse to the hold.

The young sailor glanced nervously over his shoulder, screened by the horse as he guided it up to the deck. Ahead he spotted Captain Saxon and Lieutenant Peruzo, and he ducked low until the horse was at the winch. With a backward glance at the monk he had brushed past, the young man sneaked down into the hold below and out of sight.

CHAPTER SEVEN

Rashid

△ I △

The *Iberian* rocked along the sea, ploughing through the heavy swell as the sails billowed full. William held on to the rigging and looked ahead, his eyes tired. He had slept little during the first night on board. Neither Peruzo nor Jericho had slept much either, as a night of bad weather had tossed them about in their makeshift hammocks surrounded by squealing pigs in their cages. The dung smelled strong and it seemed they would never get used to it. Brother Jericho made the best of their situation by nursing a farrow of piglets after their mother died one day into the crossing.

On the third day the weather broke and the sun came out. It was the warmest weather William had known in months, and it cheered the crew. Captain Gerard encouraged high spirits where he could, for the sake of morale. The *Iberian*'s captain was gruff and entertaining as usual. He regaled his guests with stories that bordered on the preposterous, yet William said nothing, nor did he attempt to correct the gregarious captain when he described at full length their first meeting seven years ago: the voyage from Southampton to Naples that had almost cost them both their lives. The battle on the *Iberian* had been embellished over the years, yet Gerard's account over dinner reminded William what a savage struggle it had been.

Andreas listened attentively, strangely muted as Gerard spoke animatedly about the skirmishes, the vampyre and the strange creature that interceded. At the mention of the Dar'uka, Andreas glanced at William, who at once felt uncomfortable.

The Papal messenger had previously imparted to William his own orders for the journey, which were to contact an ambassador from England by the name of Henry Isaac, who was being bribed with pigs to join the Secretariat as a spy for them in northern Africa. It was hardly a dignified trip, Andreas had confessed, yet it served two purposes: one, to gain a valuable contact, and two, for Andreas to remain as liaison to William while they were in Egypt. Andreas could be used to summon additional monks from Rome if required, and to send word if any massed forces of Count Ordrane were seen disembarking in the ports of Rashid and Alexandria. William grudgingly saw this move as supportive. Andreas could be irritating, but was an astute negotiator and persuader.

Once Gerard had finished his description of the battle, he gulped down his remaining wine, and looked pleased with himself. 'So what happened to that brave friend of yours, Captain Saxon? That Kieran Harte?' he asked.

'He took a different path,' William said sadly, folding his napkin.

'Ah,' Gerard noticed. 'A friendship broken?'

'Not broken, sir,' William replied, a little too curtly for comfort, 'just lost.'

They retired soon after, and Peruzo and Brother Jericho excused themselves for some moonlight sparring on deck, one of the few training opportunities the pocket-sized ship afforded.

William elected to watch from the quarterdeck, and annoyingly, Andreas decided to join him.

'Fine men, Captain,' he remarked as he walked over, resting his arms on the deck rail. Andreas was a portly man, a few years older than William, with fine tastes in clothes. He always seemed to wear what was in fashion, disguising himself as a courtier. His fair hair was powdered and tied back with a blue silk ribbon, yet his face was craggy, and one cheek bore a scar he barely bothered to cover. The only clue to his profession was the signet ring on his left hand that held the same inscription and profile as the chain around William's neck: the seal of Pope Pius.

'I noticed some tension on the matter of Harte, Captain,' Andreas remarked.

William ignored him.

Andreas turned away from the two men sparring, the clatter of steel in the background. 'Do you see him often?'

'No,' William said abruptly.

'It must be difficult,' Andreas considered. 'I am a great observer of men – being a messenger has afforded me that pleasure. Since I have known you, I've always noticed a burden in your eyes.'

'I beg your pardon?' William said, growing irritated.

'Forgive me, Captain,' Andreas said, and raised his hands in defence. 'I only meant that it must be hard to be away from England. And from your home, especially without your good friend Kieran Harte.'

William turned angrily to Andreas. 'That is no concern of yours.'

'Quite, Captain,' Andreas said politely. 'It was merely an observation.'

Andreas fell silent and turned back to the men sparring, Peruzo disarming Jericho much to the young monk's frustration.

'You have not written home to England for quite some time,' Andreas said at last.

William let out an exasperated sigh. 'What is this about, Andreas?' he demanded.

'I have returned to Fairway Hall twice in the last year, Captain,' Andreas said plainly, 'yet in that year not once have I brought a message from its heir.'

William was struck dumb with guilt.

'As promised, the Secretariat does look in from time to time, to ensure that your family in Lowchester are not molested by the agents of Count Ordrane. Yet not once have you asked about your father's welfare, nor your mother's. Not even your sister's. I find that . . .' Andreas paused, '. . . quite sad.'

William wanted to rebuke him, but he could not. He had neglected his family, and used his exile as reason enough. But there was no excuse for not writing home. And this stung him.

Andreas stepped closer. 'It is not a criticism, Captain Saxon. Just an observation. But may I suggest that at some point you pick up your pen and write home? It must be hard for them, must it not?'

William conceded. 'If only it were that easy,' he said. 'What would they make of my life?'

Andreas shrugged. He stretched his arms and walked away to retire. At the top step he paused and looked back. 'Who knows? But don't you think they'd be pleased with the news that you're simply *alive*, Captain? Would not any parent?'

△ II △

The following afternoon William and Peruzo checked over the horses braced in stalls in the hold. The animals looked content enough, though probably impatient for dry land.

William grunted. 'My horse wants to be in Rashid and off this damned boat,' he said and stroked the animal's neck.

'I don't think it is the boat my captain dislikes,' Peruzo quipped.

William ignored him and calmed the horse as it pounded the floor of the hold with its hoofs.

'How is Andreas's company?' Peruzo asked.

'Irksome,' William replied. 'Can you believe he has inspired enough guilt in me to write a letter!'

'A letter?' Peruzo said.

'To England.'

Peruzo gave William a strange look. 'May I ask what is wrong with that?'

'No you may not,' William replied testily. The ship rocked as the sea grew choppy, the horses stamping their feet, blowing out irritably. William patted his horse again to calm it.

'I haven't written to my parents in almost a year. Andreas believes I should,' he confessed. 'And he may be right, but it isn't as easy as I hoped. How does one talk about one's calling, if one cannot mention details?'

'With difficulty, I'm sure, Captain,' Peruzo said tactfully. 'But as a challenge, sir, not harder than this mission, surely?'

William laughed. 'Yes. You're right. I'm making heavy weather of this. It's only a damned letter.'

The ship lurched to the other side and something heavy rolled astern with a crunch. It was followed by a sudden yelp.

Both men looked around.

'*Did you hear that?*' William whispered.

'Someone is down here,' Peruzo said back to him. 'One of the crew?'

'Hello?' William called out.

A barrel rolled again and there was another audible groan and the sound of someone clambering out of the way. William stalked between the horses to the rear, passing by sacks and barrels. He lifted up a nearby lamp and looked about expecting to find a crewman trying to pack away the stores. But there was nothing.

Peruzo came up behind him. 'No one here,' he murmured.

William was about to agree until he saw movement by some crates. He put a finger to his lips and pointed to the corner of the hold. Peruzo nodded and both men stepped forward.

William, angry that the fellow hadn't announced himself, jumped to the side of the crate and shone the lamp directly in his face. 'Eavesdropping, were you . . .?' he growled, but his voice tailed off.

Peruzo looked over William's shoulder and his jaw dropped open. 'I don't believe it!' he exclaimed as William hauled the listener to his feet.

It was a boy of fourteen with fair hair to his shoulders.

'Marco!' William shouted. 'What in blazes are you doing on this ship?'

△ III △

They stood nervously outside Captain Gerard's cabin.

Marco stood by William, trembling slightly.

'You've placed me in an awkward position,' William said. 'A stowaway to boot.'

'I didn't stow away,' Marco protested.

'Then what are you doing here?'

Marco fell silent, fidgeting before Captain Gerard's voice boomed from within. William grabbed the boy by the scruff and hauled him inside.

The captain looked up at them both, but said nothing, and William was surprised.

'Is there something amiss, Captain Saxon?' Gerard finally asked.

William looked at Marco and frowned. 'This boy . . .'

'Aye, sir. What has he done?'

William's frown deepened. 'You know him?'

'He was signed on at Naples. The morning you arrived, as it happens,' Captain Gerard replied, more interested in the rolls of paper on his desk.

'Signed on?'

'He is a member of my crew.'

William felt exasperated. 'Unbelievable,' he replied.

'Why so?' Gerard asked.

William let Marco go and stepped forward. 'Captain, this boy is my nephew.'

Gerard looked at Marco and barely suppressed his laughter. 'Your . . . Your nephew!' he chuckled, and sat back. 'Is this right, boy?'

Marco didn't reply.

'Your captain asked you a question, Marco,' William said, and prodded him in the side.

Marco squirmed and nodded. 'I am, sir.'

'I believe, Captain, that he is aboard your ship with the sole intention of leaving it at Rashid,' William continued.

Gerard sat up, appearing more serious. 'Is he now?'

William shot a glance at Marco, who did not deny the allegation.

'Boy,' Gerard said loudly, causing Marco to look up. 'You have agreed payment and passage on this ship. You are part of my crew and you cannot renege on the agreement. I *own* you,' he said calmly.

Marco looked fearful.

'Did you really believe you could just leave when you wished?' Gerard added.

Marco crossed his arms, holding himself aloof.

William felt equally as uncomfortable. Marco was in deep trouble and he felt powerless to intervene.

Gerard settled back and tapped the sextant on the desk.

'I'm terribly sorry, Captain,' William said. 'If I had known . . .'

'Nonsense, sir. Boys of his age are always strong-willed,' Gerard replied. 'But what would *you* do with him?'

'It is not my decision, sir. He is part of your crew, not my company,' William replied, hoping that the punishment would not be too severe.

Gerard pondered and peered down at the rolls of parchment. 'In his heart, the boy is not a sailor,' Gerard said, 'so having him aboard will do little for me. But nor can I just rip up his contract on a whim. It would serve as a bad example.'

'He is to be punished then?' William said.

'And then delivered into your care,' Captain Gerard replied. 'Everyone will expect a whipping, you know?'

'If that is your decision, then Marco will take the whipping, *bravely*,' William said through clenched teeth. He hated the idea.

'There is an alternative, Captain.' Gerard looked up at Marco. 'If he is man enough to cheat his way onto my ship, then he is man enough to perform some *hard* chores. Let him work the rest of the crossing without payment as punishment. It might be difficult, perhaps harder than a whipping, but it will be a lesson he will not forget.'

William sighed with relief. The punishment sounded fair, and at the very least it would occupy the boy's time.

'Thank you, Captain,' William replied. He placed his hands on Marco's shoulders. 'I'll leave him to you then.'

As soon as William left, Gerard broke into a smile.

'Why did you cheat your way onto my ship, boy?'

Marco shrugged, a little embarrassed.

'Seeking adventure, were we?'

Marco shrank. And then nodded miserably.

'I hope it was worth it. Captain Saxon has left your punishment in *my* hands,' Gerard grinned. 'You will not enjoy it, but by God you will *learn* from it!'

△ IV △

The next day Rashid appeared out of the morning mist, a quiet port that had seen busier days. The *Iberian* sailed gently in, passing smaller dhows and other merchant ships across the calm waters, buoying them up and down in the frigate's wake.

The crew of the *Iberian* set to immediately, hauling in the sails and rigging, making ready to unload their cargo. William leaned out from the ship, his hands resting eagerly on the rail as he watched the town come into view across the flat expanse. From the quarterdeck he could see all the way into the suburbs, ranging over the tops of the houses to the golden minarets of the mosques that appeared like shimmering candles in the sky.

Captain Gerard bellowed out across the ship and the anchor was weighed, ropes flung out to the quayside, as the ship lost way and came to a gradual stop. He put his hands behind his back and walked over to William. Both men turned from the quay to the main deck where the sailors began to ready the gangplank and unload the cargo.

Amongst them was Marco, dishevelled, sweating, his shirt opened and his face red with exertion.

'It is a pity he is leaving with you,' Captain Gerard said aside to William. He gestured with the hilt of his sword to where Marco was toiling. 'The boy is a hard worker. I should not have torn up his contract so readily.'

William had to check Gerard's expression to see that he was joking. 'Hard worker or not, he is a problem,' he replied.

'And what will you do with that problem now that *you* are burdened with it?'

William shrugged. 'I do not honestly know. I have to hope that a reputable merchant can return him to Naples . . .'

Gerard walked around William, pausing at his shoulder. 'And if you cannot?'

William breathed heavily. 'Then he will stay with us.'

Gerard nodded. 'He may be an asset to you, Captain.'

William disagreed. 'He is a petulant child.'

'But one with fine swordsmanship,' Captain Gerard remarked.

William looked startled. 'How do you know this?'

'I have seen him sparring alone on the deck. Last night, incidentally. He looked quite competent.'

'Where the heavens did he get a sword?'

Gerard feigned innocence. 'This is a merchant ship, Captain. There are always swords on the *Iberian*.' He put a hand to William's arm. 'We know each other a little, sir. May I impart some advice that will serve you well?'

William hesitated, but had grace enough to accept.

'This boy of yours is headstrong and courageous. Among the lessons I've learned throughout my years at sea is that a great captain should harness such bravery and strength. Not to do so would be an awful waste. Marco is fiercely devoted to you, sir. He would follow you to the ends of the earth. Not many leaders of men have had such strength and loyalty in support.'

William nodded but was as stone. 'Loyalty will not be enough, Captain Gerard. Not on this mission.'

'Not even an asset?'

'His vulnerability is something I find most unpalatable,' William confessed. 'Would you bring a relation on board your ship knowing that you sail into peril?'

'No, Captain, I would not,' Gerard agreed. 'Yet I have no relation with the strength or will of this boy.'

Andreas climbed the steps to the quarterdeck, rubbing his hands together eagerly, interrupting the debate. 'Captains,' he greeted jovially. 'How are the pigs?'

William did not know whether the Papal messenger was addressing him or not, so he replied anyway. 'They smell most foul, Andreas.'

Gerard broke into gruff laughter. 'Spoken like a gentleman, sir!' he said, and slapped William hard on the back. 'They're being unloaded as we speak.' Gerard pointed down the gangplank to where several cages and carts waited for them, a squad of British soldiers standing by.

'The ambassador's escort I believe,' Andreas mused.

'Then this is goodbye?' William said, relieved.

Andreas seemed genuinely sorry, but he nodded. 'I'm afraid it is, gentlemen. Thank you a thousand times for an *uneventful* crossing, Captain.'

Gerard bowed.

'And to you, Captain Saxon . . . I look forward to seeing you again in a few weeks' time. Hopefully with some success,' Andreas added and winked.

William shook the messenger's outstretched hand. 'I hope so.'

'Remember . . . Should you need anything, I will be at the consulate in Alexandria. Do not hesitate to contact me,' Andreas whispered to him. 'And perhaps you will have a letter for me on your return?'

'Perhaps,' William said and smiled sharply.

'Good day, gentlemen,' Andreas said, and swanned away down the main deck to the gangplank.

'Pleasant fellow,' Gerard mused.

'Quite,' William replied.

△ V △

As the horses were unloaded, Peruzo spotted two riders dressed in grey coming along the quay. They waved over and Peruzo shot his hand in the air, shouting out to William. As William expressed his thanks to Captain Gerard, Brother Jericho and Marco carried their possessions down the gangplank and waited by the horses.

'Fair sailing to you, sir,' William said to Gerard as they shook hands.

Gerard smiled brightly. 'And to you, Captain. All my prayers for you and your mission. I thought you should know: a colleague of mine who captains the *Vesper* will take your boy back to Naples if you wish.'

William looked hopeful. 'Excellent. When?'

'In three days, if you can spare them. He is a trustworthy man and he may only ask Marco to perform some deck work, which he has already shown great competency for.'

William nodded, though three days was far too long a time to spend in Rashid. Still, it was better than nothing.

Gerard looked to Peruzo next and patted him on the shoulder. 'Look after your captain, Lieutenant. He is a fine officer. Worthy of any army.'

'You can count on it,' Peruzo replied cheerfully.

'And be sure both of you return in one piece, you hear?' Captain Gerard added as both officers disembarked down the gangplank to the quay.

Marco held the bridles of two horses, sheepishly avoiding William's gaze while Jericho put their belongings across their saddles. The merchants along the quay began to part as the two riders appeared.

125

Peruzo looked over at William tentatively. 'Lieutenant Vittore,' he murmured.

William nodded, wondering also what the lieutenant would make of Peruzo's presence. The two monks dismounted and marched over to William.

'Captain,' the lieutenant said, slightly bowing.

'Lieutenant Vittore, it is a pleasure to see you again. You are well?' William replied.

Vittore, a tall fellow with oiled black hair and a fine moustache that curled under his nose, nodded in reply but glanced at Lieutenant Peruzo hesitantly. 'Lieutenant Peruzo . . .' he began and then fell silent.

'Lieutenant Peruzo is here at my request. He is not replacing you, Lieutenant,' William clarified. 'With the size of the company larger than usual, I have taken steps to ensure I have two lieutenants under my command. I trust that will be acceptable to both of you.'

Peruzo, as ever, was content with the arrangement, but Vittore looked slightly irritated.

'Lieutenant Vittore, you will take the Spanish contingent. You know those men better than I. Lieutenant Peruzo is familiar with the rest of the brothers and will therefore take them,' William continued, and then paused. 'I need not remind either of you of the perilous nature of this mission, so I will leave the care of our men in your hands. As for myself . . . I must concentrate on other matters, such as finding our contact and then our prize. Understood?'

Both men nodded, yet the monk behind Vittore screwed up his face. William did not recognize the man, but surmised he was from the Spanish contingent.

'Something wrong?' William asked directly.

Lieutenant Vittore turned to glare at the monk, who looked away.

'I'm afraid there is, Captain,' Vittore conceded.

William waited for him to elaborate. 'Well?' he insisted, looking to the second monk after Vittore was not forthcoming.

126

Vittore looked about in case there were eavesdroppers. 'It's about our informant . . . He was discovered floating in the Nile many days ago, before we even arrived in Rashid. Charles Greynell is dead, Captain.'

△ VI △

They moved like ghosts through the town, passing through the crowds sombrely. Throughout the journey William brooded, barely looking to their surroundings and the colourful locals as they talked and gestured, smoked and bartered. Some squatted in doorways, others stood in groups, casting furtive glances towards the six strangers. With their pale skins and grey garb, the monks had the mark of foreigners upon them, and there was a tangible sense of hostility and wariness.

Under the occupation of the French and the British, the people of Rashid had looked on with similar distrust, yet it was tempered with a fearful respect. Since Viceroy Ali had taken control of the country, the self-respect of Rashid had waned. Foreigners were treated with suspicion and hatred, and yet Ali's intervention had proved disastrous to the port. After building the Mahmudiyah Canal, Alexandria's star was rising and Rashid was in decline. Its people looked on their own with contempt, much as they did on foreigners. It was just a matter of whom to blame.

Above them came the long melodic yet alien call of the muezzin from a nearby mosque, his voice carrying far over streets that turned eerily quiet. Marco looked up, cowed by his surroundings, and this warm and exotic world.

Eventually, having passed through much of the Arab quarter, they arrived at their lodgings, a tall building with slatted windows and cracks along its aspect. It was the colour of sand, though stripes of vibrant paint ran along the entrance, attempting to make it inviting. The detritus of rotting food and broken crates nearby only added to the feeling of poverty.

A young lad half Marco's age came scuttling out of the inn and took hold of their bridles, talking excitedly as though it would encourage William to hand over their horses.

'What is he saying?' William asked.

Vittore listened intently and frowned. 'I think he wants to stable our horses.'

'At a price I suppose,' William said as he swung himself out of the saddle and landed on the ground, dust erupting around his boots.

'Everything in Rashid has its price, Captain,' Vittore remarked. 'It was Alexander himself who said that the Persian and African states are the most beguiling yet the most corrupt. They would sell their own families into slavery if it turned over a few gold coins.'

William glanced at Vittore, regarding the officer as well as the remark. The lieutenant was bronzed and his face showed lines of exposure to the sun. He was an experienced soldier by reputation and spent much of his time in North Africa as well as in Spain.

'Can you speak Arabic?' William asked him as he opened the drawstrings of his purse.

'I know a little dialect from the west, enough to get by. But the language here is a mystery, I'm afraid. Brother Leone serves as our translator.'

William looked down at the boy who was struggling to hold his horse. William took out two coins and showed them, but the boy looked unsure. William added a third and the boy grinned, snatching them from his fingers. He then led the horses down the side of the tall building to a stable hidden at the rear, singing a song with unfamiliar words.

William shook his head dismally. 'I've served with Brother Leone before. He is a fine soldier. I hope his Arabic is as good as his sword arm,' he confided to Peruzo. 'We are in a strange land with no guide.'

'Yes, Captain,' Peruzo agreed.

'Lieutenant Vittore,' William said, turning to him. 'Arrange for guards to be posted at the door.'

'I already have, Captain, two men . . .'

'Double it,' William interrupted. 'If Greynell is dead, I doubt it was a natural cause.'

'We do not know how . . .' Vittore began.

'We will by tonight,' William interrupted again impatiently. 'Arrange for the men to meet me downstairs. Is there a room where I can address them?'

'A dining room,' Vittore replied.

'In half an hour, gather them. I need to tell you all what we face.'

Vittore half bowed and marched away, looking slightly aggrieved.

Noting that his captain was in no mood to discuss the situation further, Peruzo put his head down and carried their belongings inside, with Jericho close behind.

Only Marco waited with William outside the inn. 'You will stay with us for the time being,' William said.

'Are you sending me away?' Marco asked.

'If I can, I will,' William replied. 'This is no place for you, Marco.'

The boy looked as though he might complain, but William pointed to the two bags on the road and then pointed to the inn. 'Get me a room, and be quick. If you're going to be here with us, I may as well make use of you.'

Marco muttered something under his breath as he picked up the bags, wincing slightly as he carried the weight over his shoulders. William watched him leave, waiting until the innkeeper's son had taken the last of the horses to the stable. Then he put his hand inside his jacket and pulled out Charles Greynell's letter, his eyes running over each word, down each line.

'Well, Mr Greynell, I hope you left some clues in this letter, because hope is all we have at the moment,' he said to himself before leaving the street for the cool hallway of the inn.

★

Their room was simple like the hostel, with just a bed, a rusty lamp on a nearby table and an ancient rug on the floor that looked as though it might fall apart as soon as you stepped upon it. Full-length folding doors looked out onto a balcony. William opened them as soon as he and Marco were inside, letting in some air and churning the dust into miniature tornadoes that swirled and sparkled in the afternoon light.

William heard a murmur of effort behind him and noticed that Marco was straining again as he stowed their belongings under the table with the lamp. He went over and took the boy's arm.

'Let us see those hands,' he said.

Marco looked up, a little ashamed, his hands balled into shaking fists.

'Let me see,' William insisted gently. Marco unclenched them and he saw they were red and raw, with cuts on both. He smiled and looked proudly at Marco. 'Captain Gerard certainly had you working hard,' he remarked. 'Ask one of the brothers for salve to soothe the skin. They'll be fine in a few days.'

'Yes, Uncle,' Marco said dutifully.

William regarded the boy for a moment. There were times when Marco appeared older than he was, and sometimes in the half-light and shadow he would seem like a man. Yet his petulance and boyish pouting whenever he was chastised quickly dispelled the illusion. He was naught but a child in a growing body. If he was physically maturing enough to continue with them then so too must his attitude, William mused, surprising himself that he should even consider keeping Marco on this mission. The alternatives would cost time, looking for a merchant who was reliable enough to return the boy to Naples, time that was now required to investigate Charles Greynell's demise.

Someone knocked at the door.

'Come in,' William said, his sword only a short reach away.

Peruzo appeared at the doorway. 'They are assembled, Captain.'

'Very well,' William said, moving past Marco. He paused

130

to look at the boy as he began unpacking their belongings. 'You'd better come with me. If you are staying with us, you need to know what we face as much as the other men in this company.'

Marco spilled the clothes from his arms in his enthusiasm, gathering them up quickly to dump them on the bed before rushing after his uncle.

△ VII △

The dining room was crammed. Where there were stools or benches, the monks sat. Where there was a place to stand, a brother did so. There was space enough for William to address the men, but the room was only built to house two dozen people at any one time, not forty-two. Thirty-nine of these were monks, and William looked over each and every one of them. He recognized some: Brothers Gregory, Cristiano, Nico and Leone amongst others. Brother Leone had served with him in Aosta and many others had been with him on missions in Spain and France. The Spanish contingent led by Lieutenant Vittore was largely unknown to him, but there were a couple of faces he had seen at St Laurence, and the men assembled had a fierce reputation.

William cleared his throat. 'Gentlemen, I wish our first meeting was under better circumstances. Time is short, so I will be brief. Our mission is to locate and capture the Hoard of Mhorrer.'

There were murmurs at this, but no surprise. The rumourmongers at St Laurence and the Secretariat were all too efficient.

'I will not deceive any of you. The journey will be hard and I expect we will lose many before the job is done. But this is what you have trained for. This is what you have devoted your lives to. If we prevail, then the War will near its end. If we fail, then we risk the destruction of everything we cherish.

'Unfortunately I believe our enemies, the servants of the Count, are already here in this town . . .'

(Again there were murmurs, perhaps more audible than the first.)

'. . . And that our contact, Charles Greynell, has been murdered by them. This I intend to settle tonight. Brothers Nico and Leone will accompany Lieutenant Peruzo and me in the investigation.' He paused and placed his hands on his hips, regarding each monk in turn, studying the strength of the company.

'Days of toil and hardship lie ahead of us. The desert is unforgiving to the weak, as most of you know at first hand. And when we find the Hoard, there will be another trial to overcome: the Rassis Cult. You will need all your strength and courage to meet them. Prepare yourselves. Both here' – he tapped his head, 'and here' – he tapped his heart. 'I know we will prevail, for there are no better soldiers on this earth than the brothers of St Laurence . . .'

The monks were stirred by William's words. Their expressions were hopeful, their eyes glittering with confidence. William looked to Marco, who had been enthralled throughout the address. His eyes sparkled too with adoration and enthusiasm. 'Let me come with you tonight,' he whispered to his uncle, 'so I can prove I too am worthy of this mission.'

William shook his head. 'If you really wish to gain favour, take my orders without argument. You must stay here. Talk to the men. Learn from them. And heal those hands.'

Marco's first instinct was to sulk, but he learned fast and his expression changed to obedience. He bowed and stayed silent.

At the other side of the room, Brothers Nico and Leone spoke to Peruzo and then left to prepare while William talked to Lieutenant Vittore.

'I've heard little of the Rassis Cult,' Vittore said, 'but what I've learned makes me believe we need more men, Captain.'

'This is our company, Lieutenant,' William replied. 'There are no more. Cardinal Devirus believed that time came first. To wait for reinforcements would deliver the Hoard into Ordrane's hands.'

'I am certain the Count's men aren't here, Captain,' Vittore said. 'We would know if they were. I've had my men searching this town for the last five days. There's been no sign of them. Charles Greynell was probably killed by a local thief.'

'Where is Greynell's body now?' William asked.

'He was cremated,' Vittore explained. 'He had begun to rot. The heat is terrible here.'

'Did you see him?'

'Brothers Filippo and Adams did.'

'What did they find?'

'Nothing too unusual. He was murdered by a weapon of some sort. I wager a knife.'

'What would bring you to that conclusion?'

'His throat was cut,' Vittore replied.

'That was the killing stroke?'

'Brother Filippo could not be sure. He said the wound had putrefied from lying in the river so long,' Vittore explained, and then hesitated. 'There were more wounds across the arms and shoulders, but not deep enough to kill him.'

'Bring me Brother Filippo,' William said to Peruzo. He nodded and walked away to fetch the monk.

Vittore breathed out heavily. 'I'm not sure what more I can tell you, Captain Saxon.'

'You haven't told me a great deal, Lieutenant.'

'I am not a physician, Captain. I've only relayed what Filippo has told me.'

Brother Filippo came over. 'Captain,' he said, and stood to attention.

'I want you to describe Greynell's throat wound to me,' William said impatiently.

'It was deep and . . .' Filippo hesitated.

'And?'

'Not a straight cut. It was a little inaccurate.'

'Too inaccurate to be done at close quarters?'

Filippo thought about this. 'Most of the throat had been torn out. The blade would have been barbed, or jagged . . .'

'Not the usual blade a thief would carry, then?' William said, and glanced at Vittore, whose cheeks reddened. 'What of the other wounds?'

'Jagged again, but shallow.'

'In your opinion, were the wounds random? Did they suggest an expert attack?'

'Not really. They were quite wild, Captain. Across the shoulders and arms. There was a raking blow across the chest, but again it was shallow.'

'Not something you expect at close quarters,' Peruzo suggested. 'Especially from a vampyre.'

'If it was a vampyre,' Vittore said.

'They could have been delivered at a distance,' William said.

'None of the wounds could have been made by a firearm or throwing knife, sir,' Filippo said. 'The cuts do not match those types of weapon.'

'What would be able to strike a man across the neck and deliver unusual wounds at a distance?' Peruzo asked.

After some moments of thought, Vittore said: 'There is one weapon, sir.' He looked at William apologetically. 'I don't know why I didn't think of this before.'

'Go on, Lieutenant,' William urged him.

'We of the Order do not use it, for it requires a skill greater than we possess. It is a half-moon flail. A weapon with long chains, almost ten feet in length, that are swung until highest momentum is attained. At the end of each chain is a sharpened half-moon blade, the width of your hand. They are flung forwards or sideways and can cut through armour. If used by a skilful arm, they would deliver such wounds.'

'Half-moon flail,' William repeated to himself, imagining it. 'You'd have to be a giant to use that. Or extremely strong.'

'I've seen it used only once. Its wielder slaughtered several tribesmen in a heartbeat. It was something that defied your eyes,'

Vittore replied with a certain tone of dread, 'and something that I would not wish to face a second time.'

William looked at him long and hard. 'A vampyre?'

Vittore nodded ruefully. 'Yes, Captain. The half-moon flail is a vampyre's weapon.'

CHAPTER EIGHT

The Sins of the Quarter

△ I △

Brother Nico slipped a dagger into his bootstrap and then stowed the hatchet at his hip, before pulling his coat about him as he stood with Brother Leone in the cool air outside the inn. They spoke in hushed voices to the guards at the doorway, harmless quips that were the banter of any soldier, religious or not.

When William and Peruzo appeared the chatter abated and discipline returned. Silently the four men walked off into the evening, William leading the way.

'Vittore has provided directions to where Greynell was last seen,' William said at the end of the street. 'He was lodging at an inn called The Sun over Kadesh. It lies a couple of miles east of here.'

They said little as they made their way under darkening skies, the diverse buildings leaning over them as the four foreigners slipped down street after street with only a few curious glances cast their way from locals as they retired inside for the night.

After an hour's walk, they found the street Vittore had described, a long winding avenue of tall houses and shacks. Here rich and poor seemed to exist side by side within an assortment of styles that clashed in the throes of construction and corruption. There were women there, selling themselves to passers-by,

136

and it jarred with the fine balconies above them, draped with lush fabrics.

William was relieved to find The Sun over Kadesh marked out clearly from the rest – no need to consult with some local whore or vagabond. The inn stood, or rather appeared to lean, as though its architect had forced its construction to swagger upwards against its neighbour. It was painted in a lush green and yellow that put the nearest buildings to shame. Along its walls were foreign symbols or words, and a painting that William recognized as a king of Egypt, a Pharaoh, at the head of a vast army.

'A fine picture,' Peruzo remarked.

'It depicts Ramses's victory at Kadesh,' William replied, quite pleased with himself. 'We will look here, I think.'

The innkeeper and his staff were less than helpful. When they unearthed the owner skulking in a small grubby room, he looked afraid. William asked about Charles Greynell, but the conversation was protracted and arduous. While Brother Leone did his best to translate, neither party truly understood the other and talk was further hampered by doubt and fear from the innkeeper.

Eventually they came to an understanding, or rather William parted with several gold coins and was shown where Charles Greynell had been living in recent weeks. The owner did not stay, not even to open the door to the lodgings, but dashed away with one of the staff in tow.

'Did you see how terrified that man was?' Peruzo remarked.

William nodded. 'Something has happened here,' he said, and stared down suspiciously at the door. The innkeeper had given him a key.

'There's nothing to show the door was forced open,' Peruzo said after examining it.

'Vampyres don't always knock,' William replied.

'The window?'

William nodded and tried the lock as the monks readied their swords.

The key turned and the door opened.

The room before them was in turmoil. Paper littered the floor like oversized confetti, and clothes were strewn from the door to the open window, hanging from the bedposts and the back of the chair. Peruzo walked cautiously across it all.

'Someone has been busy,' he said.

William ordered Leone and Nico to stand guard in the hall, and then closed the door behind him as he stepped inside.

'What were they looking for, do you think?' Peruzo asked, staring down at the shirts and breeches scattered on the floor.

'It's hard to tell.' William knelt down. There were spots of dried blood on the bare boards. 'There was a struggle here.'

Peruzo looked over to the window where the blinds swung from one broken hinge. The slats were splintered, and several lay shattered on the floor.

'They came in through the window . . .' Peruzo began, tracing the attack through the air. He noticed another spot of blood on the chair. 'Greynell was sitting. He wouldn't have known they were coming.' The lieutenant found more blood on the shattered mirror strewn over the table top.

'They didn't kill him here,' he said finally.

William stood up. 'Why?'

'Too many people around,' Peruzo said thoughtfully. 'No. They took him away from here. Once they couldn't find what they wanted.'

'But what was it they were searching for? A map? Directions to the Hoard itself?' William said and sighed. They spent some time sifting through the debris but found nothing.

'So where next?' Peruzo asked.

William sat down on the chair and pulled the letter from his shirt. He read it again, hoping a sign would reveal itself after standing in the man's room. Peruzo looked on curiously.

'What does it say?'

'Riddles. Or nothing of the sort,' William admitted, deflated. He read the letter aloud to Peruzo.

'Fires? And "wanderers of the desert"?' Peruzo remarked.

'You think it's a clue?'

'As a riddle, it signifies something. Though what, only a scholar or Greynell himself would know,' Peruzo confessed.

William was forced to agree. The mere thought of the riddle had him racking his brains, with an irritation born out of desperation and frustration. He cast his eyes around the room again in case there was anything he had missed. They had turned out everything, from drawers to bags and cases, yet it only revealed that Charles Greynell was a man of expensive tastes. Whatever clues had been in the room had since been removed by others.

Peruzo kicked a discarded bottle at his feet and it rolled across the boards to collide with William's chair with a loud clink. William looked down, and his eyes alighted on something. Plucking the bottle from the floor he regarded it closely: it was plain brown glass, but marked with a moon and sun around its neck. He stared at it for a moment and then rose from the chair.

'Recognize this?' He pointed at the symbol.

Peruzo shook his head.

'Me neither,' William said. 'I wonder if the innkeeper does.'

Leaving the room, they went downstairs and found the owner counting his coins, still with that haunted expression as though he expected someone or something nasty to pay him a visit.

William thrust the brown bottle onto the desk top with a sudden thud that made the man start in surprise, scattering the coins with a wayward hand. William stared at him and pointed at the symbol.

'Leone, ask him where this bottle comes from.'

The innkeeper frowned and his hands began to shake. He shook his head slightly and turned back to gather the coins. He ignored Leone as though the monk did not exist.

William clattered the glass against the wood again. 'Greynell . . . This bottle . . . *Where?*' he said, bringing out three more gold coins.

The innkeeper's hands hovered over them and then he smiled weakly. 'Babel's,' he replied.

△ II △

The streets to Babel's were narrow and smelt of rotting refuse. Dogs skulked in the gutters competing with vagabonds who loitered in doorways and eyed the four strangers who walked by.

The map scrawled out by one of the innkeeper's staff was crude, yet William had marvelled how Leone had managed to gesture and encourage someone to draw directions. It had cost them though, in gold and time. Night had fallen by now, and the streets were dangerously gloomy.

'I think this is the road,' Peruzo said, a little too unsure for William's comfort. When his lieutenant began turning the map sideways, he grew concerned.

'Are we lost?'

The elder officer ran his fingers across his grey-flecked beard and smiled. 'This is not the finest map of Rashid,' he conceded.

'It will have to do,' William replied. 'So which way now?'

Peruzo studied the map, and then looked back at the street. Up ahead it narrowed to a point so that several sandstone buildings were leaning over towards each other, their balconies almost meeting. To the left was a side street reeking with refuse, while to the right was a wooden gate that had aged to the point of collapse.

'The map tells me nothing,' Peruzo sighed finally, 'but my instincts tell me to continue straight ahead.'

'I would trust your instincts any day, my friend,' William grinned, leading them down the diminishing sand track. As they passed under the balconies above, they heard sounds around the corner, followed by raised voices and the cackling of women.

The four men marched into the next street and were surprised by its brilliance. The street was short, but considerably wider than the last one, and flanked by numerous buildings. In

140

every window were lamps and candles that gave off a glare that eclipsed some of the shapes before them, blurring the street people's outlines in shadow and light.

William brought his group to a halt as he looked about. One building was unconventional, a layered monstrosity of balcony after balcony, receding to the top of four storeys, until the highest point seemed to shelve away into the night. Hanging from each balcony was a tapestry that was Byzantine in style yet covered in bestial depictions that flickered in the lamplight, a parody of saints and martyrs in a maelstrom of nature that wrapped itself around each figure with roots and rivers, toppling with moons and stars.

'Babel means chaos,' William murmured to Peruzo. 'What is the most chaotic building in this street?'

Peruzo nodded towards the one with the tapestries. As they came closer, the depictions were blasphemous and Peruzo appeared uncomfortable. 'Greynell would find himself *here*?'

William studied the foot of the building, noting how the women seemed dressed in neat yet baggy clothing, so that by the merest reach or gesture, a thigh would be uncovered, or a breast would peek out. One wore a gown that was transparent in the lamplight so that the dark triangle of her pubic hair showed as a shadowy cleft between her thighs.

'Whores,' William murmured. 'Babel's is a brothel.'

Peruzo grinned, but both Brothers Nico and Leone looked worried, something not lost on William.

'Peruzo, wait outside with Nico,' William said. 'Brother Leone and I will go alone.'

Peruzo nodded, but William could sense he disapproved.

As William and Leone walked to the steps, William inclined his head to him. 'I wasn't sure if you had taken the vow or not,' he whispered.

'I have, Captain. But do not worry, I have faced sterner tests than this,' Leone replied quickly. 'Any man who has ventured into the piazzas of Rome can be tested any moment of any day. I am no different.'

William chuckled, the first light moment he'd felt all day.

Several women at the steps noticed the two strangers, and began to detach from their admirers, local men or scruffy-looking merchants. These same men regarded William suspiciously, as rivals might.

The women sidled up to William, brushing against him, a hand touching his arm, his hip, his rump. One woman, not much older than Adriana and quite beautiful, confronted him and began purring some suggestion in his ear. The words were unfamiliar; the gestures were not.

He grew uncomfortable with the attention and pushed through them. At once the women's demeanours turned from pussycat to gorgon, hissing and insulting them both as they never looked back. One woman spat and gestured with her fingers, while another insulted their sexuality.

'Friendly, aren't they?' Leone said uncomfortably.

'Only when they want something,' William replied as they passed through the entrance and into a cavernous atrium beyond. It was as high as the building, and the balconies outside opened up onto terraces built inside the atrium. Here staircases ran across levels of landings grafted randomly against the walls of the enormous space, a web of steps and balconies without much logic or respect for architecture. It was simply babelesque in design.

On each landing and stair were women and their customers. Some were laughing, teasing and caressing, while sexual acts took up corners of the layout where customers either could not afford a room or in their lust had not made it to a place of privacy.

Around these acts were others equally flagrant, yet as William's eyes roved from one to another, they seemed to dull into the background, a moving picture of carnal urges, dampened only by the heavy veil of pipe smoke and the smell of burning incense mixed with the tang of sex.

Leone's eyebrows had not lowered as he looked about, quite in awe. 'I have seen decadence before, Captain, but *this* . . .'

142

William nodded, impressed and repulsed in equal measure. They walked through a throng swallowed up in its own desires. When William bumped into one coupling, the two of them barely noticed, so engrossed were they in each other. For a moment the newcomers were trapped in a ring of people; merchants with money to burn and plenty of women ready to be bought, bottles of wine spilling over tables and across the smirched wooden floors.

As William and Leone looked for a way around them, arms appeared out of nowhere and began wrapping themselves around William like pairs of tentacles. They were of different sizes and ages, and the moaning at his ear caused him to back away, turning to the three women, short, tall and large, who continued to advance with looks of greed.

'That way,' William said quickly to Leone and they made their escape, smiling outwardly like gentlemen, yet secretly dismayed by the women's advances.

Finally, they came to a bar where several women bare to the waist served drinks to the customers. A voice nearby slurred words, but they were unintelligible. William wasn't even sure if it was they who were being addressed. He turned to his left and found the speaker, a tall man in a well-tailored suit and broad-brimmed hat. His hair was long and curled, and his short beard ended in a point. He seemed to be drunk.

Again the man spoke, but the words were lost on William. He shrugged and then shook his head. 'I'm sorry, I do not understand.'

The man in the hat nodded and smiled quizzically.

Leone was feeling harassed. There were only so many ways he could say 'No' to the women about him, and he questioned his own ability to speak Arabic when even saying 'no' did not dissuade them. 'Captain, do you really think we'll find any clues here?' he whispered.

William started to believe they would not. 'Most of these people are fishermen.'

Leone nodded. 'Rich fishermen, by the looks of it.'

'It certainly is an odd place for a man like Greynell to frequent,' William added.

'Do you speak English?' interrupted the tall man in the broad-brimmed hat.

'English?' William replied, nodding suspiciously.

The man in the hat clapped his hands together and laughed out loud. 'Wonderful!' he announced, drawling so that the 'er' seemed to drag on. 'I haven't met anyone who can speak English in days,' he said and slid some way along the bar top, his hand gripping a long jar of wine.

'My name is Tom Richmond, sir,' the man said, and put out a hand. 'My friends call me Thomas.'

William looked down at the hand for a moment, then summoned his manners and shook it. 'William,' he replied.

'William? A gentleman's name, sir.'

'Mr Richmond,' William greeted.

'Please! Call me . . .' the man paused with difficulty, staggering a little, '. . . whatever you like.'

William gave him a courteous nod.

'Are you a merchant?' Thomas Richmond asked, looking William up and down.

William felt suddenly stung, memories of his family life coming back to him in a flood. The Saxons had been one of the greatest merchant families in all of England, yet William had turned his back on this tradition when he joined the army.

'I am,' he replied finally.

Thomas Richmond suddenly looked relieved. 'Thank God. I haven't met another merchant in days, sir. It's nothing but locals that smell of fish around here.'

William smiled, though he felt exasperated. Time was dwindling and he was no nearer to finding out the cause of Greynell's death.

'And how do you like Rashid?' Thomas Richmond asked. Before William could reply, he added, 'It's sadly in decline. Merchants are going elsewhere. Alexandria, I suspect. This is the last

144

fortress of decadence left in this damned placed. But I fear even Babel's will close its doors soon. A shame.'

'You look at home here,' William remarked politely, glancing around the room.

'You see, I can understand every sordid conversation and squalid promise in this room, William,' the Englishman replied, leaning casually on the bar. His hat slipped a little and William guessed the merchant was inebriated. 'I am fluent in Arabic, sir. It helps when negotiating with these fishmongers.'

Leone backed into William as another whore began wrapping her arms around the brother's waist. Leone shrugged her away.

'Captain . . .' he began, wishing he had stayed outside.

'Is this too much for you?' William asked him.

'I feel I am a target for their affections, Captain.' Leone sighed, appearing awkward.

'It would be harder to hit a moving target,' William remarked and looked around the room. 'While I speak to this gentleman, maybe you can mingle with the patrons. See what information you can gain from them.'

The suggestion was unappealing, but another woman reached out to Leone and he struggled away from her. 'I'll do my best, sir.'

William waited until Leone had pushed his way from the bar, standing out amongst the customers in his European attire, before he returned to the conversation with the English merchant.

Thomas Richmond grinned. 'Your friend is not happy,' he observed.

'Too much attention for one man,' William replied. 'My friend is shy.'

'He should take a girl,' the Englishman suggested, gesturing to the women as they walked past, sizing up the rich and extravagant customers. 'They could even show an old man a thing or two.'

'Indeed,' William said, and turned to a bare-breasted woman

behind the bar counter. He held up two fingers and the woman nodded, retrieving a bottle and two glasses. 'Will you drink with me?'

Richmond's smile broadened. 'It would be my pleasure.'

After pouring out the drinks, William toasted the Englishman.

Richmond downed his drink also, coughing slightly at the end of it. He then relaxed again and looked William up and down. 'It is agreeable to meet a fellow Englishman,' he said.

'If that is so, then maybe you can help me,' William said directly.

'Of course. A fellow merchant must always be helped,' Thomas Richmond slurred.

'I am looking for someone. A friend. I understand he drinks here,' William began. 'If you could help me find him I would appreciate it.'

Richmond nodded quickly. 'Of course! Of course! Anything for the company. There has been only one Englishman here in weeks.'

William listened. 'Just the one?' he asked. 'Who was he?'

'Here they called him "Charlie". A good man. A good merchant. He liked drinking. He liked whores. He has not been here for several days,' the Englishman lamented.

William's look was urgent as he clattered his empty glass on the bar counter.

The Englishman noticed the transformation. 'Is it Charlie you're looking for?'

'If his full name is Charles Greynell, then yes.'

'I confess I knew not his last name. Charlie was the only . . .' Richmond began, but William interrupted.

'Did he speak to you about anything of interest?'

'No. He was a silent man. Spoke little,' the other replied. 'He was private. Would not even say where he was going. Nor where he had been.'

William looked disappointed. 'Nothing at all?'

Richmond shook his head. 'Who knows where he is now?' he added.

William looked to Leone, who was busy defending his honour. 'Mr Richmond . . .' William began.

'Call me Thomas,' the Englishman broke in.

'Thomas then . . . I must know everything about Charles Greynell,' William said. 'If there is anything you recall, no matter how trivial, please tell me.'

'Why? Is there something the matter?' Thomas asked.

'Charles Greynell is dead,' William told him.

There was a pause, maybe of contemplation or something else, but the Englishman's expression soon began to crease into confusion. 'I do not understand. You are here to find Charlie. You asked me about Charlie. So Charlie is not dead . . .'

'Charles Greynell was found murdered several days ago,' William told him quietly.

'No . . .' Thomas murmured, sobering fast.

'I need to know everything about him. I have to discover how he was murdered,' William told him.

'Of course,' Thomas said distantly.

'Will you help me?'

Thomas nodded.

'Is there anyone else here who might have known Charles Greynell?' William asked.

Thomas pointed across the bar to a rotund man in a long beige gown. 'That man owns Babel's. He would know.'

William watched the bald fat man, his laughter high and almost effeminate as he massaged a young woman's nipples, nuzzling her neck at the same time. '*Him?* I thought he was a client,' William mused.

Thomas leant over the bar and began hailing the man. 'Khayyam! Khayyam!'

The fat man ceased nuzzling and turned to the voice. He seemed to sigh and walked over to the bar, muttering to himself quickly. His voice rose as he began addressing the Englishman.

'Ask him about Charles Greynell,' William interrupted.

Thomas spoke and Khayyam answered hurriedly, going on to launch into a tirade.

'What did he say?' William asked.

'He wants to know where Charlie is,' Thomas replied, 'for he has many debts to pay.'

'Tell him I am not here to pay Charlie's debts. Tell him I want some information.'

Khayyam listened, hoping the response would be profitable. At once he frowned, growing angry again. He threw up his hands and began to turn away. William dipped into his money pouch and put two gold coins on the counter. The brothel owner paused.

With his attention caught, William said, 'When was the last time he saw Charles Greynell?'

Khayyam replied quickly as Thomas translated, the fat man pausing only to take the two gold coins from the bar.

'He says it was several days ago. With me,' Thomas replied.

'And before? How long has he known Charlie? Did he say anything about where he was going?' William asked.

Thomas translated and Khayyam shrugged, saying barely a few words. 'No. Charlie said little of his business. He went away for a few months but returned recently. Now he has gone again.'

William felt tired. It was all he could do to control his frustration. Scratching his head, he weighed the purse in his hand. He was running out of money.

Khayyam grew agitated again.

'He wants recompense,' Thomas said. 'He wants to know when his debts will be paid.'

William ignored him. There were no clues here. A dead-end and wasted time. No one seemed to know about Charles Greynell and it was looking increasingly likely that the knowledge of Mhorrer's Hoard had died with their contact.

William turned to the brothel owner, his shrill voice irritating him. 'Tell this man he won't be paid because Charles Greynell is dead.'

Thomas paused, surprised at the vehemence in William's voice. But he translated all the same and watched Khayyam crumble, whimpering theatrically about the loss of his money.

William turned his back on the bar and looked across the room. Leone was picking his way through the crowd, appearing more and more bewildered by what he saw. The debauched acts in every carnal corner were making him increasingly meek, and William doubted he would have the nerve to ask about Charles Greynell, and disrupt the patrons as they wallowed in mutual desire. If William was honest, he felt a little out of his depth too. None of these gentlemen would pay them any attention if there was better sport to be had.

On closer inspection the clientele were mostly Arabs, but he did see the occasional European, dressed in creased linen and sporting days of beard growth. Most of the non-Arabs appeared down on their luck, apart from Thomas Richmond, who was simply drunk. Again William asked himself: why Babel's? Why come to a place like this, where the drink was terrible and the patrons were just as bad? The women weren't anything special, those whom William could see anyway. But what about those he could not?

He raised his eyes up the length of the atrium past the staircases that joined each random landing with the next. There were more rooms up there. Perhaps there were other whores in those rooms, for special customers. Customers like Charles Greynell.

William turned to Richmond, who was fending off curses and accusations from Khayyam.

'Mr Richmond, did Charlie have a favourite? Someone he would visit here often?' William interrupted.

Thomas tapped his lips thoughtfully. 'A girl? I don't know. They are all pretty.'

'Can you ask Khayyam?' William said. Thomas gestured over to the fat man, whose ranting turned suddenly to hope as he scuttled over. He listened to Thomas by cupping his hand around his ear, but when Thomas was done, Khayyam looked at William and spat on the floor.

149

William pulled out another gold coin and slapped it down on the counter, seething.

'Malika,' Khayyam said as he snatched the coin from the bar.

'I want to meet her,' William said.

Thomas beamed. 'Finally, you are taking pleasures from Babel's!' he said and translated to Khayyam.

Khayyam pointed at William and held up six of his fingers.

'Six coins?' William said as he reached into the emptying purse again. He looked down at the coins and shook his head. 'Very well . . . Six it is.'

The coins were stacked on the counter. 'And you too, Mr Richmond,' William added.

Thomas raised his eyebrows and patted his breast pocket. 'Me?'

'I need your help,' William said. 'I cannot speak to her, remember?'

'You wish *only* to speak?' Thomas said, amazed. 'You have not *seen* Malika . . .'

William pointed at the Englishman, gesturing to him as company. Khayyam looked surprised but nodded and pointed at the coins, raising six more fingers. William breathed hard as he dug for more coins, thinking he was probably paying off 'Charlie's' debt anyway.

With the transaction complete, Khayyam led both men across the room, past further scenes of drinking and fornication until they arrived at the stairs. Brother Leone marched over to William after spotting him from afar. He was flushed and beads of sweat were collecting on his forehead.

'Anything?' William asked him.

'No, Captain, but . . .' Leone hesitated, then glanced at both Richmond and Khayyam, who were listening.

William inclined his head. 'Continue, Leone. I doubt they will understand you.'

Leone nodded, but lowered his voice all the same. 'I was going to say that the locals are ignoring me. They won't even

acknowledge me when I speak to them. And the women . . .
well.'

William smiled sympathetically. 'You've done enough.' He
patted Leone on the shoulder. 'Wait for me outside with the
others. Inform Lieutenant Peruzo that we have a possible lead.
This gentleman speaks Arabic and can translate for me. I won't
be too long.'

Leone looked hopeful again and gave a quick nod in reply
before braving the gauntlet of the whores outside. Before
William could contemplate his decision, he was led upwards,
over the creaking wooden steps to the first landing, and then up
another flight to a second. It was there, overhanging the far end
of the landing, that Khayyam gestured to a doorway veiled by a
long scarlet sheet that billowed a little in the breeze.

William swept back the curtain and stepped inside.

The room was long and low, and night air buffeted his skin
from an open window. In the middle of the room was a four-
poster bed, veils of white muslin hanging on every side. The
smell of incense was heady here, and with each breath the scent
flowed like wine down William's throat.

For a moment he thought there was no one else in the room,
and then from the bed came movement, the folds of sheets and
veils rustling and shifting until a figure emerged from within
them like a ghost. She rose deliberately slowly from the bed, her
shadow and outline only glimpsed in the flickering light of a
nearby lamp. Curling her fingers around the left post at the foot
of the bed, she stepped around the corner.

William heard Thomas gasp behind him; he understood why.
Malika was almost as tall as William, with long black hair as thick
as Adriana's. Her face was oval-shaped, and her eyes shone like
the brightest of stars, staring with a desire that was quite daunting. Her body was slim and curved in such a way that William's
hands would almost have spanned her waist, yet her rump was
round and lush, matching her deep and heavy breasts, dark-
rimmed around the nipples that jutted beneath her transparent

gown. Even the dark triangle between her legs appeared perfectly shaped.

Regarding both men, she raised her slender arm and pulled the clasp that held her thin gown to her shoulders. It fell away like feathers, floating gently to the floor at her feet. Naked, her legs parted slightly, she waited for them to approach her.

William found himself staring and stirring, and felt suddenly ashamed of himself.

'Thomas?' he gasped.

The Englishman hesitated, locked into the spectacle of her standing there, imagining carnal acts with this woman. William reminded Thomas of his purpose with a sharp nudge in the side. Thomas cleared his throat as William walked boldly over to Malika and bent down to pluck her discarded gown from the floor. He straightened up and pushed it into her hands. 'Tell her to dress,' William said, turning his back on her.

Thomas did so under sufferance.

They waited until the woman was dressed, her expression changed from desire to bewilderment. She muttered something and Thomas translated.

'She wants to know when you wish to taste her pleasures, sir,' he said.

'I don't want her pleasures, Thomas,' William replied wearily. 'I only desire some answers.'

Malika sat down on the edge of the bed.

'Ask her about Charles Greynell.'

At the mention of the name, Malika seemed to cringe. She glanced nervously past William to the door and then to the window.

'Why is she afraid?' William asked.

Thomas spoke to her and she paused for a moment. Then, with her head bowed sheepishly, she told them.

'She says her owner would whip her if he knew that Charlie was being pleasured without paying,' Thomas replied.

'Tell her not to be afraid,' William said, and put his hand under her chin, raising her face to his.

Malika flinched like a scared child.

'Does she know where Charles went during his journeys from Rashid?'

Malika listened to Thomas but said nothing.

'Well?' William said after a silent minute passed. 'Ask her again.'

Thomas did so, and this time she looked at William and then at his purse. She said something to the Englishman and then looked up at William, her expression hardening.

'She says that Charlie confides in her, and his trust cannot be . . .'

William had an inkling of what she wanted. 'Can it be bought?'

Thomas asked. Malika nodded. William brought out three gold coins and looked at them with disdain. 'This entire town is for sale,' he growled as he drew out a fourth.

'Did you expect otherwise?' Thomas remarked casually. 'She is a whore.'

William put them on her opened palm, and she gripped them tightly. She began to speak to Thomas, though she could not keep eye-contact with either man.

'She says Charlie went away for months at a time. He would travel to the south. He would follow the Nile down to Cairo and Luxor.'

William looked at her, and understood. He nodded, trying to appear encouraging, but he was losing patience.

'Ask her if Charlie ever gave her anything. A letter, a message . . . Anything at all,' William said as he stepped away.

'She says "No",' Thomas replied.

William sighed. '*No*,' he repeated and turned to leave. 'Very well . . .'

'Wait,' Thomas said, as Malika murmured something more. 'She says that he gave her a gift.'

William looked back. 'What was it?'

Malika rose from her bed and went over to a stand where other gowns hung. On one hook was a length of string and a pendant. She lifted it from the hook and came over, talking all the while. 'He said it was a good-luck charm he bought for her,' Thomas continued.

William looked down at it. It was unremarkable, a carved wooden symbol on a cord. The symbol was of a primitive sun and a wing wrapped underneath it.

'What is that?' William asked, showing Thomas.

The Englishman shook his head. 'It could be tribal.'

'Tribal?'

'Bedouin tribes of the deserts visit Rashid. They sell such things in bazaars. They are worthless.'

'Bedouins?'

'Arabs who live in the deserts,' Thomas explained. 'Nomads.'

William felt a sting of recognition: nomads; *wanderers*.

'She says you can buy it from her,' Thomas said and laughed.

'I thought it was a keepsake. Something for luck,' William replied.

'To her it is worthless,' Thomas said. 'She cannot spend it.'

William turned the pendant over in his palm. 'Three gold coins,' he said and put up three fingers.

Malika put up four.

Controlling his temper, William agreed and gave her the coins. He took the pendant from her hands and left without another word, Thomas pausing only to look once more upon her beauty.

On the way out, Thomas laughed. 'You're the only man I know who has come to Malika's, spent much money, yet has left as he came!'

William ignored him and trudged down the stairs, the pendant clutched in his fingers.

As they made their way to the entrance, a man came in, bent and with a withered demeanour, but his face was younger than his posture. William took him to be a servant of the brothel, yet he approached the English merchant directly, waving with some urgency.

Thomas Richmond frowned. 'Hammid? What does the fool want now?' he hissed, just loud enough for William to hear.

William was hardly interested as the stooped man spoke hurriedly, his eyes not once settling on the Englishman's newfound friend.

'My servant,' Thomas grumbled to William, 'and a foolish one. But he does have some uses. I'm afraid I must leave you now.'

'Is there anything wrong?' William asked.

Thomas glanced at Hammid, who moved away, more aloof than before. 'It appears there is some trouble with my shipment. A merchant's life is an exciting one!'

'I'm sorry to hear that,' William said, shaking Thomas's hand. 'I hope it is no great nuisance.'

Thomas seemed indifferent. 'Rashid is a town of thieves, sir. Remember that. Do not trust any of them, or they'll steal the clothes from your backs and the boots from your feet. Good night, sir.'

As Thomas Richmond left him, William felt glad to have met the kindly merchant. He had been an affable fellow, and perhaps they might have shared a conversation under different circumstances.

Yet the position was now clear: they had no further leads, and little prospect of finding the Hoard of Mhorrer.

CHAPTER NINE

Blood and Babel's

△ I △

Malika's gold coins would be spent on lavish gowns and luxurious food. Not the clothes lent to her by her lecherous and repugnant master, Khayyam, nor the slop brought to her room every morning and evening. She would buy real food, fresh fruit and bread. And a robe that brought out the shape of her body and hid its sins. Studying herself in the hand mirror, Malika recognized she was no longer young like some of the other girls. There were lines under her eyes and her breasts sagged a little. She cupped them, wishing they were pert once more, as they had been in her prime.

'Ah, perfection . . .' came a murmur from the window and Malika leapt in fright, dropping the mirror, which shattered into tiny pieces.

'Did I startle you?' the voice came again, the echoing from the impenetrable shadows that lay between the window and the faint lights of the buildings across the street.

Malika rose from her bed and nodded slightly, her arms about her chest.

'What a glorious beauty you are. Why so modest?' the voice remarked and came closer. As it neared her it seemed to solidify, stretching from the shadows at the window across the room until it almost touched her feet. Then from the shadow emerged the flesh, wrapped in a long raven cloak. It seemed to extrude itself from the night until it was whole, clad head to toe in black, topped with a white face crowned with curled, red hair.

'Please . . .' Malika began and then started to sob.

'No tears on my account, Malika,' said the man before her. He gave a crooked leer, with teeth like the shattered glass on her floor. His white skin was like the surface of the moon and enhanced the crackling of his deep yellow eyes, alive with blue flecks of lightning that made them dance.

'I told them nothing,' Malika wept.

'I know, Malika, I know,' the stranger said as he seemed to float across the room to her bed. 'But isn't it what we do that tells the truth? Not what we say?'

Malika crawled onto her bed, scattering the abundance of silk pillows before her. She grabbed one, as though it might offer her some protection. The man with red hair halted at the bottom of her bed, and then seemed to bend impossibly forward, until he towered over the mattress, his face and hands not so far from her. She let out a whimper, looking for a place to escape. The curtain to the hubbub of the brothel outside was tempting, but the man was between her and it. And at the window grew more shadows, and from them came murmurs of excitement.

One of the shadows broke from the others and drifted over, a woman as tall as the man, with lank, black hair. Her skin was the colour of bone and her lips were a dark grey.

'She lies to us, Baron,' the woman said as she came to the man's side.

'It is the nature of every frightened animal to lie, Ileana,' the man replied, and reached out to Malika, his finger stretching so that it touched her just under the chin, the same spot William had felt minutes before.

'I have not lied!' Malika protested, the pillow now pulled up to her jaw, forcing the man to retract his hand.

'No?' the man asked, and straightened up to run his spidery fingers through his flame-red hair. He threw his head back, folding his arms. 'I asked only for two things, Malika . . . *Dear Malika*,' the man said, his eyes crackling with light.

'And I did both of them, my lord,' Malika cried.

'Yes, I suppose in some way you did,' the man chuckled. 'You introduced me to Charles Greynell, and you have not told a soul of what we both know.'

'Then I have not lied?' Malika asked hopefully.

'Not with the tongue . . . But you *have* with your actions,' the baron insisted. 'What did you give to the man who was here?'

'It was nothing . . .' Malika cried. '. . . Something worthless.'

'Worthless?' the man with the red hair said. 'Yet he paid you for it. He must have found it *worthy.*'

'It was a necklace. A tribal necklace. It meant nothing!' she sobbed.

The man stared down at her, trying to search her soul for more lies. 'Worthless to you, maybe . . .'

The woman at the man's side snarled and hissed something into his ear. The man flinched and scowled at her. 'Do not forget your place, Ileana. This is my coven. *Mine!* Do you think I have not made plans?! Do you think . . .?!' he ranted at the woman called Ileana. She shrank back into the shadows as another came to him. He was a bald man, also dressed in black, his skull tattooed with a giant crow's wing that reached from the neck, over the crown towards his brow.

'The men of the Church are still here, Baron,' he said.

The man with the red hair gave him a cursory look. '*Still?*'

The bald man nodded.

'Unfortunate . . .' the man replied and gestured to Ileana.

'Please,' Malika began, 'let me go. I have done all that you asked. I just want to be alone. Alone with Charlie.'

The man with the red hair grinned and looked down at her sadly. 'You wish to join Charlie Boy?'

Malika nodded quickly. Charlie was her best customer, but he was also an accomplished lover and a rich merchant. For months he had been her only chance to escape Babel's and find a life outside the brothel. A life he had once promised during pillow talk, one that would dress her in finery amongst the gentry of Europe. Since childhood, she had lived in Babel's, forced to submit to men who sickened her, or beaten by Khayyam. Charlie, sweet Charlie with his secrets and strange manner, had been her only chance. And had he not said he would reward her well if she gave the necklace to 'the men in grey coats' and not to the shadows that 'scared her the most'?

She had not seen Charlie since he'd asked her to do that one thing, and she felt horribly guilty after Baron Horia forced her to tell him everything about her lover. She felt she was cheating on Charlie with another, betraying his trust. Yet the baron was threatening and charming in equal measure. She could not refuse him.

'She wishes to join Charles Greynell, Ileana,' the man called Baron Horia said.

Ileana smiled cruelly as she pulled out something from her gown. It was a small thing, the size of the woman's palm and shaped like a pyramid. It seemed to sing with light, a soulful sound as cyan tendrils flickered along the surface of each side. It might have been made of black glass, yet for a moment it lost cohesion as something made it squirm like treacle.

Malika was hypnotized by it.

'Do you know what this is, Malika dear?' Baron Horia asked as he bent close to her, staring also at the object resting on Ileana's palm.

Malika shook her head slowly and silently.

That music . . .

'It is a Scarimadaen, Malika . . .' he told her, whispering with a voice that seemed to echo in her skull, the words filling her head, almost drowning her. She grew drowsy, spellbound, her eyes flickering rapidly. '. . . It is the giving of power unimaginable. A power that spreads such sweet corruption that many would happily die for it. Your Charlie never experienced the power of the Scarimadaen, yet he would have stopped others from doing so. I found that quite selfish, don't you?'

'It is the most beautiful thing I have ever seen,' Malika murmured sleepily.

'Yes,' the baron said as Malika crawled in a trance down the bed to be closer to the object.

'May I . . . *touch it*?' she asked.

Ileana looked positively rapturous with Malika's response and the bald man by her side, called Racinet, was equally amused. 'She is too pretty to destroy, Baron,' he remarked.

'Yes. Too pretty. But her looks will fade in time. She will wither and she will no longer be the pretty one,' the man with the red hair said distantly.

Malika hadn't heard a word of their conversation, transfixed as she was by the pyramid's disjointed song, like the low humming of an incongruous choir in mourning. No one else in the room seemed to hear it, or to care for it. To Malika it was the most beautiful song she had heard. Something to cherish. To covet. To . . .

· The baron leaned close to her, his lips by her ears. 'Do you wish to touch it?' he whispered.

Malika nodded.

'Then do so, *and join Charlie* . . .' the baron growled and reached out with astonishing speed to her arms. He seized them both, causing Malika to yelp, and then bit down on her wrist, his sharp incisors splitting open her flawless skin. Blood spurted across the bed, over the baron's white face and down his chin as Malika shrieked in agony and terror. He took the bleeding wrist and pressed it down hard on the surface of the Scarimadaen.

At once the song grew cacophonous and light spewed forth. The walls of the pyramid seemed to break open.

And then came the Fire. The Fury. *The Daemon* . . .

. . . Burning Malika's soul into oblivion.

△ II △

A whore of diminutive size, making up for her petite proportions with boundless energy and enthusiasm, latched onto William's arm and began caressing his thigh. He managed to pull her arms away, but like a limpet she only latched on to him more strongly, thinking him playful.

William drew a couple of coins from his pouch and hurled them to the floor, the sound of its landing catching her attention and alerting other whores, who scrabbled amongst the feet of customers. The patrons roared with laughter and pointed at the struggling women who fought over the coins. It was a pitiful sight.

The urge to escape the brothel grew. William found the heat and laughter stifling, suffocating. The sounds of merriment and carnalities increased until they were deafening. He was disorientated, troubled, and his temper grew. Leering, grinning faces were about him at every turn, and he might have lost patience as he forced himself away. But then something else happened that he did not expect.

Amongst the shrill hilarity and booming laughter it would have been easy to mishear a terrible scream above them. But William was attuned to such cries. He looked up to the balconies, hoping he was mistaken, the hairs standing up on his neck telling him he wasn't.

Babel's lay in ignorance, over a hundred men and women blissfully unaware of the danger so very close at hand. It was a carnal hall, and while sex and sodomy proceeded in the shadows, above them came a howl that was simply drowned out by the cacophony of copulation and sport.

Suddenly, with a shattering roar, the creature burst into view in an explosion of brick and dust. It tore away the narrow walls, and the red curtain plummeted over the edge of the balcony, carried by the weight of broken masonry. The customers below looked up in surprise or bemusement as they were pelted with shards of brick and choked in dust, still unaware of the danger.

The daemon was larger than a bear. Its arms were as long as its body and legs, its backbone so pronounced that it appeared driven through the black flesh. Its head was gigantic, out of all proportion to the rest of the body, so that its jaw hung down the full length of the torso, the gums riven by needle teeth.

Around its head fizzled the remnants of hair, giving it a coronet of smoke, while the creature's eyes burned brightly, suffused with black haze and sapphire light that blazed from the sockets in its deformed skull. It spread its arms, a winged monstrosity, and swooped from the landing. William gasped as it burst among the people below. Two men were crushed by its falling weight. A merchant's head was staved in. A woman in her black gown was caught by a stray blow of the creature's paw that ripped her in two.

Three more men turned to flee, but the daemon tore them apart in mid-step, arterial sprays and offal jetting across the floor. The daemon threw back its enormous head, its jaws stretching impossibly, and howled in triumph, not just for the chaos and death it had wrought so far but for what promised to come.

△ III △

Peruzo heard the roar of the daemon. Nico was too busy speaking to Leone to realize what had happened, but the lieutenant's heart skipped with dread at the low noise rumbling from the window above them.

Peruzo drew his sword as the first of the customers fled Babel's. Nico and Leone followed soon after and all three rushed towards the entrance of the brothel. The whores who loitered at the door appeared bewildered, while some patrons dared to look inside. They had spent their lives in pursuit of the wildest pleasures, and curiosity got the better of many, jostling to find out what new chaos was erupting inside Babel's.

Peruzo drove through the throng, the two brothers close behind.

A scene of utter carnage greeted them.

The daemon had made a butcher's block of the centre of the room. Corpses lay everywhere, while wounded spilled towards the exit clutching half-severed limbs, with faces gouged to the bone and blood on their clothes, both their own and their companions'.

While many fled, others tried to fight back. A local man was ripped limb from limb as he tried to strike at it with his sword. Another customer swung a chair at the beast, but it only shattered against its hide. The daemon lost no time but flung its attacker clear across the room, straight into the plate-glass mirror that hung over the bar. It broke both bone and glass, and the lifeless body fell onto Khayyam, who wrapped his arms around his head as though it might save him.

William had been powerless to prevent the first acts of slaughter. The room had surged with desperate fugitives, and at first he was buffeted away from the daemon on a wave of panic. It was only when most had escaped, leaving the dazed and the wounded behind, that William strode towards the centre of the room. He saw Peruzo leading Leone and Nico inside and waved them over.

'Flank it! Flank it *now!*' William cried out to the two brothers.

They nodded and ran towards the stairs, while William pointed Peruzo down the side of the bar.

A prostitute cowering in the shadows lost her nerve and broke into flight. William held up a hand, shouting, 'No! Wait!' . . . but already too late. The daemon swung itself around, its arm reached out, and the woman ran blindly into its clutch. The claws clenched and the talons on each finger skewered her, before her killer shook her like a rag doll and threw her across the room to land lifeless in the corner.

William drew his sabre from his long grey coat and looked for the creature's vulnerable spot. Above the enormous head was a limp flap of burnt flesh between the armour of its back and the skull. This was their target. William gestured to the back of his own neck to Peruzo, who nodded with understanding. If one of them could only distract it, the other might decapitate the foul creature.

Deciding to act as bait, William waved his sabre in the air and hurled a discarded bottle at the daemon; the bottle merely shattered on its armour. The creature refused to be goaded, but held William with its incandescent stare, measuring him as a threat while it pawed the ground. When William stepped leftward, the daemon stepped right. When he paused and stepped back to the right, it mimicked his movements with a snort of sulphuric smoke that fouled the air around it. William halted, feeling trapped as he looked into the daemon's glowering eyes and slavering mouth.

It would not move unless he did.

It would not attack . . . *unless William turned and fled*.

At the stairs, Brothers Leone and Nico crept upwards. Disregarded, the monks reached a position directly above the fiend and Brother Nico drew his sword. He held it in both hands, turning the polished blade against the glow of the candles until it shone in William's eyes.

William shielded his eyes momentarily and waved his sword to them.

At the signal, Leone's hand reached swiftly into his coat to draw a shining knife between his fingers. He held it above his shoulder and swung down, the blade leaving the monk's hand just as swiftly. Its accuracy was deadly and struck the daemon at the blackened, fleshy collar. It caused a faint squirt of blue iridescence and black smoke curled from the wound, sending the daemon into long choking howls as it wrestled with the steel behind its head.

With some measure of satisfaction, Brother Leone brought out another knife. He aimed it and . . .

. . . A sound like a thousand insects buzzing at once came tearing through the air around Leone and Nico. Nico was sprayed with blood, blinded by the arterial spray from Brother Leone's throat. The monk threw his hands about the air, appearing to brush away invisible flies as blood poured down his front. He stumbled and fell past Nico, his body tumbling down the steps.

Bewildered, Brother Nico stared after him as the wrenching

whine of insects or something else filled the air again. The monk saw metal flashing in the darkness, crisscrossing in front of him, and only felt the pain seconds later as his ear slid down his cheek, his lips split vertically, and his jacket fell away in strips of grey cloth, followed by a torrent of blood as his stomach poured out of the hole gouged from under his ribcage.

William saw Nico collapse on his face to slide a few steps down before halting. Above him, where the balcony hung by only a few planks of wood, was a bald vampyre, his weapon singing as he twirled it around and around.

A half-moon flail.

'Good God,' he murmured and turned to Peruzo. 'Get out of here, Lieutenant!'

Peruzo saw William waving and shouting but the beast's tortured shrieks drowned any sound. He couldn't tell if the captain was signalling to attack or was warning him of danger.

Peruzo chose to advance, ignorant of Leone's and Nico's deaths. With the surviving patrons and whores picking themselves up from the ruins of Babel's, he had to push past a couple of reeling customers to get within striking distance of the beast, which was grappling uselessly at the throwing knife with its elongated claws, as if trying to pluck a minute splinter wearing nothing but gauntlets.

'You're mine,' said Peruzo to himself, raising his sword.

William despaired as Peruzo stepped out from the cover of the balcony. He could see the vampyre standing above him, only now aware that the lieutenant was closing on the daemon. With a shrill, effeminate hoot, the vampyre twirled his half-moon flail about, the bloody blades blurring in the air.

Cursing, William reached over to an oil lamp miraculously preserved at the end of the bar. He took it in his hand and whirled it around his head, replicating the vampyre and his weapon of choice.

'I shall not fail!' he urged himself and loosened his grip on the instant, launching the lamp towards the stairs. It arched over the banister to shatter against the wall mere yards from where Peruzo stood poised. The lieutenant froze as flame shot straight along the wall and across the stairs, igniting the tinder-dry wood at once. The steps burst into flames, a flood of fire that consumed and destroyed, voracious and unstoppable as it ran upwards and outwards.

Peruzo was stunned, terrified even, before he recovered his wits and ran for cover, disengaging from the daemon as its shrieks intensified.

The bald vampyre cried out as fire danced around him. Confused by the smoke and flames that leapt up the stairs, he had to halt the twirling of the weapon and the blades sank into brick and wood as the first wave of flame singed his boots. With a swift turn, he fled the balcony, dragging the flail with him and part of the wall it was still attached to.

Peruzo saw the vampyre flee, his view blocked by falling masonry and more fire and smoke. He stumbled back towards the bar and almost into William, who had backed away from the daemon now surrounded by a sheet of flame fed by spilt spirits.

'Was that you?' Peruzo gasped, horrified that the flames had got so close to him.

'The brothers are both dead,' William told him. 'And there are vampyres. I had to get your attention somehow.'

Peruzo stared at his commander in disbelief.

'I didn't think it would spread so quickly,' William confessed, looking on with awe at the growing inferno.

Above them, the landings spiralling up several floors around the atrium began to burn and collapse, showering the space below with blazing timbers and a torrent of embers.

A section of stairs collapsed not far from where William had been gesticulating moments before, and they stumbled, numbed and beaten, towards the exit. Falling over discarded tables, Peruzo pulled William back to his feet as the central ceiling fell upon the daemon below.

The weight of the fiery timbers drove the creature to its knees. Its armour split like a crushed beetle, a wooden post rammed like a stake through the fleshy sack beneath its jaw. Blue light burned within the orange flames of the wound, until both seemed to merge into one; a pyre of incredible ferocity, belching upwards, blasting away what remained of the balconies, before ripping open a huge hole in the ceiling. The column of flame gushed outwards, flooding the bar, which exploded in a blizzard of broken glass. There was a muffled scream as it engulfed Khayyam.

William and Peruzo flung themselves out of the entrance, away from the cloud of flame that flew their way. The fire licked the soles of their boots as they dived; it scorched the hairs on their necks, and ignited Peruzo's sleeve.

William pulled Peruzo's coat from him, stamping on the sleeve to put out the fire, while the lieutenant crawled away and panted for breath. With the coat now a smouldering rag, William gave up and staggered upright. Around them, the survivors watched as the flames belched from windows and from the entrance to the brothel.

But between the palls of thick black smoke William noticed a figure appear on a balcony near the roof. It was a tall figure, nearly shrouded in smoke and shadow, yet the face was unmistakable. As was the crown of red hair.

The vampyre stared down at William with pleasure.

'*You* . . .' William murmured. He felt his hand tense around the handle of his sword. And then more figures emerged on to the balcony, followed by several on the roof.

These were vampyres, more vampyres than William had ever faced, eight at least, maybe more.

'Peruzo, get up!' he said quickly.

Peruzo staggered to his feet, still dazed.

'We have to go,' William said urgently as the shadows on the roof began to leap into the air. 'Blast! We have to go now!'

Baron Horia saw the two men stumble away down the street, uncoordinated, running like terrified dogs.

It pleased him to see the enemy so desperate. His sport had been curtailed too quickly by this foe of Count Ordrane, this man who had pursued him from Vienna to Prague, who had almost killed him on two occasions.

Baron Horia grinned viciously. 'A hundred pieces of gold to the one who takes Captain Saxon alive!' he called out to his followers, the eight black shapes dividing to swoop over the street and after their prey.

△ IV △

'It was him!' William insisted as they fled down the narrow road.

They were clumsy in their escape. Peruzo's head was still ringing, half-stunned by the explosion at Babel's. Every few steps they would stumble, sliding in the dust, liable to collapse in full view of their enemy. As they turned the corner, a crash and further screams rang out behind them, and Babel's brothel caved in with a ball of fire that mushroomed into the black night sky.

Neither man turned to look.

Into the following street they ran. Peruzo's leg buckled and both men fell, rolling head over heels in the dust beside a dwelling. With his mouth full of dirt, William saw Peruzo on his back and breathing desperately, yet it was the lieutenant who rose first, shaking his head to clear it.

'Madness . . .' he slurred as he rolled onto his knees, coughing harshly, and put his palm against the brickwork of the building nearby. He swayed from his knees to his feet, then reached down and hauled William to his, just as a sudden whining noise tore through the air. William instinctively ducked, and fragments of wall exploded near his cheek. He cried out and Peruzo pulled him away, as the weapon flew at them again, ripping more chunks out of the wall. They staggered into the open, retreating again, their hearts in their throats, pounding blood into their heads so hard it felt as if it might spurt from their ears and noses.

Peruzo glanced over his shoulder to see several figures

skipping impossibly across the roofs of buildings flanking the street. 'They're following us!'

William slid to a halt and pressed himself against the wall of one building where a narrow alley led to another street. 'There!' he shouted and broke into a run, hoping to God that Peruzo was on his heels.

Over their heads came the thrum of the half-moon flail, the wielder shrieking as it hurtled towards them, shredding the air only a few feet behind them as both men threw themselves down the alley, falling over discarded crates and pots of rubbish and filth.

At the end of the lane, William turned right and ran blindly down a street that was wider than the last. He had no idea where it would lead to, only that it lay in the direction of Greynell's inn, and beyond that their own inn and a measure of safety, if there was such a thing.

'Horses!' William pointed to where several mounts were tethered under the canopy of a deserted building.

'We can't just steal them,' Peruzo protested, but the vampyres had appeared at the end of the street and were sliding down the walls like spiders out of a web. 'Can we?'

William turned, half tripped, and saw there were six vampyres in the street behind them, their long cloaks billowing and unravelling at their feet. Above, the bald vampyre leapt, shrieking with laughter that all but drowned the lethal whine of metal blades slicing the air.

William drew a throwing knife and hurled it into shifting darkness. It struck the vampyre at his waist, causing the creature to lose control of his descent and his weapon. The half-moon flail skittered off target and struck a nearby building. Racinet uttered a screech, no longer in rapture, before he plummeted into an adjacent lane and out of sight.

'The horses . . . No choice,' William insisted.

As the vampyres quartered the distance between them and the horses, a figure fell from the sky to land before William and Peruzo, one foot forward, one back, in a perfect crouching

169

position. It was a woman with long black hair which had fallen over her eyes and cheek. She flicked the locks back and straightened majestically, a broad smile on her smooth white face.

'You are the one they call Saxon,' she said.

William was stunned momentarily by his own fame.

Peruzo was not and dashed forward, drawing his shortsword. The female vampyre regarded him with utter disdain and leapt into the air, turning full circle to kick him across the jaw. William winced as his lieutenant flew a few yards, rolled across the road and lay still.

William spat on the ground and drew his sword nervously from under his coat.

The vampyre licked her lips. 'I will enjoy this . . .'

He threw himself at her, twisting the sword about, missing her by inches. The vampyre hissed, leapt and drew two long knives about the length of William's forearm from two sheaths at her back. She then dipped and began swinging them back and forth, a crazed blur of metal that swirled merely feet, and then inches, from William, who parried one blow with his sword and then another. After dodging again, she struck out with both blades, clashing with William's sword. The blow jarred up his shoulder and numbed his arm.

Any normal blade would have shattered under the impact, but this was Engrin's sword, and William thanked his old friend for the gift.

Still, he was shaken and driven to one knee as the woman attacked again. He parried one blade, locked the sword against the hilt and tugged her arm groundwards, pulling her off balance. William used the respite to rise to his feet, but she recovered almost instantly and rained blow after blow upon his weakening arm.

Behind him, he could hear the six vampyres approaching. The woman was teasing him now, striking William's sword playfully as she sought to tire him. In turn, he grew frustrated, before seizing an opportunity as she rounded to slap his sword away again. Instead of being goaded into the attack, he feinted and struck through, cutting one knife from her fingers. She cried out, a strangely sad human cry of pain, and whimpered as she regarded her severed digits, meeting his eye with reproach. He should have followed through, but her demeanour had disarmed him: she looked so helpless.

And he hesitated.

The vampyre noticed this, and her eyes flashed through the smoke rising from her fingers. She leapt into the air, kicking past his sword and into his groin. William fell to his knees and gasped, the wind rushing out of him in strangled breaths, his hands splayed on the floor, his sword spilling from his fingers.

Ileana landed a yard in front of William and began taunting him again. 'You don't even have the courage to kill me!' she teased as she toyed with her knife. 'Your fame is all wind. What is the matter, little man? Have you never killed a woman before?'

'I have,' said a voice to her side, and a blade ran her through. This time there was no pause for pity, just screams of bestial pain as Ileana was impaled. The blade withdrew and she staggered away, clutching at her stomach. Behind her, Peruzo was leaning slightly and shaking his head while his bloodied shortsword trembled in his hand.

William pulled himself to his feet, groaning from the nauseating pain between his legs. His fingers groped blindly along the floor for Engrin's weapon.

'I thought I'd lost you,' he grunted as both men used their failing strength to lurch towards the horses. They each clambered onto a horse as the six remaining vampyres rushed forward, shrieking in anger.

As William and Peruzo kicked their heels in, the sound of the hoofs drowned out a single command behind them. A command that only the vampyres heard.

'I said "*Enough!*"' the red-haired vampyre shouted again. By his side stood Racinet, William's throwing knife in his hand.

Ileana came over, sobbing from the wound through her stomach. 'Look what they did! *Look what they did to me!*'

Baron Horia looked down at the wretched creature. 'You

were careless, Ileana,' he said. 'You cannot be so careless when we face the Rassis.'

Ileana's whimpers turned to sullen growls and she snarled at Horia petulantly. Racinet came over and shook his head. 'Do not worry, my dear Ileana,' he said, and pressed his hand against the wound. 'It will heal.'

Ileana pushed him away. 'I want blood!' she cried.

'*No*,' Baron Horia replied, and grasped her arm. 'Not now.'

'But you wanted Saxon alive,' one of the six complained.

'I wanted *sport*,' Horia retorted and broke into laughter, 'and I have had that. But Saxon is only a whim.'

The vampyre with the long red hair sauntered down the street for a few yards, gazing into the dust that was settling in the wake of the fleeing horses.

'We cannot waste more time pursuing these men,' Horia began and turned to the eight vampyres gathered around him. 'I am quite certain these followers of the Church have no clues to the whereabouts of the Scarimadaen. We have achieved our purpose in this town, so now we must move on.'

Ileana was delighted, and despite her grievous wound she clapped her hands like a child.

Only Racinet seemed displeased. 'What of Saxon? What should happen if he discovers the path to the Hoard?' the bald vampyre asked.

Baron Horia smiled and dramatically put his ear to the wind. 'Do you hear that?'

They listened.

'Those are the sounds of crying and fury in the streets of Rashid, my friends. The witnesses will speak of four strangers who entered Babel's this night.' The baron's smile broadened, almost splitting his face in two. 'The people of this town will be looking for murderers; foreign men in grey clothes, who destroyed a brothel and killed many. These men of the Church will be fugitives; I will make sure of it . . .'

Racinet nodded slowly, imagining what the local militia

would do to them once caught. Militia justice was notoriously barbaric.

'. . . Leaving us to follow the directions that Charles Greynell gave to us,' Baron Horia added, to the delirium of the coven. 'Within days, we will have the Hoard of Mhorrer for *ourselves*.'

CHAPTER TEN

The Flight Eastward

△ I △

As much by luck as judgement, they found their way through a web of dusty streets and narrow alleys back to their own inn. The flight from Babel's had been nothing less than a rout, a headlong dash for some margin of safety. It was undignified, but William and Peruzo had learnt to survive; in such a fight, they could do nothing more.

When eventually they came to their street, already familiar in its own way amongst the multitude of other streets, there was relief, short-lived under the circumstances but enough to allow William a rueful smile as he saw the four guards rush out to meet them.

William dismounted and tethered the horse to a post at the corner of the inn, Peruzo beside him. The lieutenant touched his aching jaw. It felt stiff and swollen, and the pain was nauseating when he tried to move it too far. He pressed his lips painfully together, as if his mouth was full of broken glass.

William knew that the monks were waiting to learn the fate of their missing comrades, but they would not press, such was their discipline. He paused at the entrance to the inn, resting his hand on the doorway. 'Nico and Leone are dead,' he said solemnly, 'just so you know what we face. Don't make the slightest mistake tonight if our enemy comes looking for us. There are vampyres in Rashid. Many vampyres.'

Singling out one of the brothers, Peruzo gave instructions to get rid of the two horses, knowing too well what would happen if they were found outside the inn. As he and William went to their rooms, the lieutenant forced words out from between his compressed lips; the effort seemed to hurt him. 'We cannot stay in Rashid,' he said.

'You're right,' William agreed. 'We must push on at first light.' 'To where?'

'East, to the Sinai. We know that much from Greynell's letter.'

'I will have them ready at first light, Captain,' Peruzo promised, and hobbled away down the sloping hall.

'Peruzo,' William called after him. 'I haven't thanked you for saving my life back there.'

The lieutenant paused and looked over his shoulder. 'I save your life; you save mine.'

'Still, it bears thanking,' William said and smiled.

Peruzo nodded, and was about to walk away, but there was something else on William's mind.

'Have you *really* killed a woman before?' he asked.

Peruzo halted. He walked back towards William, still holding his jaw, the ache almost tangible. 'Yes,' he confided. 'I killed my wife.'

William was shocked, but did not show it. In all the years he had known Peruzo, this admission was the most startling, yet was he really surprised that such a ghost dominated his history? Peruzo was William's senior in the War by many years, and had come to the Papacy with a background largely unknown. That something dark should lurk in his past was perhaps the mark of such a veteran campaigner.

'She was lying with another man,' the lieutenant explained. 'I was as young as you are now, and wild at heart. I was certain I could never hurt her ... yet she deceived me, and I was angry.

'I followed her to a villa in Naples and found them naked together. So I did what any man would do: I challenged her lover there and then. We fought; I was driven by savage rage. When he was wounded and could not fight further, I would not spare him. I cut him again and again, left him to bleed to death as he begged for mercy. But my wife threw herself in the way of a death-blow that would have finished it. I killed her by chance. Just by chance . . . You see, even in my rage I would never have harmed her.'

William looked at Peruzo sadly.

The lieutenant composed himself. 'Most of the old soldiers in the Order have similar tales to tell, Captain. Mine is no different. We came here for absolution. I had the choice to join this War, but I did so out of guilt.'

William nodded distantly, considering his own path that had led to the Order.

'Good night, Captain,' Peruzo said, a little brighter than before, as though unburdened by the confession.

'Let Filippo look at that jaw in the morning,' William replied casually. He wanted to say more, to say they did well to survive, that despite the loss of Nico and Leone they had destroyed a daemon. But it was scant comfort. For the first time in almost seven years, William felt out of his depth.

△ II △

Marco stirred in his bed and opened his eyes. The room was impenetrably dark, silent but for one monk's snores on the other side. He rubbed his eyes and tried to close them again, but whatever had caused him to wake, either the snoring or his own thoughts, he felt too alert to try sleeping and instead stared up at the ceiling, his vision adjusting until he could make out the outline of coving and angular cracks.

After some minutes had passed, he pushed himself up and swung his legs from under the blanket. Pulling on boots that were a little too big, just like the uniform borrowed from Brother Jericho, he stepped silently across the floor and out of the door. The hall was as dark as the room, except for a small window at the end where the moon was attempting to shine through. Marco peeked down to the opposite end and saw a faint glow from the last doorway. Curious, he slipped quietly towards it and, taking the edge of the doorframe with his fingers, peered within.

Inside the room, sitting across from a plate littered with crumbs of cheese and a crust of bread, a hunched figure bent over a piece of parchment. One hand held a quill, and his face flickered in the candlelight.

'Who is that? Marco?' William said as he looked up into the gloom.

Marco felt embarrassed. 'Uncle,' he replied gently.

William faced him, displaying his unease. 'Why are you awake?'

'I can't sleep,' he replied.

'Try,' William grumbled, and looked down at the paper again.

'You can't sleep either,' Marco remarked with a shrug.

'No,' William said. 'I have things to do.'

Marco shrugged again. 'Would you like me to go?'

William scowled and was about to tell him 'Yes', but found he was glad of the company. He'd been scribbling in silence for an hour now and had managed just a few botched attempts at writing a letter to England.

'No, come in,' he accepted, and beckoned the boy forward. Marco took the chair opposite and sat down, accidentally knocking William's jacket from the back. He went down quickly to gather it up and hung it securely again, his hands shaking a little in his haste.

'What woke you?' William asked.

'Someone was snoring,' Marco replied.

William laughed. 'That would be Jericho,' he said.

Marco smiled, but said nothing out of respect for the monk. 'What are you writing?' he asked, glancing down at the paper in front.

William looked as though he too had just made acquaintance

with the sheets. Flustered by the question, he tidied the paper into an organized pile. 'Oh . . . just a letter to England,' he replied. 'I thought it would be a splendid time to write home.'

Marco nodded, peering over. He noticed the mass of crossings-out.

'Is it hard to write?'

William's cheeks reddened. 'Very,' he said and then sighed. 'The hardest letter I have ever attempted. I haven't written home in so many months I don't know where to start.' He paused, appearing a little overwhelmed. 'They probably believe I'm dead by now. I have conjured so much illusion that unravelling it would seem impossible. I have lied about the fates of those near to me, and lied about my own welfare. I've lied so much to my own family that my conscience is stained. I need to scrub it clean, Marco. I need to explain truthfully why I haven't written to them, not the fantasy I contrived before.'

'You deceived them?'

'I had little choice. I cannot avow my true profession. How would they understand? For instance, if I wrote to them about the fates of Leone and Nico, what could I say?' As he spoke, William remembered that Marco did not know what had happened mere hours before.

'We lost two men tonight.'

'Two brothers?' Marco whispered, scarcely believing.

'Nico and Leone,' William confided. 'Leone served with me at Aosta. He was a good man, trustworthy and strong. I still marvel how we escaped Aosta when so many did not. Providence I suppose.' He looked down at the paper and ripped the scribbled page into shreds. 'But not now,' he said and put his weary hands to his head. 'Providence has deserted us it seems.

'For this mission I was promised three Arabic speakers. Vittore confessed he is having trouble understanding the dialect here, and Leone and Greynell are both dead. With vampyres in Rashid, we have little time to find another translator.'

'Vampyres?' Marco was horrified. Vampyres were a distant rumour, creatures in the shadows that no one in Villeda had seen in recent years. Yet to be so close . . . To *know* someone murdered by one brought the myths one shuddering step closer. Marco shivered.

'Are you scared?' William asked.

Marco nodded awkwardly.

'The idea is terrifying, I know,' William agreed. 'It is a fear every man in the Order must face. The fear of the unknown, the unusual and macabre. But we must take that fear into our hearts, and understand it. Use it against our enemy.'

'How?' Marco whispered, wrapping his arms about him.

William grinned. 'The enemy uses surprise and terror as a weapon. If you forget the terror, then you disarm the enemy.'

Marco shook his head. 'I'm not sure I can.'

'Nor are many initiates in the Order. But they do. Eventually,' William said. 'I was terrified when I first met a vampyre.'

'You were?' Marco said, drawing some hope.

'All men are,' William said.

'I will be different. I promise,' Marco said.

William reached over and placed his hand on Marco's shoulder. 'You hope to be,' he said, 'but there is a difference between hope and what happens. I would not be angry if you panicked and ran at the first sight of a vampyre, Marco.'

Marco shook his head. 'I wouldn't . . . I . . .'

'You would,' William insisted, though not in a cruel way. It was comforting and sympathetic. 'But that is why your company on this journey could be folly.'

Marco shrugged off William. 'You're sending me away.'

'No . . .' William said, holding up his hand. '. . . I'm considering – *only* considering, mind – sending you back on the next ship to Naples with one of the brothers. Probably Jericho.'

'I will not run!' Marco insisted.

William rubbed at the side of his head, wearied by Marco's protests. 'I cannot protect you,' he admitted finally. He looked up fondly at Marco. 'If I cannot protect you, then you will die here, Marco.'

'I can protect my—'

'You are quick with a sword, but it takes more than that,' William interrupted him. 'It takes wits, experience and a talent for survival.'

Marco gazed around the room, his mouth open to retort. But he couldn't. There was no instant reply to these accusations.

'Tonight was a trap. The vampyres were waiting for us, as I suspect they waited for Charles Greynell,' William told him. 'Even experienced men like Peruzo and me stepped straight into it. They are deceitful, manipulative and wily. And there are more here than I have ever encountered before. I do not know if I can protect you from them.'

Marco nodded. 'Then maybe you should send me home. If they scare you so much, I should leave.'

William was surprised by the reproach. 'It's not about a personal fear . . .'

Marco looked back, saddened. 'Yes it is! It's about what *you* fear, not I!'

Now it was William who fell silent.

'You think you are the only one who has something to fight for? What about my family murdered in Tresta? How about them? And how about *you*? I've seen how Adriana is sad when you leave. She never says it, but she fears you will not return. She fears you'll be killed. I don't want her to fear any more. I don't want to see you killed. You are our *family*. My *uncle*.'

William looked taken aback. His throat went suddenly dry, overcome with remorse. He hadn't expected this at all. 'She said that?'

'She thinks that you have been lucky so far, and that one day . . .' Marco stopped himself as William's expression hardened.

'. . . One day my luck will desert me,' William said and looked away, somewhat guiltily.

'I am not afraid to die,' Marco told him.

William didn't look at him straight away, fearing what he would see. If it was just bravado, Marco's eyes would falter, and that contrived demeanour would crumble. A brave boast that was beyond him, used to convince William to keep him in Egypt. And then William could send him home.

But if it was genuine . . . What then?

William looked up, and his heart sank. Marco didn't flinch, didn't falter, earnest with his expression. Marco *believed* what he was saying.

'Damn it,' he murmured and got up from the table. Marco rose and William pulled him into an embrace. 'You have grown up *too* damned quickly.'

Marco let out a sob of relief. 'I can stay?'

'You can stay,' William conceded.

'You will not regret this,' he said with boyish enthusiasm.

William winced, and wondered why he had conceded so easily. 'Go,' he said. 'Get some sleep.'

Marco was giddied by the prospect of adventure and stumbled off the chair to reach the door. With one hand on the handle, he turned to his uncle. 'I meant what I said,' he told him. 'I'm not afraid to die.'

William nodded. 'We will not die, I promise you.'

△ III △

Next morning, the men assembled hastily. With calm precision, the horses were aligned at the front of the inn. Peruzo checked the two waiting wagons and saw that each one was loaded with equipment and provisions. William watched nearby, stifling a yawn. He was battling the lack of sleep that had dogged him almost all night long. It was always the same during a mission; his mind was restless, constantly thinking of tactics, of the strategy to succeed. Rarely did he allow himself the simple luxury of rest.

Feeling fastidious, William stepped forward to look over the wagons in his turn. There were rifles, other specialist weapons, crates of ammunition and something else: a small cannon that was hooked up to a mechanism that appeared to swivel from left to right as well as elevate, all stored and compact within each inch of deck space.

'A dwarf-cannon,' Lieutenant Vittore said by his shoulder. 'I brought it from Spain. It's quite effective against daemons.'

William patted the barrel. It was made of hardened metal and was three feet in length.

'We will need it,' he said solemnly, casting his thoughts to the night before. 'But cannon will not address more immediate concerns: our route to the Sinai, and how to find the Hoard once we get there.'

'How big can the Sinai be?' Peruzo said, overhearing the conversation.

'It is vast, Peruzo, and featureless,' Vittore boasted. 'I have maps of the region. The Sinai is a desert of rock and sand, and very little else.'

'In the absence of Greynell, you have become our guide and translator, Vittore,' William told him. 'We are fast running out of time, gentlemen. Ensure we are ready to leave within the hour. What is this?'

Both lieutenants came over to where William was now standing at the second wagon, pointing at several kegs at the rear.

Vittore shrugged. 'They accompanied the brothers from Villeda. No one knows their purpose, except for a letter addressed to you, Captain.' He passed the note to William, who stepped aside and opened the letter in private. It was written in English.

Dear William

I promised I would provide you with an alternative. Contained in each keg is a compound derived from the finest chemists in Rome and the brightest minds. Be warned, its strength is ten times that of conventional gunpowder, and a small quantity could bring down a building or even a hillock. I would think such a material would be helpful to you, whether in battle, or in barter should money fail, or for use as a last resort on the Hoard itself.

Remember, the final destruction of the Scarimadaen is paramount.

How this is done, with whom and where, is a decision you will make on your own.

Good luck, my dear friend.

And good hunting,

Engrin

William folded the letter with renewed hope. It was a comfort, almost as though the old man was watching them, and he held the letter in his hands for a few more moments to dwell on this spark of optimism.

William turned briskly to the officers. 'Vittore, plan a route that will take us through villages, oases and any place that can provide respite from the desert. I don't wish to be without water or food on our journey. We may have a hard battle to fight at the end of our travels.'

'It will be done.' Lieutenant Vittore left to find somewhere quiet to plan.

Peruzo waited patiently.

'Those kegs could mean our salvation,' William told him. 'Put them under guard. And whatever happens, keep flame away from them, lest we wipe out the *entire* company by a fell accident.'

Peruzo looked surprised. 'Gunpowder for Vittore's cannon?'

'No. Something else,' William replied as two riders appeared at the top of the street. They were dressed as local men, in gowns and headscarves. At first William suspected aggression and reached for his sword, but quickly brothers Paolo and Orlando pulled away their garments to reveal the grey uniform of the Order, tossing their headscarves and disguises to the ground.

'What news?' William called out.

'The local militia are looking for us, we think,' Paolo reported.

'*You think?*' William echoed. He didn't want opinions.

Orlando explained. 'We saw armed men in the streets around the Arab quarter – soldiers who carried more weapons than normal regimented men. They accosted people in the road not far from where the brothel stood. We could not approach in case our deception was uncovered. A French merchant told us they were looking for men in grey who burned down Babel's.'

'*Blast* . . .' William cursed quietly.

'And we've been marked as thieves, Captain,' Paolo added nervously.

'Thieves?' Peruzo frowned.

'The horses,' William said. It was another decision that was beginning to blight the mission, like so many over the last few days.

'Will they be coming after us?' Peruzo wondered.

'Only when they know where we are,' William said. 'And they will know eventually. If rumours spread so fast around Babel's, they'll spread fast from here. Have the men mount up, Peruzo. Our stay in Rashid is over.'

△ IV △

The sun climbed from the east and burned across the road out of Rashid, shortening the shadows of the forty men riding away, two wagons trailing behind them. The suburbs of Rashid ended abruptly. Ahead lay a dusty track dividing green plains and hills. The land here was lush and plentiful, with tall grass that leant over in the morning breeze.

William had imagined that beyond the town would be this great expanse of desert he had heard about. To find this was not so was surprising, yet the heat from the morning sun still caused the summits of hills and the horizon to shimmer. This early in the day its effects were not apparent, but later the intense warmth would make a man feel sluggish and grubby; and then the enemy of all soldiers, lethargy, would creep into flesh and spirit.

William's instructions to Vittore and Peruzo were to keep the brothers mentally and physically primed for action. The riding by day would lull their physical selves into a latent hibernation, having only to sit and let their mounts plod on. There was little he could do to stop the general indolence of the flesh. The mind, however, could be trained, and here William requested that each lieutenant devised games to test a man's initiative or memory. These could be anything from reciting passages of the Bible from memory, to debating the pros and cons of weapons, the tricks of swordsmanship or any other martial art. It was hoped this would keep them focused on the mission ahead.

Vittore had mapped out their journey, estimating times of arrival at each rest, ensuring that each day's end brought somewhere to bed down. On the first night it was a village stable which they paid the owner generously for. Even though Vittore had tried his best to interpret William's wishes, something was lost in the translation and the price of the lodgings grew alarmingly. Vittore later apologized for whatever errors he'd been ignorant of, but his confidence had been dented and from that moment on he was reluctant to speak any Arabic to the local people, fearing another debacle.

Of the money they had started out with, a little over half remained. It was a matter William was all too conscious of. He considered that the rest should be held back to buy provisions, yet such frugal desires could not always prevail.

On the second day out from Rashid, the company reached the Nile delta. It was very wide and the waters were moving rapidly towards the coast. There were no bridges and two small fishing villages were perched on the river's banks opposite one another. To find another way round would take days, so William and Vittore rode into the village to negotiate a crossing.

After two hours of translating and impasse, a price was finally agreed on and the local fishermen transported them across the water. Progress was painfully slow. Two horses here. A wagon there. A few men at a time. The village had but three boats and each crossing and return took over an hour.

The sun was falling by the time the last of the monks had landed at the fishing village opposite. By then they'd created quite a stir among the locals, who had gathered on the banks to watch the foreigners and their horses being ferried across the

Nile. William urged Vittore to find a place to stay, but when Brother Paolo found a boy spying on them with a reward poster in his possession, William abandoned that plan.

On the poster was a likeness of a European, dressed not dissimilarly to the company. Peruzo joked humourlessly that the picture looked very like William. And it did. Vittore did not need to translate the words. It was obvious this had been sent by the Rashid militia. Somehow word of their presence had overtaken them.

From that night on the company avoided communities, squandering much-needed time in circumventing the villages that littered the roads around the Nile. When the river was bridged and forded they crossed unhindered. Where the river was impassable they paid for crossings, taking risks to get further away from Rashid. And they paid dearly. Their money was running out.

They spent almost every night under the stars, where the temperatures fell so low that men shivered themselves to sleep when they could, or just stayed awake to stare into the fathomless sky.

They could not do this all the way to the Sinai, so on the sixth day having finally crossed the Nile delta they approached a village, hoping that here at least they had not heard of the foreign marauders. Luck was with them and the villagers took them into their homes, though again at a cost. The bag of money clinked pitifully now there were only a few coins left. But it was a small price considering the evening's comfort and the chance to rest somewhere warm.

Invigorated by the respite, the following morning they set out again, and the land before them began to change from lush green grass to dunes of sand, sparse at first, then stretching as far as the eye could see.

It was on the tenth day that two scouts galloped up the line. Their horses kicked up dirt and sand, and several brothers threw jovial curses in their direction as dust engulfed them. Both men's faces were running with sweat, and their horses were blowing.

The first scout, Brother Ludovico, addressed William. 'We've seen a column of men.' He gestured westwards. 'At least one hundred men.'

'So many?' William frowned, seeking confirmation from the second scout, Donato. The older monk agreed.

'A hundred. And they were armed.'

Vittore looked unconvinced. 'Are you certain?'

'All carried weapons of some kind,' Donato told him. 'Muskets I think. Swords as well. All of them mounted, and riding in columns of five.'

'As wide as this road,' Peruzo remarked, looking down.

'Are they following us?' William asked.

Ludovico could only shrug.

William beckoned Peruzo and Vittore closer.

'Best guess?' he asked.

'If they're militia, they will be hunting us,' Peruzo replied.

'We could make a stand,' Vittore suggested.

'We are not here to fight the locals, Lieutenant,' William chided.

'We may have little choice, Captain.'

'Can we not take another route?' Peruzo ventured.

Vittore looked aggrieved by this. 'The route I devised was specific . . . Measured out to the mile . . . An oasis for every other night . . .'

'But *can* we take another route?' William cut him short.

Vittore glowered at Peruzo and then looked back at William jadedly. 'I could try.'

'Do so,' William said. 'I don't fancy facing over a hundred militiamen, no matter what the odds are of victory. Imagine, gentlemen, what would happen if we were to fight them.'

Peruzo nodded, but not Vittore.

William explained. 'This whole country is in the grip of war from one moment to the next. If not with Napoleon's army, then the British. Now there is a viceroy, Muhammad Ali. He's a hero to them, driving all enemies before him. And he *despises* foreigners. If the people adore him as much as I am told, it means his militia will hate us. They'll be burning to hunt us down and kill us. And if not this company behind us, then a greater army, or a greater one after that. We cannot stand against them, understood?'

Neither man could refute his summing-up.

'Vittore will find an alternative route and we will conceal our tracks,' William ordered. 'Even if it means losing ground on our enemies.'

△ V △

The new route took them south. They missed the next oasis by fifteen miles and were forced to sleep under the wagons and the canvas that had been used to screen the weapons. It was a bitter cold night, and no one slept. William sat shivering on a dune, observing the horizon. It was a full moon and this world of great hillocks of sand was calm and pale and eerily quiet. He felt lost in its vastness. The decision to head south brought risks, and he sensed that conditions must soon worsen.

Next morning, they decamped and rode on, turning east down a little-used track that was soft and sucked at feet or hoofs. Vittore did nothing but grumble, though with a promise they would arrive at their next oasis as planned.

As day began to fade, the company arrived at the crest of a hill along a shallow track. One of the scouts began waving back to them. Straining his eyes, William looked to the sky and saw a grey smudge against the fading blue. He pulled out his spyglass to focus on the smoky blur and saw a large black plume against the halflight. And there was more, a deep orange glow from some great fire that raged unhindered.

'What do you make of that?' William handed the spyglass to Peruzo as he pulled his horse up alongside him.

Peruzo looked long and hard, and frowned. 'A fire. But too big to be a campfire. It looks like . . .' he paused.

'Like a bonfire?' William suggested.

'Or several fires close together, Captain. A fire that is out of control.'

'What's wrong?' Vittore called over as he galloped up the line.

'Are there any villages here, Lieutenant?' William asked Vittore.

Vittore shook his head. 'Nothing on the map. But that doesn't mean there *couldn't* be any. This isn't the most dependable map that I've steered by.'

'If it isn't a village . . .' William said.

'Then it could mean trouble,' Vittore agreed.

'There's an oasis near here. And that fire and smoke is sure to attract attention. Trouble or not, we must investigate,' William decided.

Half an hour passed and the sky darkened further. The smoke was close enough now for an acrid reek to reach mouths and nostrils.

As they crested one more dune they found the reason.

Below them, more than fifty yards away, was a scene of chaos. What light remained as dusk fell lit a slaughter site of grim shadows and sinister stains. Several tall palms were alight or smouldering. The lake itself was dyed by some dark liquid, and bodies floated on its surface. Around it were more dark shapes, more bodies caught in rigor mortis, shrouded by twilight's shadows. A couple of wagons had been overturned, another was on fire and the hot embers of the smouldering vehicle glowed like scattered orange eyes in the gloom.

The company ranged itself along the dune like a macabre audience, its voices hushed, absorbing the horror below.

'Any survivors?' Peruzo hoped.

'We must find out,' William said as he edged forward.

Peruzo reached over and pulled at his arm. 'It could be a trap,' he urged.

189

'Vittore can stay here with half of the company. The other half rides down with me,' William said decisively.

The brothers divided themselves efficiently, every other man riding down the slope of the dune. Marco made to follow, but Peruzo moved his horse in front of him and shook his head. 'Your place is here.'

Marco made to protest, but a warning glance silenced him. He stayed reluctantly in place as Peruzo followed William down the steep bank.

The first wagon's contents lay spilt along the sand: elaborate and delicate rugs, and fine clothes fluttering in the evening breeze. Just beyond it lay the first body. William signalled for Brother Casper to dismount and the burly monk jumped to the floor, pushing the body over with his foot.

'His throat's torn out,' Casper called back, and spat to the side.

William nodded. 'Who was he?'

'A peasant, Captain.' Casper walked onward, pausing to look down at each corpse he passed.

Peruzo cast his eyes around, trying to make sense of it.

'The wagons were loaded with fine cloth. It looks like a merchant's caravan,' William remarked.

'So who would attack merchants?' Peruzo said.

'Robbers and thieves infest these desert roads,' Vittore suggested. 'I've seen this before, Captain. Out here there's little law and order.'

'Would thieves tear out the throats of their victims?' William asked, and looked back at Vittore, reminding the lieutenant of his previous oversight.

They continued to scour the campsite, noting the many bodies sprawled in death. They found one man who was not yet dead. In his last breath he spoke just a couple of words, but William did not understand them and was grieved by the knowledge that the fellow's last words would never be understood, nor recounted again.

At the centre of the camp, the monks separated and began

an independent search. William dismounted, his hand on the hilt of his sword. He came to one of the tents, noting its once fine quality before it had been torn through and bloodied. Inside were baskets that had been knocked over, yet not ransacked. Most of the camp's goods had been left in disorder, but little had been plundered.

After some minutes of search and consultation, Brother Eric trudged over to brief William.

'They are all dead,' he announced. 'We counted about twenty bodies.'

'No evidence to say who these people were?'

Brother Eric shrugged. 'Most have been mutilated. In the darkness, they could be anybody, Captain.'

'*All* mutilated?'

The monk nodded.

'Send Brother Filippo over, would you?'

Brother Eric returned with their surgeon, who looked sorrowful. 'There is nothing I can do for these people,' he lamented.

'I understand,' William said. 'But their wounds . . . Do you recognize them?'

'Similar to the wound I found on Charles Greynell, Captain,' Brother Filippo confided out of earshot of the others.

'I thought as much,' William said and expelled a long breath. He rubbed at his eyes and nodded. 'Keep searching for survivors and post sentries on the surrounding dunes. Fires also. I want every yard of this oasis lit tonight.'

Voices rose loudly from across the water and William looked through the gloom to the group of silhouettes.

'A survivor?' Brother Filippo asked hopefully.

'Have Lieutenant Vittore join me,' William said, and hurried to where the monks were gathered. Some of them were looking down at the figure of someone sitting in the spill of an opened bale of cloth. As William approached he recognized the man, with his bent back and hooked nose. His face and clothes were covered in loose sand, sticky with sweat and grime. He looked up suspiciously and somewhat guiltily, turning his head away as William stood before him.

Vittore rode over and halted, looking down at the only survivor.

'I know this man, Lieutenant,' William confessed, but couldn't place the man's name for a moment, and then some spark of memory flashed, an image from Babel's brothel.

'Hammid, isn't it?' William said, surprising Vittore and causing Hammid to glance up. He knelt in front of the Arab. 'Where is Thomas Richmond?'

The Arab looked fleetingly at William, but then his eyes shifted, anywhere it seemed except William.

'Mr Richmond where?' William said again and spread his hands in question.

Hammid got up labouredly from the bale and wiped the sand from his face. Then he turned and began stepping through the carnage, careful not to look down at the mutilated bodies about him, avoiding pools of blood as if by instinct.

They came to a tent and William feared the worst, but then Hammid sidestepped this to head past one more body, the burning wagon, and on towards the sand dunes beyond. William and Vittore followed but hesitated, thinking the Arab was crazed, as they left the oasis and mounted the nearest dune to its crest, where the giant moon shone.

Vittore gave William a weary look, but they followed Hammid over the crest and looked out across the desert. William frowned, not understanding why Hammid had brought them there, but then his eyes fixed on a figure in the shadows sitting bolt upright at the foot of the slope.

They left Hammid and hurried down the dune, their boots gouging grooves in the sand. As they came within a few feet, the figure had not moved and William feared the worst. Was this Thomas Richmond, stone-dead?

Taking a shivering breath, William rounded the motionless form and turned to see. Even in the dark he could make out

Richmond's now sunburnt skin, his black beard and broad shoulders. And his eyes. His *opened* eyes, staring into the distance.

William breathed out with relief, and beamed at Vittore as if his lieutenant shared his joy. Vittore seemed unmoved, and perhaps for good reason. Despite his staring eyes, the man who sat before them failed to register either newcomer's presence.

'Mr Richmond?' William said.

There was no response.

'*Thomas Richmond?*' he repeated, waving a hand in front of his eyes.

Again nothing.

He knelt down in front of the Englishman. 'Thomas?' he said. 'Do you remember me?'

Slowly, the Englishman blinked and looked up at him. William noticed drops of blood on his cheek and brow. His shirt and jacket were splashed with dark red and William thought he was wounded.

'Are you hurt?' he asked.

'No,' Mr Richmond croaked almost inaudibly. He frowned and his eyes rolled up to see William. 'Do I know you?'

'Babel's,' William replied.

The Englishman grimaced as though thinking was painful. He narrowed his eyes, studying William's face, and then he seemed overcome, gripping him by the arm. 'Of course! Of course! William, wasn't it?'

William nodded, smiling softly. Thomas Richmond's smile broadened and then he began to weep. 'Thank you, sir. God thank you . . .'

William held the Englishman's arm, pleased by the gratitude, though still recognizing that danger lurked near. 'What happened here?' he asked urgently. 'Your servant has not been helpful.'

'Do not blame him,' Thomas murmured. 'He's scared, that is all. He hid when the killing began.'

'What happened to you?'

Thomas looked up at William. 'I *did try* to help my men . . . But they fell upon us. They murdered them all.'

'When?'

'In the dead of night.'

'You've been sat here all day?'

Thomas nodded. 'Hammid sat with me for a time, and then night fell, and he hid again. He thought they might come back. Whatever they are.'

'They?'

'*Shadows*. Three shadows came out of the night. They slaughtered my servants.'

'Are there any survivors apart from you and Hammid?'

Thomas shrugged, his mind elsewhere.

'Mr Richmond?' William insisted.

The Englishman's attention revived. 'There may have been a few left wounded, but they would be dead by now. I am no surgeon, sir.'

William was thwarted. The merchant was in shock, but who could blame him? His whole entourage had been massacred. 'We need to know more. If this is vampyres' work, then where are they now?' he said quietly to Vittore, who nodded. He turned back to Thomas and laid a gentle hand on his shoulder.

'Mr Richmond,' he began, 'does Hammid know anything about what happened?'

'Why would Hammid know more than I?' said Richmond, picking himself up from the sand. He brushed himself down automatically, despite the blood dried on his clothes. He stared up the hill to where Hammid was rocking on his knees, his eyes tight shut. 'Poor Hammid knows nothing, I assure you.'

'He knew enough to hide when night fell,' William said.

'He's afraid of the darkness,' Thomas answered. 'Aren't we all?'

'Afraid or not, you need to come back to the oasis,' William told him.

'Back to that *death*?' cried the other, and waved a despairing hand in its direction. He shook his head. 'I cannot.'

194

'The bodies of your men will be buried,' William assured him, 'but we can't protect either you or Hammid out here.'

The Englishman began to chuckle, a deep terrible laugh that was harsh with sorrow. 'I fear, sir, that you won't protect us at all!'

'You are certain to perish if you stay here,' William assured him. 'Either by what lurks in the night, or by the sun. Your skin is burnt, and you look famished. We have food and drink.'

'I have food enough, sir,' Thomas said, and touched his tender face, wincing where it burned. Brushing off William's hand, he climbed unaided to the crest of the dune to where Hammid was kneeling and muttering a prayer. The Englishman put a hand softly upon the Arab's scalp and the prayer stopped abruptly. Hammid looked up at Thomas, who smiled and said something in Arabic that seemed to give the man some hope.

'Do you think he has a right to know?' William said aside to Vittore.

The lieutenant watched Thomas and shook his head. 'No, Captain, I do not. He is alive, and that is all that matters. Better to allow him that ignorance than tell him the truth.'

'But his suffering may be our fault. He helped us at Babel's. This could be his punishment for aiding the enemy of the vampyres.'

'That may be true,' Vittore admitted, 'but we must keep him ignorant. Anonymity, remember?'

William relented and led both Thomas and Hammid back down to the oasis where already the brothers were building pyres of tents and wrecked wagons, burning what could not be salvaged. A chain of men was working to carry the dead from the watering hole to a place beyond the dunes. Around the perimeter stood guards, armed with their Baker rifles.

Thomas Richmond did not notice this until they wandered down into the hastily erected camp. He looked to his right and found a man in a grey uniform studying the black horizon, the weapon in his hands.

'Who *are* you?' he demanded of William. 'I took you for a merchant when we first met. But somehow I doubt you are.'

'We are monks, Mr Richmond,' William told him, 'on a pilgrimage.'

'What kind of monk cradles a gun?' Thomas retorted, unconvinced.

'The kind that will protect you tonight, Mr Richmond,' William replied a little too abruptly, so that his first reaction was then to apologize to the merchant.

Thomas looked outraged. 'I knew it!' he began and then started to rant. 'You have something to do with this!' he shouted. 'I heard what happened at Babel's. Burned to the ground, did it not? That night you were there . . .'

William winced under the hail of abuse and accusation. He raised a hand for calm, but the gesture only prompted further ranting.

'Get Hammid some food and water. He needs to rest,' William murmured to Vittore.

'And him?' Vittore nodded to Thomas, who was now shouting to the stars.

'I'll calm him. See if you can find some wine or something stronger. He will need it tonight.'

△ VI △

They sat upon the sands, mesmerized by the flames that reached higher and higher. A smell of burning fat blighted the air, and the whole place stank like an abattoir.

Thomas turned to William as he sat down next to him, passing the weary merchant a tin cup of gin.

'It's not wine, I'm afraid,' William confessed.

Thomas sniffed it suspiciously, then sipped, before knocking it back, coughing at the end. 'Gods, not wine indeed! Gin? Monks with guns? Monks with *gin*?'

'I'm not a monk,' William replied.

'You said . . .'

'I said these men were monks. I am not.'

Thomas shook his head dismally. 'Too many riddles, sir. Too many riddles in the night. Please, be frank with me.'

'I am *Captain* William Saxon,' he began. 'These men are monks, and are under my command. I am not a priest, nor a man of the cloth, yet they follow me, for they are not monks in the conventional sense. We are more . . . *physical*.'

Thomas looked at William in bewilderment. 'You sound like Inquisitors.'

William laughed out loud. 'Dear God, no. The Inquisition was a means to one man's end, a paranoid and skewed belief. Ours is less sinister. Yet unfortunates sometimes become embroiled in our conflict.'

'*Unfortunates?* That is a fine word to describe my dead servants,' Thomas said sadly. 'What conflict could cause such devastation?'

'A secret conflict that has lasted thousands of years, Mr Richmond. A war between Heaven and Hell,' William explained.

The Englishman frowned and made to joke, but the words would not come. 'You jest with me,' he said finally.

'I do not,' William said plainly, and refilled Thomas's cup. 'The shadows that attacked you are vampyres, half-daemons with the strength of many men. They have a murderous disposition.'

'Why should they attack *me*?' Thomas protested. 'I have done nothing to them! I am simply a merchant. A merchant who sells cloth to the Bedouins, and certainly not a man of great threat.'

William agreed. He waited for Thomas to drain the cup again before refilling it. As the Englishman sipped, William told him his suspicions. 'You aided us at Babel's.'

Looking up from the gin, Thomas stared at William. It was a reproachful expression, a mixture of deep regret yet anger as well. 'And for that, I am marked?'

William nodded. 'I never thought your services as translator would condemn you. Nor did I know that vampyres were watching. You see, it was the vampyres who destroyed Babel's, not us. That woman, Malika, was murdered by them. They also murdered Charles Greynell.'

Thomas looked aghast. 'The Rashid militia believe that *you* destroyed Babel's. Did you know that two armies track you? One from Rashid and one from Dumyat?'

Now it was William's turn to look anxious. 'How do you know this?'

'I have been travelling through the villages and townships around the Nile. Since I was a foreigner, they asked about "men in grey",' the Englishman replied candidly. 'I told them nothing of course.'

'My thanks,' William murmured, though it worried him intensely that two armies were searching the region for them. Shaking off the first militia had been a feat in itself . . . But two?

'The militia from Dumyat search the northern coast, while the Rashid army sweeps south,' Thomas said. 'It is led by a brutal and ambitious man. The Viceroy Ali has put Rashid's protection in his hands. Your arrest is crucial to this man's reputation.'

'Who is he?'

'He is called Haidar. He was a regular customer at Babel's. For him, this will be personal, *Captain* Saxon,' Thomas said, dwelling on the title with unease.

William was alarmed. He hadn't expected to face three enemies on this mission.

'Shouldn't we leave now? Whatever brought you to this oasis will certainly bring them, don't you think?' Thomas said.

'The vampyres could still be out there, so we must wait until sunrise. Vampyres dislike daylight. Some are unnaturally sensitive to it. Unfortunately that is their *only* weakness,' William told him.

Thomas wrapped his arms about him and hunched his shoulders. 'You have dangerous enemies, Captain.'

'Yes,' William agreed, his thoughts elsewhere.

'And now so do I,' Thomas added.

William breathed hard and rested his cup on his knee.

'Whatever your destination, we will escort you there. It is the least we can do.'

Thomas did not appear comforted by this. 'For what good it will do me, I accept. But I suspect even monks with guns will not stop these creatures, Captain.'

CHAPTER ELEVEN

The Ayaida

△ I △

On the fifth day since the slaughter at the oasis, a great storm whirled down from the north and struck in the late afternoon. It was Thomas who saw it first, a great murky wall, as though the clouds had merged with the horizon, and he began gesturing and shouting.

'A *haboob*, William – a sandstorm,' he warned, pulling his horse about. The animal grew restless, as did the rest of the horses. 'We must take shelter.'

William ordered the men to dismount and enclose themselves using the three wagons as a palisade. They rigged the canvas sheets from the wagons to make a canopy in the centre. It was makeshift and patchy, and the horses had to be tethered to the wagons firmly and blindfolded in case they should try to stampede into the desert.

It took many minutes to build, and the last sheet was still being lashed to the wagons when the storm fell upon them with a sudden furnace blast. The monks hunkered down and put their hands over their heads as the fine grains rushed over the wagons, under the decks and into the centre, battering them with dust and sand. William put his hands to his eyes and squinted out as the canopy thrashed about. For a moment one sheet was torn free, but a brother leapt up and caught it in time, pulling it back in place and clinging on.

And as suddenly as it began, the sand settled and the storm passed over.

Thomas straightened up and pushed aside the sheets, sighing with relief. 'We were lucky,' he said. 'I've heard of storms that have lasted for days. Some have erased entire villages.'

William didn't take his words lightly. 'We need to find some refuge and soon,' he agreed, and addressed his lieutenants. 'Where are we?'

Vittore studied the map, a little bewildered, and for a moment he seemed lost. Then he gestured to a point that was many miles still from the Sinai. Nearby was an oasis, yet it was more than a day's ride.

'We are running out of water,' Peruzo remarked quietly, as the monks around them began pulling down the sheets and inspecting the frightened horses.

'And food,' Vittore added, glancing at the horses again.

William could see what he was suggesting. 'That is a desperate solution, Lieutenant,' he warned. 'We need all the horses to carry us to the Sinai – and to fight when we get there.'

'Captain . . .' Vittore said, sounding tired, 'we might never reach the Sinai. We could die of starvation. Of thirst . . .'

William walked out between the wagons, his lieutenants close behind him. 'Many things could strike us down between here and our objective,' he said as he passed by the horses, gentling them while they struggled and shook the sand from their hides. 'We're deep in peril. But let us think of practical matters.' He turned to Peruzo. 'We have water to last how long?'

'If we ration to a few sips a day, we *could* last until we reach the oasis,' Peruzo replied.

'And food?'

Vittore appeared grim. 'Enough for a small bowlful this evening. Just rice.'

'Then make sure we ration the portions. Save as much rice and water as we can.' William paused, and then added: 'I will decline to eat this evening.'

The two men objected, Peruzo the louder.

'I have faced harsher conditions than this,' William explained, though he doubted he had.

△ II △

That evening William sat alone as the monks ate their meagre meals. Not one of them complained of going hungry, though Hammid made peevish noises until Thomas silenced him and he backed off into the shadows with his small bowl of rice.

As William watched, his lieutenants came to join him. Both were empty-handed.

'Have you not eaten?' he asked them.

'We chose to follow your example, Captain,' Peruzo replied. 'We need the men to be fit and healthy.'

'That's right,' said Vittore, and gave a wry laugh. 'For the sake of the mission.'

William noted the sarcasm but could not help but agree. They were moving in one direction, but with no idea whether it was the right one.

He reached into his jacket to take another look at Charles Greynell's letter to Rome. As he withdrew it, something fell out onto the sand. It was the pendant the woman at Babel's had given him. He picked it up to study it in the firelight.

'Any clues?' Peruzo asked, watching his captain.

William glanced at the lieutenant and shook his head. 'Only another riddle.' He sighed as he lamented his own ignorance. He had shown the pendant to the officers several days before and they had passed little comment on it, other than Vittore saying it looked 'tribal'. William wasn't sure why he had kept it, whether it was a curse or a talisman. Other than the cryptic letter to the Secretariat, it was the only possession they had of Charles Greynell's.

'Thomas Richmond believed it could be Bedouin. In his letter, Greynell mentions "wanderers in the desert",' William told them as he slipped the pendant back under his shirt.

'And you think he meant the nomads in this region?' Peruzo asked.

'It's a hope,' William replied.

Vittore sighed. 'Not a high one, Captain.'

William did not answer.

'You've turned things around before, Captain, you will do so again,' Peruzo said confidently, dismissing Vittore's cynicism.

Lieutenant Vittore sat back and eyed Peruzo. 'If I had the companionship of angels, I too would feel confident, Lieutenant Peruzo. But I have not seen them on this mission. And I'm sure my captain would agree that it's safer to count on things you can believe in.'

'Just because you haven't seen them, Vittore, doesn't mean they don't exist,' Peruzo growled back.

'And you say *I'm* naïve?' Vittore mocked.

'I never said—' Peruzo retorted.

'Enough!' William said, loud enough to stop them both, quiet enough so the brothers below them could not hear.

Both men looked abashed, unable to meet their captain's eye.

'I will not have this bickering in my company, understood?' William said.

The two lieutenants nodded sheepishly.

'As for this talk of angels . . .'

'*Do* they exist, Captain?' Vittore asked.

William looked at the lieutenant, measuring his choices. Rumours of angels would surely grow under these desperate conditions. William didn't want to raise false hopes, but he had to say something.

'They exist, Lieutenant. But I would not call them angels,' he finally replied.

Peruzo crossed his arms with a small measure of triumph. Vittore grunted, still unconvinced.

'I first met them seven years ago, on a voyage to Naples on board the *Iberian*,' William explained. 'This was before my years of service in the Order, before I knew about the war between

Heaven and Hell. Kieran Harte and I were taking a Scarimadaen to Rome, under the protection of Engrin Meerwall.

'Off the coast of Sardinia, we were attacked by a ship crewed by kafalas and a vampyre. Many of our crew were killed, and the vampyre almost took the Scarimadaen. If he had, everyone would have perished.

'But in the midst of battle, a creature of light intervened. It fell from the skies and into combat, destroying the vampyre, its ship and the kafalas. A terrible thing it was; inhuman, with power unimagined. And it was utterly *merciless*.'

Vittore had fallen silent now, listening closely.

William hunched his shoulders against the cold. 'It scared the hell out of me.'

'Are they invincible, as the stories say?' Peruzo asked.

William grunted. 'You would think so. But I saw one perish in battle at Aosta seven years ago, and another has perished recently, so I understand.'

'What about Lieutenant Harte, Captain? Are those rumours true as well?' Vittore asked.

Again, William nodded.

'So you *do* keep the company of angels, Captain,' Vittore remarked.

'No, Lieutenant, I do not,' William objected. 'That would imply they come at my bidding or at my request, and they do no such thing. I cannot call them when I wish. They are certainly not my friends. And we cannot rely on them for this mission to succeed.'

'The men believe they will come to their aid. It is a hope they cling to,' Peruzo said.

'Then I will tell them no differently,' William replied.

'You would lie to them?' Vittore said, uncomfortably.

'I will give them no grounds to believe that celestial intervention is guaranteed, Lieutenant,' William countered. 'The Dar'uka are aware of our task, and they too have sought the Hoard. It *is* possible they will be our salvation. So the brothers can continue with their stories and their rumours. I will not fuel that hope, but nor will I take it away from them.'

'And what of us?' Vittore said. 'We're in the middle of nowhere, hunted by three enemies, with a fourth at the end of this road. The brothers of the Order are the finest fighters in Europe, Captain, but we are hardly an army. And starvation and thirst will soon weaken as. We may not be fit to fight either man *or* beast.'

'We will continue in the spirit of this expedition, gentlemen, because too much is at stake to do otherwise.' William's sheer determination reached them like a rising tide. 'With luck we will arrive at the next oasis and will replenish our supplies. And if luck favours us that far, then perhaps it will shine on us further when we reach the Sinai. We will find the Hoard, defeat the Rassis and return to Rome without the militia ever finding us.'

The lieutenants nodded dutifully.

William got to his feet and stretched his arms, feeling the creak of muscle and bone. 'If you'll excuse me . . . I must sleep. We'll move out in a couple of hours.'

Peruzo rose also and walked with William a few yards. 'Captain?' he said gruffly.

William turned.

'Do you think they'll come?' Peruzo asked him. 'Honestly?'

'They haven't for some years,' William replied. 'But they said they would if they could. That's all I can say.'

Peruzo watched him go, and returned to Vittore's company.

'I could have done with some food,' Vittore grumbled, patting his belly.

'As could we all,' Peruzo said.

'I am surprised he is so . . . *optimistic*,' Vittore marvelled.

'That is why he is our captain, and we are simply lieutenants,' Peruzo said. 'A good soldier will see a hopeless cause. But a good captain will see a way out.'

Vittore nodded. 'I hope you're right, Peruzo. Right now, I see no way out for us, except across the River Styx.'

△ III △

Thick dust clouds flew up as the column of horses cantered down the stony track that wound its way through sand dunes and chunks of weathered rock. Marco kept his covered head down as the intense heat made him feel drowsy. He wished for water, but would not ask for it. The monks had drunk less than he and were soldiering on. The belief that refreshing waters lay ahead seemed to spur them.

William cantered with Peruzo to the front of the column, and then further ahead, aiming for the top of a ridge. He grunted in dismay as the hard skin of the dune simply cracked and his horse's forelegs sank in, forcing him to dismount. Peruzo too swung himself from the saddle and both led their weary horses back down the dune.

'We'll go on foot,' Peruzo suggested and William nodded, trampling through the deep sand as they climbed to the peak of the dune.

Covered in sand and with sweat glistening on their faces, they arrived at the summit and looked eastward. Desert stretched as far as they could see, until the wasteland struck a horizon black with mountains.

'The Sinai?' William said.

'I think so,' Peruzo replied.

'There,' William said and pointed to a small roll of dust between them and the black shadows.

'I see it,' Peruzo replied. 'Militia?'

William pulled out his spyglass, lowered it again to wipe sweat from one eye, then closed the other and tried to focus.

'I see men,' he said vaguely. 'Men on horseback.'

'How many?'

'Fifteen, maybe twenty.' He handed the lieutenant the spyglass.

Peruzo scrunched up his face and held still. 'Yes. Twenty men.'

'What do you make of them?'

'Can't be sure. Arabs . . . But their purpose . . .?' Peruzo shrugged.

After one last look, William shut the spyglass and sighed. 'The scouts said over a hundred men pursue us again from the west,' he mused as they trudged back down the dune, 'and it would be fair to say in our current condition we would not defeat so many. Twenty we could manage.'

'There is the question of provisions, Captain,' Peruzo reminded him.

William nodded thoughtfully, mentally digesting this further concern. Climbing back onto his horse he waved Vittore over.

'Where is the nearest oasis?'

Vittore pulled the map from his saddle, and laid it against his horse's neck. 'There is one here, behind that long bank of dunes I suspect,' he said and then gestured towards the clouds of newly formed dust near the horizon.

'Straight to those riders,' Peruzo groaned.

'A perfect place for a trap?' William suggested.

'I would say so,' Peruzo agreed.

'I said before, we can handle twenty militia,' William said confidently.

'Only if we have to,' Peruzo reminded him.

'We have no choice. We need food and rest, Peruzo,' William told him. 'And without water, we will soon perish.'

The water skins were all but spent, while the heat cooked the brothers in their saddles. Several monks looked ready to topple from dehydration.

Thomas Richmond did his best to share out his water with those near him. He handed Marco his canteen for a sip, and the boy almost refused, but his mouth was so dry he could feel the skin tearing when he moved his lips in anticipation of just a trickle of water. He took the canteen shamefully, tempted to gulp down the remaining drops, but the other monks around him watched patiently, and Marco halted as he lifted the canteen to his lips. He felt on trial and wondered if Brother Jericho had told them he had been wasting water. He had learnt to sip over the last few days, but that would not matter to thirsty men.

Uncomfortably, Marco tipped the canteen back just to wet his lips and tongue. He passed the canteen back to Thomas, lamenting he hadn't taken a bigger sip as he saw him take a longer swig.

William trotted by the side of the lead wagon, the dwarf-cannon hidden under canvas. Two brothers manned it, while two more sat behind, their Baker rifles hidden at their feet. William glanced behind them, examining the rest of the company. Despite the desert's ravages, all seemed ready to fight.

The sun was beginning its steady decline again and William considered their situation was grave. On the one hand, pursuit by a native army that believed them murderers. On the other, trailed by vampyres. Yet it was this latter thought that provided a strange glimmer of hope. William reasoned that if the vampyres had already found the Hoard they would have returned to the Carpathians with their prize. That they still hunted William and his men might imply that the vampyres were as much in the dark as they were about the Hoard's location.

It was a fragile hope, but one he clung to.

'I will not fail,' he told himself.

△ IV △

The company rounded the corner of a large humped dune that towered over them, shading them all for a moment before they rode out into blinding light. The heat was punishing, and William put a hand to his eyes to shield against the glare. As the dazzle persisted, there came a chorus of shouts and the monks began loading their rifles. Now his eyes began to focus; outlines took shape . . .

William was aghast.

Spread out along the ridge were some forty riders, all of them armed. *Not* the twenty his spyglass had found.

'*Damnation!*' The cry was torn out of him. He spurred his horse towards the head of the column where Peruzo and Vittore sat, and stared back at the Arab force waiting above.

'Where the hell did they come from?!' William griped.

'They used the sun to set a trap, Captain,' Vittore replied and laughed bitterly. 'And we rode straight into it.'

'Get the men ready to fight.' William drew his sword halfway out of its scabbard and gestured for Marco to hang back with Thomas. But the Englishman was galloping towards him.

'Trouble, Captain?' Thomas rasped as he squinted towards the men on the ridge.

'This is not your fight, Mr Richmond,' William replied. 'They came for us. Only us. You will not be harmed.'

'Are you sure?' the Englishman said. 'I'm a foreigner here, am I not?'

William compressed his lips. The merchant was right. In battle, the Englishman would look much like the monks, and was just as apt to be cut down. William pulled his horse about, his hand on the hilt of his sword, before Thomas reached over and took his shoulder.

'I'm not afraid of a fight, Captain, but . . .' he began, and then looked over to where Hammid was cowering in the wagon, staring wide-eyed at the riders on the ridge, '. . . we could use my servant.'

'Hammid?' William said.

'He was inconspicuous enough during the slaughter of my caravan. I wonder if he has the courage to step up and parley,' Thomas mused. 'It's worth trying at least.'

'If he doesn't get nailed through the heart before he opens his mouth.' There was no humour in William's grin. 'I'll go with him.'

'Hammid is *my* responsibility,' Thomas asserted. 'We will both go, Captain.'

William conceded. 'Very well. Peruzo?'

Peruzo steered his horse through the two ranks of brothers, all with their rifles in their hands, tense with the expectation of the fight.

'If this fails and I am killed, get the company out of Egypt,' William instructed. 'Somewhere we are not being hunted as criminals. Our mission is as good as over anyway. I think the Hoard is now beyond our grasp, and I won't lose more men in a hopeless cause. Maybe if Charles Greynell had been with us . . . If we hadn't wandered this desert for so long without food or water, we would have stood a chance. Vittore was right. The men are not fit to make a stand.'

'I hear you,' Peruzo replied, and could not hide his sadness. 'Captain, I . . .'

'No further words, Lieutenant. Good luck,' William said abruptly.

'And to you, Captain,' Peruzo replied.

William pulled his horse about as Thomas reappeared with Hammid, slumped in the saddle behind him. 'Shall we go, William?' It was a breezy invitation.

They rode ahead of the company and down the track towards the ridge. As they arrived at the foot of the dune, they kept their eyes on the riders above them. The Arabs were dressed in long silk robes and keffiyehs, their faces veiled, eyes dark and foreboding. They sat like flamboyant executioners, resplendent but deadly.

William glanced nervously to Thomas as they came to a cautious halt. The Englishman licked his lips and said a few words to the cowed man sitting behind him. Hammid looked afraid as he stared up at the riders; reluctantly he dismounted and shuffled along the side of Thomas's horse. As he came to the horse's head, he paused, looked back at the Englishman for some prompting (he met only a glare from Thomas) and then walked slowly up the ridge.

'What did you instruct him to say?' William asked quietly, his eyes never straying from the riders.

'I told him to say we are foreign merchants bringing cloth

to the Bedouin tribes in the Sinai, and could they tell us the way to the nearest tribe.' Thomas grinned.

'Subtle,' William laughed lightly. 'Do you think they'll believe him?'

'They have only to search our wagons.'

'And find them packed with weapons and ammunition.'

'Quite, Captain. Quite,' Thomas sighed.

Hammid crept closer to the men on horseback, their outlines dark with the sun at their backs. They seemed to view Hammid with indifference, and William held his breath, his hand hovering near his sword in case these strangers came charging down the slope. The sun sent rivers of sweat to trickle down his brow and neck, and down the small of his back.

The sunlight blurred what happened next, the distant talk too quiet to be heard, the words too alien to be understood. William was left in tantalizing ignorance. Hammid stumbled back to them, half upright and then tumbling down the loose sand.

William waited as the line above parted and several more riders emerged, armed to the teeth and carrying muskets. 'Blast!' he murmured. '*It's bad.*'

Hammid fell at the feet of Thomas's horse and was gabbling to his master.

'What does he say, Thomas? What does he say?' William demanded urgently as the newcomers lined up on the ridge and drew their swords.

Thomas looked up blankly.

'Thomas?!' William shouted.

The Englishman said something quickly to Hammid as the riders with formidable curved swords began to descend the slope towards them. Hammid shouted back breathlessly.

'*Are they attacking or . . . ?*' William yelled as he drew his sabre.

'No, wait!' Thomas said and lunged at William to pull his arm down.

William's instincts were to push the other away, but the merchant's hold was strong and threatened to unseat him, pulling open his jacket and shirt. 'What are you doing, damn you!' William cursed him.

'I think they wish to talk!' Thomas insisted.

Behind the riders came a booming voice, an order to do something that William hoped neither side regretted. The mounted Arabs lowered their swords and began to part. From the centre appeared two more riders, one broad with a large curved sword at his side, while a lone rider dressed in loose white robes and jet-black keffiyeh appeared just behind. Both men began to descend towards them.

As they came closer, William saw that the Arab in the white robes had a narrow face with gleaming eyes. He was clean-shaven and probably younger than William. Judging by his clothes and the scimitar gleaming from his saddle, he appeared to be someone of prominence, spearheading the body of riders as they descended.

Was this an officer of the militia? If so, he was grander than William had expected.

Thomas moved his horse away, with Hammid half stumbling and scampering behind him. William backed away too, his hand still hovering near his sabre as the riders converged around them, now only yards away. They were dark-skinned and dark-eyed, apart from the single rider in the white robes who stared at William with bright blue eyes, quite distinctive amongst the other riders.

William glanced at Thomas. 'Ask them what they seek,' he prompted.

Thomas cleared his throat and asked.

The man in the white robes stared at William with an intense and threatening look. 'Where did you get that?' he said, pointing to William's chest.

William was taken aback. 'You speak English?'

The other man nodded. 'You are surprised?'

'Very,' William murmured.

'Where did you get that necklace?' the speaker asked again.

William looked down and found the pendant, revealed beneath his shirt after Thomas had grasped at his arm.

'It was a gift,' he answered.

'Who gave it?' the man in white pressed.

'A good friend,' William ventured.

'A foreigner like you?'

'A *merchant* like me. A man called Charles Greynell.'

The man in white eyed William for a few moments and then he reached into his robes and pulled out the selfsame pendant.

'That necklace was a gift,' the man said. 'If you have it now, it means that you are either a friend of Charles Greynell or a thief.'

William was both relieved and delighted. 'I assure you, the former.'

The man nodded slightly, not yet sure about this stranger's honesty.

'You knew Charles Greynell?' William asked quickly.

The man nodded.

William found himself laughing. 'Then you know what this symbol is?'

'Of course,' the man in white replied. 'It is my tribe. *The Ayaida.*'

△ V △

Brother Jericho sat with Marco, watching as the Arab riders explored the wagons.

'We don't have to fight?' Marco whispered.

Brother Jericho shrugged. 'Not at the moment,' he replied. 'They seem friendly enough.'

'*Now* they do,' said Lieutenant Vittore nearby. 'These people can turn in an instant, Brother Jericho. Keep your wits about you. Both of you.'

Brother Jericho nodded and winked at Marco, smiling a little. Marco didn't find the situation amusing, but then Jericho was thinking that at least they could get water or food from these Arabs.

Lieutenant Peruzo galloped up and Marco tried to listen as he began speaking with Lieutenant Vittore. Following the short exchange, both officers set about rousing the company.

'Mount up, we're heading out!' Vittore bellowed. 'Stow the rifles and the cannon!'

At the head of the wagons, William and Thomas were still speaking to the Arabs' leader, Hammid having scuttled away to hide again.

'You say you are Ayaida?' William said.

'My name is Sheikh Fahd. You are on my lands,' the sheikh said, his tone aggressive.

'Of course,' William said, trying to ignore the veiled threat. 'Forgive me for being rude, Sheikh Fahd. If I had known these were your lands . . .'

'You would have been more polite than to come here armed?' Sheikh Fahd smiled thinly. 'I understand English etiquette well enough, Mr . . .?'

'Saxon,' William replied. 'William Saxon.'

Sheikh Fahd nodded perfunctorily.

'This is Mr Thomas Richmond, a merchant from England,' William went on. Thomas nodded, also disarmed by the current turn of events. 'As you can see, we are not hostile.'

'As for what I see . . .' Sheikh Fahd said, and looked at William's sword. 'You are well armed for merchants. We know the militias are following you.'

William glanced at Thomas, who was not so surprised.

'We have friends in Rashid and Alexandria,' Sheikh Fahd declared. 'It does no harm to keep an eye on your enemies.'

'We are not your enemies, sir,' William insisted. 'And if you are a friend of Charles Greynell, you are certainly a friend of ours. As for the militia . . . It is just a misunderstanding.'

'Many men have been executed for misunderstandings, Saxon,' Sheikh Fahd said. 'But I am no friend of the militias, and you are not the enemy I watch for.'

'We are not?' William said, relaxing again.

'We fight for the Ayaida. Not for Muhammad Ali,' Sheikh Fahd told them. 'If you are their enemy, then perhaps you have some use.'

It was William's turn now to be wary. 'I see,' he said and pondered. 'What use might that be?'

'Later,' Sheikh Fahd said and smiled broadly. 'These are dangerous lands, Saxon, perhaps too dangerous for the likes of you. I suggest we escort you to our camp. Including you, Mr Richmond?'

Thomas shrugged. 'Sheikh Fahd, you are the very people I wish to trade with. I have no need to venture further into the Sinai.'

'Then our meeting is fortunate for all,' the sheikh said. He shouted to the riders, and like ripples of water the call passed swiftly from those waiting at the side of the dune to those on the ridge, who began to descend.

'You will come with us and enjoy our hospitality,' Sheikh Fahd told William and Thomas. 'After that, we will decide what to do with you.'

William was now on his guard. 'I suppose this is not a choice?' he said, sitting erect on his horse and trying to appear unmoved by their predicament.

'You are astute, Saxon,' the sheikh replied. 'No, it is not a decision for you to make. The moment you rode onto my lands was the moment your choices were removed. Whether or not you are friends of Charles Greynell, I will decide your fate when we reach my camp.'

CHAPTER TWELVE

Raiding Party

△ I △

Questions . . .

William had plenty of these, yet he dared not ask them. Instead he did as he was bidden, and rode side by side with this Bedouin chief who watched him with calm suspicion. It was clear Sheikh Fahd did not trust William, that he regarded him as dangerous. His guards rode close to the company, flanking them carefully, watching the monks' every move. They would surely attack if given cause.

But despite this new jeopardy, William was overwhelmed with relief. Yes, they were captives, but willingly so. Outside of Rashid, this royalty of the desert was the sole surviving contact of Charles Greynell. That Greynell had chosen to leave a gift from the Ayaida with Malika had not been fortuitous. It had been providential.

William just hoped that Sheikh Fahd saw it that way.

Feeling the need for diplomacy, William urged his horse on a little quicker so he was shoulder to shoulder with the sheikh.

'I must say . . .' William started, the days of riding through scorched lands hoarsening his voice, 'your English is fluent, sir. May I ask where you learnt to speak it?'

Sheikh Fahd eyed him briefly but did not reply. For a moment or two William felt snubbed and awkward.

'My father fought alongside the Mamelukes against

Napoleon,' the sheikh said finally. 'He was not the only sheikh to do so. Many Bedouins believed the French would steal the desert, the mountains, and our women and children. So we fought and we fought hard. There were victories, but many defeats. Eventually, my father retired to the Sinai to rest.

'And then the British came, and the Ottomans, and there was faith again. And the French were driven from the sands as they were from the seas. There were victories, and not so many defeats,' Sheikh Fahd remembered. 'After serving alongside the British, my father realized once the French had been driven from Egypt that our only enemies were our allies.'

The sheikh turned to William, his eyes drilling into him. 'The British are weakened by war, but they look upon this land with a conqueror's gaze,' he said, and then shrugged. 'My father was a great man. Some say he could see into the future. He sent me to Dumyat to be schooled by an Englishman. I learnt your customs, your philosophy, history and your words. And after I was done, I knew then that the British *were* coming. It is their nature to conquer.'

William suddenly wanted to shrink back into that Papal world, to express himself in Latin, to shed his British past. From experience he knew that the sheikh was right. He knew the machinations of the British empire, its ambition to go to the corners of the world. William had once believed that it was simple adventure and exploration that drove that machine forward. But with years outside of the empire, he saw a greater motivation: the greed of possession and the will to dominate and subjugate.

'They might leave Egypt alone,' he suggested sheepishly.

Sheikh Fahd studied William for a moment and then dismissed the conversation with a wave. 'We do not fear the British,' he said. 'It is Ali who is our enemy now. Ali threatens to drive us from our lands. The Mamelukes are all but dead and Ali rules Egypt. We have no allies now.'

'I too fought against Napoleon. At Waterloo,' William said. 'My enemy was once the French as it was your father's. And I am no friend of the viceroy, as you know. You could consider *me* as an ally.'

Sheikh Fahd's eyes widened. 'You were a soldier?'

William nodded.

'A British soldier? *Very* interesting, Mr Saxon. You almost fooled me. I had taken you at your word, a "merchant's" word. Not a soldier's,' Sheikh Fahd added triumphantly and cocked his head back. 'I was right to suspect your intentions. Your deceit is now revealed, and a flimsy deceit it was.'

William went to protest, but the sheikh flung his hand in the air and rode away, leaving William with a sense of foreboding.

△ II △

The sheikh's men guided them down a rock-strewn ridge and William was surprised that their surroundings changed so quickly. The landscape was still a waste of sand, but they had risen into the highlands as the sun began to fall behind them. Here the hills were rugged and the path was arduous, but as they moved down they discovered a plateau that was strewn with trees and bushes. Some patches of grasslands still existed, and nestled between them was a large camp by the side of a lake, busy with people moving about their daily work.

As they neared, William spied children playing, women carrying clothes and babes, while guards milled around, muskets over their shoulders, long blades at their hips, chatting to herders who were standing idly by.

Nearby were homes like cloth buildings, made of striped blankets. The camp seemed spun, like a spider's web, with guy ropes crisscrossing the paths between each tent. Fowl strutted between the ropes and pegs, and goats stood tethered to posts, blinking in the setting sun.

'Is this your tribe?'

Sheikh Fahd turned about in his saddle and nodded. 'Yes, Mr

Saxon. Welcome to the Ayaida. There are some of us who are nomadic, but most live here under my protection.'

At the centre of the camp was a giant marquee surrounded by several other large and elaborate tents, dwarfing the clusters of tents nearby. The camp seemed to have its own sets of core communities, with tents facing inwards in circles, or clustered together.

At the perimeter of the camp were small enclosures: makeshift fences hemming in horses, sheep and chickens that scattered whenever someone walked near. These were tended to by elderly men, their faces dark and weatherbeaten, staring indifferently at the foreigners as they rode into the heart of the tribe.

It was difficult to see whether these simple nomads regarded the monks of the company as trophies or objects of curiosity. Plainly, most had never seen Europeans before, and there were expressions of instinctive suspicion from some, downright hostility from others.

Fearing for his captain, Peruzo tried to move his horse closer to William, but several Bedouin riders closed in front of him, casting looks of warning. Peruzo relented, hoping they were trying to protect their sheikh, rather than remove contact with his captain.

'Out of the pot, into the fire,' Thomas murmured to himself.

They came to a halt by a paddock and Sheikh Fahd shouted to the riders, who dismounted and became quickly garrulous, joking with each other, while some glanced warily at William and the monks.

The sheikh pulled his horse around to William's. 'You are now the guests of the Ayaida, Mr Saxon.'

'I am honoured,' William replied uncomfortably.

'As a condition of my hospitality, I request you surrender your weapons,' Sheikh Fahd told him.

William frowned. 'I am not sure I can allow that.'

'It is not a choice,' Sheikh Fahd replied. 'I could have made this request when we first met, but in the desert every man has the right to defend himself. Here there are families and there are children. I would feel content if the only armed men here were my bodyguards.'

William studied Sheikh Fahd's expression. He appeared sincere, but William still didn't trust him. Far too much had gone wrong of late for him to trust anyone.

'Your weapons will be returned to you, Mr Saxon, once you leave this camp. If they are needed in a hurry, I will give them back,' Sheikh Fahd offered. 'For urgent use only.'

William considered the options and realized there were none. 'Very well.'

Sheikh Fahd barked orders. The Bedouins moved towards the monks. William turned his horse to address the rest of the company.

'They want us to disarm,' he shouted.

The brothers gave a stir of unrest.

'Captain?' Vittore said, quite worried.

'We have little choice, Lieutenant,' William told him. 'Hand the weapons over to the Bedouins. Let them store the munitions. The sheikh assures me they will be safe.'

After the weapons began to fall to the floor, Peruzo dismounted and marched over to William.

'This is not a good idea, Captain,' he protested. 'How do we escape now?'

'For the moment, we don't,' William replied. 'We are not in good shape, and we need rest. We have too many enemies out there to make the Ayaida one of them. And . . .'

'*And*, Captain?'

'This sheikh knew Charles Greynell. He has been suspicious of us so far, but with persuasion he could be helpful. Remember what is said in the letter about the "wanderer"?'

'Greynell *could* have meant this man . . . Or our hosts could sell us out to the militia,' Peruzo warned.

William felt his chin, touching the stubble again. 'I could do with a wash and a shave, not to mention something to eat and drink,' he said, dismissing Peruzo's concerns. 'Privileges of captivity, wouldn't you say?'

'If we're lucky,' Peruzo said grudgingly as he watched the natives gather their weapons. 'Even if this sheikh is friendly, we could be wasting precious time.'

'At this moment, Peruzo, the Hoard is out of our reach,' William pointed out. 'The brothers are starved and weak. What we need now, more than time, is luck. And we're fast running out of both.'

△ III △

As promised by their hosts, they were treated to a place to wash and shave and then to change their clothes. The monks of the Order applied themselves with zeal simply glad to be out of the blistering heat of the sun and the saddle. But William tempered his graciousness with caution.

He shared a simple tent with Thomas and Marco within the inner circle of the camp, not so far away from the sheikh, something that Thomas took as a privilege. He changed into courtier's clothes, making sure his appearance was impeccable.

Apart from his oversized monk's shirt and breeches, Marco had no other clothes that were fit to wear. Thomas lent him a spare shirt and trousers that were again too long, much to the Englishman's amusement. Eventually, with the cuffs turned up, they fitted well enough.

One of the sheikh's bodyguards appeared at their tent and Thomas translated. 'A summoning from our hosts, Captain Saxon,' he said as his fingers caressed his long pointed beard.

'All of us?' William asked.

'Just you,' Thomas said and gave a long sigh.

'A private audience,' William murmured, and regarded the severe expression of the Bedouin, his chest crossed with long knives. 'Or interrogation.' He buttoned his grey jacket, still grubby from the sand and sweat. There were splotches of blackened blood on the cuffs from the battle at Babel's, but at least his shirt was clean and fresh.

While Thomas glowered, William beckoned Marco to him. 'And you . . . Keep out of trouble, understood? No wandering about. This place is dangerous.'

Marco nodded.

William followed the bodyguard outside. The evening was warm even though the sun had fallen behind the hills an hour or so ago. The day was beginning to darken, coloured now only by the sand and the orange rocks that walled in the valley. There were plenty of places to hide out there, William observed, but hoped the vampyres were not foolish or ambitious enough to attack them while they stayed with Ayaida.

William and the bodyguard ducked under ropes tethering the large and impressive tents to the ground, passing by Bedouins who would not look at the infidel in their midst. Only a few children playing in the dust outside the inner ring of tents dared to look at him, and then it was with a mixture of curiosity and fear, some laughing and pointing with infantile glee.

The bodyguard led him around another tent and over to the largest, which was striped, and trimmed with gold thread. He stopped at the entrance and then stepped back, silently gesturing William inside.

William ducked underneath the flap, parting another curtain into the central chamber. Beyond was a room that was large and cool; extravagant yet not dazzling. There was a smell of spice in the air. It went to William's head and made his mouth water.

Apart from himself, the chamber was empty.

He stood for a while and then frowned. 'Hello?' he called, somewhat impatiently.

At first there was no reply; then at the other end of the chamber, a curtain parted and the sheikh appeared, wearing his spotless robes.

'Mr Saxon,' he greeted.

'Sir,' William said, and bowed.

Sheikh Fahd studied William intently before reaching down

222

to a gold jug on a table to his right. 'Would you care for some coffee?' he said.

William nodded courteously, though secretly his throat was screaming for something cooler. He had not drunk for many hours, and his insides felt as arid as the desert about them. The sheikh clapped his hands and instantly a woman appeared with two gold jugs, steam dancing from both. They gave off a rich smell, spicy and inviting. William began salivating and watched all too eagerly as the serving girl lowered the jugs to Sheikh Fahd's side.

'I'm afraid we do not have tea here,' Sheikh Fahd said, but William could tell he was teasing.

'Coffee will be fine,' he replied.

The sheikh poured some into an ornate cup and lifted it. William walked over, bowing to take it from the sheikh's hands. The cup was hot, and William had no doubt that its contents would scald his mouth if he drank too soon.

'Is something wrong, Mr Saxon?'

William shook his head graciously. 'Not at all, sir.'

'Would you like some water first?' Sheikh Fahd said and smiled.

William looked up. He was testing him. 'I am fine, thank you.' He sat down opposite the sheikh, hoping that his coffee would cool down soon enough.

'Who is the boy who travels with you?' Sheikh Fahd asked.

William pulled an uncomfortable face as he blew on the coffee. 'No one of consequence.'

'Really?' Sheikh Fahd said. 'I find that hard to believe. Is he your . . . Now how would you say it? Your serf?'

William laughed, almost spilling the coffee in his hands. 'Definitely not, sir.'

'Then who?'

'He is a stowaway. He hid on a boat from Naples to Rashid. He has been in my care ever since.'

'A stowaway . . .' Sheikh Fahd pondered.

'Seeking excitement and adventure,' William added irritably.

'I know that feeling, Mr Saxon,' the sheikh replied. 'My younger sister, Jamillah, is the same. She teaches herself to fight with the sword and rides when she should not. She's like a wild animal. Not a sheikh's sister.'

'She sounds *trying*, sir,' William mused.

'I have told her she must marry soon, yet all she wants is adventure.' Sheikh Fahd shook his head. 'The waywardness of youth, Mr Saxon.'

'I understand it well, sir. The boy suffers from a similar affliction,' William smiled.

Sheikh Fahd snorted with amusement, and began a deep chuckling as he considered the common problem between them. But as he relaxed on an elaborate mat surrounded by large, embroidered cushions, the laughter faded and the sheikh's manner grew graver.

'You should let my people wash your clothes while you are here,' he said. 'Appearances matter, especially when you're in a position of power.'

'Your offer is gracious, sir. But we will not be here long enough to accept it.'

Sheikh Fahd looked surprised. 'You are leaving us so soon, Mr Saxon?'

'I have another engagement.'

'Still on the run from the militia?'

William didn't reply.

'You haven't asked me why I chose to save you and your friends, Mr Saxon. I could have easily sold you to the militia, or left you to die in the desert. You looked quite lost,' the sheikh remarked.

'Then why didn't you?' William asked.

'Because I don't believe you are a merchant.'

William smiled. 'Who do you think we are?'

'Dangerous men, Mr Saxon,' the sheikh said, and grinned.

'Dangerous to the Ayaida?' William said, more nervous now.

'That remains to be seen,' the sheikh replied casually. 'Do you believe in ghosts?'

224

William shrugged. 'During my career I've seen many things most men would scarce believe, sir. But ghosts? I have never seen one.'

'My brother was killed by ghosts, Mr Saxon,' the sheikh said and paused, watching William closely. Not a flicker of doubt crossed William's face, even though his first reaction was to think of such a claim as superstition. The sheikh smiled and continued his story.

'Months ago now, my brother sought an alliance amongst the southern tribes against the Viceroy Ali. Some of us believe that Ali means to drive all Bedouins from the Sinai into the sea. Those who see the danger have agreed to the alliance in case his armies come here. But there are other great families who are blinded by greed and ignorance. One of these tribes is the Myabela.

'The Myabela have been paid to spy for Ali. They knew my brother would eventually approach them, so they lured him to their camp and tried to kill him and his men. He escaped with only half of his personal guard. The rest were murdered.

'But the Myabela scented their quarry. They chased him north, through the gorges and darkest valleys. And one by one, his bodyguard perished. Finally, my brother headed east, towards a region of ill fortune where not even the Myabela are so foolish as to follow. They know what lies in that terrible place.'

The sheikh drew breath sharply and looked at William with sorrow. 'My brother was not killed by the Myabela. He was ambushed by ghosts who for three days attacked him and his remaining bodyguards in the mountain passes. One by one they were killed until only a few survived.

'And then on the fourth day, my brother's guards sacrificed themselves so that he and his servant, Dawud, could make their escape. In the end, their sacrifice was in vain. My brother was struck twice in the back by arrows. Dawud fled, cowardice taking hold of him. When he found his courage again, he returned to my brother, but only to see these ghosts cutting him apart.'

225

William sipped the coffee, forgetting that it might still be hot. The heat burned his tongue, and he winced. 'That is . . . is *terrible*, sir,' William said. 'And ghosts did this?'

'Dawud believes so,' the sheikh replied.

William blew down on the coffee again and thought about the story. 'So Dawud lived?' he said, surprised that anyone could survive in the desert alone.

'Barely,' Sheikh Fahd replied. 'A passing caravan of foreigners from St Catherine discovered him. He was almost blind with thirst when they found him.'

'He sounds like a lucky man,' William remarked.

'We *both* were, Mr Saxon,' Sheikh Fahd insisted. 'The leader of the expedition agreed to search for survivors of the massacre. When this man arrived at the valley he was able to retrieve my brother's body, and my family have been in his debt ever since.' The sheikh paused, his expression distant for a moment or two. William tested the coffee again, and content that it would not burn the roof of his mouth, he drank thirstily. Sheikh Fahd smiled and offered the jug again.

William looked apologetic but crossed over to refill his cup. 'Thank you,' he said and sat down again.

'The leader of that expedition was Charles Greynell,' the sheikh said as William made himself comfortable.

William almost choked on his coffee. 'Greynell?' he gasped and lowered the cup. 'Truly? *He* found them?'

Sheikh Fahd nodded, pleased by the reaction.

'But what was he doing there?' William asked impatiently. 'How did he come across Dawud?'

'I never asked him, Mr Saxon,' the sheikh admitted. 'I merely believed it was providence he was there at all.'

William looked struck, dazed even. 'And you say he was travelling from St Catherine?'

'That is what he told me.'

'And he returned *here*, bringing Dawud and your brother with him?' William guessed. Again the sheikh nodded. 'So that is why Charles had the pendant.'

226

'We would have given him much more, but he refused,' Sheikh Fahd replied. 'He is a good man. And a friend of the Ayaida.'

William nodded solemnly and rested the coffee before him.

'So tell me, Captain, how is it that *you* know Charles?' the sheikh asked.

William looked up from the cup. He knew this moment would come. He could only be truthful. 'I don't know him, sir,' he confessed. 'I didn't have a chance to.'

'Explain,' Sheikh Fahd demanded.

'Sir, I'm sorry to tell you this, but Charles Greynell is dead.'

The sheikh stared at William, the words sinking in slowly at first, but once past that wall of incomprehension, the revelation was rapid. Sheikh Fahd looked devastated. 'Dead?'

William nodded.

'How?' the sheikh asked.

'Murdered, sir,' William replied. 'Murdered by the same people who hunt us now.'

'The militia?'

'No. Someone else,' William told him. 'You were right to think that I wasn't a merchant. I am someone quite different. I really am a soldier. And Charles Greynell was my contact in Rashid. But our enemies got to Charles first. He did not survive.'

The sheikh nodded, though William doubted he understood everything he was saying.

'What is your real name?' the sheikh asked.

'William Saxon *is* my real name, sir,' he replied. 'Though I am a captain.'

'*Captain* Saxon,' the sheikh said and seemed pleased with the title.

William shuffled closer. 'Sir . . . Charles was meant to lead me to a place deep in the Sinai, and I wondered if you have ever heard of the term "Mhorrer's Hoard"?'

The sheikh shook his head. William sighed.

'Is it a treasure?' the sheikh asked.

'No sir, it is not,' William replied. 'I would call it a curse.' His mind was busy.

'Who killed Charles, Captain Saxon?' the sheikh asked.

'Creatures of greed and darkness, sir,' William replied cryptically. 'They are called vampyres, and I hope you will never have to meet one. They are responsible for the deaths of Charles, two of my men, not to mention many innocent people in Rashid and in an oasis many miles from here.'

'They sound dangerous,' the sheikh replied. 'Like the ghosts that murdered my brother.'

William's eyes widened. 'Yes. That's right. *Just like vampyres*,' he said eagerly. 'These ghosts of yours, what can you tell me about them?'

'I know very little. Only rumour. The legends say ghosts steal the souls of men and leave their corpses to rot in the mountain passes. They attack who they wish. Men, women, anyone. Other than that, I have nothing more to tell.' The sheikh watched William's expression deflate. 'You wish for more?'

'*Is* there more?' William replied hopefully.

'There may be,' the sheikh said and clapped his hands loudly. 'Hisham!'

At once the broad bodyguard entered and bowed before his sheikh. Words passed between them, the bodyguard left quickly, and Sheikh Fahd settled back.

'Dawud will know more,' Sheikh Fahd remarked. 'He was near them when my brother was murdered.'

'What is the name of the place where your brother died?' William asked as they waited for Dawud to appear.

'It has many names in Arabic and Egyptian, yet in English you would call it "the Valley of Fire".'

William heard the name and then something registered. The name began to unlock something, clues, doors, *words written in a letter* . . .

'Is there something wrong, Captain?' Sheikh Fahd remarked.

William found himself beaming as though something wonderful had just occurred. 'I'm not sure,' he replied distantly. 'It might be nothing. Or it could be the answer to a riddle . . . possibly the greatest riddle of all.'

The young servant known as Dawud was urged into the tent, flanked by two of Sheikh Fahd's guards. The Bedouin bowed to his sheikh but gave William an uneasy look.

Sheikh Fahd asked a few questions and Dawud answered, his speech spluttered and now and then stumbling as though he had plenty to say but was reluctant to speak it.

Presently after several exchanges, Sheikh Fahd addressed William. 'Ask away, Captain. He is nervous and still afraid, but he will speak.'

Whether it was the effects of the coffee swirling inside him or the lightning strike of sudden revelation, William felt eager, hungry for what only Dawud could tell him. 'What can he tell me about these ghosts?' he said forcefully, staring at the wretched young survivor.

The sheikh asked and Dawud rocked on the balls of his feet, putting his hands together, pleadingly reverent.

'They were dressed like the sky. They wore strange armour about their bodies and across their arms. And they had no faces to speak of, just one eye . . .'

William frowned. 'A Cyclops?'

Sheikh Fahd agreed. 'Yes. Like the legends. He says they had a single eye, painted with fire.'

William balled his hands, searching for the relevance. The references to fire in Charles Greynell's letter . . . The Valley of Fire . . . The ghosts with a single eye of . . .

'*A riddle of fire*,' he muttered. 'So it is true.'

'Captain?' Sheikh Fahd said, but William was lost in thought. Sheikh Fahd growled under his breath and sent Dawud away.

William got to his feet and began pacing the tent.

'Captain Saxon, what importance is this to you?' Sheikh Fahd demanded.

William thought for a moment, considering the consequences, yet the temptation that this Valley of Fire could be the domain of the Rassis was so great that he could not refrain. He drew the letter from his jacket and held it out to the sheikh.

'What is this?'

'It is Charles Greynell's last letter.'

Sheikh Fahd opened it and read, frowning with concentration. While William waited he brooded on the turn of events. Was the Hoard truly so close to them now? Might the mission prove a success? It felt at least possible, and he had to control his emotions as he waited for the sheikh to finish reading.

Sheikh Fahd lowered the letter and looked solemn again. 'A mystery,' he said.

'Indeed a "riddle",' William said. 'A "riddle of fire", no less.'

Sheikh Fahd did not reply, but stared at William with further questions. William had already told the sheikh too much, yet he could see a friend in the making. He remembered Kieran's parting words, their wisdom confirming his resolve: '*In our absence, you should find allies where you can . . .*'

'Sir, I believe your brother was not murdered by ghosts,' William said plainly. His host must know the truth.

The Bedouin looked back patiently, still holding the letter. 'Then by whom?' he demanded.

William took his time to reply, hoping to make his suspicions sound credible. 'I believe he was murdered by a sect called the Rassis Cult. The Rassis are not ghosts, but men like you and me.'

'If they are flesh and blood, then they can be killed,' Sheikh Fahd said. Clearly the notion appealed to him.

'I believe so,' William replied. 'But I might add, this is not your fight, Sheikh Fahd, but *my* mission.'

'For honour, Captain Saxon, I believe it *is* my fight,' Sheikh Fahd replied. 'I wish to add revenge to my song.'

'Your song?'

'When someone of great prominence dies in my tribe, a song is written about their death,' Sheikh Fahd said. 'If you stay, I will have someone sing it to you. My own voice does not carry a melody, but there are some in my tribe whose voices would shame the greatest of songbirds.'

'I would be honoured to hear it, Sheikh Fahd,' William replied.

'But the song is incomplete, Captain Saxon,' Sheikh Fahd said and sighed. He stared at his guest so searchingly that William wondered what he was seeing.

'The reason I did not let you perish in the desert was that Charles promised to send me a weapon,' Sheikh Fahd said at last. 'A weapon of vengeance to strike down my brother's murderers. And I prayed to Allah that such a weapon would come.' He walked over and placed his broad hand firmly on William's shoulder.

William looked up at the sheikh. 'A weapon?'

'*You*, Captain Saxon. And your men,' the sheikh explained. 'And now you are here, I *will* be revenged on these ghosts.'

△ IV △

Marco woke with a start to the sound of voices. When he emerged from the covers he found two figures standing at the entrance to the tent, their outlines blurred by shadow and campfire. He slowly pulled the blanket back over him and listened.

'I've elected to move our camp away from the Ayaida,' said a whispered voice.

'The men aren't at their best. If the vampyre were to attack now . . . Wouldn't the Ayaida offer us the protection we need?' said the other.

'Camping away from the Ayaida is a condition of having our rifles returned to us. Other than Thomas and Vittore, no one in the company has the faintest understanding of these people. A diplomatic incident between two armed parties is bound to end in tragedy.

'Besides, camping at the ridge will provide a better vantage point. It looks out across the whole valley.'

'What about Marco? He should camp with the brothers if you want him to learn anything.'

'Not now,' came the reply. 'He is not ready to fight. He might do something rash and then we'll all suffer because of it.'

'If you may permit me, Captain, you should give him more credit.'

'Peruzo, he is *my* responsibility.'

Marco realized he knew these voices.

'I am still surprised the sheikh ceded to such a request, Captain,' Peruzo said. 'Didn't he ask why?'

William sounded wary. 'He is no longer suspicious. We're allies now.'

'*Allies?*' Peruzo sounded alarmed. 'But how? What have you told them?'

William stepped closer and Marco strained to hear.

'Do you trust me?'

'Of course. You are my captain.'

'How about as a friend?'

'You have done right by me ever since I've known you, William.'

'Then trust me now, my friend. I take all responsibility for breaking the charter of the Secretariat. We need the sheikh's help. With it, we could achieve our mission. Without it, I fear we have already failed.'

'If you bring these people into our war, the Papacy will surely banish you.'

'That is my burden, Peruzo. But do you really think they would cast me aside if I brought them the Hoard of Mhorrer?'

There was something else said, something that Marco wasn't able to hear. He leant forward and knocked over his uncle's kit, which clattered to the ground.

'Marco,' William said. 'You've been listening?'

Marco rolled over and sat upright. 'What is happening?'

'Go back to sleep.'

'But Uncle!'

William said something under his breath to Peruzo, who slipped off into the night. Now William came to Marco, stepping over Thomas, who was fast asleep. He sat down near his nephew, and yawned. 'I've moved the company up the ridge above the valley,' he whispered, and stretched his arms.

'Should I go as well?' Marco asked as he tried to get up.

William held up his hand. 'No. You'll be staying here.'

'But I should be with the brothers, shouldn't I?' Marco protested.

'You should stay with *me*,' William snapped, feeling tired. 'You are my responsibility, not the Order's. And certainly not Peruzo's, nor Vittore's.'

Marco looked crestfallen. 'You don't want me here.'

'I want you *safe*,' William insisted. 'If Sheikh Fahd turns out to be an ally, then I intend to leave you here while we go further into the Sinai.'

Marco felt his face flush red, and his eyes burned with anger. 'No!' he said. 'I'm coming with you!'

'Marco . . .' William groaned.

Thomas snorted, stirred and muttered something unintelligible.

William glanced over his shoulder and shook his head.

'You promised!' Marco whispered as loud as he could, lest he wake up the English merchant.

'I did no such thing,' William growled at him. 'This mission has become more dangerous than I could have imagined. This is not a game, Marco.'

Marco stared at him, tears stinging his eyes. 'I will go where you go.'

William shook his head. 'No, Marco, you will not. And should you try, I will have you tied up here. Is that what you want?'

Marco rolled over, pulling his sheets over him. He sniffed and wiped the tears from his eyes, ashamed that he should be crying, but angry about being betrayed.

'Marco,' William said, but the boy's icy silence spoke enough.

William spent the next half-hour staring at Marco, watching him slowly fall asleep, hearing Thomas's muttering behind him, yet feeling no comfort. His head was a mess of possibilities and considerations. Fatigued though he was, he could not hope to sleep. Yet after an hour, weariness had taken its toll and William curled up in the corner, his eyes closing for whatever rest was afforded him.

△ V △

It took time to move the wagons and horses up the ridge. Their weapons were returned eventually, but not all at once. The Bedouin had taken a shine to the Baker rifles and handed them over reluctantly, but hand them over they did.

Peruzo was still suspicious of their hosts, but for the next hour he concerned himself with setting up camp a quarter of a mile away from the Ayaida. It was hard going in the dark and the monks seemed weary. Yet, despite their fatigue, and despite lapses in concentration, the company seemed in good spirits. Tomorrow they would rest and replenish.

Vittore posted Brother Angelo for first watch. The young monk grumbled, but obeyed and trudged to the ledge of rock that looked out over both the valley and the dunes to the west. He checked his rifle and squatted down against the rocks, wrapping his arms around him against the cold.

There were other sentries around the camp, other pairs of eyes that would be watching for vampyre attacks. Angelo would not be the only one. Perhaps that was why the young monk found himself dozing off, lulled into security by the respite after the preceding days. After fighting to stay awake, he succumbed to the night and slumped over his rifle, slipping into a shallow sleep.

Angelo woke with a start. Brother Tore had shouted, hadn't he? Wasn't that his voice? His cry? There were more sounds in the dark and Angelo struggled to the edge of the outcrop. Rubbing his blurred eyes, he peered out into the night. Below him the darkness seemed to swarm with movement.

'Vampyres!' He loaded his rifle, drowsiness making his hands

234

clumsy. When it was finally loaded, he raised the rifle and pointed it towards the shadows. And then the dark separated and several men rushed towards him.

They were not vampyres, though. They were Arabs.

Hesitating, Angelo wasn't sure whether to fire or not. Lieutenant Peruzo's orders were to shoot *only* at vampyres. And definitely *not* Arabs.

The hesitation cost him dear. After he lowered his rifle, more men appeared on the ledge. Silently they scrambled up to Brother Angelo and wrestled him to the floor. Angelo kicked out, knocking two or three away, but the weight of their numbers had him pinned down. Then they began to beat him. Blood filled his mouth and pain filled his head with each kick and punch.

There was a sudden loud bang and one of the Arabs on top of Angelo whirled away in a spray of blood. The others fell away from the monk, retreating as another shot ripped through the air.

'Get off him, you savages!' Lieutenant Vittore shouted.

Angelo pushed himself up, but his head was spinning and the rusty taste of his own blood filled his mouth.

'Stay down!' the lieutenant ordered as he reloaded his rifle. He looked like a hero, broad-shouldered and fierce. He had a determination that was unequalled amongst the brothers.

He would save them.

'When I tell you, you must . . .' Vittore ordered but his instruction was cut short. There was a series of sudden reports, like firecrackers exploding around them. Angelo watched Lieutenant Vittore twitch horrifically, pulled in every direction as a fusillade of bullets tore through his body. The lieutenant staggered back for a moment, bleeding profusely, before falling to the ground.

With blood blinding his eye, Brother Angelo's world turned over for a final time, before he passed out.

Peruzo heard the shooting as he was settling down inside his tent. He leapt to his feet, half-dressed, his braces down his legs, and snatched up his Baker rifle then ran outside. Other monks had dashed from their tents with the closest weapon to hand, just as the Rashid militia poured into the camp.

It was only exceptional judgement that stopped Peruzo from shooting down the first rider. Instead he dropped his rifle to the ground and ordered the rest of the company to do the same. Jericho looked at the lieutenant incredulously.

'We're not here to fight Arabs, Jericho,' Peruzo shouted over to him. The monk relented and laid the rifle at his feet. 'Don't give them any reason to harm you.'

For some minutes the camp was in chaos. Peruzo silently cursed the Arabs as several monks were kicked to the ground despite having laid down their weapons. Brother Filippo emerged with Angelo over his shoulder and told Peruzo what had happened.

The militia had tracked them to the Ayaida and attacked under cover of darkness once the opportunity arose. For whatever reason, exhaustion or bad light, none of the sentries had seen the first wave of militia until it was too late. Brother Tore had been disarmed and beaten, his bleeding body hurled into camp for Argento and Filippo to tend to while the others were corralled. Vittore's death had occurred soon after the militia stormed the camp, taking them by complete surprise. Vittore had killed two of the militia, but paid for the mistake with his life. It had all been quick and far too easy.

Peruzo listened with mounting despair. He cursed the militia again and the fortune that had led them here. He stopped short of criticizing his captain for ordering them to camp along the ridge. It had been a mistake, but the bigger mistake was to believe the Rashid militia had given up on them.

△ VI △

The man who was watching the tents burn with some satisfaction was sinewy and muscled through years of discipline. When he dismounted from his horse, he did so like someone half his age. At his back were tied two scimitars, dangerous in any man's hands, but in Khalifa's, lethal.

As the militia ransacked the camp, Khalifa looked over their prisoners with disdain, noting Peruzo in particular. He smiled as he looked down at the lieutenant with no small measure of triumph. Peruzo stared back with contempt; it was the only spur Khalifa needed. He kicked Peruzo in the head, sending him sprawling in the dirt.

'That was for Babel's. Bind them,' Khalifa commanded.

The sight of the tents burning in the darkness gave special pleasure to one onlooker, a man with a pot belly and dressed in expensive robes. His name was Haidar.

Ali had tasked Haidar personally to protect Rashid, a post that was worthy of a prince. While Ali was away, Haidar had been treated as royalty, courted by men of wealth and position. He had taken a bride and other women (especially in Babel's), revelling in his status. There had been nothing to contend with in many months, except for the foreigners who corrupted the town.

The captain of the militia stared at the approaching riders from the camp below. At the head were around a dozen men and horses dressed like Mamelukes, but Haidar could see that more were gathering. A camp like this could have several hundred Bedouin riders. He was outnumbered.

Haidar turned to Khalifa and beckoned him over.

'We've plundered the infidels' tents and arrested the murderers,' Khalifa announced.

'Well done,' Haidar said. 'Your skills are beyond measure, Khalifa. I will reward you for this.'

Khalifa bowed. 'What about them?' He gestured to the horsemen approaching.

'I will be both kind and forceful. These savages would not dare make war on Ali. But to be sure, send some of my men back to Bastet with news of our prisoners. If we do not return

to the main camp, they are to go to Dumyat with word of insurrection.'

Khalifa bowed again and galloped in haste to the riders at
the top of the ridge while Haidar with his personal guard of
eight men trotted slowly down the track, one hand raised in
peace to the approaching Bedouins. He halted before the tribal
riders reached them and waited for them to halt a few yards
away.

'I am Haidar, first captain of the Rashid militia, under Ali,'
Haidar greeted.

'I am Sheikh Fahd of the Ayaida,' the sheikh retorted, his
white robes in disarray. 'What do you want here? This is *our* land.'

'This is the land of Ali, my sheikh,' Haidar corrected him.

'Not yet it isn't,' Sheikh Fahd replied angrily.

Haidar noticed the tension and smiled. 'You are right, of
course. My apologies.'

'Accepted,' Sheikh Fahd said coolly. 'I ask again, what do you
want here?'

'You are harbouring fugitives,' Haidar replied.

'We have done no such thing,' Sheikh Fahd retorted.

Haidar pointed up the track. 'Then what are these?'

'Neighbours,' Sheikh Fahd said. 'They've done us no harm,
so we allowed them to camp there. What business is it of yours?'

'These men are murderers, Sheikh Fahd. Surely you have
heard?'

'We take no notice of the affairs of others,' Sheikh Fahd
replied.

'Of course you don't,' Haidar said wryly. 'No matter. They
have been arrested on your land, and I think you should be
pleased they have been taken. After all, you would not want
them associated with your tribe, would you? As enemies of the
people of Egypt?'

Sheikh Fahd narrowed his eyes and compressed his lips. He
knew what this man, Haidar, implied. His hand tensed on his
sword.

'There is no need to be aggressive, Sheikh Fahd. Any act against my militia is an act against Ali. You know this.'

'No one will know what happens here tonight,' the sheikh threatened.

'My scouts have returned to our camp with news of the arrests. If I do not return soon after, it will be assumed that your people have massacred my men. That would be unfortunate,' Haidar said. 'Do not mistake my army to be the only one in this region. There are other militia searching for these murderers. *All* follow Ali.'

Fahd hesitated, and after a while his hand relaxed. 'If they are your prisoners, take them,' he said.

'Oh, we will,' Haidar said, as though this was not up for debate. 'I would very much like to search your camp for other offenders.'

Sheikh Fahd's hand returned to his sword. 'And I tell you there are no such men.'

'I would like to see this for myself,' Haidar insisted.

'Do you call me a liar?' Sheikh Fahd said politely. At once the dozen Bedouins behind Sheikh Fahd tensed, and so did Haidar's guard.

Knowing that his bluff had been called, Haidar could only smile. 'I meant no offence, my sheikh. I will leave you in peace.'

△ VII △

William hastily strapped on his sword with a creak of leather.

'Where are you going?' Thomas said groggily, still half-asleep.

'I heard shooting from the ridge.'

'Vampyres?' Thomas asked.

'Vampyres don't have muskets,' William replied and hurried from the tent. The camp swarmed with men, and he quickened his pace until he was almost running to his horse. Something bad had happened.

As he got to his mount, the animal pawed the ground

impatiently. He loosed the tether, swung himself into the saddle and set out at a gallop towards the ridge, but he hadn't gone far before he met the sheikh and his bodyguard on their way back. William slowed, and the sheikh turned his horse to bar his path.

'Do not go up there, Captain,' he warned him.

William gave a start. 'What has happened?'

'Your militia friends have arrested your men,' Sheikh Fahd told him gravely.

'Every one?'

Sheikh Fahd nodded. 'I am sorry, Captain. There was nothing I could do. I told them nothing of you, the boy, or the merchant. *You* at least are safe. But if you ride up there, they will take you too.'

William crumbled in the saddle, his arms falling slack in desperation. 'What will happen to them?'

'They will be tried for murder, Captain Saxon, if they are lucky,' Sheikh Fahd said. 'If they are not . . .'

'They will simply be executed,' William said.

Sheikh Fahd put his hand on William's shoulder. 'You may yet succeed in your mission, Captain.'

'With my men gone, I don't see how,' William murmured.

'You have at least one ally now, remember?' Sheikh Fahd insisted.

William looked back at him, noting his sincerity. 'Those are more than just monks, sir. They are the finest soldiers you will ever meet. If we are to defeat the vampyres and the Rassis Cult, then I *need* those men.'

Sheikh Fahd shook his head. 'Impossible. Ali needs only the slightest excuse to drive all the tribes from the Sinai. If the Ayaida attack the militia, it could start a war.'

'Damn it, sir!' William said desperately. 'Don't you see? The War has already begun!'

240

CHAPTER THIRTEEN

A Perilous Liberation

△ I △

Lieutenant Vittore looked up into the dawn sky, his lifeless eyes catching the light all too briefly as it brimmed up over the ridge and across the valley, extinguishing shadow. And then a veil of scorched tent cloth was drawn over his face and Vittore was gone.

William's expression hardened.

He had spent much of that night preparing to leave, and as the first rays of light shone over the mountains to the east he rode up to the smoking remnants of the camp, driven to see what was left. The swords and the cannon were gone. Those tents that were not reduced to ash had been torn apart. Pots and pans lay scattered, clothes had been trampled by horses. Amongst all this was only one body: Vittore's. But that was still one body too many.

William pulled his belt tight while looking down at the shroud of the lieutenant.

'I see your resolve is unchanged,' Thomas noted. The Englishman had accompanied William to the camp, along with Hisham and several riders who stood aside and watched as William made his way forlornly around the site of struggle.

'They've stolen all the weapons and the bastards have killed one of my officers!'

'He would have died protecting the company, Captain, I'm sure,' Thomas suggested.

'He should not have died in the first place,' William growled, kicking a dented tin across the dust.

After several minutes of calm, William said: 'I need help to carry Vittore to my horse.'

'Of course,' Thomas said and dismounted.

The two men struggled with the lieutenant's body, and as William lifted him over the saddle of his horse, Thomas recognized his resolve. 'Your death will mean nothing, Captain,' he remarked.

'I'm sorry?' William said, his tone rejecting the observation.

'Your reaction to this man's demise might be your undoing,' Thomas remarked, and shrugged dispassionately.

'This is not about vengeance, Thomas,' William retorted, looking at Vittore's body draped before him. He mounted his horse. 'I only want my men freed.'

Down at the Ayaida's camp they were met by Sheikh Fahd and several other Bedouins. Marco came up at the rear and helped with Vittore. Once the lieutenant's body was laid on the ground, Sheikh Fahd addressed William.

'Again I ask you not to go,' he said. 'It is a foolish errand. Three men against an army?'

'One man,' William corrected him. 'Marco and Mr Richmond will stay here, if I may intrude on your hospitality further?'

'As you wish, they will be treated well,' Sheikh Fahd said. 'What of your fallen friend here?'

William stared down at Vittore, the sight of his shrouded body arousing barely contained fury. He wanted to scream, but he would save all that for the militia.

'I would be honoured if you would bury him here. Lieutenant Vittore was a man of the desert,' William replied, his voice breaking. 'It would be fitting for him to stay here permanently.'

'It will be done,' Sheikh Fahd promised.

William took a blanket, several canteens and a long coat from

his tent. He tied them to his horse, Marco looking on in anticipation. 'You will stay here under the sheikh's protection,' he said
to him as he packed.

'But I want to go with you.'

William seized his shoulders and shook them angrily. 'No,
Marco! No! You *will* stay here, by God!'

Marco looked at his uncle pleadingly.

'If you are to serve with me, you must take my orders. *Understood?*' William told him.

Marco could not refuse. 'I will stay.'

'Prove to me you are growing up, Marco. Show me that, and
I will consider letting you join the Order,' William said as he
swung himself up to the saddle.

Marco brightened, but only a little. He was not too green to
realize that his uncle was riding into peril and might not return.
He wanted to reach up, to give him a hug as he had when he
was younger. But the other part of him cried out to be a man,
and he reined in himself and his doubts.

William saluted Thomas with a casual hand, smiling faintly.
The Englishman simply shook his head but smiled also, looking
quite hopeless.

'Good luck, Captain,' Sheikh Fahd said. 'As I prayed to Allah
to bring you here, I will pray you are returned to us.'

William nodded and kicked in his heels to gallop along the
valley, leaving them all to watch the dust erupt and then settle
in his tracks.

△ II △

This was a disaster.

Even if he could somehow free the brothers – and William
did not see how it was possible – they would need rearming by
Sheikh Fahd. The company's weapons had been all but removed
and they would face the Rassis and the vampyres with sticks and

stones (though at least Engrin's gunpowder had been saved, hidden away in the Ayaida tents).

While his thoughts strayed to the tipping balance between success and failure, he continued to track the militia slowly, though the coming dark made progress slow. Then as twilight crept up behind him he heard a voice call his name.

William pulled up his horse and turned about to see two riders on the horizon. He brought up his spyglass and squinted, his tired sight causing the image to blur. When he focused again, he groaned, but smiled inside.

'*Thomas* . . .'

'You shouldn't have followed,' William said as he greeted the Englishman.

'You would go by yourself?' Thomas grinned.

'It isn't your risk.'

'Yet if you fail and are killed, what would *I* do, Captain? Stay for ever in that God-forsaken camp?' The Englishman laughed. 'I am a gentleman, not a tribesman. You are my escorts, as I see it. So any help I can provide will be repaid in kind.'

William was only too grateful for the assistance, yet as he looked over to Thomas's companion he felt suspicious. Hammid rode alongside Thomas, but he had done so reluctantly. If the timid Arab had his choice, he would have no doubt stayed with the Ayaida.

'Well, we should move out, don't you think?' William said finally, realizing that further argument would only waste more time.

'At night?' Thomas looked concerned. 'What about those vampyres?'

'They are the least of our worries, Thomas,' William said grimly. 'At least this way we can track our foe and gain a night's ride. They have a lead of almost a day.'

'What are we waiting for then?' Thomas enthused, and urged his horse onwards.

△ III △

To the east, the Ayaida camp roused itself as the sun came up. Marco woke to the sounds of tribesmen stirring. He sat up and put his arms around his legs, feeling terribly alone. With his uncle gone and the merchant Thomas following soon after, there was now no one he recognized, and no one who understood him.

Marco shuffled over to the tent flap and parted it. He felt like a pedestrian in a very busy market, just as removed from it all as when he had visited the bustling streets of Rome. No one took any notice of him, which was fine, but what would happen when he became thirsty or hungry? What then? Would he try to speak to these dark-skinned men? Or would he be forced to steal to survive?

Marco turned back inside the tent and ferreted for a canteen, but all were empty. Even the food that had been sent to their tent the evening before was reduced to crumbs. He groaned and sat down to think.

Presently the tent flap opened and a broad man entered. He looked down at Marco, and something he saw made him laugh. It was not a menacing sound, but it grew irritating and Marco felt belittled. He scowled up at the intruder.

The broad man clapped his hands, barked words into the air, and another man appeared. This one had a scar across his temple. In one hand was a sack which he tossed over to Marco. When he looked at it suspiciously, the broad man began laughing again and left the tent.

He opened the sack and was delighted to find food, some bread, meat and cheese, which was too creamy for his usual tastes, but he was hungry and ate it gladly. After he finished eating, he noticed a water-skin left by the curtain. Several thirsty gulps later, he relaxed again and lay back, watching the sun glint through the cloth above him.

Perhaps life in the camp was not so bad after all, he thought.

But while they might treat him well enough, he longed to be with his uncle, to fight at his side.

After dozing for a good hour, the food in his belly settling, Marco got to his feet and left the tent. He expected to find guards outside, but was amazed to see no one at all. With the entire camp open to him and nothing but freedom, he decided to explore.

The Ayaida camp was busy, far too busy to pay much attention to a single guest wandering among them. He smelled spices and cooking oils. Glancing inside the square tents as he passed by, Marco saw a woman breast-feeding a baby, men skinning sheep. Children were playing with their family's livestock. Songs seemed to flow from each home; melancholy songs.

Marco halted near the entrance of one simple tent made from goatskin and listened as a woman began singing something that sounded sad at first, but grew light-hearted. She was dressed in a long black gown over a bright orange dress, her face concealed by an embroidered veil. Marco wondered if it was a song of mourning, whether this woman had lost her husband, or even a child.

He stayed, enraptured, until the woman turned and ceased her song. She stared at Marco, and then bowed, gesturing for him to come inside, but now he felt uncomfortable, troubled by a stranger's readiness to welcome him inside her tent, and ashamed to have been caught spying on her. Marco smiled weakly, and shook his head. As the woman approached him, he bowed politely, turned and walked away.

After this encounter, he made for the enclosures where the company's horses were corralled. He found Brother Jericho's charger and began grooming him, the horse attentive to his strokes. Here Marco felt at home; here there was some semblance of normality.

Vittore's black stallion was stamping the ground, clearly upset, and Marco wondered if the animal sensed that its master was dead. He walked over to quieten the horse, which tossed its head back and forth before bowing solemnly to Marco's fingers.

He went on stroking its mane until he heard another sound, of stamping feet and quick explosive breaths, coming from behind the enclosure. He recognized that sound.

Marco patted the stallion's flank to assure him he wasn't going too far and rounded the enclosure to the point where the rear was surrounded by supply tents. Between the space of the tents and the fences was a gap several yards wide. In that gap was the source of what he'd heard: someone dressed head to toe in black, swinging a sword about them, advancing and retreating. The blade was short and narrow; it shone as it turned in the wielder's expert hands.

Watching the warrior were four young women, chattering to each other with words that Marco did not understand. They seemed distracted, not concentrating on the swordplay in front of them, and Marco found it odd they were not mesmerized as he was, by the blur and flash of steel cutting the air. He did not realize that he'd strayed from the shadows in the enclosure and was just a stride or two from the display.

One of the girls stopped speaking and pointed in alarm.

It was enough to halt the warrior. He lowered his sword and half-turned to Marco. Behind the veil, his eyes were narrow, elegant and young, and Marco was reminded of Marresca for a moment. Around his head was a black scarf that contained his hair and hid his nose, cheeks and lips. As he turned fully to Marco, the warrior loosened this head-dress and Marco watched as a mane of long black hair cascaded from it down to the shoulders. The warrior shook the last strands of hair and pulled the scarf completely away, to stare at Marco.

Marco was stunned. It was a woman who stood before him; a woman who had wielded the sword so gracefully that it transfixed him. He knew that women could fight (Aunt Adriana for one), but to see it done so . . .

'*Beautifully,*' he murmured, surprising himself by speaking his feelings aloud.

The girls listened and then fell about laughing, some saying words that were clearly just mocking him.

The woman walked over to Marco. She was a little taller than him and perhaps just a little older. She had deep brown eyes and flawless brown skin. While Marco had been gripped by her swordplay, he was now taken by her beauty, his eyes straying down from her face to her shoulders, the curve of her breasts, down to her waist.

The woman said something to Marco and began to smile. It was not so scornful as her friends, but deferential and perhaps inquisitive. She repeated herself again, but he did not understand.

Then she pointed at Marco and shrugged, opening a hand to him.

Marco looked down at it, speechless, transfixed, not knowing what he should do.

One of the girls standing nearby started shouting, and the woman turned at the sound of feet approaching. She looked to Marco and shook her head, pointing to the horses. Then she gave him a gentle push, urging him to leave, which he did eventually just before the first of Sheikh Fahd's bodyguards appeared.

He hid behind the nearest fence post and watched as the thickset man who had laughed at him in his tent raised his voice to the female warrior. The exchange was heated and the women were led away by other guards. Finally the female warrior lowered her head, petulantly wrenching herself from the restraints of a guard before marching away under the watchful eyes of Marco's morning visitor.

Marco wasn't sure what had just happened, nor who this female warrior was. Throughout the raised voices, the anger and reprimand, there was only one word he remembered; a word he believed was a name. Perhaps even the name of the woman in black.

Jamillah.

△ IV △

Hammid sipped from the water-skin, eager for more before Thomas snatched it away. He slumped in defeat in the saddle, as sweat trickled down his temple.

They had ridden for much of the day, following the never-ending tracks that did not break for rest. Just like themselves, the militia had ridden all night.

'At least the hoof prints are still fresh,' Thomas said, trying to lighten the mood. 'Maybe they're not far away.'

William nodded wearily, but he did not truly believe they were any closer to the army. The desert surrounded them and it seemed the whole world had turned to sand.

Hammid cupped his hand over his eyes and then began to gabble something, at first in an undertone, then louder, standing up in his saddle.

'What is it?' William asked as the Englishman pulled his horse about. Thomas angled to their left down the steep side of a dune and galloped up the slope of the next one, eyes trained to where Hammid was pointing. William followed at a canter. At the top of the ridge, Thomas gestured to a shape in the sky.

'See?' he shouted. 'A bird, Captain! We must be near a farm or a village . . .'

'Or an oasis?' William said eagerly.

They rode to the peak of the next dune, and there William almost sobbed with relief. The bird had indeed flown from an oasis. It lay a few miles distant in the dip between several giant dunes and surrounded by large boulders. Among them, along the shore of the water, a body of men had made camp.

Soldiers.

'The militia?' Thomas ventured.

William pulled out his spyglass and stilled his breathing as he focused on the encampment, hoping for some sign that these were indeed the militia they were tracking. As he focused on sentries dressed in dusty robes and armed with rifles and swords, he found nothing. He swept the site and still there was nothing, just a camp of militiamen. If his monks were being held prisoner there, there was no sign of them.

He turned to Thomas. 'I can't see them.'

'It will be night soon. We should search the camp now,' Thomas suggested, restless at the thought of waiting any further.

Ignoring the advice, William lifted the spyglass again and looked harder, studying every horse, every tent, even the packs and bundles half-hidden in the shade of boulders. Then he went to the guards, studying their clothes, their faces, their . . .

'Rifles,' William said and a smile peeled across his lips.

'Rifles?' Thomas said.

'Would the militia have access to firearms like a Baker rifle?' he said, more to himself than to Thomas.

The Englishman stroked his chin. 'Militia are usually poorly armed. How should I put it? Cannon fodder.' Thomas was curt but objective.

William was pleased. The militia had taken great pains to hide the presence of the brothers, yet in their greed they had plundered their weapons, and this was the signal he needed. 'They *are* here,' he said as he snapped the spyglass shut.

△ V △

A gully curved from behind one arm of the dune in the direction of the oasis. William and Thomas dismounted and led their horses down to it. Here, out of sight of the camp, they left Hammid, fearing that so devoted a coward would only give them away. The oasis was ringed by rocky outcrops which provided adequate cover at the perimeter, but the nearer approach was in the open. They tethered the horses in the shade of some boulders, and made their way on foot to the edge of the oasis. Here they hid in some shade and waited.

Thomas looked up into the brilliant sky, squinting as the sun

250

moved overhead to burn the grains of sand barely inches from the tips of their boots. 'I admire your tenacity,' he whispered.

William made no reply, his mind set on other things.

'Coming here to rescue your men – it is admirable,' the Englishman continued. He looked down at the empty water-skin that lay between them. They had given Hammid the half-full skin. William planned to fill the empty one at the oasis.

'Do you think Hammid will run?' William asked.

Thomas smiled. 'Hammid is a coward. It's a fact we both recognize. But he will stay as I ordered.'

'You sound quite sure of someone you can't trust.'

'Oh I trust him, Captain,' Thomas said confidently. 'I trust his greed. The prospect of reward will keep him loyal.'

'Then why leave him out there?' William said, gesturing back to the dunes behind them.

'Because he screams like a girl whenever there's danger, Captain. A scream that can travel for miles.' Thomas's chuckle was an empty sound that gave William no comfort.

'Cold?' Thomas said as he watched William chafing his arms.

'It's cooler in the shade, and I'm tired.'

'You should sleep,' Thomas suggested. 'You're no good to your men if you need rest. I can keep watch.'

'Well, if you insist,' William said gratefully, reaching to take the empty skin of water. 'Maybe after I get this filled.' He winked at the English merchant and left their hiding place behind the rock, creeping around the other side and down a narrow track that wound between small rocks and some stunted bushes.

Thomas peeked around the corner with a mixture of delight and fascination as he watched the captain slip like a cobra between two points where sentries had been posted. They didn't see his shadow sneak by rock and sand, and then Thomas too lost sight of him.

William returned nearly an hour later, his clothes spilling sand, his forehead dripping with sweat. He was smiling broadly and clutching a full skin of water.

'I wouldn't have believed it,' Thomas said and took the bloated skin from his hands. 'I was beginning to feel anxious.'

'It was no easy task; the camp is well fortified. I got as close as the horses. While they were led to water, I sneaked in,' William said. He breathed out and then relaxed.

'So you filled our skin while the horses drank?'

William shook his head. 'Look at it,' he said.

Thomas looked down at the skin, and then looked closer. 'This is not ours,' he said finally.

'I traded our empty skin for a full one,' William said, satisfied. 'They will think nothing of it. Perhaps think that one of their men was too lazy to refill it, but they won't know I've been inside their camp.'

'What else did you find?'

'They have around one hundred and fifty men. Most are in tents, but there are about two dozen sentries, all armed. I think the brothers are at the far side. I saw some cages there with men shut inside.

'Their weapons are being stored in the centre of the camp, though they've pillaged what they could.' William chuckled. Thomas could not see the funny side. William held up a hand to explain. 'Our weapons are beyond them, Thomas. I saw one fellow stab himself in the thumb with a throwing star.'

'Throwing star?' Thomas asked, bewildered.

'One of our more specialized weapons.'

The Englishman sighed. 'You really *are* the strangest monks I've ever come across.' He passed the water back to William, who declined, and Thomas spoke again. 'It may be none of my business, Captain, but what exactly *is* your mission here?'

William glanced at him. 'I'm sorry, I cannot say. Only that should we succeed tonight, I am to lead these men into the heart of the Sinai with Sheikh Fahd.'

'Are you treasure-hunters, Captain?'

'Treasure-hunters of a *sort*.'

'I knew it!' Thomas applauded.

William leaned back against a rock while he planned the

brothers' rescue. Then the short desert evening came, and he thought on other things, not least his still unfinished letter home. He thought about Adriana, about Marco, stranded at the Bedouin camp, and finally tailed away. His eyes closed while the sun fled the desert and the cold of night closed in.

△ VI △

William woke with the feeling that hands were running over his body. He scuttled backwards suddenly, his spine colliding with the rock behind and jolting his eyes wide open.

'Ah . . . Awake, Captain?' Thomas grinned, sitting opposite. A sliver of moon shone above. 'Bad dreams?'

William instinctively moved his own hand down his jacket to his hips. He nodded, still in a daze.

'I would have woken you myself,' Thomas began. 'You slept for a long time.'

'Then you *should* have woken me,' William reproached, his throat desiccated. He coughed, and ran his tongue around his dry lips, tasting salt and sand.

Thomas passed him the skin of water. It was half-empty already, the Englishman having indulged his thirst. William took a long gulp and then splashed a little on his face. Why conserve water when he needed all of his resources?

William cricked his neck and rubbed at his moistened face as the dregs of his dream dissolved. He rolled onto his knees and stood up to peer around the edge of their hiding place. In the distance the guards were moving.

'They're changing,' he murmured. 'This is the night watch.'

'That will make it harder to sneak in, will it not?' Richmond asked.

William nodded. 'But the chink in their armour remains.'

Thomas's silence was a question.

'Where I managed to crawl earlier on . . . If I can get to the horses, then I can divert their attentions elsewhere,' William said.

'And that is when I try for the cages you spoke of?'

William turned about. 'No. You will stay here,' he said.

'Captain Saxon! I believe you are asking me to . . .' Thomas said angrily.

'I'm asking you to keep your head down. I might need you if I manage to get back here,' William told him. 'But if I am caught, I will surely be executed, possibly tortured. You are a civilian, Mr Richmond. I cannot lead you into trouble. You will stay here, sir, until I return.'

'In the night?'

'In the night,' William confirmed.

'Do not be long, Captain. I still remember what dangers the night holds,' Thomas told him as William loosened his jacket and pulled it away, leaving only his shirt. He tied his sword to his back.

'I won't be,' he replied, and slipped away into the encroaching shadows.

William crawled on his elbows along the darker edge of that narrow track between the rocks and sand. Where the sand fell away to the foot of a supine boulder, he slid down the slope until his left foot was flat against the rock, and crept further towards the oasis, invisible to the sentries above him. Their outlines glowed from the campfires beyond and William noticed how casual they looked – alert, yes, but not expecting trouble.

They're complacent, he thought. They could afford to be. Their quarry were under armed guard now, so what did they have to worry about? William would make them pay for their smugness. He was not about to slit their throats – he was no random assassin – but should he succeed in freeing his men, these sentries would almost certainly incur the wrath of Muhammad Ali for letting them escape.

At the edge of the rock, he hunkered down and saw the other boulder a few yards away. Clenching his teeth, he breathed in and dashed towards it, soundless as he got to his target and slid quickly to the ground, into a shallow hollow and then past it.

Here lay a patch of tall grass, thick and green at the roots but dried at the tips. It was coarse, and while William used it to screen him he made sure not to disturb it. At the edge of the grass was a short track of dirt and then another patch of grass that led down to the water. He dashed across it and lay flat again, keeping his head below the level of the lowest stalk of grass. There he waited, breathing quietly as he listened to the sounds of the camp. There was joviality, sounds of laughing and singing.

William heard movement close by. He crawled back into the grass and held his breath as he spied a militiaman looking about where he'd just been. For a moment he thought he might have been discovered, but the Arab only pulled aside his baggy robes to urinate into the grass. William did not move, and could only pray that the fellow did not piss on him. The stench made him grimace, but he was grinning as the Arab walked away. William watched him leave, and breathed more deeply.

Praying that his luck held, he turned about and crept through the tall grass until he arrived at the lake's edge. The water rippled under the evening breeze, stretching some fifty yards to the heart of the camp. At the far side, by the edge, under a stand of palm trees, was the Order's wagon of weapons, the dwarf-cannon still perched upon it, half covered by a blanket.

To skirt around the lake would take him past several tents of militia, the horses, and four sentries who were standing around just chatting. William narrowed his eyes. Turning to the sky he saw the moon shining down towards the camp. From the opposite side, its reflection would highlight each ripple. There was some movement on the lake, but not enough. He must wait for a stray cloud to cover the moon and turn the water black.

A silent wait, and finally a cloud. He seized his chance and crawled to the water's edge. Like a hunting crocodile, he eased into the liquid. The chill made him shiver, but he lowered his body into it up to the chin.

Swimming out from the shore with slow easy strokes, he looked around and no one was watching. William took a deep breath and submerged completely, leaving only an eddy in the water.

△ VII △

Thomas sat and waited. He could do little else, even though it was clear to him that if Captain Saxon failed, then so did he.

There was a sound of movement nearby and Thomas shuffled further into the shadows, making himself as small as he could so that a passer-by would simply see darkness and nothing more.

'*Hiding are we?*' came a voice.

Thomas froze. He closed his eyes and cursed . . .

. . . And then the curse became a laugh as he straightened up. 'You took your time getting here,' Thomas said as a figure emerged into the moonlight. He was quite tall, dressed in black with long red hair. His skin was pale and deathly, but his expression was grimly good-humoured.

'Where is he?' Baron Horia asked casually.

'He has gone to free his men,' Thomas replied.

'And you didn't think it wise to follow him?'

'He asked me not to,' Thomas replied derisively.

Baron Horia stroked back his red mane and walked out to the edge of the rocks, planting a heeled boot on the nearest one to stare out into the night and the oasis beyond, lit by many glowing fires.

'He will fail, won't he?' Thomas said.

Baron Horia shrugged. 'He is Captain William Saxon, a man of infinite surprises. There have been many times when the Count thought he might fail, yet still he survives, while many of my brethren have perished.' The vampyre returned to Thomas and his smile twisted. 'This time, we want him to *succeed.*'

'And if he does, the plan continues?'

'It does,' Baron Horia replied. 'This man and his rabble are close to discovering the Hoard of Mhorrer, and we must let him achieve that aim. Only when the Rassis Cult is destroyed will I act.'

Thomas nodded his understanding, only to pause and frown as though there was something neither had considered. 'Why would he succeed where you failed?' he dared to ask.

Baron Horia glared. 'Because they are prepared,' he snarled.

'But you are vampyre . . .'

Baron Horia seized Thomas by the throat and lifted him a foot from the ground. '*And we were not ready!*' he growled. 'When we assaulted the Valley of Fire, the Rassis already knew we were coming. Of my coven of nine, two were shot from the air as we approached and their heads cleaved by those who hid below. Three more were destroyed when we attacked the summit. There wasn't even time to loose a daemon upon them. Dahlquist tried and perished doing so, and I almost lost a hand retrieving the Scarimadaen. It was a *disaster.*' Baron Horia found he was choking Thomas and he relaxed his grip, letting the Englishman fall to his knees and claw for breath.

'You doubt me, I see. But would you like me to show you how *efficient* I can be?' Baron Horia warned his gasping acolyte. 'As I did with Charles Greynell? He was in agony for quite some time, you know.'

'Not . . . necessary . . .' Thomas bowed his head.

The vampyre strolled a few steps and then stopped. 'Only Ileana, Racinet and I remain, Thomas Richmond. Alone we cannot defeat the Rassis. But with Saxon and his monks, not to mention the savages helping him, we may yet succeed.'

'Have you *seen* these monks of the Order, my Baron?' Thomas said behind awkward breaths. 'They are a shadow of an army. Gaunt and thin. They haven't had a decent meal in days. They could hardly defeat you, let alone these Rassis you speak of.'

'They may seem weak on the surface; their skin may be pale, their bodies slender, but their wits are sharp, and they are all muscle and sinew.' Horia licked his white lips and smiled. 'They are much stronger than you know. And besides, I have no choice. If Saxon does not defeat the Rassis, then no one will.'

'And if he does succeed?' Thomas said, rubbing his bruised neck.

'If he does, Thomas, then we will ambush the survivors and take the Hoard for ourselves,' Baron Horia vowed. 'Something I should have planned all along. I was foolish to think we could defeat the Rassis by ourselves. My master had failed to do so on a number of occasions. Even those winged menaces the Dar'uka have not succeeded. Does that not tell you enough?'

'Are the Rassis *that* powerful?' Thomas asked.

Baron Horia turned to the Englishman, the surface of his yellow eyes seething with light. 'Oh yes, Mr Richmond. They are the stuff of human nightmares.'

△ VIII △

William was alone in the black abyss. Occasionally his feet would kick against the bed of the lake, but the sensation was of tumbling and then floating, with nothing but darkness about him. Apart from the occasional sandbank, the water of the oasis was deeper than he had expected. He strove to swim further, but after a few yards his hands only clawed at the gloom and the cold was constricting his chest. He lifted himself and swam shallow, careful not to leave strong ripples on the surface.

Above him in the silence was nothing. It was night up there, and only the occasional flicker to either side reminded him he was swimming between the campfires by the lake's edge.

William paused for a moment to breathe and take note of his surroundings, before he submerged once again.

He swam towards the far bank where the glow of the fires was weakest and shadow prevailed. There was no one watching the lake; the sentries he spied were talking amongst themselves, unsuspecting. He reached the sandy shore, his knees resting in the silt. It sank as he put his weight upon it, and as he knelt the water rose up to his chin again.

On either side were patches of tall grass with tents nearby. To his right two guards stood by a fire. They were laughing and joking, their gestures grand and playful, but something in their voices told William they were describing something malicious. One man made jabbing movements, then punched and kicked out as if at a target on the ground.

William felt suddenly desperate as it dawned on him that they were describing the torture of his own men. He felt his top lip curl angrily and his body flushed with fury.

Another sound caught his attention: footfalls directly ahead. In front, only yards away, was the wagon of weapons and munitions. William had first planned a diversion by stampeding the horses, but seeing the cannon again had provided a better idea.

The footfalls he had heard came from another guard who was singing a strange off-key song while he paced around the wagon. This man was in his way.

William eased out of the water and crawled up the bank, flattening himself against the sand. He waited for the sentry to turn and retrace his steps, before he raced quickly across the tall grass to the side of the wagon. Placing his fingers on its timber sides, he was comforted to touch it again, so essential to their mission. If his suspicions of the Rassis were correct, he would need all the weapons they could lay their hands on, but could he possibly liberate their cannon, and would it be worth the risk?

No horses stood nearby, and it would take some minutes to hitch one to the wagon – minutes they would not have in the heat of the rescue. The choice was clear: *the cannon or the men*.

It was no choice at all.

He waited until the sentry turned about and walked to the left. High above, the cloud crept away from the moon and lit the oasis with silver. It caught William out in the open. Cursing his carelessness, he fell to his knees and rolled beneath the wagon. He waited for a call of alarm, but nothing broke the jocular chatter and the sound of insects clicking in the night.

William crawled to the rear of the carriage. The sentry was marching to the front, his pace regular and monotonous. William rose to his feet and flattened himself against the back of the carriage. He listened to the sound of steady footsteps, pulled out his sword and waited.

When the sentry appeared, William moved close and swung his sword down, the butt connecting hard with the man's head. William caught him as he fell, then rolled him under the wagon and out of sight before taking his weapon, a poorly kept and antiquated musket which he slung over one shoulder. He would check it was loaded later, but first he needed a diversion.

He looked about quickly, spotted no other guards, and climbed into the wagon, ducking under the canvas sheet that half hid its contents. He scanned the floor of the carriage looking for one of the small crates of munitions required to serve the cannon – no easy task in the poor light.

The dwarf-cannon was a piece of ingenuity taken from the Far East and tempered by the skills of Villeda's engineers. It used gunpowder and a wad, but the loading took seconds rather than minutes, and the ball was the size of a fist and would splinter into shrapnel within a dozen yards of the barrel. From Lieutenant Vittore's description of the cannon in action, William knew how devastating it could be, and again he thought of the harm it would cause the militia. He turned the barrel so it was pointing over the water. At that range the shot would explode harmlessly over it, not hurting a soul, but doing a good job of scaring these sleeping fools out of their skins.

Eventually he found a crate of shot and levered it open with the hilt of his sword. Inside it the balls were packed in wood shavings. Each one felt light, considering its size and purpose, and William was reminded that it was the scatter effect, not the range of the cannon, that made it so effective. He pushed the crate aside with his boot and looked up from under the canvas to check his bearings again. Then he dived back under and rummaged for powder and wads.

After much fumbling in the dark, his hands discovered the basket of wads, and he scrabbled for the keg of powder. He was running out of time. In his haste, he pushed some more crates aside. One of them toppled with a crash, and he swore quietly. The one keg he was looking for was not there.

Pausing to calm himself, he breathed out and peered desperately down into the darkness at his feet. Without the keg of powder his plan was useless. Cursing again, he straightened up and pushed the canvas back just a little, hoping to use the moon to light his search.

As the canvas shifted he found the barrel of a musket pointing straight at him from a couple of feet away, and next to it another.

William froze at the cocking of the flintlocks, and heard the heavy beating of his heart. He closed his eyes for a moment, then rose up slowly and pushed away the canvas, holding his arms above his head. He was struck suddenly by the sweet smell of something cooking far away, the sound of laughter around a campfire, and a bird calling in the distance. He was hungry, tired and he could do with a drink.

William was tugged from the wagon to land sprawling in the sand. His belt was cut away from him as he struggled, winded by the fall, before someone kicked him in the belly. He felt pain rip through him. Another kick sent him sprawling across the sand and blood flooded his mouth. He put a hand to his jaw before it was pulled away, and then he was yanked onto his feet by his hair. He staggered, but felt many hands upon him pulling him in opposite directions.

Finally one man took control and rammed his musket into William's kidneys, causing him to cry out, before he was pushed and dragged away.

After being hauled across the camp, tripped, kicked and punched in the process, William was hauled into a tent and thrown to the ground. There was a rug there, simple but soft compared to the coarse sand, and his fingers reached out to touch it, calming himself and letting the pain of his beatings drain away.

As he concentrated hard to lock the hurt in the back of his mind, he became aware of a voice, proud, mocking and clearly pleased by something. He peered up and found the leader of the militia, a man older than William by a few years. He stared down at William with dark eyes, edged with red veins like a drunkard's, although his expression and posture were far from inebriated.

Haidar viewed the infidel with contempt. 'Ignorant bastard,' he growled down at William in Arabic. '*All* infidels are ignorant.'

The guards that had brought William nodded in solidarity.

'This is the scourge of our people,' Haidar announced, and spat on the ground in front of William. 'They come from overseas to subjugate us, to take our wealth, our women, and then destroy us!'

'*Kill him!*' snarled one of the guards.

Haidar looked up at the outburst, but far from being angry, he looked pleased. 'Yes. Yes. And we will. But not before I make an example of this one. He has come to set his people free. Was that your plan, infidel?'

William looked up. He didn't understand the words, but the tone was far from friendly.

'We will see,' Haidar smiled coldly. 'We will torture him, and then find the truth. And then if we cannot find the truth, we will torture his friends some more!'

The guards nodded, laughing quickly. William recognized their intent. He was in dire trouble, and although he wasn't bound, he didn't know if he had the strength to escape, outnumbered as he was inside the tent, and without a weapon. As he knelt on the soft rug, blood dripping from his swollen lip, William realized that his only hope of getting through this mess alive lay with Thomas Richmond.

CHAPTER FOURTEEN

The Battle at Bastet

△ I △

William stared at the floor, waiting calmly now. The pain from the kicks and punches had grown numb. As the rhythm of his heart began to slow, he felt a sense of detachment. He regarded his fate lucidly. As the minutes passed he knew that Thomas was not going to save him. How could he? What could one civilian do?

In the past it was luck that had intervened; and in recent months it was Marresca who had made the difference. 'Where are you now?' he found himself asking aloud. At that moment he would have given anything for a mere fraction of the Dar'uka's strength.

Haidar looked down at William with scorn.

'What should we do with him?' one of the guards said.

Haidar tightened a red sash about his waist, then caressed the gilding of his sword. 'We make an example of him tonight. The Europeans once hanged their enemies, then cut them open before drawing their guts out as punishment. I think we will do the same to this one. Then we will parade his head to his friends.'

The guards murmured in agreement, their eyes resting on William voraciously. They wanted blood. So far they had been content with beating the men in grey. This time there was promise of death.

'Take a rope and bring Khalifa,' Haidar ordered. 'He has the hands of a surgeon. Let Khalifa remove his guts while the infidel still breathes.'

One of the guards bowed and left the tent. The others swooped down and held William fast where he lay. William looked up at Haidar and spat a glob of bloody phlegm on the Arab's boot.

Haidar made an almost effeminate moan of outrage and his hand went to the handle of his sword. 'I'll cut you, dog!' he shouted out. But his words were overlaid by an inhuman howl of rage that sounded for an instant far away, but suddenly wailed across the camp. The guards looked about nervously as a dreadful silence followed.

For many seconds it felt as though the entire oasis was holding its breath . . .

. . . *Then the shouting and screaming began*. The musket fire, the chaos, the running feet, the cries of dying men . . .

The guards were rattled. Only Haidar responded. He grabbed William by the neck and lifted him up, shouting into his face so that spittle rained on his cheeks. 'You are doing this!' he ranted. 'You have brought fire upon my men! Tell me, who are you?'

William stared back at him, meeting his gaze resolutely. He did not fear, and he knew what was coming for them. 'The Devil is here. And I will soon be dead,' he told the leader of the militia, 'but so will you . . .'

Haidar's anger grew and he let William drop to the ground. He did not understand William's words but saw the defiance. 'I will not wait,' he shouted and drew his scimitar. 'The infidel dies now. Pull his arms back and show me his neck!'

William saw the sword begin to rise and he looked down, his mind filling with what would be lost: the company, Marco, Adriana. For a moment it didn't seem to matter, as if this was the fate that luck had denied so often over the years.

The blade swung down. Time to die.

△ II △

The militia knew nothing. No one saw the sentry's blood being spilt. No one saw the vampyres swoop upon him, holding him tight before slashing open his wrists, his blood flowing down upon the Scarimadaen positioned before him in the sand.

The daemon's spirit burst through the sentry's body, warping flesh and bone out of all resemblance; then with a roar it rampaged down the bank of the lake, its burning hide splashing across the water, leaving a trail of steam.

Then . . . *Then*, the militia knew. They could do nothing else but face this shrieking force of preternature. With each yard covered, the daemon brought pandemonium. A tent was torn apart, horses cut loose and left to stampede, guards disembowelled or torn limb from limb. One sentry had bravely leapt upon its back, but one swing of the creature's scaly arm sent him through the air and into the nearest fire.

A few of the militia aimed their muskets, but the leaden balls made no impact on the beast. The survivors of the first few minutes' carnage fled headlong into the desert, screaming and sobbing unintelligibly as the daemon spread havoc behind them. Yet flight brought no protection; the bald vampyre, Racinet, struck down the panicked militiamen, his half-moon flail winnowing souls in the darkness, slaying one, then two and then a third desperate runner, who abandoned first their posts and then their lives.

The female vampyre, Ileana, swept through the air after launching herself from the highest dune. She skimmed overhead, her arms outstretched with two long daggers in her hands, delivering swift deep cuts amongst the scattering soldiers with a 'snick-snick' sound. None of them knew what was happening, only that random countrymen were falling to the sandy floor, blood gushing from neck or stomach wounds. The night was a dance of death. Each soldier who fell, each man who perished, saw as his last a veil of night descending followed by the swift wet rip of steel through flesh. And at the centre, the daemon continued its onslaught, butchering all who came its way, hacking, severing, shovelling up horse and man to toss them into the air like rag dolls.

Baron Horia looked on with satisfaction. The defeat by the Rassis had blunted his appetite, yet now that blood was flowing, the thirst returned. The daemon was wreaking havoc across the oasis. It would burn itself out in time, but by then William Saxon's gaolers would be no more.

The battle was bloody, and terribly one-sided.

△ III △

Thomas sprinted through the confusion, skirting the daemon's path. He ran past several tents, and in one the occupants came at him with their swords. He cut them down with ease. Ahead he saw men leaving the largest tent in the centre of the camp, and it struck him that perhaps he was too late, and Captain Saxon was already dead.

A militiaman crashed into him and both men fell. As the other man rose, Thomas slashed him across the arm and then grabbed him by his robe and swung him down. 'Where is the infidel?' he shouted.

The man looked up in agony and terror.

'The tent. Haidar's tent!' Thomas shouted again, and followed the gesture that pointed to the largest tent.

'Much obliged,' he drawled in English, and thrust his sword upwards into the man's ribcage. He made for the tent again as more musket-fire echoed about him.

It is possible that when Thomas entered the tent he did not fully grasp the scene that faced him. Had he paused to consider, everything might have turned sour, his master's plans included. Had he been rash, there would have been no escape for any of the monks of the company.

When he entered he saw Haidar's blade fall upon William. He swung his own sword upwards in the instant, an arcing slash that cut through Haidar's wrist. The scimitar fell to the floor a fraction short, shaving hairs from William's bowed head, but little else. Haidar stumbled back and saw his wrist spurt blood across his fine rug.

Seconds had passed. William's two guards turned dumbstruck to Thomas, but he cut them down, cleaving one across the face, and spinning to thrust his sword into the stomach of the second.

William opened his eyes and stared down at the large scimitar and the hand that still held it. Firmly and swiftly, he was pulled to his feet.

'Good, you're not dead,' Thomas grunted as he slashed William's bonds.

'Thomas?' William choked. 'I only hoped . . .'

'As did I, Captain. As did I,' Thomas replied and handed William a sword – it was one of the brothers' sabres.

Haidar was rolling about in agony, jetting blood across the tent and himself. Thomas marched over and put the side of his sword against his neck. 'Shall I kill this one?'

Haidar stopped screaming and was now looking up in terror at both men. He gestured wildly, sobbing for his life.

William felt sickened. He wanted the bastard to suffer, for beating him, for killing Vittore and imprisoning his men. But the sounds of battle outside brought different thoughts. 'No, we need him alive,' he replied.

Thomas couldn't see why.

'Our enemies are with us,' William told him. 'Those sounds are daemonic.'

Thomas recoiled, drawing his sword back as though the mere mention of these creatures evaporated his courage. He stepped away from the tent flap. Haidar scuttled into the corner of the tent and whimpered.

'What did you see?' William demanded.

'Very little,' Thomas whispered, trembling. 'I was inside the camp before the first shots were fired. Then it turned to madness.'

'We have to free my men, Thomas. This fellow can help us.' William jerked a thumb towards the snivelling Haidar.

There was a trample of footsteps and three men rushed into the tent, all of them armed. They froze at the sight of the infidels. No one moved, until Haidar cried out and the oldest of the Arabs stepped forward, a lithe-looking man with two swords at his back. He drew one and stepped towards William.

'Quickly, Thomas, tell them!' William said, raising his sword in defence. 'Tell them we know who's attacking.'

The oldest man raised his sword. His eyes glared and William took guard, but he felt weak and his sword-arm was heavy. He could defend himself, but he wasn't sure for how long.

As Thomas translated William's words, the militiaman paused, surprised to hear an infidel speak their language. It was that pause William sought to exploit. He could have lunged in, could have thrust his sword into the man's belly, but there was a greater enemy. 'Tell them we're not to blame,' he added, 'and we can help.'

One of the other militia spoke fast and then pointed at William, bellowing with rage.

'Tell them we didn't destroy Babel's,' William persisted, words flying out of his mouth in desperation. 'It was . . .' Before he could finish there was a catastrophic roar and the tent collapsed about them to the sound of snapping poles and cries of anguish. William was dragged to the floor and turned by chance to see the militia's commander skewered by several talons through the stomach. Haidar shrieked over and over until blood rose in his throat and spilled over his lips.

William rolled away from the daemon as it shredded the Arab into pieces, the tent-cloth staining black. All was gloom and shadow until William pushed past the last layers of tent, grabbed a discarded spear and escaped into the dark of night.

Thomas was struggling out as William ran. He too scrambled for safety as the daemon rose from under the tattered fabric which had ignited and was starting to burn away. Now the blackened bulk of the creature emerged, smoking and animated with embers that spat and danced across its skin.

Thomas and William stared, the former in utter terror, the latter in awe.

William was certain it was the daemon they had faced at Babel's, yet its head had shrunk and the mouth hung open to belch smoke and ashes that sped like tiny fireflies into the air. It shook what was left of Haidar from its enormous paws, and bent over to delve in the tent for the others. It caught a guard who was twisted up in a curtain and tossed him high into the air and out of sight. The second guard was crawling away when the daemon stamped on his head with a sickening crack.

The last man, the oldest, pushed himself from the wreckage of poles and fabric and stared up at the daemon as it dropped its head towards him. It opened its jaws and the man was engulfed in smoke and the stink of sulphur.

Despite the pain raking his body, William found himself running towards the militiaman. He swung his spear to waist height and then shouted at the monster a few feet before he reached it. The daemon lifted its head just as William's thrust drove the spear into its mouth. It seemed to choke, and the spear was swallowed inside a spray of sparks and blue fire. The creature's bulk vanished for that moment in a huge funnel of smoke and with growls of hoarse discomfort. In the confusion, William grabbed the militiaman by the collar and hauled him out from under the flailing talons.

Half dragged, half stumbling, both men lurched away into the shadows where Thomas was hiding.

'Damned foolish!' the Englishman chided.

'We need every ally, Thomas!' William shouted. 'Ask his name.'

Thomas did so, but at first the man would not reply, simply staring at William with little comprehension.

Finally he spoke. 'His name is Khalifa. And he thanks you for saving his life.'

'Tell him he can thank me later,' William replied. 'I need my men freed *and* our weapons, or we'll all die from this creature!'

Khalifa nodded, pulling himself upright, the ordeal leaving little mark upon him. That same dangerous determination in his eyes had returned. He gestured to the rear of the camp where the fighting was less, and spoke with frantic speed.

'He'll send a man to free them,' Thomas translated, surprised at the turn of events. 'He wants to know what that creature is and how to kill it.'

'No time to explain,' William answered. 'We should worry about the vampyres, Thomas. They unleashed the daemon and I doubt they'll be far away. Tell Khalifa to gather his men and shoot anything that comes at them on foot or on the wing. We'll deal with the daemon ourselves.'

As Khalifa dashed away, William bent down to take a discarded sword from the sand. Its previous owner had fled, and probably died. But William would not run, he would not cower, and he would fight to the death.

△ IV △

There were three cages. Each one had barely room for five or six, yet into each were crammed over a dozen brothers of the order. When William got to them, all the rage swelled up into his chest and he ran the last few steps until his hands gripped the bars of their prison. 'We're here! We're here!' he kept telling them. 'Are you harmed? Is Peruzo there?'

'Here . . .' came a faint reply from the third cage. William went over to the hand extended through the bars. He took it and held it.

'Are you hurt?' he asked.

'A couple of bruises,' Peruzo said. 'There are others in worse condition. They haven't fed us and they kept us short of water.'

'Bastards!' William growled. 'I will free you all, I promise.'

'They . . . They beat some of the brothers . . . *Badly*,' Peruzo began.

William could not speak.

'Brother Casper is blind,' Peruzo said miserably. 'They burnt out his eyes when he would not talk.'

William gripped the bars tightly, as though with all his rage he might pull them apart with his bare hands.

'Others were tortured. I think Brother Gregory has died. We cannot rouse him.'

William turned away, tears pricking his eyes. 'Open the cages, you bastards! Open these bloody cages now!' he screamed into the night.

Khalifa loomed out of the smoke with another militiaman, keys in his hands. As they approached, William snarled at Khalifa, who appeared unmoved, before he snatched the keys from the shaking militiaman and shoved him to the ground. The Arab scurried off to find a hiding place as William tried the keys to the padlock of Peruzo's cage, cursing in Italian, English and any language that came to mind as he babbled words of utter rage.

At last the padlock opened and William hurled it away, tugging the door open. He helped out Peruzo who wobbled on his feet. 'Can you walk?'

'I think so,' Peruzo replied.

'Help the others,' William said as he went to the next cage. He unlocked it and then went to the following cage, all the while shouting words of support to his men.

Behind him Thomas watched with admiration, stealing glances at Khalifa, who looked wary that these freed men might soon take their revenge upon him. William and the several monks whose strength remained were laying out the wounded. One of them fetched water. Six men were in such bad shape that they hardly seemed able to walk, let alone fight.

Brother Casper, though blind, would not hear of it. 'I can fight well enough as long as someone tells me where the enemy is!' he yelled indignantly.

William tried to calm him, but understood his frustration.

'My weapons!' he shouted at Thomas, but it was more to the man called Khalifa. 'Tell him I want my weapons back! *Now!*'

Khalifa pointed to the wagon nearest the water. William remembered the dwarf-cannon, but didn't recall other weaponry.

'What about our rifles?' he demanded.

Khalifa shrugged when Thomas asked.

'Bastard!' William spat at the Arab. 'The throwing stars, the knives . . . Tell him, Thomas . . . *Now!*' William seethed; they were getting nowhere. He beckoned to Peruzo. 'Get every man who can fight over to the dwarf-cannon. Tell them to scour the oasis for weapons. Anything they can get their hands on. We can reclaim our own weapons later.'

'What are we facing?' Peruzo asked.

'At least one daemon, and almost certainly vampyres.'

'It will be done,' Peruzo said and trudged back to the monks who waited by the cages.

'Thomas? Get this—' William began, but his effort to find an insult fit for Khalifa came out as a growl. 'Just send him back to his men. Let them fight the vampyres alone. We'll help when I see fit.'

Thomas sent Khalifa away and waited. 'Where should I be?'

William regarded the Englishman for a moment. He handled a sword well enough, but this was a daemon they were fighting. 'Go with him.'

'But, Captain . . .'

'Make sure they don't do anything stupid, Thomas. If they can occupy the vampyres long enough, it will give us more time,' William explained.

Thomas reluctantly followed Khalifa to the periphery of the oasis, looking over his shoulder at the men making ready for battle.

William addressed his troops. 'This has been rough, and there is worse to come. You have suffered greatly and I would not ask more of your courage if our mission did not demand it. Our enemies have attacked us at a time when they think we are at our weakest. We must prove them wrong. We must show them there will never be a perfect moment to attack the men of Saint Sallian. We are men of the Order. This is what we have trained for.'

The monks nodded, galvanizing themselves.

'There is a daemon out there, and we *can* bring it down,' William insisted. 'We only need a plan. And I have one.'

△ V △

Brothers Ricardo, Paldini and Adams scrambled into the wagon and tugged away the canvas that covered the cannon. Fortunately, the gun was already aimed in the direction of battle. Looking out from the deck of the wagon the brothers noted flames shooting up around the camp, one conflagration totally out of control.

In the shadows, figures dashed about in panic as something huge and baleful lumbered after them. Shriek after shriek pierced the air as these men were torn apart along a path that was coming closer.

The brothers stationed themselves in a perimeter that stretched not far from the water's edge down two flanks, leaving open the way to the wagon. Peruzo marshalled the men, those few who had found muskets at the front, while those with hand weapons waited at the rear. Some of the men appeared ready to collapse from exhaustion, and William had water supplied by means of discarded canteens and water-skins.

'Who's the rabbit?' Peruzo asked as he looked down the path to the water.

'That will be me,' William answered.

Peruzo shook his head vehemently. 'You cannot . . .'

'I am the only one of us who can run, Lieutenant,' William told him. 'You are in no shape yourself, and nor are the others. If I had my choice, none of you would be fighting.'

'There are no choices here, Captain,' Peruzo reminded him.

'Exactly,' William smiled ruefully. 'We only have one shot at this. If it fails, we could lose many more men trying to bring the daemon down. I've already lost more men on this mission than I bargained for. We are in poor shape, Peruzo.'

The lieutenant conceded.

'Fire the dwarf-cannon within four yards of the daemon. Anything further away will have little impact,' William said as he tucked the sword under his belt. He rued the loss of Engrin's sword, but now was not the time to hunt for it.

'Just make sure you get out of its way,' Peruzo called after him as he marched towards the water.

William did not linger. Why delay the inevitable? It came to him that the plan was crazy and folly at best. And at worst . . .? He jogged silently over the sand.

The brothers looked on in admiration. This was not just their captain; it was a man who was prepared to sacrifice himself. Every last one of them prayed inwardly that he would survive.

Closer to the water, William retrieved a musket lying in the sand. It was rusty and he doubted it would fire a single shot. But shooting the daemon was not his first thought. He stepped into the water up to his ankles and began to wave the musket in the air with one hand, the sword in the other.

The daemon was wallowing in carnage, yet throughout the destruction wrought, it exulted little: there could never be enough. Around its arms hung rags that might have been the host's clothes, or the vestiges of those it had murdered. The necrotic abomination only halted its mindless demolition of the camp when distracted by the sound of William's taunting. The daemon snarled in the back of its swollen throat and then roared to the challenge. Picking up its splayed feet, it hauled its smouldering hide into the water and towards its gesticulating prey.

'Come on, you bastard,' William shouted. 'Come and get me.'

The creature waded out until the water came up to its breast, flooding its jaws so that the water boiled and pulses of steam gushed out. At first the daemon was slow, impeded by the depth of the water, but too soon the bed of the lake rose again and its momentum increased. As the water fell away, it opened its dripping mouth and exhaled a rolling gust of sulphuric breath, darker than night. Behind it the fiery glow of its slanted eyes burned like volcanic gashes in its blackened skull. It uttered a primordial growl as it surged forward through the lake.

The hulking shape came on, and William's heart beat faster. The daemon was no longer marching towards him, it was *charging*.

'Oh, bloody hell!' The words spluttered over William's lips as he turned and ran. He had not rehearsed every step of his plan, his path to the mouth of the cannon. There were obstacles to pass: debris, dismembered bodies, discarded sacks . . .

And a heartbeat behind him, the daemon trampled through the grass, the tips whipping its hide.

William was out of the tall grass and hurdling over the body of a militiaman. Ahead of him, his vision blurred and shaking, he could see the wagon half lit up by a nearby fire. He felt the ground trembling as the daemon came after him; he could almost feel its heat on the back of his neck now and smelled the sulphur fuming from its throat.

He put his head down and ran harder, every breath, every move, focused on self-preservation. He could not tell whether he would make it, or what folly the plan might have been. Death had reached for him already that night. Would he cheat it once more?

As the cannon came into view, he saw Peruzo rise and take aim with a musket. Looking to his captain for an instant, he fired over William's head, the single gun making a weak report. His aim was true and the shot rebounded off the daemon's shoulder, but not hard enough to slow it. William did not look back as he came to the cannon and dived to the floor . . .

. . . Just as the daemon reached out for him.

Peruzo dropped the empty musket and yelled: 'FIRE!'

The dwarf-cannon exploded. Smoke spurted from the weapon with a low rumble, followed almost simultaneously by an ear-splitting crack as the cannonball flew through the air and split into shards a moment later. The shrapnel tore through the daemon's head, which burst with a muffled crunch . . .

. . . But even decapitated it continued its charge, its frenzied momentum throwing it headlong towards the wagon. William rolled away just as one armoured foot crashed down mere inches from his skull, before the hulk ploughed straight into the cannon. The wagon was lifted into the air, before it rolled over completely, spilling the three monks inside. Brother Ricardo landed winded, as did Brother Paldini, who was thrown a few yards clear. But Brother Adams – Vittore's trusted second in command – landed under the wagon. The left rear wheel slammed down on his chest, crushing his ribcage and flattening his mid-section. As Brother Ricardo fell he saw only briefly the jet of dark fluid spraying from Adams across the deck of the wagon as the dwarf-cannon tumbled out, followed by the powder and shot.

The headless daemon, wreathed in flames and smoke, lost cohesion and slumped upon the wreckage, its dead weight smashing the side of the wagon.

Brother Ricardo lay only a few feet from the burning mess of bone and flesh, watching it with utter disbelief, while Brother Paldini got up groggily. Punch-drunk, he staggered over to get a closer look at the burning corpse, grinning with triumph.

'We killed it!' he yelled. 'It's dead! It's dead!'

Several monks broke from the flanks and cautiously approached for a closer look. William too stared up and began laughing. The plan had been poorly conceived but it had worked. It had . . .

'Wait!' Peruzo shouted and waved to the monks. 'It's still on fire! The powder! The . . .!'

There was a sudden explosion as the flaming torso of the daemon ignited the first gunpowder keg. The blast tore apart the midsection of the wagon; flying splinters killed Paldini instantly.

Then the next keg exploded as Brother Jacque made to

escape. He was engulfed and his flaming body hurled several yards away.

William was thrown too, the blast wave lifting him from his knees to send him sprawling across the sand. Bright light filled his vision. He lay there prostrate and deafened as the oasis around him silently burned.

△ VI △

Baron Horia saw the glowing cloud erupt over the oasis, the light of the explosion reflecting against his pale skin. At that moment the Scarimadaen in his palm began to tremble and shake violently.

The daemon had finally been destroyed by the men of the Church. It was time to leave.

△ VII △

Brother Casper, a sightless giant of a man, stood aloof from the other monks resting by the cages. He looked out into the dark with cauterized eyes; the wounds were raw but a healing crust had coated them. He could hear the pop of muskets in the dark, the crash of battle rupturing the night.

Brother Samuele sat on the edge of the cage, his torn leg causing him pain. 'Hey, Casper . . .' he called. 'What are you doing, brother?'

'Waiting,' Casper grunted back.

Of the other monks, Stefano, Angelo and Goffredo were in bad shape, with Angelo running a high fever. Brother Tore sat quietly to Samuele's right, his face disfigured by torture with a flaming brand.

'The battle won't come to us, my brothers,' Samuele assured them.

'The captain will prevail,' Tore said hopefully. 'He'll do right by us all, mark these words.'

'Angelo is worsening,' Stefano whispered, the brother as white as the moon. He held his stomach and all had noted the dark stain on his side. Stefano carried his injury well, but was in poor shape himself.

Tore got up and trudged over, bending down to pull open Angelo's shirt. The monk's body was marbled with bruises and other wounds. There were burn marks, shallow cuts and other signs of torture. The brother had been particularly stubborn, and had been made to suffer following Gregory's interrogation and murder at the hands of the militia.

Samuele looked on in despair.

'He won't survive much longer, Samuele,' Tore said.

'He *must*,' Samuele implored.

Suddenly, the camp was lit by a tremendous explosion followed by a thunderous wave of sound that drove Casper to retreat.

'Oh my . . .' Brother Samuele murmured and limped from the cage. He searched the sky and saw a ball of fire blossom across it. Then came another light, a bright glare of cyan that screamed as it fled the camp, twisting and arcing across the sky into oblivion.

Samuele punched the air. 'I told you! Did I not?! The daemon is slain!' he shouted and began to dance about haphazardly on his sounder leg.

Casper beat the air blindly, elated that some victory had come.

Above them, the vampyre wheeled, catching the night with all the skill of a swallow on the uplift. She too had seen the daemon destroyed, and it angered her. Below, the wounded men of the Church celebrated and all she could think of was her fallen comrades in the Valley of Fire.

And it angered her so . . .

Filled with rage and blood lust, she plummeted down, shrieking like a banshee.

Brother Casper heard her coming and fell to his knees, feeling the air part near his ear with a snick-snick sound. Brother Samuele tried to flee, but his leg failed him. The vampyre swooped to his left, flung out her blades and cut open the monk's side. Crying out, Samuele fell to the floor.

Brother Tore made to leap up from Brother Angelo, but his wounds caused him to double over in agony and he too fell to his knees as the vampyre came about for another pass on Samuele, who was struggling in the sand, blood pouring out of the wound.

'Samuele! Samuele!' Tore shouted desperately.

Brother Casper got to his feet. 'Where is he?!' he yelled back.

'Directly behind you . . .' Tore replied, '. . . three yards away.'

The vampyre came out of the darkness and landed suddenly, the momentum causing her to skip off the sandy floor like a stone off water, before she found her footing and broke into a run that was impossibly fast. She reached Samuele as he made to rise again. The monks let out a unified cry of warning but Samuele was in no state to defend himself. She took him by the neck, pulled him up so that he could stare with terror into her eyes, before she laughed and ripped him from collar to navel, letting the blood gush over her.

Casper heard Samuele die and smelt the stench of death taint the air around him. Sniffing the air like a sightless dog, he put his head down and heaved himself to the right, his large hands outstretched; his face contorted in fury.

The vampyre had not seen Casper lurch towards her as she savoured the killing, but on seeing him now, merely feet away, she almost retreated before she realized the monk was blind. Laughing in anticipation of the game in prospect, she skipped over Casper, treading the air to land behind the brother and gash open his back with a fluid movement of her blades. Casper let out a groan, but the giant responded by turning as quickly as his bulk would allow. His big hands grappled in the air, but she ducked playfully and cut off his thumb.

Howling with pain, Casper would not stop as he reached for her again and again, guided by her mocking and laughter.

'You're playing with me!' Ileana cackled. 'I can play too!' She ducked and lifted into the air, gracefully kicking her right foot out. Her boot tip connected with Casper's chin and the giant stumbled back.

Brother Tore tried desperately to find something to defend Casper with, but there were no weapons at all. He gestured to Stefano to conceal the two other monks in shadow, then had to look on helplessly as Casper was wounded time and time again.

Ileana brought out both blades and looked over Casper's shoulder to Tore. 'Your friends are begging to be murdered,' she said, and gestured to the monks behind him, hoping the monk would understand. 'I will gladly offer this service.'

'No!' Brother Casper shouted and he swung his hands towards her.

She dodged his great paw, and then thrust both blades into his chest. The Bear of Corsica, as he was known to all in the Order, bayed in agony, but his strength remained. Thinking she had dealt the death blow, Ileana did not reckon on the monk's long reach. She only realized her complacency when by chance he lurched forward and took hold of her in a hug of iron. She could not move, her arms locked to her sides.

Screaming with rage, and then with pain, Ileana struggled. Casper clung on as long as he could, hoping to snap her spine, or at least delay her for the brothers to escape. But the burly monk grew weaker with every breath.

'*Casper!*'

'Must hold on . . .' he began to murmur, blood filling his mouth.

'Casper!' came the voice again. He recognized Lieutenant Peruzo.

The vampyre began to shriek again, squirming in his grasp.

'Do it, Lieutenant!' Casper growled through the blood that was filling his throat.

Peruzo hesitated.

'*Now,*' he growled as she began to spin loose.

Peruzo thrust his sword into her chest. The blade ran straight through her and impaled Brother Casper, who let out a last breath. The two bodies tottered for a moment, and then Casper fell forward, trapping the vampyre under his weight.

Peruzo stood back with terrible comprehension. Looking down at his handiwork, he fell silent, not noticing William at his side, his face black as night from soot. There was a long gash on William's forehead and blood was running freely down one cheek.

'Bind her!' William shouted furiously.

'We should kill her,' Brother Tore cried back.

William shook his head. 'No, we need her alive. Bind her, Peruzo. We'll stake her out to the east, by God.'

△ VIII △

Brothers Jericho and King returned to the cages as William surveyed the scene of battle.

'The enemy have fled,' Jericho told him. He gestured to the silence that was descending on the oasis. 'If the vampyres are still out there, then they're waiting.'

Peruzo was leaning on one cage, exhausted and saddened by their losses. As William approached, he did not look up.

'We're victorious,' William murmured sadly.

'Gregory, Paldini, Adams, Jacque, Samuele and Casper . . .' Peruzo said, recording the men who had perished. 'And six are wounded. We are not victors, Captain.'

William patted Peruzo on the shoulder. 'We could have lost many more,' he suggested.

Peruzo would not reply. The death of Casper was weighing heavily on him. He had heard the monk's last breath, a breath he himself had taken from him. There hadn't been a choice, but Peruzo had never killed a brother before, even in pity.

'Is the vampyre staked out?' William asked.

'She is,' Peruzo replied.

'*She?*'

'A female, Captain.'

William hesitated. This must be the vampyre they had faced outside Babel's.

'I've seen that look before,' Peruzo remarked. 'She is *still* a vampyre. She murdered Samuele and tortured Casper.'

'I know, I know,' William agreed quickly, though the idea of staking out a woman still repelled him.

Peruzo got to his feet and straightened his jacket. 'I have no qualms about killing her, Captain. Let me deal with it.'

'No,' William said. 'I am the senior officer. I must question her. Just make sure Thomas and the one called Khalifa are there to see it.'

'I understand what you say, William, but what makes you think they *won't* attack again?' Thomas asked as William led him to the edge of the oasis, the man called Khalifa following at a distance with several armed guards. Dawn was an hour away.

'They won't. Not even to rescue their friend here,' William replied. 'They are running out of time.'

'Yes, yes, you have said this before – "Sunlight destroys them." They need shelter . . .' Thomas repeated.

'This is our only chance to gather information,' William added. 'For a soldier it's a rule: Know your enemy. We have to discover what we are facing – numbers, weapons, anything.'

William spoke over his shoulder as they marched up a dune to where some monks were gathered, silhouetted against the dawning sky.

'And torturing this animal will give you that information?' Thomas said, screwing up his nose in disgust.

William tried to hide his own distaste. 'You wanted vengeance, didn't you? She destroyed your whole entourage. All your servants, your goods . . .'

'She?' Thomas said and stopped in his tracks. '*A woman?*'

William couldn't look Thomas in the eyes. 'We're not torturing her, Thomas. We just need information.'

Peruzo stood at the crest of the dune and waved down to William with his sword. They came up, but as they neared they could hear the cries of the creature clear enough.

'Bastards! Swine! Sons of whores, all! You will die! YOU WILL *ALL* DIE!'

Thomas glanced at William in dismay. 'Her voice . . .' he said. 'It's terrible.'

'Aye,' William replied quietly.

Thomas shivered and faltered. 'I'm not sure I can do this, Captain Saxon.'

The man known as Khalifa looked equally pale. He had lost many men to these monsters, yet the sound of her shrieks drained his resolve. William turned to them and told Thomas to translate his words.

'Tell him this evil creature killed his men, as she did the people of Babel. It was she who caused the death of his commander, she who would gladly have murdered the militia.'

Thomas paused, his mind racing.

'Tell him, *please*,' William pressed.

Thomas considered altering the words, but then what was the use? What was done was now done. Ileana had been caught.

Thomas translated and Khalifa nodded, his anger overriding the desire to leave.

They climbed to the top of the dune and looked out. At the foot, surrounded by campfires, was the vampyre, tied on the sand with great chains and rocks, staked out and spreadeagled. She writhed and pulled, and each time it seemed she might break free, a monk would strike the creature across the leg or arm, the wound deep enough to weaken the vampyre as she tried to mend herself.

'Must they?' Thomas said.

'Yes,' William insisted. 'She would break free if she were left alone.'

'It is torture,' the Englishman murmured.

'It is necessity,' William replied sadly, looking away. 'By wounding it, we sap its strength. But the creature can heal itself quickly, so we must deliver wounds at regular intervals to keep it from escaping.'

'She is in agony,' Thomas murmured.

'It is not a woman,' William reminded him. 'We cannot show it pity. It would have shown us none.'

The female vampyre arched her back and whimpered. She turned her head to look behind her and found William standing there, the other two men just out of view. She shouted something in her old tongue, and then in Latin, which William understood.

'Please! Please release me! I will never harm any of you again. Please, it *hurts*! It hurts *so* much! I don't want to die like this . . .'

William flinched at the cries for mercy, but looked away, hardening his resolve.

'Surely this is wrong,' Thomas said.

'It *must* be done,' William replied, but his own determination was weakening. 'Its friends are out there somewhere, and they will attack if we show weakness. If they do, we will be ready for them.'

'And if they don't, what then?'

'Then we kill it,' William replied.

'No further torture?' Thomas asked.

'None.'

'Then tell me when it's done, Captain. I want no part of this.' The Englishman turned away and walked back to the camp, leaving William to stare after him. He could understand pity for a woman, but not a vampyre. But then William understood the vampyres far better than Thomas Richmond ever could. Their words were lies, sympathy was weakness. You must deal with them as you would any dangerous animal.

Even a woman.

'Captain?' William turned away from the writhing creature and walked over to where his lieutenant stood with Jericho and several brothers. 'Dawn comes quickly here,' Peruzo said,

285

and gestured to the horizon. The thin glow of light was now advancing steadily. The sun would reach them sooner than expected.

The vampyre had realized this as well.

'Please!' she squirmed. 'Please don't do this!'

William tried to ignore her. 'Has it said anything about our enemy's strength?'

Peruzo shook his head. 'It only babbles. Nothing we can use.'

William nodded.

'Why did the merchant leave?' Peruzo asked curiously.

'Doesn't like dirty work,' William said and knelt down by the vampyre. He regarded the creature, her appearance, her stench, the way her eyes crackled with light but were growing dimmer.

'Do you understand what will happen to you?' he said in Latin.

The vampyre arched her back and looked back with a mixture of hatred and pain. 'Shit-eater!' she screamed at William.

'Is that a No?' William asked politely. '*Et si nous parlons français?*'

The vampyre stared at William and nodded slowly.

It wasn't often William spoke French, and when he did it was only privately to Adriana. So the conversation with the vampyre came out stilted and wrong to his ear, perhaps because he was no longer using French for affection; it was difficult to sound threatening.

'You understand me now?' he said. 'No more games. I want *answers*. Where are your friends?'

'I was born in Paris,' the vampyre replied, disregarding the question completely. 'I was a girl then. I lived in the lanes with my family by the river. I was happy then . . . *So happy.*'

William tried to ignore the sentiments. Tried to ignore how human and fragile she . . . it . . . sounded. 'I don't care for your life story. *Where are the other vampyres?*' he demanded.

The vampyre wept and began writhing again. 'Release me! Release me now!' she implored. 'The sun is coming! The sun!'

William nodded. 'Yes, the sun. I see you are afraid of it. Some

286

of your kind have a particular weakness for the sun. I hear it burns you. Your skin. Your flesh. Your bones, even?'

The female vampyre stopped struggling and looked back at William, tears smudging her cheeks. 'It is our curse.'

'No,' William said and shook his head. 'Your curse is to hold the rest of Humanity in contempt. How many have you murdered?'

'My family were murdered,' the vampyre moaned. 'Have you ever seen your own family killed in front of your eyes?'

William shuddered and suddenly thought of the family he'd left behind in England – of Father, Mother, Elizabeth. He looked away, afraid of revealing his own weakness. *God, how he missed them.*

He rose and stared over to the horizon. 'You have murdered more people than I can possibly know. Other families, I expect. And you probably enjoyed it, correct?'

'LET ME GO!'

'Never,' William replied nervously. 'You can *never* be released!'

'AAARGH!!' the vampyre screamed and raised her right arm, lifting the chains further and further, and then the rock that was holding them down.

'Wound it!' Peruzo yelled.

Jericho darted forward and thrust his sword through the creature's shoulder, enjoying the sensation in revenge for brothers Samuele and Casper. The vampyre screeched and sank back sobbing to the ground.

'Keep an eye on her, damn you!' William implored. Breathing heavily, he kicked the vampyre's leg to get her attention. 'How many more are there?' he demanded. '*How many more of you?*'

'In Hell, shit-eater!' the vampyre cried, and spat towards William.

He looked over his shoulder to the horizon and back at the vampyre. '*You first.* The sun is coming.'

She looked ahead and wept like a child.

'Enough games!' William growled, and drew Engrin's sword. It had taken him over an hour to recover the weapon from the field of battle, yet it had lain with the lion's share of the company's weaponry, hidden in a tent that had not even been touched by the combat. If ever a weapon had a charmed existence it was this sword, a weapon that William now lowered over the vampyre. 'You *will* tell me your strength, or there will be no mercy.'

She sobbed and rolled her eyes. 'They will come. They will save me!' she implored.

William thought about this for a moment. It had been hours since they had staked her out and yet no attack had come.

Not yet.

'Where are you camped, vampyre?' William asked.

She looked up at William with a grimace of terrible fear.

'Yes,' William suddenly realized. 'You are camped far away, too far to stay out here for long. Your friends have gone because they would be caught in the daylight if they strayed too far away. They've abandoned you.'

'No.' The vampyre shook her head. 'No. They haven't. They can't!'

'They have,' William said coldly. 'Now if you tell me how many there are, I promise a quick death.'

'Let me live!' she cried.

'How many of your kind came tonight?' he demanded again. 'How many?'

The female vampyre gibbered a little, staring at William and then through him. 'We are only three.'

'Lies,' William replied. 'I saw more in Rashid . . .'

'No! No!' she sobbed. 'I tell the truth. Now there are only three of us.'

'Where are the others?' William pressed.

'Gone,' she replied after a lengthy pause, her eyes darting about.

'Where?' William said, growing irritated and disgusted by the whole process.

'Gone,' she repeated and began sobbing again.

'That's not good enough,' William growled and walked away.

'*I don't know any more!*' she cried, the voice sounding pitifully human. William almost turned, almost resolved to cut her loose, but Peruzo was like a rock and glanced at his captain. His expression was clear.

'You think he can trust you?' Peruzo asked the creature.

'Oh yes!' the vampyre replied, glancing nervously ahead as the first rays of sunlight began peaking from the brow of the horizon. 'Please release me.'

William shook his head. 'You murdered those people in Rashid. You murdered my friend's whole company. And you murdered my men,' he said. 'Your request is denied.'

'*No!*'

'You would only come back and kill us all,' William added as he walked away.

'Not true! Not true! I swear!'

Peruzo joined him a few yards from where the vampyre began writhing again, pleading as loud as she could to be set free. William gripped his sword. 'Time to end this.'

'You would put that creature out of its misery?' Peruzo said and frowned.

'There is no need to prolong it,' William replied.

'It serves a purpose, Captain,' Peruzo told him. 'A lesson to the other creatures out there. A lesson on who they face. It might even stir them into error.'

'We are soldiers . . .' William protested.

'And soldiers must sometimes commit distasteful acts against their enemy, Captain,' Peruzo replied.

'I have never tortured anyone in my life, Lieutenant,' William said under his breath.

'This is not torture, Captain. It is justice. It's nothing less than it deserves, if I may say so,' Peruzo told him. 'Remember the brothers it has killed. Poor Casper is dead, killed by this bitch. How many others has she butchered? She laughed when she murdered Samuele. She is guilty as hell, Captain. Maybe we should send her there.'

William sighed bitterly. 'That she is,' he replied and sheathed his sword. 'And as much as I deplore such an act, it *would* serve a purpose.' He looked to the horizon and grimaced.

'Very well, Peruzo. Let the sun take its course and this wretched creature's body.'

△ IX △

William did not stay to the end.

The sun came up gradually, the starry sky lightening bit by bit until only the strongest stars struggled within the dawn-blue. Finally the few clouds in the sky turned from black to gold, their bellies streaked with crimson. On their heels came the sun, its first peep touching the horizon with a dazzle of light that made the vampyre scream.

Peruzo sat on the sand and waited. He didn't know how long it would take; minutes maybe, sometimes it took an hour or more. But it was almost always a violent end. Most of the brothers waited with him, mainly to be sure that their enemy died, but perhaps also for a glimmer of retribution.

The new commander of the militia, Khalifa, also watched, transfixed by the sight of the fettered woman thrashing crazily in the growing light. He too had lost men, many more than the company of monks. Forty-six militiamen had perished in the assault and another twenty-three were badly wounded.

The vampyre peered up, her eyes now only narrow black slits, devoid of the light that once crackled within them. The creature's powers were utterly spent; no more strength to mend itself, no more strength to escape.

'Please help me,' the female vampyre whispered to Khalifa, who stepped back, afraid. 'You *can't* leave me like this.'

'Just ignore it,' Peruzo called over.

Khalifa looked up in trepidation. It seemed to the Arab that these men in grey were more dangerous than the creature slowly cooking in the rising sun. It was absurd that they should just leave this wretched thing to burn in the desert.

'I once had a family, you know?' the vampyre keened. 'I had no choice. I was forced to become this way. My family was murdered by this *curse*. Please . . . *Help me . . .*'

Khalifa backed away up the dune and held himself still.

The sun began to advance, casting long shadows before it. The vampyre recoiled, pulling her legs up as far away as possible, but the chains held her in place. The light moved slowly over them, creeping up little by little, and the vampyre held her breath as if the act would repel the approaching rays.

Her skin began to smoke.

Khalifa walked away when the shrieking started. Before he crested the dune he glanced behind him, seeing the threads of smoke rise from the creature's clothes. He had seen people die before, had killed many himself. But this was unholy, terrible, and for the first time, Khalifa felt his soul being soiled by participation.

Peruzo and the brothers watched the female vampyre writhe and spit, screaming obscenities as the sun crept up further, now up to her waist. Then it rose up to her chest, then to her neck.

'NO!' she screeched. 'NOT MY FACE!'

The vampyre's denials were cut short as her lower jaw caught the sun and was suddenly on fire, bright blue flames seeping from every pore to lick around the skin and hair. The vampyre's scalp ignited and her head became an inferno as it shook about, still alive, still screaming. Blue flames leaked out of her ears, her nose, and then her tongue, leaking as though the creature's body could no longer contain it. Fire gushed from every pore in its body now, burning the clothes that dressed it.

The vampyre's head was black, devoid of eyes or lips, the tongue now just a gurgling froth of brown slime sliding down the back of her throat that was liquefying under the rising heat. Though still barely alive, it rocked for one last time and then stayed put as her muscles shrank or burst. Then the brain fell apart inside her burning skull, followed next by the heart and lungs that had not beat or breathed unaided since she had been turned by Count Ordrane.

It didn't end there, the bones still acting as a cage for the half-spirit within that struggled to be released, twisting around rib and skull with livid, violent rasps of cyan light that ruptured and charcoaled all that would burn.

The smell was repellent.

Peruzo, feeling nauseous, got up from the sand to walk away. The other vampyres had not tried to rescue her. They had let her die, and it dawned on Peruzo that her slow death really had served little purpose.

'When it's done, bury the remains,' he ordered the remaining monks, the smoke of the burning vampyre twisting into the sky as the sun rose higher.

CHAPTER FIFTEEN

Allies and Avengers

△ I △

Three days had passed since the battle at Bastet, the name of the oasis that would be indelibly imprinted on each survivor's memories. Every man had left something there, a friend, innocence or a misconception. For some, it had been the bloodiest engagement they had faced, for others a harsh reminder of what could be lost if they failed.

Peruzo rode quieter than most, racked with the guilt he felt over Brother Casper's death. He had lost men in the past, but Casper's demise was *his* fault. *His* blade. *His* neglect. They should never have been captured by the militia in the first place. He should have seen them coming.

The torture of the vampyre had not moved him. It was she who had been the death of Casper, or rather it was she who caused Peruzo to kill them both. In his eyes she was not a woman. And her agonizing death was deserved.

William felt differently. The interrogation and torture of the female vampyre had stained his conscience. He knew he could never tell Marco about what had happened, let alone Adriana. It was something he would never discuss, not even with those who had witnessed it. And it had damaged his relationship with Thomas.

The English merchant had not spoken a word to William since Bastet. He kept himself aloof, riding alone with Hammid.

William could not understand why Thomas blamed him so much. After all, the vampyres had been responsible for murdering his people, so why was revenge so unpalatable?

Despite William's protestations that the remaining vampyres could attack at any time, both Thomas and Hammid rode at a distance from the monks, sometimes ahead of them, sometimes lagging behind.

Deciding to mend the relationship and discover Thomas's grievances, if only for the Englishman's safety, William broke off from the column, hanging back until the two forlorn riders caught up.

Thomas gave him a cursory look as he approached.

'Peruzo believes we could be lost,' William said to him.

'I see, Captain,' Thomas said perfunctorily.

'We have water enough for two more days at best,' William said. 'We must have rejoined the Ayaida by then.'

'We should have arrived this morning,' Thomas remarked.

William couldn't tell if it was a criticism or not. 'You're angry at me, aren't you?' he said.

Thomas looked surprised. He regarded William for a moment, debating inwardly whether to reply. Finally he nodded. 'I cannot reconcile what you and your men have done.'

'With regard to what, may I ask?' William pressed.

Thomas licked his dry lips and stared at William silently.

'She was a vampyre, Thomas,' William said. 'She helped kill your . . .'

'I know what her crimes were, Captain,' Thomas said abruptly. 'She was still a woman.'

'Chivalrous, Thomas, but not practical. In this war, women are just as deadly,' William replied.

'I noticed that,' Thomas remarked bitterly. 'Did you stay to the end?'

'I didn't have to. I could hear her die.'

'We *all* heard her die, Captain Saxon. Every living soul in the oasis could hear her.'

William stared at Thomas witheringly. It was enough that he

felt guilty for what had happened, but that he should be judged by Thomas angered him. 'Feel lucky you were not part of it,' William barked back at him. 'When we leave you with the Ayaida, you can forget all this happened.'

Thomas frowned. 'Really? So easily? You're looking to unburden yourself of me there?'

'I believe that was our arrangement.'

'It was,' Thomas said, 'but other matters have complicated it. I don't believe the arrangement was to include me in a rescue mission and a battle.'

'No,' William admitted, 'it wasn't.'

Thomas straightened up in his saddle. 'As for abandoning me to the Ayaida . . . Do you think a man can so easily escape his destiny?'

William appeared mystified by the question.

'I am now involved in your war, Captain Saxon,' Thomas explained. 'It was inevitable that when I helped you escape, the enemy would see me as *their* enemy. They have already destroyed my merchant caravan for aiding you at Babel's. And my hands are bloody too, Captain Saxon. Her death falls on all who let her perish. I am quite aware there is no escape for me from your war.'

William stared at Thomas. It was brutal. It was honest. And it was also right. The vampyres would not show mercy if they caught him.

'What will you do?' he asked.

'I will travel with you,' Thomas said and shrugged. 'You may yet have need of a translator with a sword.'

'I might,' William agreed. 'But the danger . . .'

'. . . Is obvious to me, Captain,' Thomas said. 'I have little choice in the matter. Perhaps it would be wise to tell me of your mission, now that I am part of it.'

William nodded reluctantly. For the next hour William recounted the particulars. As it stood, success now depended on Thomas, who would translate any orders he had in case Sheikh Fahd fell in battle. William knew the Rassis would not be easy opponents. It was this matter he had mulled over during the ride from Bastet.

'I may need to change our initial objectives,' he confided in Thomas. 'I have lost more men than I expected. If I am honest, I think I will lose many more in the battle with the Rassis. More than I can afford, and still come safely back to Rome.'

'How so?' Thomas asked.

'The original mission entailed returning the Hoard to Rome. If the vampyre was telling the truth, there are still at least two more of them out there, and they're sure to attack us on the return to Rashid. So if by the grace of God we manage to liberate the Hoard from its guardians, we may well lose it because only a few at best have survived the battle with the Rassis. However, there *is* an alternative.'

Thomas listened close.

'We could destroy the Hoard at the Valley of Fire.'

'But you said there are no conventional means of destroying these artefacts,' Thomas said.

'As I understand it, there aren't. But I have been provided with unconventional explosives that may serve.'

Thomas masked his alarm. 'You would destroy the Hoard? Even if that meant disobeying your superiors?'

'To stop it falling into the hands of Count Ordrane?' William said and smiled. 'Yes. Without hesitation.'

△ II △

Ahead the sky was darkening and the brightest stars were beginning to appear, yet there was still no sign of the Ayaida. Then, to the relief of all, they saw four riders coming towards them.

At first they thought it might be militia, those from Dumyat that might still be pursuing William and the company. The relief on recognizing Sheikh Fahd's guard was overwhelming, and William choked back his emotions as they galloped towards them.

The bodyguard addressed them and Thomas translated cheerfully, the words greeted with laughter and relief: they were only two miles from the settlement.

The men in grey were treated to an overwhelming welcome when they returned to the valley. The scouts had seen their trail twenty miles away, dispatching riders to intercept the company, while other scouts returned to the camp with the announcement that 'the man called Saxon is alive'. Word quickly spread and Sheikh Fahd dressed himself in the grandest of robes.

And with good cause.

He had other guests with him that morning; other sheikhs who had come to join him the night before as allies against the Rassis. For Saxon to live and to lead them in revenge against his brother's killers marked a truly triumphant day. But first the sheikh had to tell Saxon's kin of the news, and he sent Hisham to Marco's tent.

Marco did not understand a single word Sheikh Fahd's bodyguard was saying to him that morning, but he caught his uncle's name and saw a beaming smile. Surely his uncle was alive and was returning. He might have cheered out loud, but wanted to wait until he saw William riding into camp. In this world of alien customs and language, Marco took nothing for granted. Only when he could see his uncle in the flesh would he be convinced of his safety.

Marco stood alone in the chill of dusk and watched the approach to the camp as the valley was drenched in golden light from another setting sun. At first there was nothing, until orange puffs of dust erupted at the apex and began to billow down the mouth of the valley, dispersing soon after to reveal the column of riders.

He found himself running, jumping over guy ropes and around baskets, dashing past livestock and their owners, before he passed the perimeter of the camp and kept on running. He had sprinted many yards before he made out the gaunt

297

expressions of the riders. Lieutenant Peruzo, Jericho, the English merchant and . . . Marco beamed. His uncle too.

As the company rode by, Peruzo did not look down at him, his face as grim and grey as his hair. Jericho winked at Marco but he too looked exhausted. When William drew level he halted his horse and peered down. 'You are well?' he asked him.

Marco nodded, noting the blood on his uncle's jacket, the dirt on his face and the dust in his hair.

'Come,' William said, putting a hand down to him. Marco took it and was pulled up onto the horse behind William. He held on in silence as they trotted into the Ayaida camp, the tribespeople cheering and waving. For William it was most unexpected, until Sheikh Fahd arrived, flanked by an escort clad in their finest robes.

It made William crave a bath and shave.

'I am glad you are alive, Captain Saxon,' Sheikh Fahd greeted and bowed slightly.

'As am I, sir,' William replied wearily.

'And the militia are not in pursuit?' he added.

William shook his head. 'We came to an agreement,' he replied, recalling Khalifa's parting words. The company's weapons had almost all been returned by the militia at Bastet, save for those exchanged for horses to carry back William's men to the Ayaida. But it was Khalifa who told William that he would send word to the militia from the nearby towns that they were not to harm the men in grey. He also told William that should he need anything in Rashid, then he had only to send word and it was his. Khalifa believed that Allah had shown clemency and that William was a friend of Egypt, rather than an infidel.

These assurances almost made up for the terrible conditions and torture of William's men, and like a diplomat, William was outwardly grateful. But deep down, he hated Khalifa and his rabble. What they had done to the monks was unforgivable.

'Your losses were great?' Sheikh Fahd continued.

'They were too high, yes,' William said softly. 'But the company remains strong.'

'Later we must hear of your exploits,' Sheikh Fahd insisted. 'My guests would very much like to hear them.'

William looked to the Arabs who were remarking his travel-stained state. Compared with their finery, he felt uncomfortable and scruffy. He was feeling far from sociable. But he mustered a bow, and Sheikh Fahd was satisfied, he and his guests bowing back before they turned away.

Once out of sight, William wilted in his saddle.

'A celebration, with you as the centre of attention, Captain? Most fortunate,' Thomas teased. 'I envy you.'

'I am not going alone, Thomas,' William insisted, staring back at him.

Thomas's smile waned and he studied William for a moment. The smile that followed was grudging but then warm. 'Very well. If you wish me to attend, I will be honoured.'

Thomas and Hammid dismounted and led their horses away as William let down Marco and then dismounted himself.

'Pitch camp at the edge of the settlement,' William said to Peruzo. 'Not too far away this time. And keep an eye on Marco if you can.'

Peruzo nodded silently. He had not said a word in hours.

'Is something wrong?' William asked.

'No,' Peruzo replied, and then he corrected himself. 'You spend much of your time with the Englishman now.'

William almost reprimanded Peruzo, his tone insolent for an officer in the Order, but the events of recent days had been hard on them all. 'He is an ally, Lieutenant. He may have his uses,' William explained calmly.

'Perhaps,' Peruzo replied, 'but I do not like his servant.'

'Hammid?'

'Unsavoury. Untrustworthy. No good will come of it,' Peruzo said gruffly.

'Let me decide that, Lieutenant,' William retorted. 'Just be sure the camp is pitched and our wounded looked after. I have a feeling our rest here will be short.'

Peruzo brightened a little. 'We move out soon?'

'If these guests are allies of the sheikh, then we surely will.' William looked along the line of monks who were stretching from the days of riding or helping with the wounded. 'What do you make of the company?' he murmured.

Peruzo turned to them and rubbed at the stubble on his left cheek. He shrugged a little as he thought about it. 'I would say that a day and a night of rest would much improve their constitutions, Captain. But even then, only twenty-four men would be fit enough to travel.'

'Just twenty-four?' William was dismayed. 'I hoped there would be more. Not exactly the force I wanted to lead.'

'You don't believe there are enough men, do you?'

William looked at Peruzo. He could not lie to him, not after all they had endured. 'It never was, my friend. Against the Rassis in a straight fight, the full company had a slim chance. But now that we've lost so many . . .'

'The mission ends here?'

'That depends on our allies. The Bedouins are our last hope.' William paced a little and shook his head. 'What of our wounded? Is there any chance they can recover quickly enough?'

'Some may never recover, Captain. More days of riding like this will surely kill them.'

William noted the anger in Peruzo's voice. 'See that the others are ready in the morning,' he ordered. 'And gather what weapons remain.'

'What of the gunpowder Engrin sent us?' Peruzo said out of the blue.

'Hopefully, it is still with the Ayaida. If it is, we take it with us.'

'We are disobeying Cardinal Devirus's orders?'

'Yes,' William replied. 'I hoped that it wouldn't come to that. It would be some achievement, riding into Rome with two hundred and fifty Scarimadaen, would it not?'

'But if the Dar'uka came to our aid . . .' Peruzo said.

William bit his lip. 'Did you see them at Bastet, Peruzo?' he said. 'Did they come when we needed them the most?'

Peruzo shook his head.

'We cannot count on them,' William said. 'Vittore was right. We must trust in what we believe. And I can only believe that somehow we will find allies here in the desert that are more dependable than "angels".'

△ III △

He bathed, but did not shave. Even after washing away the days of dust and blood, dirt still felt ingrained in every pore. A long soak was what he really needed.

Marco dressed nervously, having been invited to the evening meal too. His hands shook as he pulled on the man-sized shirt and jacket that Thomas had lent him. He hoped there would be one particular guest at the meal – one he looked forward to seeing the most, but was worried that others would suspect his feelings for her.

William sensed the nervousness in Marco. 'What did you do while I was absent?' he asked.

'Not much. Nothing at all,' Marco spluttered and his cheeks reddened.

'Just kept to the tent?'

'Pretty much,' Marco murmured. He hated to lie, but his uncle would lambast him if he found out; just as the sheikh would be furious with Jamillah if he discovered they had spent the last two nights sparring.

Jamillah was more than Marco's equal, a master of the sword who would impress even his uncle. Neither of them understood the other's words, but that was fine. The dance they made with their swords was language enough, especially with someone as beautiful as Jamillah. He had learned more from striving to match her graceful movements than he had learned under his aunt's or Peruzo's tutelage. He learned how to feint, how to use balance to wrong-foot his opponent, how to move half as grace-fully as she . . .

And more: Marco learned how to fall in love.

He hid these facts from his uncle as they left the tent with Thomas and strolled through the twilight air to the mouth of the great pavilion. The bodyguard called Hisham stood before them. He regarded them quite fleetingly, eyeing their shabby clothes, and only Thomas noted the subtle criticism in his expression.

The tent flaps were tied back so that music and laughter flowed out undiluted. As they walked in, men appeared with dishes spilling over with meat and fruit, while empty plates left the pavilion. Inside the main chamber of the tent the guests had been arranged in a circle, lying or sitting cross-legged on great cushions or mats as they reached for their food.

Sheikh Fahd sat opposite, two others by his side, including a woman in white and yellow. The sheikh gestured for them to sit and the three made themselves comfortable to his left, in the space between the woman and an older man resplendent in bright clothes gilded with gold and silver. The jewellery about his neck could have bought an entire village; such prosperity William had never considered possible for simple nomads. He wondered at Sheikh Fahd's standing with these men, and whether these were his allies or his masters.

For over an hour William watched as the sheikh wined and dined Sheikh Mazin (who sat next to Thomas) and a second sheikh who was not much older than Marco, called Anwar, who sat with the third sheikh, Galal, facing them. Anwar was a bright enthusiastic man–child who had swaggered into the tent all blus-ter and display, which Thomas translated as: 'You're not starting a war without me!' Galal was content to sit quietly, smiling politely, while Mazin looked uncomfortable, scowling at his neighbours.

William was in no humour for the finer aspects of the evening. For every song that was harmonized, and for every dancing girl that Sheikh Fahd paraded in front of them, he could only think of Adriana and how long he had been away from her. He longed to get back to her, he wanted to finish this mission.

Marco had kept quiet throughout the meal. He had so far managed to avoid eye contact with Jamillah, who had been sitting veiled in her white and yellow gown. Like Marco she had acted indifferently, quietly looking to the other sheikhs when they spoke, listening to her brother when he made an announcement. Yet those eyes gave her away. Now and again he felt them upon him. Fear and his pounding heart forced him not to look back.

After another dancer finished her performance, the women guests were dismissed. Marco tried his best not to watch Jamillah leave, looking after her for just a moment as she departed, flanked by bodyguards. But his eyes lingered longer than they should have, and William cursed his nephew under his breath, praying that Sheikh Fahd had not noticed.

To William, this woman could only be the sheikh's wife or someone of equal importance. That Marco was captivated by her was both unexpected and dangerous. William hoped it was a fleeting thing, yet it dawned on him that more had happened while he was away than Marco had let on.

Thomas leant over to William as Sheikh Fahd addressed the guests. 'Sheikh Fahd speaks of his intentions and how the tribe's elders have allowed him to summon the sheikhs of neighbouring tribes, their allies,' Thomas whispered. 'He says that a great curse has fallen on these lands. Greater than the poison spread by Ali. For this curse has claimed the lives of his people, including his brother. And throughout legend, the area known as the Valley of Fire has been a place of ghosts and spirits who deal only death . . . But now this man . . .'

Sheikh Fahd was gesturing towards William and the three other sheikhs and their henchmen stared across. He stared back, a little nervous. '. . . This man says they are not ghosts, but flesh and blood,' Thomas continued to translate. 'This man who knows about such matters says they *can* be killed.'

The older sheikh, Mazin, with a short beard that was grey-ing at the tip, a single scar across his brow, began laughing.

'What is funny?' William whispered to Thomas.

'He thinks you're a liar,' Thomas replied.

William blushed. 'Tell him I speak the truth.'

'Perhaps it is not wise to speak yet, Captain,' Thomas cau-tioned. 'This is a precarious meeting. We would not wish to speak out of turn.'

William blushed even deeper but nodded. 'Of course.'

Sheikh Fahd gestured again to William and began to speak directly to the older sheikh.

'He is explaining why they are flesh and blood,' Thomas translated and smiled. 'He tells this sheikh he is a fool to ignore your words.'

William's face cooled and he crossed his arms, glancing at Sheikh Mazin, who glowered back.

'Now the older sheikh thinks Fahd has been bewitched . . .' Thomas said.

William shook his head, frustrated more and more by the palaver. Marco just found it tiresome. He forgot himself and yawned.

Sheikh Fahd broke off and laughed. 'I see our youngest guest is tired,' he remarked.

William prodded Marco and he straightened up. 'If he wishes to be dismissed, let him go, Captain Saxon. This is a matter for soldiers, not boys,' Sheikh Fahd acknowledged.

'Thank you, sir,' William said and turned to Marco, signalling that he could leave.

Marco got to his feet and walked from the gathering. William watched him leave, suspicion mounting about what the boy might have done in his absence. He remembered the woman in the white and yellow dress. He remembered Sheikh Fahd's talk of a rebellious sister.

Jamillah. Wasn't that her name?

With Marco gone, the youngest sheikh began speaking.

'Captain Saxon,' Sheikh Fahd said, and gestured to Anwar.

'These are the words of Sheikh Anwar. He asks why he should follow you to the Valley of Fire.'

'Please tell Sheikh Anwar, sir, that should I fail in my mission to destroy the evil in that valley, then that evil will spread like a flood over the Sinai. It will destroy everything in its path. Long before my lands are touched by this evil, the Sinai and all of Egypt will burn.'

Sheikh Fahd paused before translating, the horror of that threat all too apparent. He told Sheikh Anwar, who began to lose his sceptical expression, but whose question remained.

'Sheikh Anwar asks again, why should *you* lead such an army into battle?' Sheikh Fahd said, while the other sheikhs nodded their agreement.

'I've been fighting this war for a long time, yet here I stand. My men are battle-hardened. Three days ago we killed a daemon. And time is running out, Sheikh Fahd,' William replied.

Sheikh Fahd relayed the message, and the youngest sheikh responded. He rose to his feet and gestured to the sky.

'He will join us,' Sheikh Fahd announced to William. 'He has twenty warriors in his entourage and another six hundred can be called upon. He deems it an honour to fight such a foe.'

William bowed to Sheikh Anwar.

The second sheikh, not much older than Fahd, had short curly hair and wore the plainest robes of the three. He stood and spoke quickly. Sheikh Fahd bowed gratefully and looked back to William. 'Sheikh Galal pledges his thirty men here, and another five hundred riders.'

William nodded again, bowing to Sheikh Galal. 'And what of Sheikh Mazin?' he said, and glanced at the oldest sheikh who sat seemingly unmovable.

Sheikh Fahd asked a question that Mazin seemed to dismiss, before Anwar said something curt to the older sheikh that made him rage.

'A fine insult,' Thomas chuckled by William's side.

Sheikh Mazin sprang to his feet, hurling abuse at the amused Sheikh Anwar, and then glowered in fury at William.

305

'Sheikh Mazin promises his entourage and another five hundred and fifty men,' Sheikh Fahd announced, 'but he refuses to bring his cannon.'

'Cannon?' William said, a little surprised.

'Relics of an old war, Captain Saxon. I doubt they could even fire in a straight line, but the Suwarka have kept these antiques for generations,' Sheikh Fahd said pleasantly, without any hint of mockery that would enrage Mazin further.

'Even without his cannons, it will do,' William assured the sheikh. 'That's over eighteen hundred men.'

'Two and a half thousand men,' Sheikh Fahd corrected, 'including my riders.'

'Very well,' William said and bowed to each sheikh in turn. Finally he addressed Sheikh Fahd. 'We should leave tomorrow, sir.'

Sheikh Fahd clapped his hands together. 'I agree. Tomorrow *morning*, Captain,' he insisted. 'Why should vengeance wait?'

△ IV △

Racinet raged.

'I want blood!' he snarled as he looked down on the Ayaida from the gloom of the rocks.

'No, Racinet. You cannot,' Baron Horia replied.

'They murdered Ileana! They tortured her! At least give me the one with the silver hair. His head at *least* I must have!' Racinet implored.

'You will do nothing. And if you disobey me, I will take *your* head instead, Racinet,' Baron Horia promised angrily, agitated by the bald vampyre's constant threats and profanity. Two days and nights of Racinet's outbursts had tormented Baron Horia to distraction. Had he not needed him so badly, he would have beheaded the troublesome creature some time since.

'Ileana disobeyed me and paid the price. I forbade her to prey on the monks,' Horia declared. 'My orders were simple: only the militia to be harmed. We need the monks to live to fight the Rassis, or my plan is redundant. Ileana weakened Saxon's little brigade too much. I should've kept her on a leash, don't you think?'

Racinet snarled again and stepped forward, but faltered as Horia's hand brushed the hilt of his sword.

'You exhaust me, Racinet,' Horia said wearily. 'And you bore me. I haven't come all this way to fail. If you challenge me as Ileana did, I will leave you to die here as well. I will not waste one dark hour considering your fate. And it would be unpleasant, Racinet – oh yes, quite unpleasant. This is a land of little shelter, and a sun that would burn the skin from your bones, as it burned Ileana's.'

Racinet bit down on his lip with his jagged and rotten teeth. The shards drew blood, but it was black and coagulated, a sludge that oozed from his mouth and down his bone-white chin. 'When this is over, Baron, there will be a reckoning,' he promised. 'You left her there to die.'

'You heard Thomas Richmond's warnings, Racinet,' Baron Horia said. 'They were waiting for a rescue. It would have been folly.'

'You didn't even *try*,' Racinet lamented.

'I know you loved her. Your lust for Ileana was not unnoticed by me. But do not forget our prize: *a world of our own to rule for ever.* Lords of *all* men, Racinet. Such a prize surpasses the mourning of one lover. I will let you loose upon them in time, but isn't the prize of success worth the price of delay?' Baron Horia tossed his long red hair. His eyes flashed blue in the darkness and he radiated confidence. But in his arrogance he did not notice Racinet's implacable expression. If he had he might have acted.

'Come now, the sun arrives in a matter of hours and we must return to our caravan,' Horia said, rising from the outcrop of rock, his long limbs straightening up with fluid movements. Many miles distant lay the haven of their covered wagon, hidden in the deepest desert away from curious eyes. It would take hours to reach it, but there was no alternative. Nothing could survive without shelter in this wasteland, be it human *or* immortal.

Twisting away, Horia receded into the night, away from the camp, away from the fires and the stirring of life. Racinet hung back as his master slid into shadow; his fury was out of control. His long fingernails had dug deep into the dead skin of his hands, drawing the same lines of blackened blood. His eyes flashed wildly, and tears would have flowed if they had not dried up many, many years ago.

It was Horia's mistake to suppose that he could curb a being like Racinet, a creature so reckless, so predisposed to irrationality and raging emotion. It was not just lust that governed Racinet's actions. He had cared for Ileana, and she for him.

He had truly *loved* her.

As Racinet advanced from the rocky outcrop, the handle of his half-moon flail was already at his fingertips. 'Sometimes, my Baron, vengeance is more important,' he murmured and loped through the night towards the camp of the Ayaida.

△ V △

Marco waited until the last of the guards had gone and then slipped out of the tent. He could not tell how long his uncle might be absent, but he'd take that chance to see Jamillah again. With a pounding heart, all of his senses alert, he crept through the gloom, hugging the shadows in case any guard or other Bedouin was still awake, before stepping silently over guy-ropes, past rugs that shifted in the midnight breeze, past tethered goats and baskets of grain.

Dinner with the sheikh and his guests had tried his nerves, all the more so with Jamillah in attendance. She was the sheikh's family, and whatever he felt for her was forbidden, yet Marco didn't care.

He had feelings for Jamillah that were far greater than any

308

desire he had felt for a girl in Villeda. He had once led a girl called Helena to the Maldinis' barn, and they had fooled about, touching each other's hitherto secret places until the sounds of Tustio Maldini approaching scared her away. But with Jamillah he wanted something else. With Jamillah there was a terror inside that made him feel sick with excitement. He didn't want to just touch her; he wasn't just curious about what she concealed under those gowns, or behind that black veil. He wanted to hold her, to talk to her, and finally kiss her gently on the lips. Nothing more.

As before, Marco arrived at the corral and waited, looking about in case the sheikh's guards lay in wait. He didn't believe his luck would last for ever; sooner or later their forbidden meetings were bound to be interrupted.

Like the moth drawn to her candle-flame, Marco did not care.

He hunkered down between two horses and waited, stroking the animals as they grew restless and pawed at the ground. Footsteps approached. Macro stood up and sidled past the edge of the closest horse. He paused at the edge of the corral, waiting to be sure. Then, from the gloom, came the woman in white and yellow, her handmaidens behind her.

Marco grinned and straightened up. He brushed a hand over the clothes that Thomas had given him, ran his fingers through his hair, and started forward.

'Marco . . .' came a whisper.

Marco froze in mid-step. The voice did not come from Jamillah.

'Marco!' it came again, this time a hiss.

Marco turned slowly and someone grabbed him by the collar.

'Why are you here?' the voice demanded suddenly, and Marco realized who was holding him.

Lieutenant Peruzo stared gravely at the boy, then glanced over to Jamillah and her two attendants. Luckily he and Marco were still in shadow.

'Speak! What are you doing?' Peruzo prompted.

'Nuh . . . Nothing!' Marco protested.

'Your uncle told me to keep an eye on you,' Peruzo said. 'I certainly didn't think why!'

'He doesn't know,' Marco replied and held his hands together hopefully. 'Please . . . Don't tell him.'

Peruzo eyed Marco with the same demeanour as an older brother might. He was loath to hide Marco's secret, yet he knew it was a trivial one compared with the other problems that had plagued the mission.

'Were you following me?' Marco whispered indignantly.

Peruzo shook his head. 'I was checking the horses. We may leave here tomorrow. The captain wants everyone ready.'

'Including me?' Marco said hopefully.

Peruzo shrugged. 'He did not say. Though no doubt after tonight, he may think twice.'

'Please!' Marco protested, raising his voice. 'Please don't tell him, Peruzo! He doesn't have to know!'

Marco forgot himself, or rather their situation, and his raised voice caught the women's attention. They began to call over, and when no one replied, Jamillah and her women walked towards the horses.

'Blast it, Marco,' Peruzo seethed, and clamped his hand over the young man's mouth.

Marco had other ideas. He tore loose from the lieutenant's grip, stepped out into the corral and waved at Jamillah, a boyish smile on his face, hoping that the gloom might mask his nervousness.

As Jamillah closed to within a couple of feet, Peruzo appeared at Marco's shoulder and she froze. The sight of her clothes and her two attendants told him that she was someone of importance – someone dangerous. So he laid one steady hand on Marco's shoulder and said calmly: 'We must leave.'

Marco was caught in two minds. He knew that Peruzo was right, yet how could he leave Jamillah, with her smiling eyes, her dance with the sword? He wanted to be with her, and knew, just knew, that she wanted the same.

'Say goodnight to your friend,' Peruzo insisted, his tone a command.

Marco sighed and smiled apologetically at Jamillah. 'I'm sorry . . .' he began.

Whatever else he thought of saying was stopped short as something whined in the air. Peruzo heard it a fraction sooner, and before Marco registered danger the older lieutenant had grabbed his shoulders and pushed him to the ground, just as the air around them erupted in a swathe of ripping sounds like fabric rent apart.

Trapped by Peruzo's bulk, Marco heard screams.

'Jamillah!' he shouted.

Peruzo looked up to see one of the handmaidens stagger to one side, her eyes looking into darkness as blood brimmed over her lips, the front of her dress glistening in the half-light, running dark red. The other handmaiden simply stood and screamed, her hands over her mouth, as the first fell face-down in the dust.

Jamillah was uncomprehending, frozen in disbelief. Peruzo leapt up and rushed towards her, seizing her hand as the half-moon flail whipped out again. The crescent blades carved through the air she had stood in a heartbeat before, and struck the second handmaiden, severing all four fingers of her left hand and gouging her shoulder.

More screams and sobbing, and Marco got to his knees.

'Stay down!' Peruzo shouted.

Marco stopped his rise, and it was enough for the vampyre to miss him by mere inches as he soared overhead and landed in the sand several feet beyond. Racinet looked down at the handmaidens, the first lying dead in a spreading pool of blood, the second crawling away with choking sobs, before the vampyre twirled his flail again. Peruzo was unarmed and could do nothing but dash towards the vampyre with outstretched hands. He managed to grip one arm before it could release the flail, but the struggle at close quarters was one-sided. As Racinet roared defiance into Peruzo's face, his fury transformed into strength that picked up Peruzo and hurled him against a corral post. He hit it with a crack that snapped the post and felled Peruzo too. Inside the corral, several of the horses bolted, barely missing Peruzo in the small stampede.

The clamour brought cries of alarm from around the camp.

'Vengeance!' Racinet roared, ignoring the growing danger, and he advanced on Peruzo's prone body. The lieutenant did not move . . . Out cold, or dead.

As the vampyre approached, there came another cry, this time from Marco.

'Jamillah! No!' he shouted.

Her attack caught the vampyre unprepared. Jamillah's blade hissed past his cheek and he stumbled back, astonished by the speed of the sword that spun patterns against him. For a moment, Racinet thought it was the spirit of Ileana. But as Jamillah attacked again, the life in her eyes told him different.

Jamillah followed her quick feint by a slash with her sword that cut through the vampyre's sleeve and gashed his arm. Racinet recovered his instincts and kicked off into the air, surprising Jamillah, who failed to take guard as she marvelled at such a feat. He turned in mid-air, pulled out a dagger and plunged it into her shoulder. Marco ran to her, catching Jamillah's body before it could hit the dust.

By the corral, Peruzo stirred. Racinet turned back to the lieutenant. 'Now you will pay your penance for Ileana . . .' he hissed and set the half-moon twirling once again.

Behind him, Marco pulled the knife from Jamillah's shoulder. She cried out in agony and fell unconscious, blood gushing from her shoulder and over his hands – so much blood. Jamillah was surely dying, and utter fury welled up inside Marco, driving the tears from his eyes. The colour had drained from her face: he was losing her.

To that creature . . .

Flaring with rage, Marco turned to the vampyre, his vision

312

blurred. In that maelstrom of wrath and fear, he remembered fragments of vampyre lore: their strengths, their weaknesses. In that moment, nothing mattered but his own vengeance. Vengeance for his family in Tresta, vengeance for Jamillah who was lost. He would not lose Peruzo as well.

Leaping to his feet, Marco cried out as he hurled the dagger at the vampyre. It was a wild throw, a crazy throw they might tell him later, but it was lucky. The blade struck dead centre in the back, and the vampyre howled.

He turned with a look of disbelief. How dare this boy attack him when retribution's work needed to be done? Did he not know what he was? *Who* he was? He was Racinet of the Crags. Racinet, third in line to the duchy of . . .

In a single swift movement, Marco took up Jamillah's sword and charged. Racinet had not expected this from a boy and was caught in slow suspension as the blade swung about.

Peruzo saw vaguely what happened next; saw the flash of metal and the head of the vampyre leaping from its neck before a thin spark of light jetted out, followed by tendrils of cyan that writhed in the air. There were unholy screams, the discord of the damned and the calls of the living as the survivors struggled to make sense of the blinding glare, the chaotic pyrotechnics, while the creature burned.

Peruzo fought to stay awake and aware. Pain racked his body and pounded in his skull. He saw the fires consume the vampyre.

And then there was darkness.

△ VI △

William was running full tilt, with Thomas close behind. The commotion had begun as the guests were leaving the sheikh's tent. At first the distant screams drew little notice – the noise of children playing beyond their bedtime perhaps, scaring each other. But then the guards ran past.

Were they under attack?

William's feet pounded harder at the sound of the howling. It was unmistakable: a cry like a tortured animal; a vampyre's raucous shriek. He drew his sword as they bounded in the wake of several Bedouins who were also sprinting towards the corral. There was more commotion now, and light, a pillar of light erupting over the neighs of frightened horses.

'Vampyres!' he shouted at Thomas, who was struggling to keep up.

So many expectations and fears filled William in those moments: an attack . . . someone had defeated the vampyre, but at what cost?

And lastly: *Where was Peruzo? Where was Marco?*

When they entered the corral, slowing to weave their way among panicked horses, William's head whirled in desperation at the sight. In front of him was Marco, bowed fearfully while the bodyguard known as Hisham stood over him holding a scimitar's blade against his neck.

'No!' William yelled without thinking. At once the other bodyguards sprang forward, their drawn swords menacing William. Thomas halted in his tracks, his hands in the air.

William stared at the Bedouin; each had a look of murder in his eyes. The slightest command would turn these sometime allies into his executioners. This was the direst trouble.

When he saw Peruzo also on his knees, William rated the situation even worse, until he noticed that his lieutenant wasn't under guard, though badly shaken.

'Captain . . .' he said, struggling to get to his feet. William moved to help him up.

'What happened?'

'A vampyre . . .'

'And Marco?'

'I don't know,' Peruzo replied. 'I was out cold for a moment. When I came round, the vampyre was burning up.' The lieutenant pointed to the pile of smoking corruption the others were shunning fearfully. The stench of rotting meat and sulphur was gagging.

Thomas stepped forward and stared down at what remained of Racinet. He screwed up his face as he looked away.

'Why do they threaten Marco?' William said urgently.

'He was holding the girl when I woke,' Peruzo said, nodding to where a slender figure lay crumpled on the ground, her elegant robe more crimson now than yellow.

'Jamillah . . .' William gasped, a precarious situation grown steadily worse. His mind raced and he pulled his lieutenant to his feet. 'Go to Brother Filippo. Tell him to come at once. He can examine you while he's at it. You don't look well, my friend.'

'Just groggy . . .' Peruzo grunted and staggered away.

'Thomas,' William called, bewildered by the turn of events. The Englishman appeared at his side. 'I can't allow this.'

'We have no choice, Captain,' Thomas said. 'They blame the boy for her wounds.'

'It was not him,' William protested.

'It will not matter to them,' Thomas said. 'He has her blood on his hands.'

Then came more shouting from afar, a commotion that sounded terrible yet softened into relieved weeping as a guard appeared carrying a bundle of rags.

Another death? William thought fearfully.

The bundle was lowered gently to the ground, and unwrapped from the blood-stained garments came another woman, one who was shaking and weeping. She burst into speech, reaching out for Sheikh Fahd's sister with a fingerless hand. Then she gestured frantically to Marco, and William's blood ran cold. In his ignorance, he believed it an accusation: this woman with the ruined hand had sentenced the boy to death. He was about to lose his nephew, and that was something William could not let happen, regardless of the repercussions.

The bodyguard raised his sword, and William steeled himself, before Thomas's hand grasped his shoulder. 'Stop, Captain,' he said firmly.

William froze and watched as the bodyguard sheathed his sword and pulled Marco to his feet.

'What . . .?'

Thomas laughed; it was cold, perhaps bitter, and lost on William. 'Marco killed the vampyre,' Thomas said. 'He saved the sheikh's sister.'

William gasped. *Marco killed the vampyre? Could it be true?*

The Bedouins lowered their swords as William sheathed his own and ran to Marco. He took the boy in his arms and held him tight.

'By God, Marco!' he breathed, his eyes closed. 'You've aged me, boy!'

Marco hugged his uncle back. 'I had to save her,' he cried. 'I had to, Uncle.'

'I know,' William murmured, and released him. 'But you could have been killed.'

'I don't care,' Marco said truthfully and looked down at Jamillah. Tears were running down his young cheeks as he stared down at the sheikh's sister, the pallor of her skin. 'She's dead, isn't she?'

William could not say. 'Brother Filippo will tend to her,' he promised, hoping the monk was on his way.

△ VII △

More people did arrive, but the monk was not among them. Instead Sheikh Fahd appeared. He flung himself to the floor and took Jamillah's body from one of the guards, pushing the man away. Fahd was beside himself, cursing in every tongue he knew, gesturing to the sky and to the ground with great moans and sobs. His sister looked lifeless, limp in the burly Arab's arms.

When Brother Filippo arrived, with Peruzo not far behind, William motioned towards Jamillah. Sheikh Fahd at first could only glare at the monk with contempt and fury, causing both Filippo and William to step back.

'Sir, Brother Filippo is a physician. One of the finest,' William explained. 'Let him look at her, *please*.'

Sheikh Fahd was hesitant, but Brother Filippo looked in-offensive. Looking down at his poor sister, the sheikh groaned for a moment, his once affable expression driven from him. Then he handed her reluctantly to Brother Filippo, who laid her gently upon the sand.

For many minutes, too many for those apprehensive men, the Ayaida prayed to Allah for Jamillah's deliverance, while Filippo trusted not in God but in his own skills as a physician. The first moment of relief came after the monk roused her with a phial held under her nose and signalled to all that she was still alive. Yet her pale complexion and the thickness of blood on her dress did not bode well.

Finally Filippo gestured to Marco, who wavered at first, but then came over. He spoke a few words and Marco gathered her up in his arms. 'We need to move her to a tent,' Filippo said to William.

William asked the sheikh and they were allowed to follow Hisham to one of the harem's tents, leaving Sheikh Fahd to stand and shiver in the chill of night.

'Will she live?' he asked William.

'Brother Filippo is her only hope,' he replied.

'That is not an answer, Captain Saxon,' Sheikh Fahd seethed.

'I know little of her condition, only that she is badly wounded,' William admitted. 'I'm sorry.'

Sheikh Fahd shook his head. 'You have nothing to be sorry for. I am in your debt,' he said. 'And in your nephew's debt. He saved her life.'

William could only agree. Marco was a hero. By morning everyone would know this. And by morning William would have little choice but to take the fearless young vampyre-killer to the Valley of Fire, despite every warning in his soul. Marco had earned it.

Sheikh Fahd retired, the bodyguards moving after him in procession. If these Bedouins had a judgement on this evening, it was not offered. William wished that he knew right now what they all thought, both of his company, and of the war he had dragged them into. Would they be enraged and bring more men? Or would William and the company be blamed for the attack, for the wounding and maybe the death of the sheikh's beloved sister?

Part of him believed the fault was his, just as it was his fault that Thomas's entourage had been attacked by vampyres, the militia at the oasis almost slaughtered, and Marco brought close to execution after saving Jamillah's life. William had brought them all here, into his own little war with Count Ordrane of Draak.

'A dark business,' William found himself murmuring to no one as his thoughts rambled. Only Peruzo and Thomas remained near the corral.

'You should get some rest, Lieutenant,' William suggested, noting the drained look in Peruzo's eyes.

The lieutenant agreed, too tired to argue, and rose shakily to his feet again, lurching away into the shadows, making for the company's tents at the edge of the camp.

Thomas stared down again at the scraps of rag, the ash dispersed and trampled by the numbers of Ayaida who had rushed to the scene. The vampyre's remains had been kicked about, reduced to dust for horses to tread on. Even his burnt clothes were strewn like rags. The half-moon flail lay a few feet away, half buried in the sand.

'Just one vampyre,' William said to him. 'The prisoner at the oasis said there were two.'

'Yes,' Thomas said distantly.

'I see you are wondering as I do,' William whispered. 'Why only one vampyre attacked, and what has happened to the other.' William patted Thomas comfortingly on the shoulder and then followed Peruzo, pausing to pick up the vampyre's flail on the way back to their tent.

Thomas watched William until he disappeared behind the pavilions and their shadows. He shivered in the cold, as he looked out to the horizon. Thomas did wonder why just the one vampyre had attacked, and indeed why it had attacked at all.

But not for the same reasons as William.

CHAPTER SIXTEEN

Myths from the Fire

△ I △

Like any boy his age, any boy with a half-formed perception of devotion and responsibility, Marco intended to stand his ground all night by Jamillah's tent, and would have done so if not for William. It took the promise of allowing Marco to accompany him to the Valley of Fire to coax the boy from his vigil. Even then, Marco slept little, pacing outside their tent, or watching the stars as though some sign of Jamillah's fate would be unveiled.

Brother Filippo had tended her for several hours. He sewed up her wound, applied some of Villeda's finest ointments to salve it, and brewed a herbal tea to cope with her fever. When eventually the colour returned to her cheeks, relief ran all through the camp.

'Can I see her?' Marco asked early that morning.

Brother Filippo, somewhat fatigued himself, shooed the boy away. 'She needs to rest,' he said, stifling a yawn.

'I want to speak to her.'

Brother Filippo indicated Hisham, who barred the way. 'These people have their customs. You might have saved her life, but it is not yours to order, it is theirs. They are Ayaida and you are but a boy from Villeda. Return later.'

Marco looked over Brother Filippo's shoulder, the desire to see her almost too great to restrain.

'Marco,' said the monk, taking his shoulders, 'you did a great thing last night. You are a hero. Yet soon we may be leaving this place for ever. Take comfort that you have saved a life and be grateful for that.'

Marco sagged but he understood. If they did return, he would see her. If they did return he would be with her, and he vowed to become so brave a man that even Sheikh Fahd would not refuse him.

William roused the brothers as the first threads of dawn warmed the gully. Despite their maltreatment at the hands of the militia, they readied themselves quickly, reunited with their Baker rifles, weapons they had sorely missed in the battle at Bastet. Many of the brothers appeared refreshed following a decent night's sleep and with good food and drink in their bellies.

William visited the brothers too wounded and battered to ride. Some protested and insisted they were well enough to serve. William did not relent, but offered them a chance of heroism: to help to protect the Ayaida while they were away. There was, after all, 'still a vampyre loose in the desert'.

With Jamillah mending, Sheikh Fahd appeared purposeful and urgent. Earlier that morning he had convened a meeting with the tribal elders, who had blessed him and the battle ahead. For Fahd, the vampyres and the Rassis were one and the same. The destruction of the Rassis would lift the peril from the Ayaida, especially his sister, as well as satisfy his vengeance. He did not delay rousing his men, and the seven hundred were mounted and ready to travel as quickly as William's monks.

As the sun rose a quarter up into the blue sky, the long column of Bedouins and monks left the camp. Most had their minds on what might lie ahead. Marco looked back through the clouds of churned-up dust to the harem in the centre of the camp and the woman who lay there.

By the end of the first day, the army had cleared the beige-coloured wastes of Bir Gifgafa. On the second day, the extra riders promised by Anwar and Galal finally arrived, their appearance marked by a broad bank of rolling dust as hundreds of horses lined up on the plains of Yalliq just in front of the sandstone and limestone mountain that shimmered in a midday haze.

The Suwarka appeared soon after the Tarabin and Aquila Bedouins, the six hundred riders galloping through the pass of Ain-Heim dragging several carts, and behind them three cannon. Sheikh Mazin galloped down the line, not to embrace his men as Galal and Anwar had, but to berate his eldest son for bringing the tribe's artillery with them.

William hung back with Thomas, and both began to laugh as Mazin chased his son around on horseback, the former yelling abuse, the latter cowed and in full flight.

'So Mazin brings his cannon,' Sheikh Fahd said, quite pleased.

'As I recall, you said they would not shoot straight,' William remarked.

'So I did,' Sheikh Fahd replied, 'but at least it will provide the proper noise for the encounter. What is a battle, Captain Saxon, without cannon?'

'As long as Mazin doesn't fire on *us*, they might be of some use,' William said.

'Then we will be sure to let the Suwarka charge first, Captain Saxon,' Sheikh Fahd said, and chuckled as they watched the Suwarka join the long column of Bedouin riders.

The allies of the Ayaida brought much celebration from Sheikh Fahd's men and gave great hope to the company of armed monks; it was now truly an army, and William's confidence was rekindled for the long journey ahead.

The hours of riding through fractured landscapes of barren rock and over vast plains of scorching desert blurred and merged the following days together. Only the cold of night could call a halt to that urgent drive into the heart of the Sinai; then there was time to speak with Thomas about matters other than their immediate mission, the pleasures of a merchant's life. His friendship with Thomas invigorated him, a reminder of how much there was that lay outside the clandestine conflict between Heaven and Hell. There was a life back in England. In the ignorance of the outside world, there was the chance to be happy, to aspire, achieve, gossip, even to take leisure.

When he began once again to write that difficult letter home to his father, mother and Lizzy at Fairway Hall, it came surprisingly easily, in a torrent of blurred facts and credible fictions. There were lies in that letter, yes, but only because William believed in them, only because he *wanted* them to be true. On the third night of writing, with the letter almost complete, he realized that his ardour for the War had waned. He wanted to be back with his family in England, and was ready to start a new life with Adriana.

If, that is, he survived the mission.

△ III △

Four days out and Sheikh Fahd announced to William they had passed into the El-Tih highlands and were taking the hidden roads to the foot of Gebel Musa, and the Monastery of St Catherine.

Despite their progress, conditions were growing ever more severe. The brothers' remaining wagon was battered but intact. Not so with Mazin's wagons. Of the four carts, one fell down a gully in a rock slide while another's wheels buckled twice under the strain of travelling narrow paths and rocky gorges. Had it not been for the wheelwright skills of several brothers, the Suwarka would have lost the cart and its cannon by the end of the first day through the highlands.

On the fifth day, the heat in the highlands rose and water was running short amongst the monks of the Order. Even the Bedouins, masters of conserving water, were flagging. On the sixth night, Sheikh Fahd appeared unusually subdued when he invited William to eat with him in his grand pavilion that had burdened the camels riding at the centre of the army.

'We must find an oasis,' he confided as a wind grew about them, howling through the gaps in the mountains and down the passes, causing the walls of the tent to billow and the lamp-flames to flicker and waver. 'There are smaller wells in these mountains, but it would take a day to change direction and seek them.'

'An extra day?' William said. 'Time is everything, sir.'

'So is surviving, Captain Saxon,' Sheikh Fahd reminded him.

'Are there alternatives?'

'To dying?' Sheikh Fahd laughed humourlessly. 'We could head for Ain Umm Ahmed.'

William frowned.

'It is an oasis. One of the largest in this region. But other Bedouin tribes use that area. Tribes that are often hostile.'

'Hostile against two and a half thousand men?'

'Even then,' Sheikh Fahd admitted. 'They would see our army as an invading force. They would not tolerate us.'

'Then it is a risk,' William admitted. 'But a warranted one.'

'Agreed,' Sheikh Fahd replied. 'Tomorrow we will head east towards Wadi el-Ain. There we will drink and feed. After that, I am not sure when we'll find another place to rest. This land has a stone heart. And it will betray us with thirst and hunger. I will pray to Allah that we find the Valley of Fire soon, Captain Saxon.'

'What about this monastery?' William asked.

'St Catherine?' the sheikh said. 'Why would you wish to go there?'

'You said St Catherine was visited by Charles Greynell,' William said. Sheikh Fahd nodded. 'Then it lies not far away from the Valley of Fire?'

'We do not need directions to the Valley, Captain,' Sheikh Fahd said.

'No,' William agreed, 'but we need a place to rest before we assault the Rassis. And I would like some information. Maybe those who live at the monastery can tell us more about the Rassis Cult.'

'What more could you wish to know?'

'A friend once told me the Rassis are cunning and strong. A good soldier will learn about his enemy before he engages it. I just want to know whether they are desperate men or cold killers.'

'Does it matter so much which they are?' Sheikh Fahd asked.

'If they are desperate, they will fight to the last and offer no mercy because they believe they will receive none themselves. And if they are cold killers, then they will slaughter all of us if they can.'

Sheikh Fahd began to laugh. 'As I said, it does not matter so much! We are doomed either way, my friend.'

William smiled and then grew serious again.

'Do you fear them, Captain Saxon?' Sheikh Fahd asked, noticing William's solemn expression.

'I do not fear the Rassis, sir. But I fear the consequences should we fail,' William replied and then wrapped his arms about himself as the winds outside blew stronger.

△ IV △

The track heading to Wadi el-Ain was narrow and snaked around shattered mountains and mammoth chunks of rust-coloured rock. It was littered with boulders and smaller stones which made the going strenuous. For almost a mile of track, the going was so poor that the wagons threatened to slide from the side of the mountain into the gully below, impeding their progress and slowing the army to a crawl. Amongst the waste-land there were spots of green, but little lush vegetation, just golden scree and brown rock with tufts of weeds daring to peek from clefts in the hard terrain.

The brothers' mouths grew parched. Their jackets were no longer the grey of the Order, but the colour of the dust and rock about them; their faces rough and gaunt, as if the journey's few days had aged them. Even the Bedouins whose land this was looked relieved when they made the oasis of Ain Umm Ahmed before sunset. The leading riders leapt from their horses and ran to the pool's edge laughing and jostling to sip from the water and fill their skins, but they were quick to make room for those behind them.

With so many thirsty men, William was impressed by their discipline. He allowed the monks to drink their fill, then dismounted and led his horse to the water to drink while he filled his own water-skin. Marco knelt by him and did the same, accepting the wait as he had accepted the hardships of the journey. William was proud of him. Any remnants of his former petulance had been shed along the way. Marco had suffered like the others without a word of complaint.

'*Easy*,' William warned, as he took great gulps from his water-skin. 'Don't drink so quickly. You could choke. Take small sips, like this . . .'

Marco watched and nodded, sipping as his uncle did.

Thomas sat in the saddle while Hammid filled both their skins of water, keeping away from the rest of the Bedouins and monks. He handed one skin up to Thomas and then sat in the shade to sip from his own.

William came over. 'Well, we have water,' he said.

'But there is a cost?' Thomas asked.

'Two days' travel. I fear we will not arrive at St Catherine for another three days.'

'Three days of *this*?' Thomas looked bewildered. 'Perhaps I should have stayed at the Ayaida camp.'

William ignored him. It had been Thomas's choice to join them after all. 'When we reach St Catherine you can stay there until we return. The monastery should have lodgings of some sort.'

Thomas brightened and stretched his aching arms. 'That is appealing. And yet I think I'll continue with you to the Valley of Fire.'

'If that is your wish,' William said, secretly thankful.

'It is, Captain. It is,' Thomas insisted as they made their way to the circle of tents.

△ V △

After two more days of hard riding, they sighted St Catherine's monastery. The army journeyed down a valley Sheikh Fahd called 'The Plain of el-Raha' – a vast expanse of tanned stone and sand that stretched from one rocky crag to the other, giant broken mountains walling in the plain. The floor was bare of life. The vision of civilization squatting amid this wilderness came as a relief.

The chatter amongst Sheikh Fahd's men grew as they neared the walls of the monastery. William knew by the sheikh's description that the monastery housed Greek Orthodox priests, yet he felt confident they would not turn away even an army of well-intentioned Arabs such as these.

Even so, he felt the need for caution as they came within half a mile of the monastery. He signalled for the monks to halt and Sheikh Fahd's hundreds of riders followed his lead.

'Is something wrong, Captain?' Sheikh Fahd asked.

'An army of this size might be intimidating,' William told him. 'Should the monks of St Catherine see two and a half thousand Bedouins descend towards them, they might lock their gates against us. Or those guards there on the wall might shoot down at us.'

Sheikh Fahd looked to the soldiers William referred to, tall shapes clustered at intervals along the wall, some dashing between towers. 'If I looked upon this magnificent army, I too would take fright. The monastery has suffered small attacks from bandits over the years. It would be a crime against Allah should a battle occur between us over a misunderstanding.'

'I will go alone with several monks. We will pave the way forward. Just wait for me,' William suggested.

'I will come with you,' Sheikh Fahd told him.

'You do not trust me?'

'Of course,' Sheikh Fahd replied. 'I am simply curious.'

William picked five men to ride with him, leaving Peruzo in command. Sheikh Fahd took Hisham and two bodyguards. As they rode nearer, William spied the soldiers high on the walls. They were armed with rifles, and there was little cover on the approach to the monastery; a well-trained guard could pick them off quite easily.

About forty yards from the walls, they slowed their approach. 'We should draw near gradually, so that they can see who we are. That we mean no harm.' As the formidable walls loomed higher, William felt apprehensive. 'I just hope these men understand Latin,' he added more to himself.

'They are Greek,' Sheikh Fahd reminded him. 'Do you speak Greek?'

'No. Do you?' William replied, foreseeing a major problem.

Sheikh Fahd shook his head and laughed.

'Well, it's too late to turn back now. The main gate must be over to the left.' William steered his horse towards an opening in a low stone wall, fifty feet from the leading wall. They made their way through, and noticed a number of men gathered by some narrow stone steps beyond it, some armed with guns, others dressed in long black gowns with long grey beards.

Brother Jericho gestured to them. 'Monks?'

William nodded and spurred his horse into a trot. He put one hand in the air and began to smile nervously. *Here goes*, he thought to himself as they closed on the steps, praying they understood Latin.

'I am William Saxon. Of the Order of Saint Sallian, Villeda. Sent here by the Papacy. Whom am I addressing?' he shouted.

There wasn't an instant reply, but a chorus of murmur, then shuffling, and finally one man with a grey beard longer than the others stepped forward. 'I am Brother Stephanos,' he shouted, 'of the Order of Saint Catherine. State your business, brother, for you came bearing weapons, and that throws doubt on your story.'

'I apologize for my appearance, Brother Stephanos. We are monks of an unconventional kind,' William called back.

'I see. And from an Order none of us have heard of,' the Greek monk replied cautiously.

'I admit you will not have heard of the Order of Saint Sallian prior to this day. There are few who have. But there is good reason for this, which I might venture to explain if you allow us refuge, or at least to camp within the grounds of your monastery.'

The Greek monk stared down at them and then cupped his eyes to look down the plain towards the thousands of riders massed there. 'What evidence can you offer, to show that you are telling the truth?' he called back.

'Evidence?' Brother Jericho murmured by his captain's shoulder.

William frowned. He then remembered the Papal seal around his neck. His hand reached up to touch it. 'Stay here,' he said to the brothers and rode ahead.

Brother Jericho held his breath as the soldiers on the walls trained their guns on his captain, Sheikh Fahd was equally worried that William would be shot from his horse without warning.

As William neared the steps he brought out the chain with the seal attached. 'This marks an envoy of the Roman Catholic Church, Brother Stephanos,' he called out a few yards from the steps.

The Greek monk shuffled down the steps and crossed the ground to William's horse. William pulled the chain from around his neck and handed it down to him.

'Pope Pius,' Brother Stephanos remarked as he looked over the seal. 'You appear to be genuine, yet you lead an army.'

'Yes,' William admitted, 'but on a holy cause, Brother.'

'There is nothing holy about war,' the monk decried.

'You may feel different when I tell you what our cause is,' William replied. 'We are looking for the Rassis in the Valley of Fire.'

The monk's expression changed suddenly as though an invisible hand had slapped him in the face. 'Not many would dare speak of the Valley of Fire, nor of the ghosts that dwell there. Are you chasing the Devil himself?'

William grinned ironically. 'That we are, Brother. That we are.'

'Very well. You may come inside the walls. But your army stays where it is,' he replied, the main gate opening wider to admit the ten arrivals.

△ VI △

'Let us sit,' Brother Stephanos suggested, lowering himself down upon a rather old and fragile stool behind a simple wooden table. William sat opposite, feeling his own stool wobble under his weight. Sheikh Fahd sat next to him, finding the experience amusing, not quite trusting the whole of his weight to the chair he sat on.

Brother Stephanos called for water for their guests, while William introduced his monks first, and then Sheikh Fahd.

'A Bedouin sheikh?' Brother Stephanos said. 'And those are his men to the north?'

'Not just him, but three other sheikhs ride with us,' William told him.

'Then you *are* soldiers and this is an army,' Brother Stephanos concluded.

'That notion does my cause a disservice, Brother Stephanos,'

William objected. 'You speak as though we are invaders or conventional conquerors. We are neither.'

'Then explain to me who you are,' Brother Stephanos said as several monks in black gowns brought jugs of water. 'Drink?'

William nodded and took a wooden cup filled to the brim. 'My thanks.'

'Thanks be to God,' Brother Stephanos corrected. 'This is His will, Brother Saxon. For while the seasons have been dryer than most, our wells still hold water.'

'A miracle, Brother Stephanos,' William replied formally and sipped. He tasted sweet cold water, far purer than anything he'd drunk from the oases, and so he sipped again, thirstily draining the cup, much to his own embarrassment.

'You have travelled long, I see, Brother,' Brother Stephanos said, with a hint of surprise as he regarded William's now empty cup.

'Yes,' William replied, and added: 'Though I confess, I am not a monk.'

'You said you were . . .'

'I said I came from the Church, and the men I lead are monks. A common misconception,' William explained. 'I am Captain William Saxon. I was recruited by the Vatican while I was serving with the British army seven years ago.'

'A soldier?'

'An officer,' William corrected.

'That explains why you are dressed in such a manner,' Brother Stephanos said, and gestured to William's clothes. 'And what is that I see on your sleeve? Blood? You have the air of bandits.'

'The Order of Saint Sallian is an Order with a different task,' William told Stephanos. 'Since we left Rome some weeks ago, eleven of my monks have been killed. Four others are terribly wounded and are resting at this sheikh's camp.'

'How did this happen?'

'The infernal, Brother Stephanos,' William replied bluntly. He felt no need to play games with this fellow. Either the religious men of St Catherine knew about the infernal, or they did not. Time was slipping by. He needed answers quickly.

'You speak of evil men,' Brother Stephanos parried.

William could see deception in his eyes. He narrowed his own, and leant forward. 'Not men. These are monsters, Brother Stephanos. Creatures with no soul.'

Brother Stephanos sat back and shook his head slightly.

'Do not feign ignorance,' William warned him. 'I see it in your eyes.'

'I know only of ghosts, Officer Saxon,' the monk protested.

William recalled the same conversation with Sheikh Fahd. 'Of course. And they dress head to foot in dark blue? And they murder?'

Brother Stephanos nodded. 'There are stories of such terrors.'

'And what stories have you heard?' William tried to curb his impatience.

Brother Stephanos locked his fingers together and directed a cautious gaze at William. 'The story I have heard is told among the nomads to the south. They speak of silent ghosts who come down from the mountains to raid their camps. They kill the men and rape the women, and then they fade away into the night. After several years, the ghosts return.'

'Why?' William asked.

'To reclaim their progeny,' Brother Stephanos replied. 'Those children who have not been killed at birth by angry tribes are then taken away by these ghosts once they are weaned. The children are never seen or heard of again.'

'But how? Ghosts do not have children.'

'There lies the flaw in the story,' the monk agreed.

'Do you believe these "ghosts" are flesh and blood?' William asked.

'I believe they are *men*,' Brother Stephanos replied.

'And these children . . . How do the ghosts know which are theirs?'

'Because they carry the marks at birth.'

'Marks?' William prompted.

Brother Stephanos fidgeted. 'I have only seen one supposed bastard child of these "ghosts". They are shorter than other Bedouin children; their skin is lighter, like sand, and their hair is thick black. But their eyes tell it all – long and narrow, like knives. They are not Arabs.'

'Then from where?'

'I do not know. Far away, I expect,' Brother Stephanos said.

'So what does a soldier of the Vatican want with ghosts?'

'They are guarding something terrible, Brother Stephanos,' William replied. '*The infernal.*'

The monk folded his arms with displeasure. 'You use that word glibly, Officer Saxon. May I ask what *exactly* they are hiding?'

'Two hundred and fifty artefacts straight from the pit of Hell,' William said plainly. 'The term Scarimadaen may not be one familiar to you, but believe me, you will be glad to never hear that word again. If we fail to destroy these "ghosts" and what they are hiding, imagine what could happen should the Devil walk our streets with two hundred and fifty of his foot-soldiers alongside him.'

'You speak of the Apocalypse,' Brother Stephanos said in dismay.

'I do,' William confirmed. 'It could start here in the Sinai, unless our mission is successful.'

Brother Stephanos looked horrified. He rose slowly and ran the tips of his gnarled fingers through his beard. 'If you had been simply a man plucked from the desert, I would have considered you wild at best, insane at worst. But you are not.'

'No,' William replied sadly, 'I am not.'

The Greek monk turned to the others behind him and began speaking in hushed whispers.

'Do you believe you have succeeded, Captain Saxon?' Sheikh Fahd murmured to him in English.

'I hope so, sir,' William replied. 'We are running out of water and food. And some shelter would be a fine thing.'

Brother Stephanos said something in a language William

didn't recognize, but believed was probably Greek, and the Orthodox monks departed humbly. The old monk addressed him again.

'The Arabs may camp within the outer walls if they wish,' he said. 'We have lodgings for thirty men. Will that be enough for your Order?'

'It will. Thank you,' William said and rose from the table. 'There is also an English merchant we saved in the desert, and his servant. They have become victims of this horror also.'

'I am sure we can find lodgings for them,' Brother Stephanos said. 'But they will be simple.'

'If there is a place to rest our heads, it will do just fine,' William said, somewhat relieved.

△ VII △

After washing and dressing, William walked into the courtyard of St Catherine. It was quiet as the sun set and the sky turned a dark blue. The strongest of stars dared to waken and a three-quarter moon hung over the mountains in the distance. It was cool, but not cold, and William was stripped to his shirt, his jacket washed and drying with the rest of the Order's jackets. He had shaved, and as he stood in the evening air with Marco at his side, he ran a rough hand over his chin and felt satisfied. It was good to be housed within a building for the first time since leaving Rashid.

Peruzo arrived in the courtyard with a broad smile, the first since Bastet.

'You look revived, Lieutenant,' William remarked.

'I could have had two baths, Captain, there was so much dust.'

'And the company?'

'Resting. Talking. Eating and drinking,' Peruzo replied gladly. 'Shall we find our host, Brother . . .'

'Brother Stephanos,' William replied. 'I suppose we should.'

'What of the Englishman?' Peruzo asked as the three of them strolled across the courtyard.

'Thomas elected to stay in his room,' William replied. 'He is looking forward to a long bath.'

'He does not like washing with the others,' Peruzo remarked.

'He prefers his privacy,' William replied. 'I was once like Thomas. Most merchants are. But in the army you do things differently. Being shy whilst bathing is the last thing you think about.'

The observation tickled Peruzo, who chuckled as they walked towards a large building at the northern wall of the monastery. It was grand, with flawless walls and windows, newly built amongst the more antique buildings about them.

They entered a hall that feigned to be simple at first, yet as the eyes adjusted to the gloom, lit intermittently by tall candles and several small lamps, they noticed elegant murals and paintings on the ceilings.

Peruzo admired them for a few minutes before one of the Orthodox monks nodded for them to sit at a large table. 'Impressive,' Peruzo murmured and gestured to Marco to look up as they took their seats. The boy's eyes widened as he saw figures in historic settings, depictions of saints and their fates.

'This is nothing, my friends,' Brother Stephanos said behind them. He walked in carrying himself carefully, appearing older now than William had first believed. Beneath that thick black gown was a body fragile with age. When he sat down it was slowly, lowering himself by degrees and under strain.

'Tomorrow I will show you our basilica, and there you will see beauty. A wondrous sight, even for those who have seen the Vatican.'

'I regret, we cannot,' William said. 'We must leave at first light tomorrow.'

'Unfortunate,' Brother Stephanos replied. 'Then I will enjoy your company tonight instead.'

The conversation throughout that evening was much muted, but necessary. William found it a refreshing diversion as they

335

talked about all things secular and eventually personal as William admitted his position as an exile.

As the evening turned into night and they bade Brother Stephanos goodnight, the monk took William aside.

'Your path is a violent one, Captain Saxon,' he said.

'It is the path I must take, Brother Stephanos. I do not choose it willingly.'

The monk gripped William's arm, his strength belying his age. 'You must one day renounce this violence.'

'The violence is for the sake of Christianity,' William replied. 'How can I renounce a cause that is just?'

'Because it puzzles me that the Church would pursue such a cause,' Brother Stephanos lamented. 'Regardless whether daemons exist in this world, we cannot kill our brothers. We must use prayer and faith in God.'

'Prayer will not stop these creatures,' William told him bluntly. 'Guns and swords will.'

'Spoken like a true soldier,' Brother Stephanos remarked, exasperated.

'I beg your forgiveness,' William said and bowed, 'but sometimes sacrifices must be made. I fight tooth and claw so that men like you do not have to. What would you do if two hundred and fifty invincible creatures, taller than a man, with only violence in their hearts, came pounding at your gates? Would you pray for deliverance? Would you use scripture to attack them?'

'I would do all that I am prepared to do. But I would not raise my hand to them,' Brother Stephanos replied.

'Then be glad there are men who will,' William replied. 'Men who sacrifice much for those who will turn the other cheek. Sometimes, Brother Stephanos, simply turning that cheek is not enough.'

Chapter Seventeen

Lies in the Desert

△ I △

Hammid looked down on the camped Bedouin riders during the steady dawn, feeling torn between his allegiances. His eyes were ringed black and threaded with thick red veins as though constantly sore. But it was inside that hurt most, the terrible mass growing within him, painfully thrusting its way through his organs, making him void himself uncontrollably at times, coiling him in agony at others. Only Thomas Richmond had offered any respite, and a purpose.

The Englishman appeared at his shoulder.

'You wish to stay with them?' Thomas asked.

Hammid shook his head. 'They ask too many questions,' he replied awkwardly.

'And what answers do you give them?'

'Only those you wish me to,' Hammid replied.

'Good,' Thomas said, and smiled, a grin without humour. 'We have a long journey ahead of us, Hammid. Are we packed?'

'Yes.' Hammid bowed.

'Then stop lingering here and take my belongings to the courtyard.'

Hammid bowed again and left quickly. Thomas stayed at the turret to look towards the mountains in the distance with a feeling of expectation.

The farewells had been perfunctory at best. William had all he needed from the Orthodox monks, and the Greeks wanted the Bedouin army away from St Catherine's. Brother Stephanos did not care for ghosts, nor daemons, nor vampyres, but when an army of thousands came to his gate, headed by someone speaking for the Vatican, then it was time for alarm. The captain from Rome troubled him greatly, as did the direction of the Roman Church, and he decided he would write to the Vatican soon to express that concern.

William, for his part, had suspected that something ill would come of their visit to St Catherine. It was after the meal that evening that he confided in Peruzo what trouble there might be.

'Surely he would not stop us,' Peruzo had said.

'No,' William replied, 'but he might raise questions with our superiors. Remember that a duty of our mission is stealth. To hide all evidence of war. I have just led an army of Bedouins to the gates of an important monastery in the very name of our war. I have broken the code.'

'They will do nothing,' Peruzo said and shrugged. 'What *can* they do?'

William smiled. 'Nothing I would regret,' he said. 'If they ask me to leave the Order, I'll do so willingly.'

'Surely not . . .' Peruzo said, alarmed.

William nodded. 'I would, my friend. I would. Adriana has already requested it.' He appeared grave for a moment, almost lost. 'Everything has changed. I no longer feel righteous. My reasons to continue fighting are not so clear to me, Peruzo. Everything that has happened since we arrived in Rashid, the deaths of the brothers . . . And what we did to that woman at Bastet . . .'

'*She was a vampyre*,' Peruzo insisted. 'You had no choice. It would be a great blow to the cause if you left because of ill-founded guilt.'

'If we succeed in this mission, Peruzo, I doubt there will be much of a cause left,' William said ruefully. 'And if we fail . . .'

'We will not fail,' Peruzo assured him, 'because you are still here to lead us.'

△ III △

The day slipped by in endless hours of trotting down dusty tracks, now in shadow, and then blazing sunlight. Marco dabbed at his face with his shirtsleeve, the sweat pouring off him; he went to his water-skin again.

'Slow down,' Jericho said by his side. 'Don't drink it all at once. No one has said where the next oasis is.'

'Have you done this before? Travelled in the desert?' Marco asked after taking a very small sip that did little more than wet his lips.

Jericho shook his head. 'My first mission was to Vienna,' he said. 'The brothers around me have been to Spain, and some to other barren places. I'm not enjoying it much. I don't like the heat or the sand.'

Marco could only agree. He too disliked the endless, joyless rides and the intense warmth of the open. So far it wasn't like the adventures he had dreamt of. There were no moments of heroism, nor moments of honour, just small skirmishes in the dark where men would fall screaming and bloodied.

Killing the vampyre had been a nasty business; chaotic and far from heroic as the monks believed. It had happened suddenly, blindly, and Marco could only think of Jamillah – Jamillah who was killed whenever the moment was replayed in his dreams. Always in his dreams the vampyre would gut her in front of him, leaving Marco to sob uncontrollably.

At times he woke believing it to be true, and only once fully awake did he remember Jamillah still lived. That he had saved her life.

The sun began to set again, gliding down the back of the world until the horizon pulled it beneath the golden rocks. Marco started to shiver, yet he remained quiet until they rested at the foot of the mountains, the twilight quiet and eerie.

Even the Bedouins were unusually peaceful, their horses subdued.

Marco dismounted and his eyes followed his uncle as he strolled up to Thomas, who was lowering Hammid down from his horse. 'Another night under the stars, Captain,' Thomas said to him as he slipped out of the saddle and landed on the dusty ground.

William shrugged. 'Tonight feels different.'

'Is it expectation?' Thomas ventured, with uncharacteristic enthusiasm.

'Perhaps. *You* appear in good spirits.'

Thomas's smile broadened. 'Maybe this life of excitement is the life I should pursue. Maybe I should return with you to Rome,' he replied.

Thomas had suggested as much before, that he would renounce the merchant's life for something far nobler, and William assured him he would say a few good words about the Englishman on their arrival at the Vatican. But William had reservations too, and part of him wished to warn Thomas off this course of action. Over the last day's riding and talking, William had come to believe more and more that he should not stay in the Order of Saint Sallian. That it was time to leave. And how could he encourage the Englishman in a career that had lost its savour?

Marco stood some way away from their conversation, but he watched. He didn't know why, but he had an odd feeling about Thomas Richmond. Maybe it was nothing, but the man's true face was appearing gradually, like skin being peeled from an orange.

And his servant, the one they called Hammid, was looking sicker and sicker.

Yes, Marco thought to himself, something felt quite wrong.

△ IV △

The next day the landscape that had been flat or gradual now grew steep and severe. The sides of the mountains were steep walls of rock where no one could climb and no path meandered. Perhaps it was the heat, perhaps the brightness of the sun, but it sometimes appeared to William as though the walls of the valleys were closing in on them, shutting them into an eternal prison of red dust and brown rock. It was oppressive and the gaunt expressions of the riders grew, fear creeping into the hardest of faces as the Bedouins continued, quicker than usual, across the dry river beds and wadis.

As the day crept on, word came to William about a problem with Mazin's men. The Suwarka were struggling a mile or so down the line after one of the wagons had shed a wheel again, and a cannon had broken loose, rolling to the foot of a bank of scree. Mazin's riders had effectively cut themselves in half, three hundred staying with the cannon to pull it out, while the other three hundred rode on under Mazin. The sheikh's son had been told to remain with the cannon as punishment.

The news did not please Sheikh Fahd, nor did it please William, and both agreed that they had to continue on to the Valley of Fire without them.

After this bad news, there was some relief in the late afternoon when the army climbed the saddle from one wadi, and from the top of the ridge they sighted trees and green grass.

'The Oasis of Amin Dahir,' Sheikh Fahd said and gestured.

William rode up to him, the three sheikhs, Anwar, Galal and Mazin, not far behind. 'They say it fills with water once every four years,' Fahd remarked, 'and then turns to dust for the other three.'

'We appear to be lucky,' William said.

'Lucky, Captain Saxon? No, it is a miracle. In this time of drought, Allah is merciful,' Fahd said. The sheikh said something to Anwar, Galal and Mazin, and all three murmured in agreement.

'They think it is you who has brought the miracle, Captain Saxon,' Sheikh Fahd said. 'It shows that Allah approves our cause.'

William nodded. 'Let us hope more miracles befall us, sir.'

All talk of miracles was forgotten as they came within one hundred yards of the first trees. The riders at the head of the army had halted, and started shouting. Instantly William rode along the line with two brothers by his side, armed with their Baker rifles. Marco watched his uncle gallop away, cupping his hand over his eyes. Thomas made a move to ride forward, but Peruzo signalled him to stay. The lieutenant then glanced at Marco, and his expression was obvious: he shared Marco's distrust of the merchant and his servant.

William halted at the head of the column where Sheikh Fahd and his bodyguard, Hisham, were circling some object rammed into the rocky floor. It was a post, a notice of sorts, and William approached cautiously.

The sign was seven feet high, carved from a trunk of wood that had been eaten from within by insects so it appeared like rotten bone. There was a slat nailed across it, and at the top perched an ancient russet-coloured skull, a spearhead driven through its crown to hold it there for all eternity.

'A warning?' Sheikh Fahd chanced.

William leant closer, examining the head. He reached out and tapped it with his sword hilt. To the riders' dismay the jawbone crumbled and fell, joining the dust on the ground.

'It is old,' William deduced. 'Whoever this was, died a long time ago.'

'And these symbols?' Sheikh Fahd asked, pointing to the slat of wood nailed across the trunk.

William looked down. They were letters he could not read, like little pictures of lines and boxes, waves and other such iconography. The waves reminded him of the tattoos the kafalas scarred themselves with, emblems of rank in the Count's army: three waves were one step removed from being turned into a vampyre.

As William glanced at each symbol he rubbed at his temple with recognition. There was something here that felt familiar.

'I've seen such symbols before,' he said finally.

'Where?'

'One of the tutors in my Order, Master Yu, writes similar symbols. These are words,' William said, and pointed to them. 'Words from the East.'

Sheikh Fahd reached over and ran his fingertips along the lines, much to the clamour of the other riders who feared he was calling a curse upon himself. 'These men of the East, what are they like?' he asked.

'They are fierce warriors,' William replied. 'They fight differently than any other race. And they are very, *very* dangerous.'

Sheikh Fahd noted the caution in his voice.

'If the Rassis are men from the East, or at least trained in the same manner, the combat will go hard,' William said. 'Eastern men train in the art of fighting. They call it the Martial Art. I too have trained in the basic skills of this art, yet I confess I know only the skin, not the flesh and blood beneath it.'

Sheikh Fahd laughed. 'We have an army. You worry too much.'

'I hope you're right, sir,' William replied.

Beyond the sign, William ordered his men to reconnoitre for a mile in each direction while Sheikh Fahd sent a few of his own riders, commanded by Hisham, up the steep slopes of the mountains. This caution cost them two hours, but William knew ambush country when he saw it. They were close to the Valley of Fire, and not too far away from where Sheikh Fahd's brother had run into trouble.

As the afternoon waned and evening set in, most of the scouts returned and William conferred with the sheikhs. With the Rassis so near, William thought they were susceptible to attack. The Valley of Fire was less than a day's ride away, yet the sheikhs were arrogant and tired. For them the oasis made the perfect place to rest before battle. Even Sheikh Fahd relented, though he secretly shared William's concerns. They could not see the danger they were in, and William could only convince them to post sentries along the bluffs, while ensuring that a state of vigilance was maintained.

As the army rested and fed, the oasis suddenly became a thriving community. Tents were erected, water flowed and food was consumed in preparation for what lay ahead. The mood was subdued at first, but the idea of battle seemed to galvanize the Bedouins; songs were sung, and tall tales were passed around the fire.

The monks were more restrained than their allies, meditating at times, or talking amongst each other quietly. With the exception of Marco and Jericho, each monk had long experience of battle and each had his own routines before the coming day.

William marshalled what he knew for a while, then in the peace of his tent he smoothed a patch of sand and began to draw what he expected from the battle to come. He stared down with a strategist's eye, assessing the enemy's choices. Could he starve them out? Time said he couldn't, nor did he expect that an army of less than five thousand men could contain the Rassis. Then there were Mazin's cannons, still stranded down the road. They had not been seen since midday, and William wondered if they would come at all. Despite Fahd's teasing, the cannon would have been a useful addition to the army. They could have pounded the enemy positions at long range – enough to soften them up for a cavalry charge. But even then William wasn't certain if cannons would be enough.

Do not underestimate the cult of the Rassis. They are cunning. They are strong. They have been fighting this war longer than you.

Even though Kieran had said little, it was enough to make William think hard about the strategy ahead. He must not include the Dar'uka. Whether the 'angels' would come, as Peruzo and the brothers hoped, William could not guess. As he had remarked in the past, the Dar'uka had never intervened by request, only when it suited them.

Yet despite his pride, despite everything in his soul that warned against hope, William joined his hands in silent prayer. And prayed for deliverance from the Rassis.

△ V △

Marco squatted in their tent, re-splicing the hilt of his sword. His sparring lessons with Peruzo had finished half an hour before and there was a slight bruise blossoming above his right eyebrow.

William laughed. 'So Peruzo caught you with his back-swing, did he?'

Marco winced sheepishly.

'He used to catch me off guard with that one as well,' William said, and lay back on his mat. He rolled over onto his side and regarded Marco. 'You need to bend when he comes at you. When your opponent faces you like that, you must know he will strike you with his back to you. He uses the momentum to turn, to bring his blow against you. So dive down and then strike forward. Jab him in the ribs, or bend to the side and strike low. Always be sure that he will strike at you in an arc, his momentum and balance allow him nothing else.'

Marco nodded and imagined how the sparring might have gone if he had done as his uncle suggested. 'He would have missed me. He would have struck only air,' he said, and began to wave his hand, moving an imaginary sword in his fingers as he stroked it about, parrying and striking.

William watched him for a few moments, and then realized that their tent was one man short. 'Where is Thomas?'

'Taking a bath,' Marco replied.

'*Again?*' William was amazed. 'How many baths a day does that man take?'

'Only one, Uncle,' Marco said. 'He didn't bathe with us.'

The Englishman had yet to take his bath with the rest of the monks, and William respected his privacy. But then he recalled their precarious surroundings and got to his feet. 'Did he take an escort?' he said quickly.

Marco looked up, surprised by William's urgency. 'No, Uncle.'

'He should not be wandering this oasis alone. Not now. We could be ambushed at any moment, Thomas would not know what to do,' William considered.

'I could find him,' Marco suggested. 'I could ask him to return.'

William nodded. 'Very well. Take two brothers with you though,' he said.

◬ VI ◬

Brother Jericho agreed to go with Marco, while Brother Lucas felt the need to stretch his legs and so tagged along as they strolled from the outskirts of the camp and made their way towards the thick bank of reeds and boulders at the side of the water. The two monks argued about something that Marco understood little about, a place called the Carpathians and a great fortress that lay there. And while they spoke of names and places he knew nothing of nor cared about, Marco thought about Jamillah.

'If the Order assaulted the Fortress of Draak, we would be expelled from the Church,' Brother Lucas said to Jericho, their conversation growing heated.

Brother Jericho sighed in disagreement, not even noticing that Marco had halted at the edge of the reeds. He almost can-

346

noned into him, and turned to glower at Brother Lucas. 'At least this war would be over.'

Brother Lucas scoffed. 'Don't be naïve, Jericho. This war won't end in our lifetime.'

Marco put up a hand and both men fell silent. They could hear splashing somewhere, the sounds of bathing or swimming. Marco glanced at the two monks. Jericho's arms were crossed and he was shaking his head. 'I don't understand his hesitancy on behalf of the Church. Can you, Marco?'

Marco just shrugged.

'I think you should talk to Engrin,' Brother Lucas said. 'He has a great way of explaining things.'

'*Engrin?*' Jericho said. 'That old man?'

'A *great* man,' Brother Lucas corrected and then glanced at Marco, remembering why he was standing there. 'Why don't you look for the Englishman, Marco. I need to talk some sense into Brother Jericho.'

Brother Jericho laughed out loud. 'You can try!' he teased. 'So tell me . . .'

Marco ignored them both and walked through waist-high reeds towards the boulders that screened the shore from the camp. He picked his way along a small track, the tips of the reeds spiking his legs through the thin fabric of his trousers.

When he got to the rocks, he squeezed between two, climbed a third and jumped from the top to land in more reeds beneath. From there he could see across the oasis to the small row of trees along the far bank. Below, swimming in the water, was Thomas Richmond's pink outline. Marco walked down to the bank, passing the neat pile of clothes on the sand, and shouted out to him.

At first Thomas did not notice him. And then as he stood up in the water, Marco shouted again, before a hand appeared at his mouth and halted him quickly. It was quick, but the grip was weak, and Marco used his instincts as his uncle had taught him, and drove his elbow up into the chest cavity of his attacker.

The hand fell away with a groan of pain, and Marco turned

with his hand raised to discover Hammid, now doubled up and gasping.

'Enough!' Thomas shouted and Marco turned about. The Englishman stood naked in the water, his eyes blazing with anger, his left hand covering his right shoulder. He stormed up to the bank, water dripping from his chest hair and beard, a look of fury on his face.

Hammid struggled to his feet and was almost sick. He rubbed at his stomach and started to whine.

'Pathetic little man.' Thomas glowered at his servant and snatched his shirt from the pile of clothes, pulling it on quickly before drying himself, so that the white shirt was instantly wet.

'You, boy, are trouble!' Thomas growled at Marco as he dressed. 'Your uncle needs to discipline you.'

Marco was struck scared. He didn't know whether to run or stay.

'Come with me!' Thomas said as he marched over to Marco, his shirt half outside his breeches, Hammid moving awkwardly behind him, still holding his stomach. Marco stood by as calmly as he could, but then flinched as Thomas took his arm and tugged him close.

'Spy on me, will you?' he snarled in William's language, yet there was no familiar compassion in the words, just a cold, threatening tone. Thomas pulled Marco along by the arm, through the reeds and around the rocks. Marco stumbled a few times, once to his knees, before being hauled up again.

He slipped once more, but he regained his footing and as he did so he wriggled free from Thomas's grasp and stepped away from him. 'I have done nothing wrong!' he shouted defiantly.

Thomas glowered at Marco, his eyes incandescent with rage. Marco retreated, then froze as he backed into someone. A pair of gentle hands grasped his shoulders, and by his ear he heard: 'Is something wrong, Marco?'

Marco turned around, relieved to find Jericho standing there. The monk appeared cautious as he stared back at the Englishman, who was composing himself. Brother Lucas was nearby and looked on with interest.

The Englishman slipped the hem of his shirt into his breeches and gave them a dazzling smile. 'And I suppose neither of you understand a word I say?' he said sarcastically.

The monks remained silent.

'No. Of course not. Just the language of the Roman Catholic Church. How quaint,' Thomas added. The dazzling smile broadened and he pointed at Marco, then gestured at his own eyes and nodded.

Marco flinched. There was no humour in what Thomas had just done. The Englishman clucked something to the pained Hammid and both began to walk away.

'What was that about, Marco?' Brother Jericho asked.

Marco didn't reply but watched Thomas leave the oasis for the ring of tents fifty yards or so away.

'I don't like him,' Brother Jericho confided to Marco, feeling the boy's shoulders tense under his fingers. 'Are you sure there's nothing amiss?'

Marco nodded. 'I'm fine,' he insisted.

'We should return,' Brother Lucas said.

They walked back to the camp in silence and Marco rubbed at his arm where Thomas had gripped him. What had he done? Had he seen something? He continued to rub at his arm and then something began to surface, a sudden gesture . . . Marco frowned as he thought about it some more, Brother Jericho walking just in front of him while Brother Lucas hung back, looking up at the darkening sky and the birds wheeling above, reluctant to argue again with the combative Jericho.

Marco was so engrossed in what the Englishman had been hiding that the distant twanging sound was lost on him. There was a sudden thunk and then a cry, and both Jericho and Marco turned to find Brother Lucas with an arrow in his side.

Brother Jericho stopped in his tracks and watched as the monk fell to his knees in the reeds, his face contorted in pain, then fell backwards and vanished under the tall yellowing stems.

349

'Lucas?' Brother Jericho called out, bewildered. He took a step forward and Marco heard a whistling noise. By instinct he pushed Jericho aside, and both of them toppled and rolled, Marco to the right, Jericho to the left. The arrow struck the ground a foot away and cartwheeled into the reeds.

Brother Jericho swore as he lay face-down in the dust, his first proper curse in some years. Another shaft flew past their heads and buried itself in the ground a yard away as Marco tried to struggle to his feet.

'Stay down dammit!' Jericho yelled at him. 'We're under fire!'

His hands reached for Marco across the dusty ground; he tasted the grime in the air, and breathed it in – a musty, acrid smell. Marco did not see him, and slipped away to a boulder that was no bigger than he was. He lay with his back against it, panting as another arrow whistled between them and just missed Jericho's fingers. The monk retracted his hand at the last moment, feeling the air part close to his fingertips. He rolled frantically away, pursued by a volley that hit the floor inches from each roll until he flopped into a narrow wadi. There he lay flat as arrows smacked against the opposite bank, raising a spurt of dust with every strike.

He rolled onto his front and raised his head. 'Ambush!' he bellowed. 'AMBUSH!' He hoped his words would travel, and he almost tried again, before another series of twangs made him flatten himself again. Several more arrows hit the ground, one catching his sleeve. The arrowhead ripped cloth and nicked hairs but missed the skin. Pulling it free, Jericho rolled back over and began shouting once more. 'SOUND THE ALARM! AMBUSH! AMBUSH!'

At the edge of the camp he saw several Bedouins emerge from their tents. One stepped forward and cupped his hand over his brow. Jericho shouted to them, but arrows hissed from nowhere and the Bedouins fell to the ground with muffled cries.

'No!' Jericho shouted desperately, fearing that they all were dead or dying.

Yet one survivor rose, an arrow protruding from his shoulder, staring down bewildered at the shaft as though it shouldn't be there. Then, and slowly, he started to lurch away, calling out as he did so. Jericho heard commotion spread like a beehive disturbed, and men came streaming out of their tents, grabbing their weapons, questioning or commanding. The camp was roused. He could lie back thankful. Footsteps to the right. 'Look right, Marco, they're coming!' he called over to the boy, who lay huddled against the wall of his sheltering rock.

Jericho yelled louder. 'Lucas? Brother Lucas?'

Brother Lucas tried to speak but could only cough and utter a high groan of pain. An arrow thwacked too close in the dirt. 'Marco, we need to move!' Jericho shouted. 'I have to get you back to camp!'

'But Brother Lucas . . .!' Marco shouted back.

'Brother Lucas understands, Marco. You are my captain's nephew.'

Marco shook his head and turned over onto his knees, facing away.

'Wait! Marco, don't try it!' Jericho shouted, seeing the boy's intention. 'You'll never . . .', but Marco had sprung from cover and dived into the reeds beyond. Jericho stood up to follow and another arrow flew his way. It plucked at the heel of his boot, but he was rolling along the ground, the dust of his impact screening him from the unseen archers. When their next volley blocked his path to Marco's rock, he turned about and sprinted in the opposite direction, zigzagging his way to the tents before throwing himself face-down into a ditch near the perimeter, mere feet away from where those several Bedouins lay bleeding or dead.

△ VII △

William bolted with his scabbard clutched in his hand, the belt smacking against his legs as he hurdled tent-ropes to reach the wagon where the greyjackets stood, loading their Baker rifles in its cover. Peruzo waved him over and William slid to a halt in the dust, ducking as another arrow fell among them.

'They have our range,' Peruzo growled.

William followed the lieutenant's gesture towards the mountainside to the right of the camp. It was jagged, rocky, with many ridges, and alcoves a man could hide in.

'Pin them down as best you can. Fire into the shadows. Maybe we'll get lucky,' William ordered as he made to move away.

'And you?' Peruzo asked, surprised that William should part from them now.

'I need to see Sheikh Fahd,' William said and left them quickly, stepping past a sobbing Bedouin who was screaming whenever his friend tried to pull the long thick arrow from a wound in his thigh. Blood had spilt across the sand.

Sheikh Fahd marched with purpose through the camp with Hisham at his side. William hurried his pace and intercepted the sheikh before he could make for the horses.

'You were right, my friend,' Fahd conceded. 'It *is* a trap. They're firing from the mountains. My scouts have seen them, Captain. Sheikh Mazin's men are going up there, look . . .'

William turned to see the Suwarka gather towards the base of the slope. A shower of arrows flew and some fell screaming.

'They'll be cut down!' William exclaimed. 'Surely they don't expect to assault head-on? It's too steep, and they'll see them coming.'

Sheikh Fahd shrugged. 'The Suwarka will do what they wish, Captain Saxon. Mazin has lost control of them. It is his son they follow. Mazin has no eye for battle.'

'We *must* pull them back,' William pleaded.

'It can't be done. Do you see? Now Sheikh Anwar is attacking, and he is impetuous, a lot like your nephew I think,' Sheikh Fahd observed.

William groaned out loud. In the confusion he had forgotten Marco.

. . . *Marco, whom he'd sent to find Thomas.*

He didn't even try to stop Sheikh Fahd now, but reeled away, moving faster with the knowledge that Marco was out in the open, and Thomas too. His heart pounded harder as he fought to subdue his fears for Marco, but his path took him stumbling through chaos. The camp was in panic. Arrows kept falling sporadically amongst the tents. Now and then one would skewer a scrambling target.

William returned to Peruzo's side. 'We can't see them, Captain, and those poor bastards the boy sheikh commands are getting in the way,' Lieutenant Peruzo shouted and pointed to the Tarabin warriors.

William was only half listening.

'Captain?'

'Marco is out there, Peruzo. Dammit, I sent him to find Thomas,' William replied.

'Leave him to Jericho and Lucas.' Peruzo took William's arm and shook him to his senses. 'What are we to do?'

William's thoughts swirled – and then stilled. He felt oddly removed for a moment, and swore out loud to focus himself. 'We can't assault through Anwar and Mazin's men . . . so we take the right flank. We hit them in the side. Who are our best climbers and best skirmishers?'

Peruzo called the names, and those he mentioned stopped firing and lined up along the wagon.

'Get them up that mountain and take care of the ambushers,' William shouted. 'But be careful . . . This is the Rassis' home ground.'

Peruzo nodded. 'It will be done.'

A hard climb would face them up the scree and scattered boulders to the right, but it offered a better screen than the left. The centre was slowly clogging up with men trying to scale the rock face, and falling under methodical volleys of arrows.

As Anwar's men retreated, a second wave of Suwarka threw themselves up the steep slopes of the mountain, Sheikh Mazin screaming at them to fall back. In answer, more arrows rained down. William saw several figures fall, shrieking all the way.

With Peruzo and half the company suddenly charging from

353

the wagon across the sandy ground towards the foot of the mountainside, William kept the others firing at what he considered was the perfect cover for the ambushers: an outcrop of rocks that formed a beetling ledge on the side of the slope, halfway up the mountain. From here this was all that could be done. William slipped off and headed for the lake.

△ VIII △

Marco crawled over to where Brother Lucas was lying. He pushed through the reeds until his fingers found the monk's boot, then used his elbows for leverage to pull himself along the brother's right-hand side, tugging thick clumps of reeds away with his hands.

Brother Lucas was barely conscious, but he managed to open his eyes slightly and let his head turn towards Marco.

'What are you doing here, boy?' he said faintly.

'You've been hit,' Marco whispered.

Brother Lucas seemed almost to smile. 'Oh yes. Yes, you are right,' he said, sounding genuinely surprised as he glanced down at the wooden shaft embedded in his side. His eyes seemed to return to life. 'What can you do about it?'

'I . . . I don't know,' Marco confessed.

Brother Lucas winced. 'I know little of dressing wounds, boy.'

'But you're bleeding . . .'

Brother Lucas coughed and grimaced. 'Yes . . . *Yes*. I think . . . I am.'

'How do I stop you bleeding?' Marco pleaded.

Brother Lucas reached over with his right hand, his fingers clawing towards Marco's. He held it tight. 'You can't. Not by yourself. But you can stay here with me. Until the end, if it must come. Can you do that?'

Marco nodded and kept hold of Lucas's hand as they lay in the reeds.

★

William found Jericho running through the camp but uncertain where to go.

'Jericho! Where is my nephew?' William demanded, seizing the monk's shoulders.

Jericho was startled by his urgency and looked blank for a moment. Then he gestured behind him, to the reeds and boulders that lay between the camp and the water. 'I couldn't reach him. He's there, hidden in the reeds. With Brother Lucas.'

'Wounded?'

Jericho shook his head. 'No. *No*. But Brother Lucas has been hit. I couldn't get to them. Arrows cut us off . . . I had to find cover . . . I left them. I . . .'

'You did what you could,' William assured him.

'Yes,' Jericho said, but he was still ashamed. 'I must go back. We need Brother Filippo.'

'Filippo is on the mountain,' William replied quickly. 'We can do this without him.'

They reached the edge of camp and waited for arrows to seek them. None came, and after a few moments' pause William slapped Jericho on the shoulder and they ran, dirt spurting up in their wake as they sped across the ground, leaping over natural trenches, potholes and clumps of wild grass. Jericho put his head down and led the way.

They would have run straight to the cover of the largest boulders if William had not stumbled over Marco, while Jericho slid into the reeds, rolling on his side. Relieved to find the boy in one piece, William turned his attention to Brother Lucas as Jericho crawled to his side.

'Still alive?' Jericho asked the monk, frowning at the shaft that jutted from under his ribs.

'*Still? Just*,' Brother Lucas whispered.

Jericho studied the wound, the blood like dark red wine. He turned to William. 'I need some water.'

'Be quick,' William replied. He motioned for Marco to move aside. Only now did Marco release Lucas's slackening grip, while William took his place, holding his hand with both of his.

'Captain . . .'

'Don't talk,' William whispered to him. 'Conserve your strength.'

'I have little left . . .' he said, his voice weakening. He inclined his head, his face grey. His eyes tried to open as blood ran down the corners of his pale lips. William knew he was losing him.

'Promise you'll find . . . the Hoard . . . Promise . . . You'll destroy one for me . . .' Brother Lucas gasped, his voice now barely audible.

'I promise, Brother,' William said, his hand on the monk's growing tighter, trying to hold him in this world. But the effort was futile. William saw the light fade from his eyes, and felt his grip relax.

'Rest, Brother,' William said at last and closed Lucas's eyes.

Tears flowed down Marco's grimy cheeks. He wiped his eyes with the back of his hand.

'I couldn't . . .!' came Jericho's voice from up ahead. '. . . couldn't find anything to hold the water!'

The monk fell quickly to his knees and crawled over to them, holding his soaking wet shirt. 'I tried to carry it in this, but the damn cotton doesn't absorb enough. I need a water-skin, Captain. I need to . . .'

William held up his hand. Jericho ceased and looked down at Brother Lucas. He was not breathing. Jericho bowed in despair, his shaking hand on the monk's still chest.

'Easy, Jericho,' William assured him. 'You did everything you could.'

'It wasn't enough.' Jericho sighed.

William lifted his head and listened to the change in battle. The sounds of fighting had almost ceased. Getting to his feet, he saw the Bedouins were returning to camp, carrying the wounded and the dead. Cupping his hands over his eyes against the setting sun, he saw grey figures around the outcrop halfway up the slope. It was Peruzo and the monks. They had reached their goal and were now looking for survivors.

'We should go,' William said. 'We'll carry Brother Lucas between us.'

Silently, Jericho put his hands under the monk's shoulders and lifted. William took Brother Lucas's ankles, Marco put his hands under his back, and between them, in silence, they carried the fallen brother back to the camp.

△ IX △

Sheikh Fahd looked surprisingly calm. 'We lost eight men, and four were wounded,' he said to William once they had rested Brother Lucas's body with the company.

'I'm sad to hear it,' William said.

'And Sheikh Mazin has lost thirty-two of his riders, Captain, with a dozen more wounded.'

William stared at Sheikh Fahd. 'So many?'

'You were right. The Suwarka were rash to tackle the slope head-on.' Sheikh Fahd looked at the blood on William's hand – Brother Lucas's blood. 'How many of your brave monks died?'

'One dead, no wounded,' William said.

Sheikh Fahd looked surprised. 'One? That is just a scratch, Captain Saxon,' he said.

'Not to me, sir,' William rebuked. 'Let us talk later.' He walked away.

Peruzo and the monks were standing a few yards off, looking down at Brother Lucas's body.

'Lucas was a good man,' Peruzo said.

'What did you find up there?' William asked, not wishing to dwell on their loss.

'A single body.'

'Just the one?'

'There might have been more,' Peruzo surmised. 'They could have taken their dead with them. The one corpse we did find had fallen from his position, down into a narrow ravine. He was jammed at the bottom.'

'Where is he?'

Peruzo took William to the wagon and pulled back the canvas that had once covered the weapons. The corpse wore an ankle-length dark blue robe, and a black hood covered the head. Beneath the hood was a glazed ceramic mask shaped like a dragon's face, with a flaming cyclops eye set into the forehead; it was covered in grime, blood and sand.

William slipped his fingers under the mask. Blood had stuck it to the face beneath, so it came away with a tearing sensation and a crackling sound.

The face was calm. It belonged to a man content with death, his eyes so serenely at peace that a few of the watching brothers gave audible gasps. Peruzo stepped forward, studying the enemy.

'Like Master Yu,' he remarked, seeing the hue of the skin and the narrower eyes.

'Yes,' William said, his suspicions confirmed. 'This sect will be stronger than I feared.'

'Captain, I heard you had a prisoner,' came a voice behind them. The brothers parted and Thomas appeared with Hammid close behind. Marco noticed the Englishman was fully dressed.

'I'm glad to see you unscathed, my friend,' William greeted him warmly.

Thomas half bowed, his hand on the hilt of his sword. 'By chance more than anything,' he said and glanced at Marco. It was only slight, but it unnerved him. Marco stepped back against Jericho.

This quick exchange did not go unnoticed by Peruzo. He walked over to the boy while William went on talking.

'I feared your fate would be the same as Brother Lucas's,' William said and gestured to the body on the ground.

'Not so, Captain,' Thomas said. 'Your men are the ones who saved my life. I was in cover in the camp when the first arrows fell. I am heartily glad to see that your nephew survived.'

'Captain?' Peruzo called out.

William looked back. His lieutenant was standing next to Marco, but there was tension in his posture.

'Will you excuse me, Thomas?' William said.

The Englishman nodded, with a touch of unease.

Peruzo smiled, but the smile was false: it hid a darker purpose that only an old companion would have sensed.

'What is wrong?' William asked him at once.

'Marco has seen something,' Peruzo whispered.

'"*Something*"?' William looked from Peruzo to Marco.

'When he found him in the water, Richmond was quick to cover his shoulder. Tell him what you saw, Marco.'

'I'm not sure,' Marco said. 'I thought it was a wound. But I think it was something else. A sign.'

'What sign?'

'Like the sea. Waves. Three black waves painted on his shoulder.'

Peruzo looked for recognition in his captain's eyes . . .

'It can't be,' William murmured. 'You were mistaken.'

'And if he wasn't?' Peruzo said.

'Coincidence, surely.'

'During this mission, Captain? With the spies of Count Ordrane lined up against us?'

William rocked on his feet.

'*We have to know*,' Peruzo insisted.

William nodded, trying to compose himself. It was a little too much to take. Yet there was doubt in his mind . . . A grain of doubt and a fear that he'd been taken in too easily. The boy must be wrong, he told himself. It was a mistake in the heat of battle. Nothing more.

Sheikh Fahd came over to the wagon with the other sheikhs, curious about what the monks had found. The news of the dead Rassis had spread through the camp and everyone wished to see their enemy. But as Sheikh Fahd approached, he saw William shaken. The captain of the Order walked over to Thomas with an apologetic expression.

'I don't know what to say, Thomas,' William said, looking embarrassed. 'It appears you're hiding a secret from me.'

'I'm sorry?' Thomas replied.

'Are you wounded?' William asked pleasantly.

'No sir, I am not.'

'Then can I see your shoulder?'

'Of course,' Thomas said, taking off his jacket and unbuttoning his shirt. He pulled back the left shoulder, revealing nothing. 'See?'

William smiled and laughed weakly. 'I'm sorry, Thomas. I meant your *right* shoulder.'

Thomas stared at William and then at Marco. 'The right?' William nodded.

'Why?'

'Because I am asking you. Please?'

Thomas smiled, but it faltered.

'*Please*, Thomas?' William gestured, his other hand creeping to the handle of his sword.

'The right shoulder,' Thomas said. 'Of course.'

As his left hand moved to the right shoulder of his shirt, his right hand seized the handle of his own sword. It came up fast, but Peruzo's blade was already there. Thomas had been quick, but had not seen Peruzo's stealthy approach. The blade clanged off Peruzo's and fell to the ground when the lieutenant punched the Englishman full in the face. The sheikh's men levelled their swords.

Thomas straightened up, his hand at his bleeding lip. He spat on the ground.

Peruzo kicked away the fallen sword and then ripped open Thomas's shirt to reveal the three black waves Marco had seen at the oasis: the mark of the kafala, the servant of Count Ordrane of Draak.

William backed away, almost choking on the fetid wave of desolation that rose from his stomach.

Peruzo saw William's suffering and in anger he struck Thomas across the cheek. Thomas's head jerked to the side, and he strove to keep his feet for a moment, defiantly, before sagging to his knees with a groan. 'I owe you for that,' he snarled at Peruzo.

Peruzo stared down, unflinching.

William swung round. 'Jericho,' he growled. Brother Jericho jumped as if a sword's tip had prodded him, nervous in the face of William's fury. 'Empty the wagon and then organize the brothers to build a cage. I want this man chained and confined.'

'He should be executed . . .' Peruzo protested.

'*Now, Jericho!*' William barked. Looking distraught and pale, he brushed through the crowd of monks and Arabs and walked to his tent, murmuring to himself: 'No executions today. There's been too much death already.'

CHAPTER EIGHTEEN

The Journey to the End

△ I △

Once prayers had been spoken, sorrows conveyed and vows renewed, the monks withdrew from Brother Lucas's grave, mere yards from where he had fallen. Peruzo led William away, thinking to distance his captain from their loss. He escorted him to a fire where some of Sheikh Fahd's men sat. They looked up at the two Europeans, and it was Hisham who nodded towards them, gesturing for them to sit. Here, as elsewhere, it was a solemn gathering.

'How could I have been so wrong about Richmond, Peruzo?' William said aloud, aware that his words would mean nothing to the Bedouins around him.

'It doesn't happen often, Captain,' Peruzo observed cheerfully.

'Did *you* see it coming?'

The lieutenant shrugged and stoked the fire in front of them; the embers glowed brighter with each prod and sparks spat into the air. 'It matters not what I thought,' he said after a few moments.

'It does to me,' William insisted.

Peruzo looked skyward, as though the stars might shine on his wisdom, giving it some weight of credence. Never would he presume to lecture his captain, but nor would he refuse a request. 'I thought Richmond was a little suspicious. It was odd

362

he would always bathe separately from the others. But there was nothing to say he was an enemy.'

'I didn't even notice that,' William said distantly. 'My judgement was flawed. I failed the company.'

'You've had distractions,' Peruzo replied. 'The mission for one. Marco for another.'

'Yes, Marco . . . That boy always gets into trouble.'

Peruzo shook his head. 'Captain, forgive me for being so bold, but I think Marco can look after himself.'

'You don't know him as I do,' William replied.

'I know him well enough. He's had no motherly or fatherly guidance, with the exception of yours and Adriana's. He lost his parents at the time a boy needs them the most. And he lost them to our enemies. All Marco has known since then is your defence of the Light. He knows only of your battle against the forces of Hell. Your heroism. Your leadership.'

'You are saying he wishes to emulate me?'

'No,' said Peruzo. 'I'm saying he wishes to *follow* you. As we all have. If anything, the last week has taught you that Marco *is* ready. He's brave, he's willing . . . And he *is* old enough.'

'And yet with Marresca you believed him too young,' William remarked.

'I was wrong about Marresca,' Peruzo admitted. 'The lieutenant could handle himself well enough. My only concern was . . .'

'Yes, Lieutenant?' William said.

Peruzo locked his hands together in thought and stared into the fire. 'I believed Marresca was too cold a killer. Like a statue of a warrior with no heart. No soul. I was afraid the war was taking away his humanity, Captain.'

William understood the sentiment perfectly well. The way the lad could slay without hesitation, without a second thought. Even William, with all his years of fighting, did not relish ending a life, be it vampyre, daemon or mortal. Killing was necessary, and that was all. But Marresca had been born to slay, and did so too efficiently to be altogether human. His progression to

Dar'uka seemed right, perhaps even pre-ordained: an unnatural young killer becoming an immortal warrior.

'Yet you believe Marco would not turn that way?' William asked.

'You saw what happened at the Ayaida camp,' Peruzo said. 'He cared more for the sheikh's sister than he did about destroying a vampyre. He is unlike Marresca in many ways. He has more passion. More love.'

'That may be,' William admitted, and sighed. 'But right now we need a dozen Marrescas, Peruzo, not my nephew. A clutch of cold killers would help us against the Rassis.'

'Will the Rassis use the Scarimadaen in battle?' Peruzo said.

It was a thought William dreaded. 'Honestly? I don't know. It is written that the Rassis are keeping the Hoard for a specified time. No one knows when that will be. It is possible they have orders only to release the daemons when that time has come.'

'Not even as a last resort?'

William turned pale. 'Aye. As a last resort they may. I trust you won't mention this to the others? Not even this army could stand against two hundred daemons. Sheikh Mazin is skittish enough. So as far as anyone else is concerned, the Rassis will *not* use the Hoard against us.'

The conversation flagged while both men considered its implications. The idea of facing both the Rassis and their daemons was terrifying.

'Is there any hope the Dar'uka will aid us?' Peruzo asked finally.

'I have prayed they will,' William admitted. 'They might hear my words. Or they might not. The Dar'uka say they know everything. I wonder now if that is true. If it is, then they'll know how close we are to nearing our goal, and they will help us.'

'And if not?'

'Then we must rely on our courage and our allies. Our luck has improved of late. Maybe it will improve a little more when we face the Rassis.' William rose to his feet and stretched. 'Where is Hammid?'

'He is a prisoner of Sheikh Fahd. They will execute him in the morning.'

'I need to talk to him.'

'Why? He'll tell you little, I'm sure.'

'Thomas Richmond is a liar. He is a deceiver of the highest order. A man who was willing to risk everything against the Rashid militia in order to infiltrate our company. He saved my life, but to what end? What did he have to gain?'

'You think Richmond had a plan?'

'I am certain of it. If Hammid is going to die, he will plead for mercy, won't he? He will tell us everything to save himself.' William turned to go, bowing to the men around the fire.

'What? *Now?*' Peruzo said.

'Time won't wait for us, my friend,' William replied.

△ II △

Four men were guarding Hammid, with two more nearby. They had been hand-picked by Sheikh Fahd himself, a gesture to William that he understood the danger this man posed.

William consulted first with Sheikh Fahd, who agreed to attend the interrogation even though it was far into the night. Hisham stood nearby, his brawny arms crossed over his chest as Hammid was dragged into Sheikh Fahd's tent by the four guards and thrown to the floor.

Hammid whimpered but stayed quiet.

'Get up,' William said, gesturing to him with his sword.

Hammid got to his knees, but could not look at William.

'Sir,' William said, 'perhaps you could tell him that we need to know *everything* about Thomas Richmond.'

Sheikh Fahd agreed and looked down at Hammid from his raised chair. He shouted at him, but more with urgency than fury. Hammid turned to Sheikh Fahd; he was anxious, but William saw resignation in his eyes. He knew he was going to die, and that pleading would not save him.

After a moment or two of composure, Hammid began to speak, and Sheikh Fahd translated:

'He says they met in Rashid months ago. Richmond told him he was a friend of a count in Europe, a powerful man who was looking for a prize beyond measure. Richmond wanted two things: a guide who knew Egypt well, and the whereabouts of Charles Greynell. Hammid knew nothing of Charles, but agreed to be Richmond's guide on condition that he found a cure for his illness.'

'What illness?' William asked.

'He is dying, Captain Saxon,' Sheikh Fahd replied over Hammid's timid chattering. 'He has a great infirmity that eats away inside him. He passes blood each day and night, and knows with every setting sun his life ebbs faster. Richmond promised he would rid him of the illness. And . . . *to make him immortal*?' Sheikh Fahd began laughing sadly. 'Foolish little man. How could he believe such lies?'

'Perhaps not completely untruthful,' William replied. 'Richmond's master indeed could grant that wish.'

Sheikh Fahd frowned. 'Surely not. Only gods have such power.'

'Then Count Ordrane of Draak is a demigod,' William said ruefully, 'for he is immortal himself and can make others like him. If Richmond had succeeded in his mission, immortality might have been his prize. Yet I doubt Count Ordrane would bestow such a gift on this poor wretch.'

Sheikh Fahd got up from his chair. 'While I pity this fool, he *will* be executed in the morning, Captain.'

William looked down at Hammid again. 'Sir, before you go, may I ask one more favour?' he said. 'Could you find out if he knows anything about the vampyres? Particularly any plans they have?'

Sheikh Fahd stared at William, a little weary of his requests. 'For you, Captain, of course,' he said patiently.

He spoke to Hammid again, and the chatter resumed. 'He

says he knows only that Richmond met the "creatures of the dark" several times.'

'When?' William asked.

'The last time was four nights ago. He says the final vampyre fled to the north to find an army,' Sheikh Fahd translated and then trailed off. He said something to Hammid, and then grew angry at the man's reply. Hammid's chatter increased, now fearful.

'This army he speaks of . . . he knows little, but it will be coming,' Sheikh Fahd translated.

Hammid continued to talk, this time slower than before, his hands balled into fists, his expression furious.

'What does he say now?'

'He pleads.'

'He pleads with anger?' William remarked, surprised by the servant's deportment, the way Hammid seemed ready to strike out at someone or something.

Sheikh Fahd looked unimpressed. 'He says he should not have trusted Richmond. But Richmond threatened him. He says he should have driven a dagger into Richmond's back when he had the chance, but he was a coward.'

William heard the contempt in Sheikh Fahd's voice, but it was at odds with the anger from Hammid. William walked around and stood in front of the servant. He bent down and looked him in the eyes.

'What are you looking for, Captain Saxon?' Sheikh Fahd said, and then yawned. 'It is late. I am tired, and we will do battle tomorrow.'

'Please indulge me, sir,' he replied, 'for I think we may suffer another battle but for this man.'

'I cannot see how.'

'If there is another army coming for us from the north, Hammid may yet be of use. Tell him that I cannot save him, and that his illness will kill him. I do not offer immortality, but repentance,' William said.

Sheikh Fahd relayed this. Hammid faltered for a moment,

and perhaps it was resignation that twisted his face that way. Then a tear rolled down one cheek as he held out his hands. He said something quite gentle and deliberate, faintly smiling. Sheikh Fahd didn't translate immediately but stared at Hammid.

'He says he only wishes to atone for being in league with a devil like Richmond. He says "the blood of his countrymen is on his hands" because the illness made him weak.'

'What would he do for atonement?' William asked.

'He says anything you ask of him,' Sheikh Fahd replied.

William smiled, but it was free of compassion. 'Then do not execute this man.'

Sheikh Fahd looked angry. 'This is not your choice, my English friend.'

'I ask as a favour, sir,' William said, helping Hammid to his feet. 'This man may have stayed silent, but has he lied? No, he has been afraid, and men who fear can be useful.'

'Explain yourself!' Sheikh Fahd demanded, furious that he should be denied blood.

'He is the only link to our enemies, the only link to Richmond. If an army of kafalas rides over these hills or tries to ambush us after we have been to the Valley of Fire, we will lose, sir, and the Hoard of Mhorrer will be released. Is that what you wish?'

Sheikh Fahd opened his mouth to retort, but he stopped short. Instead he folded his arms and looked down at Hammid. 'What could this wretch offer to stop such an ambush?'

'We could use him to discover Richmond's scheme. Hammid is the only one he can trust.'

'That man is no fool, Captain Saxon. He will smell the deceit. He will not believe this coward has remained loyal to him,' Sheikh Fahd scoffed.

'Maybe,' William replied, 'or perhaps Hammid *is* still loyal to Richmond. The temptation of immortality is a strong one.'

'You think he would turn back to Richmond? You think he is deceiving us now?'

'I do not know for sure. But we can make certain it happens.

Once Hammid knows of Richmond's plans, I can make Hammid talk, one way or another. We let loose the rat to see where it scurries.'

Sheikh Fahd smiled. 'I understand your thinking. But I will keep him on a short leash, Captain.'

'As you see fit,' William said, and walked away from Hammid and out of the tent.

Outside the air chilled his skin through his shirt and Peruzo wrapped his arms about himself. 'Can you tell me what happened in there, Captain?'

'I saved Hammid's life.'

Peruzo disapproved.

'I did it to learn more about Richmond,' William explained. 'I want to know why he went to such lengths to deceive us. The vampyres could have destroyed us at any point, Peruzo. They could have left us at the mercy of the militia from Rashid for one. But they didn't. In fact, I suspect they helped to free us.'

'That makes little sense, Captain.'

'I know. But what if they weren't strong enough to take the Hoard themselves? Maybe the Rassis are more formidable than the vampyres the Count sent here. And that's what I need to know: how strong are the Rassis? Hammid can find these answers if we make Richmond believe he is still loyal to him.'

'It is a great risk,' Peruzo said, looking hesitant. 'If Hammid helps Richmond escape . . .'

'He won't. He'll be kept on a leash.'

They walked back to the tent in silence, the conversation over. William had made his decision. Peruzo hoped they didn't regret it.

△ III △

The next morning, a small sandstorm whipped up and careered down the valley, spooking the horses and causing general chaos as the first shafts of sunshine sparkled over the side of the mountains. It was the reveille they needed, and the monks of the Order decamped quickly.

Marco sat astride Richmond's horse, glancing over to the caged Englishman who sat with his knees up by his ears, his hands bound with rope. His eyes were darkly ringed, leering and angry. There was no sadness in them, just malevolent contempt for all, and utter hatred each time he looked at Marco.

The boy flinched and turned away, not daring to stare back. Jericho rode up and patted him on the arm. 'Do not worry yourself. He is harmless. See? Locked up in a cage like the animal he is.'

'What will they do to him?' Marco asked.

Jericho appeared enthusiastic. 'If we can, we will take him back to Rome. There he will be interrogated and then perhaps hanged.'

Marco glanced at Richmond again, remembering the piles of corpses at the oasis, the flies buzzing in clouds around puddles of blood and the vultures feasting on the dead servants. The Englishman had done that. And who knows what he would have done to the brothers, or him, or even his uncle?

'You are twice the hero, Marco,' Jericho said, almost reading the boy's mind. 'Enjoy it. We are indebted to you.'

Marco nodded cautiously. He felt more queasy than heroic; a sense that his enemies were growing and there was no one to save him. His hands shook around the reins of his horse and he gripped them till his knuckles turned white; no one must notice he was terrified.

Thomas's captivity had become a nuisance. It had taken much of the night, several wooden crates, a few of the scarce trees around the water, and many hands, both Arab and Italian, to build the cage. They had lost the use of the wagon and the monks were burdened with their additional weapons and ammunition, strapping them across their saddles or backs where they could. Sheikh Fahd had agreed to take the special gunpowder Engrin had sent them, roping the kegs to camels. They were strange animals, gangly and far from elegant, yet sturdy, and with far more strength than the horses. The camels could have trekked all day and night without rest.

While William spoke to Sheikh Fahd about the direction their army was to travel, Hisham rode up to Fahd and bowed. Words passed between the two men, and William sensed something wrong by the sudden rage in the sheikh's expression. Fahd was furious. He gestured down the line of monks and Arabs to the tents that had yet to be dismantled. Sheikh Mazin's tents.

'What's happened?' William asked.

'He will not come,' Sheikh Fahd growled. 'The coward is staying here.'

'Mazin?' William said and turned in his saddle. 'Surely not ...'

'He says he is waiting for his cannon to catch up with him,' Sheikh Fahd said, and spat on the ground. 'Yet he is too cowardly to tell this to my face. He has lost the taste for battle. He has lost the belief of his own men. They look to his son, not to Mazin, and he knows this.'

'Will his son join us?'

'His son is not here, Captain Saxon. He is probably missing in the mountains,' Sheikh Fahd said, waving his hands to the ridge behind them.

'So we've lost the cannon and his six hundred men,' William murmured. He blew out his cheeks. 'That is a desperate blow, sir.'

'We are Ayaida. We are Tarabin. And we are Aquila,' Sheikh Fahd boasted proudly. 'We do not need the Suwarka. We can crush the Rassis ourselves.'

William did not argue, but the loss of so many men was a severe setback. 'I must tell my company,' he said, trying to put a brave face on the news.

As he rode back to speak with Peruzo, William paused by the wagon and Richmond's cage. Richmond took hold of the bars, the wood creaking just a little. Despite everyone's efforts, the cage had been assembled quickly and given time it could be breached. Richmond had been under constant guard, and whenever he'd tried to pull hard on the bars, his hands had been whacked with the butt of a rifle until his fingers were black and blue. He had got the message quickly, but could find other ways of tormenting William.

'Do you honestly think you can take the Hoard of Mhorrer?' he hissed at him.

William shot him a cursory glance. 'Of course,' he smiled. 'And we will succeed where you have failed.'

'Failed! Pah!' Richmond laughed, and pointed at the rows of tents. 'I see some of your friends are not following you. Scared by the Rassis, are they? They should be, William. The Rassis will slaughter your pitiful little band of savages. Your defeat is but delayed.'

'I care not for your opinion,' William replied. 'You are, after all, locked in a cage. You're *our* prisoner, Thomas Richmond.'

'For now, William, *for now*,' the Englishman said slyly.

William smiled. 'If you refer to your servant, Hammid . . . He has renounced you and serves Allah, not Count Ordrane.'

Richmond fell suddenly quiet. 'Hammid would not turn.'

'Oh but he has,' William replied quickly and leant over to him. 'He was afraid of you, you know. But now he prefers the company of *good* men.'

'And you consider yourself good, do you, William?' Richmond growled and clung to the bars of the cage, rocking it slightly. 'I saw you when you tortured that woman at Bastet. I saw your expression. You hungered for her pain. You were elated when she burned to ash under the rising sun. Is that a mark of a good man? You and I are not so different. We are both soldiers of Light and Shadow. Burning in our guilt. We are alike.'

William felt stung by the accusation. He turned away.

'I speak the truth, do I not?' Richmond said and laughed.

'Tell me, Thomas, why did you turn traitor against your fellow man?'

Richmond sat back and regarded William well. 'Death, Captain Saxon. Just death. I saw everyone I knew and loved die of old age or disease. When I realized that our life on this world is nothing more than the time it takes for a candle to burn, I knew it was far too short. I wanted more.'

William said nothing.

'You think you are so righteous, but you're blind,' Richmond continued. 'There is no Heaven. There is no right hand of God. Just the Void. Immortality is the only eternal existence there is, and men will fight for that. Men like you and me.'

'Not me,' William countered. 'I believe you have only one lifetime, and you do what you must within that. You have wasted yours, Thomas Richmond. And I will make sure you will never claim your prize. You will never – *never* – be immortal.'

Richmond gritted his teeth and smiled thinly. 'We will see. We will see.'

William rode angrily away, galloping to where Marco and Peruzo sat, behind Sheikh Fahd's riders.

'Is something amiss with our allies?' Peruzo asked, gesturing to Mazin's men, who were standing by their tents and watching as the rest of the army packed and mounted.

'The Suwarka are coming no further,' William said sadly.

Peruzo nodded. He looked almost philosophical.

'You don't seem too concerned,' William remarked.

'You didn't see the Suwarka in action, Captain,' Peruzo replied. 'They were a shambles. I swear they tripped each other up in their haste to climb the mountain. They would only get in our way.'

William laughed. 'Very well, then perhaps it is no great loss . . .' he said, but his words trailed away as Thomas Richmond began taunting him from the wagon.

'Ignore him, Captain,' Peruzo advised. 'He spreads only lies.'

'It is worth the irritation,' William replied. 'He has information on the vampyres and the Rassis. If we can get that information, I can stand to lose Mazin and his men.'

'And you really believe Hammid will help us do that?' Peruzo said.

William's deal with Hammid had been clarified earlier that morning: if the Arab could learn the truth about the Rassis Cult

373

and where the kafala army intended to attack, then he would free Hammid, for whatever time he had. It was a bargain the weak little man had little choice but to make – execution the only alternative. Still, while the Arab had readily agreed, William did not completely trust the switch of loyalties and remained cautious, ensuring that several of Sheikh Galal's men were nearby at all times.

'Everything is a risk, Lieutenant,' William replied. 'From letting Hammid loose, to riding into the Valley of Fire with fewer men than we started out with. I cannot say what might happen today, whether we face victory or defeat. But this is our fate, and bitter or sweet, we play it to the end.'

The long column of Bedouins and monks began to move out and William held up his hand and then lowered it, pointing the way. The brothers spurred into a trot and began riding out of the oasis towards the mountains of the south-east, the wagon rattling at the rear, the Suwarka uneasy spectators as their allies left them.

Richmond looked out of his makeshift cage, his fingers at the bars, pulling gradually and gradually until the first one creaked and groaned loose.

△ IV △

At midday they travelled up the pass between two mountains, making slow progress as the road grew ever more narrow until they were but two horses abreast. Sheikh Fahd had sent Hisham and several other riders ahead of them to plot their way, while the monks watched the walls of the mountains for signs of an ambush. After the attack the evening before, he would not take any chances from here on.

At the top of the ridge, the road ran steeply downhill, splitting into two, one wide and one narrow. The wide road went left and fell steeper, then bent and ran roughly level to rejoin the narrow road that forked right and slanted down the slope.

Peruzo pointed it out to William and looked back at the carriage. 'The wagon is too wide for the narrow road,' he said to him.

William stood up in the saddle, watching as Sheikh Fahd's riders walked their horses gradually down the narrow road, none opting for the wider one.

'Do they know something we don't?' William said to his lieutenant.

'The wider road has no cover,' Peruzo replied and gestured to the range of boulders that formed a wall flanking the narrower path that slanted more shallowly down from the ridge.

'Cover or not, the wagon can't make it,' William said. 'And we can't wait much longer to decide. The other sheikhs are impatient.'

Peruzo nodded, noting the hundreds of restless riders still climbing up the pass behind them, a few beginning to make loud noises of complaint behind the wagon.

'Send the horses down the right, and the wagon to the left,' William said, and trotted down the narrow road with Marco. Halfway down he dismounted and tied up his horse by a boulder and one of the few bushes that dared to grow in the wastes. Marco was about to do likewise when William shook his head and pointed him down the track. Grumbling, Marco rode on reluctantly, leaving his uncle to stand in the shadow of the rocks.

William felt uneasy. He wasn't sure whether it was Richmond's words, or if something was not quite right with the way the road forked. He walked out of the shadows, slipping between two of the brothers' horses as they trotted past, and clambered along to the wider path where rocks and scree piled up in jagged hills. As William looked about he noticed the rocks were not weathered and the vegetation underneath was moist where stems had broken. There were plenty of plants there, as there were at the side of the narrow track, and it was the roots of these plants that often held the loose soil and rock together. Yet as William reached down to touch the broken branch of one bush he found it was sticky like the others, with little dust upon it. This had not happened months or weeks ago, but very recently.

A rock-fall? William thought. He looked over to their wagon moving slowly past the rocks, its wheels creaking along the dusty floor, feet away from the steep drop of the slope to its left. And then William knew – he just *knew* – his error.

'A trap,' he murmured, but his lips barely uttered the words. With his legs refusing to go forward, he managed to draw enough strength to bellow: 'HALT! IT'S A TRAP!'

The brothers on the wagon did not hear him, and only the monks who had been riding behind William did. They stared quickly over to the wagon as it continued to roll serenely down the road without a care, almost as though their captain had lost his sanity and was just yelling madly through the clouds of dust to a danger that did not exist.

And then came a rushing and a trembling, as if some force was sucking out the world beneath them, and the wagon was consumed by an enormous ball of dust. William clambered over the rocks towards the wide road as another boom trembled through the ground.

He jumped to the road, stumbling back as a fissure a foot wide ran towards him and split the road in two. The shock wave knocked him flat, and he rolled away as chunks of earth and rock tumbled into the ever-widening crack in the earth. Another tremor blew a gust of dust over him; it stung his eyes.

Disoriented, coughing and spluttering, William headed blindly for the cries of distress from horse and man. He crawled on his knees, rock fragments cutting his palms, till he came to the lip of the fissure. Here sat the teetering wagon, with only the roots of dead vegetation keeping the ground from crumbling away to send it plummeting into the chasm below.

Brother Michael was hanging from the edge of the fissure, having leapt from the driver's seat. There was no sign of the second driver, Brother Eric.

'Hang on!' William yelled as he lunged for the monk's arm. He gripped it tight and began pulling.

'I'm slipping!' shouted Brother Michael, but William clung on and heaved with all his might. Now as the dust cloud dispersed he could see the wagon . . . and its cargo. Thomas Richmond was crouched in his prison, his hand through a gap where one of the bars had come loose. He was not looking for escape at that moment, but down into the chasm that opened beneath him.

William faltered. He had Brother Michael before him, but he wanted to save Thomas as well. For too long he hesitated, and Brother Michael's hand slipped. But not before another hand was there and took hold of Michael's sleeve. It was Peruzo, timely as ever, hauling up the monk as William grabbed his other hand. They pulled him swiftly to lie gasping at the edge of the road.

William scrambled back towards the wagon. It was swinging slowly to the left, and gradually edging itself from the nest of roots that held it above the great drop below. The roots groaned; the wagon shifted again.

'Thomas!' William shouted.

The English merchant looked up. William could see he was terrified.

'For God's sake man, don't move a muscle,' William shouted and tried for a foothold below the edge.

Thomas watched William's heroics and looked down again at the chasm.

Peruzo was yelling, begging his captain not to go.

'I have to,' William shouted back and coughed on dust. 'We need him. He can help us.'

Thomas watched as William inched along a chunk of rock that had stubbornly refused to fall into the chasm, but now it was starting to loosen.

'What are you doing, William?' Thomas said candidly, his body quite still as the wagon juddered a little more. The roots were beginning to part.

'Give me your hand,' William replied. 'Reach out a little further.'

Thomas looked at William's outstretched arm. It was barely a few inches from his, and for a moment he thought he might be able to touch the captain's hand. He loosened another bar, but the effort shifted the wagon further and there was a desperate tearing sound.

'Quickly, Thomas!' William yelled. 'My hand! My hand!'

Thomas put out his hand and then withdrew it. 'What future do I have with you, William?' he said. 'If I survive the Valley of Fire, I will certainly be tortured and executed in Rome.'

William stared in dismay. 'Dammit man. Reach for my hand, before it's too late.'

Thomas looked at William, then to Peruzo and back at the chasm.

'Please!' William implored.

Thomas looked down in horror as the fabric of the wagon began to groan. He turned back to William and flung out his arms.

It was too late.

The roots tore free at that moment. The wagon seemed to hang for an age, before it canted and fell, tumbling down into the chasm below. For a single heartbeat, William had seen Thomas look up in regret and utter terror as he fell – an expression not easily forgotten.

The wagon hit the side of the chasm, to explode in a spray of rock, dust and shivered timber. The cage disappeared. Thomas disappeared. Fragments kept falling and falling.

'Thomas,' William murmured, sadly.

Peruzo reached down, ashen-faced, and pulled William up. 'You could have been killed.'

'It was a risk worth taking,' William replied. 'Richmond knew so much. *What a waste.*'

'Brother Eric is dead,' Peruzo said angrily. 'He had the reins looped around his hands. Michael said the horses pulled him down when the harness broke.'

William hung his head. 'Damn them, Peruzo. Damn those bastards.'

'*Who?*' Peruzo replied.

'The Rassis, of course,' William said and got to his feet. 'The Rassis did this. Look at it, Peruzo. They dug a trap under the road.'

Peruzo stared into the clearing clouds of dust and saw the rocks piled up almost a hundred feet down. As the air cleared the wagon appeared, smashed to pieces and strewn across the slope.

'The wagon is gone,' the lieutenant said.

'So is the Englishman,' Brother Michael added.

'No one could have survived the fall, Captain,' Peruzo told him.

'We should find his body . . .' William suggested.

'Do we have the time?' Peruzo replied.

William sagged, conceding. 'No. You're right.'

Peruzo looked at the monk by his side, his face dripping blood from a cut, and smeared with dust and sweat. 'Are you injured?' the lieutenant asked.

Brother Michael shook his head, still dazed from the rock-fall. 'Ride with one of the brothers,' Peruzo told him and patted the solemn monk on the shoulder. 'We can mourn the loss of Brother Eric later. Can't we, Captain?'

William was still staring into the fissure.

'Captain?' Peruzo said again. 'What do you see?'

'A lost opportunity,' William replied sadly, and turned his back on Thomas Richmond's grave.

△ V △

They found Hisham's head a mile down the road, impaled on a spike and surrounded by the heads of five other scouts. Already flies had clustered around the slowly congealing blood oozing down the spike's shaft.

Sheikh Fahd was enraged, his voice echoing throughout the mountains as he screamed his venom to the sky.

William rode back to the column. The riders had stopped and there were murmurs of dissension. 'What has happened?' Peruzo asked as William approached.

William swatted a fly from his face. 'The sheikh's personal bodyguard is dead. They ambushed him and the rest of the scouts while we struggled with the wagon.'

Peruzo bowed his head. 'They were fools, Captain.'

'No, Peruzo, they were not fools,' William disagreed. 'These were some of our sheikh's most trusted men. I think Hisham was close to Sheikh Fahd. He feels his death as dearly as his brother's. No, they weren't fools. Our enemy is cunning. They used the trap at the ridge as a diversion.' William took a sip of water. 'They are weakening us, Peruzo. Taking bites out of our courage, gradually.'

'It is a good strategy. Look . . .' Peruzo said, nodding to the Bedouin riders around them.

William searched their faces and saw doubt and fear. The attacks were undermining their resolve. 'We must get to this Valley of Fire before dusk. The battle *must* take place today,' William insisted and took another sip of water. He turned his horse and kicked in his heels to ride back to the front of the army, Sheikh Fahd having ridden a few yards away in private to grieve.

William hung back with the other two sheikhs, who looked on gravely. He could understand the sheikh's loss, but had no time for tact. He trotted his horse over, much to the consternation of the Bedouins.

Sheikh Fahd turned angrily in his saddle. For a moment his rage remained, and then he held up his hand to stop his bodyguards from hauling William back. 'What is it?' he demanded, and wiped his wet eyes. 'You disturb me now?'

'We have to go on, Sheikh Fahd. We have no more time to mourn. Is the valley far from here?' William said.

'It's over the next rise. And then it swings low into the gorge. Beyond that is the valley,' Sheikh Fahd confirmed. 'We could be there in two hours or less.'

'Let's make it less, sir,' William said, striving to hearten the sheikh. 'Our enemy knows our weaknesses and will continue to demoralize us if we take too long to face them. Let us surprise them instead. We no longer have the wagon to slow us down, and it has been a while since these horses galloped.'

Sheikh Fahd looked bewildered. 'These passes are not for galloping, my friend.'

'Then we will be *careful*. We cannot risk another night where the Rassis can attack us at their leisure.'

Sheikh Fahd pondered. 'I *would* like my revenge today.'

'And I would like to end my mission,' William concurred.

'So we will end this now,' Sheikh Fahd announced brightly. He shouted to the riders and smiled. 'Today I will take vengeance for Hisham, for Jamillah and for my brother.'

'And I will draw my sword with you, sir,' William told him. 'As allies.'

'As *friends*,' Sheikh Fahd corrected him, and reached over to shake William's hand.

△ VI △

The sun was over the peak and heading down to the west of the Valley of Fire. The valley lay in shadow. In the morning the rising sun would set it alight, the red and orange rocks would dazzle and shine, a thick heat haze would merge sky and horizon, and the temperature would soar, closed in by these towering walls.

But in the late afternoon, the valley was not so intimidating. It would have been ordinary apart from the single mountain that rose at the end of the gorge, its steep slopes tapering to a point where a temple sat, built of ebony-coloured stone. A single track wove its way along the valley floor to the foot of that mountain, and there it stopped abruptly against its face, secret paths snaking up from there on.

And it was quiet. So deathly quiet that only the sound of sand blowing in on a breeze could be heard.

381

Presently, as more afternoon shadows formed in the valley, there was a rumble of thousands of hoofs. The Bedouin army arrived and deployed across the valley, hundreds wide, in ranks of four.

And as they formed, dark shadows appeared on the mountain at the foot of the valley. Shadows that seemed to come alive. William knew who these shapes were, and knew that they were not ghosts, but warriors of a nature that made him tremble at the thought of battle.

They were the Rassis Cult.

CHAPTER NINETEEN

Through the Fire

△ I △

'We could have done with Mazin's cannon,' Peruzo said to William as he squinted towards the mountain, its squat mass casting a long imposing shadow across the valley. He sighted movement in the foothills, and some of the younger monks with sharper eyes noted the occasional dark figure emerge from among the rocks.

Slowly but surely, these figures drew up in a narrow line at the base of the mountain.

'What do you reckon their range is?' William asked as he watched patiently.

'With those bows? I would say up to one hundred and eighty yards, judging by the attack on the camp yesterday . . .' Peruzo grinned. 'Our Baker rifles can better that.'

Sheikh Fahd galloped down the line with the three sheikhs; all were eager to fight, despite the loss of the Suwarka. 'We will charge and take them head-on!' Sheikh Fahd announced triumphantly, waving his great shining sword above his head to the roar of approval from the Bedouins.

William held up his hand. 'Forgive me, sir, but battles are not won through rash actions. If we attack now, we are charging a fortress. We would lose many men.'

'They will die for Allah!' Sheikh Fahd barked at him. 'We are not afraid!'

'It is not bravery that I question,' William urged. 'The Rassis are strong in defensive positions. We learned that much in the ambush at the oasis. That temple at the summit must surely be their base. If it is, they will have it well defended. We will be cut down before we get within a dozen yards of striking them, as Mazin's men were at the oasis, but much, much worse.'

'Mazin's men were foolish. There is nothing weak in Ayaida steel, Captain Saxon,' Sheikh Fahd assured him.

'Indeed, sir, there is not. But the enemy have bows. They have already claimed scores of Bedouins from a simple ambush. If we charge in blindly, we could lose a quarter of this army in one volley. Then victory will be beyond us.'

Sheikh Fahd tightened his jaw and stroked the neck of his horse. He relaxed a little, replacing his scimitar in its scabbard. 'What are you suggesting?'

'I can use the rifles as a screen. When the Rassis realize they do not have our range, they will move closer, and then at my signal you will charge to meet them,' William outlined.

Sheikh Fahd appeared pleased. 'It will draw them out of safety,' he said thoughtfully. 'It gives them less time to shoot back. I like this plan.'

'We will lead the way, and then you will form up behind us,' William said. 'Pass by my men, and we will join you in the charge.'

'It will be done!' Sheikh Fahd roared and galloped away to meet with Anwar and Galal.

Peruzo waited patiently, the brothers more cautious than the hot-blooded Bedouins. 'What are your orders, Captain?' the lieutenant asked.

'How many crack shots do we have in the company?' William asked him.

'Well there's Garibaldi, Argento, Cristiano, Donato . . .' Peruzo replied, running off a list. 'The others are fair, but only really accurate up to one hundred and fifty yards, perhaps less. So, fourteen men in total.'

'*Sixteen* men,' William corrected. 'You and I, also. The others we'll hold in reserve.'

'What about Marco?' Peruzo said.

'He will join the sheikhs' camels at the rear, along with the remaining brothers.'

'That is sure to please him,' Peruzo teased.

'Pleased or not, those are my orders,' William retorted.

△ II △

The sound of the horses lining up was clamorous. At the head of the three ranks of riders were the sixteen skirmishers on their horses, their Baker rifles slung over their shoulders, other weapons strapped to their saddles. William had divided the men into four groups of four, spread out across the centre of the line. The Bedouins had left gaps to pass by the monks during the charge. William rode at the centre of these groups with Brothers Argento, Vincent and Donato. Peruzo took the left flank with three other brothers, including Brother Filippo the physician.

Their horses gained momentum as William steered the monks ahead, closing to four hundred yards from the mountain. He hoped Peruzo's calculations were correct. If the enemy could fire beyond two hundred and fifty yards, he would have no choice but to order the charge.

Ahead, William could see figures dressed in dark blue robes and armour. They were slight, like thin shadows, and emerged without ceremony, appearing at once at the foot of the mountain while more came in sight at the clefts in the rocky slopes.

The rhythm of the horse had caught him now, and William's heart pounded in his chest. For several moments he thought about Adriana, thought about her face, her lips, the smell of her hair . . . And then he remembered Marco at the rear. He had said nothing to him before leading the attack; no words of comfort, nor of farewell. He hoped he would see the boy again.

Upwards of two hundred yards. William was half-expecting

385

the arrows to fly, but none fell. Encouraged by this, he held up his hand, pulling on the reins. His horse yielded with a roll of dust. The other monks halted almost as one, and while it took time for the Bedouins behind them to register that they were stopping, halt they did, their mounts protesting.

William leapt from his horse, unslung his rifle and adjusted the belt of ammunition that hung at his hip. Brother Argento was at his heels, and then at his side, already loading his rifle as he ran. The two other monks were following close behind, their rifles at high port. At one hundred and ninety yards they stopped and raised their rifles, aiming at the dark blue figures. William took a single glance left and right to find the brothers were at the same mark, and aiming at the Rassis.

He didn't need a second look to know they were ready. 'FIRE!' he yelled.

The sixteen rifles echoed in the valley like tiny rock falls, spitting out smoke and fire.

William could not tell if they hit their targets, but then at once cheers came from the riders behind them. William turned to see Sheikh Fahd raise his sword aloft, beaming triumphantly at William. As the smoke cleared they saw the results: nine men, perhaps more, had fallen. They were few, but a start.

'Independent fire!' William shouted to the monks.

Each brother began reloading and firing, round after round after round. Their rate was impressive, taking less than ten seconds to load and discharge. Most of the rounds found their target, and one by one the dark blue figures began to fall. In a minute, William had counted almost three dozen dead.

Elated, he cheered them on, bewildered by their enemies' apparent inability to retaliate. Loading again, spitting the bullet into the barrel and then ramming the linen patch, he raised his rifle to take aim. Then as his finger tensed on the trigger, he stiffened in dismay. Up ahead of him a previous casualty was rising to his feet again – *like a ghost*.

And then, unbelievably, more 'dead' warriors got to their feet.

Some continued to lie in the dust, but in a matter of seconds, half of the previous slain were alive again.

Brother Argento faltered. He looked over his shoulder to William with an expression of despair.

'Dammit, Argento!' William shouted. 'Keep on firing!'

Argento raised his rifle and aimed. Pausing at the last moment, he raised his sight and targeted the dab of dark blue that was the head of one warrior. He uttered a short prayer and squeezed the trigger. Through the smoke he saw a fan of crimson envelop the warrior's shoulders in a cloud, and the figure collapsed.

'Aim for the head! The head!' Argento screamed himself hoarse through the smoke.

Another fusillade, and more of these ghostly warriors fell, some to rise again, others staying down. From the slopes, shadows slid out of the clefts and climbed down, moving silently to the lower quarter of the mountain. They reappeared quickly, positioned themselves at new ledges, and William saw a movement of weaponry . . .

. . . Archers.

He raised his arm aloft and waved at Sheikh Fahd, who was continuing to watch the men of the Church firing into the ranks of Rassis and almost missed the signal. With one hand holding aloft his sword, he gripped his reins with the other and yelled to the riders of the Sinai: 'For Allah!' He kicked in his heels as the first flight of arrows sailed from the mountainside.

William saw shafts rise in unison and then dip and come hurtling down. He signalled the retreat and all fell back apart from Donato, who had always been the fastest loader in the Order. He had squeezed off one shot as William signalled to the sheikh, but was now almost loaded again when William ordered them back. Donato raised his rifle as the Arabs galloped past; timing it just before one of them blocked his view, he fired.

He might have seen the target fall to the sands, and he might have heard the cry of triumph from the Bedouins as they charged towards their enemy, but the volley was on him too soon.

The brothers were halfway to the horses when the arrows landed. They struck the ground around where the skirmishers had stood. Any Bedouin rider who had reached this point was a target, and many Arabs fell to the ground, their mounts or themselves impaled by the thick black shafts. Some mounts were struck in the neck, rearing up with death cries to collapse on other horses and their riders. One fell in front of two riders and these were pulled over, rider and beast in a tangle of breaking bones.

Brother Donato was struck twice, one arrow through his thigh, while a breath later an arrow pierced his neck. Blood spurted from his mouth as he stood motionless for a moment, his right hand at his leg, the other struggling with the arrow through his throat. William turned to see him stagger as the dust of the charging horses threatened to consume him, and then he was gone.

William turned and ran for his horse. Brother Argento was there before him, the charger pawing the ground for his master.

'Another volley!' Argento shouted as William swung up into the saddle. Both watched as the sky above the riders turned grey and the hail tumbled down on the Bedouins.

'A hundred arrows,' William reckoned. 'Just a hundred. But they'll take many men with each volley.' Between them and the rear of the charging mass of riders were dead or dying Bedouins and their horses, scores of them. The first volley had been timed well.

William dropped his rifle to the ground and pulled his sword free: Engrin's sword – the blade the old man had entrusted to him so many weeks ago. 'The day we have been waiting for is upon us, gentlemen,' William said. 'This is the day we take the Hoard of Mhorrer!'

The monks drew their weapons. Peruzo pulled his short blade free and pointed it towards the charging Bedouins.

'For the Church! For God! For all of Mankind!' William yelled and kicked in his heels.

Marco saw the battle unfold as he sat with the remaining five monks of the Order. Jericho waited nearby, his fingers flexing on the reins.

'Donato has fallen,' said Brother Michael.

Brother Jericho nodded sadly.

'We should attack!' Marco cried impatiently. '*Why are we waiting?*'

'To watch after you, boy,' said a gruff monk behind them. Marco did not know his name, just another face that they travelled with.

'It is your uncle's orders, Marco. We are to stay here and wait,' Brother Jericho said, but he too felt impetuous, itching to charge.

'For what?' Marco said.

'For the next battle,' Jericho replied, though he was unsure as well.

'Do you think they'll leave some for us?' Brother Michael asked.

Jericho didn't know, and continued to watch as another volley of arrows fell upon the charging Bedouins, the greycoat line closing in fast behind them.

△ III △

It was like riding an earthquake. Each charge was the same, chaos in one direction, the dead piling up behind them. William saw Bedouins fall in front of him, fearing their tumbling bodies would trip his horse, but the animal was instinctual, dodging this way and that, bending around the fallen.

Before him two Bedouins were slain, one with several arrows in his chest, another colliding with the rider's horse. William's horse leapt, its hoof catching the trailing leg of another mount.

There was a sickening snap, and William believed his horse must fall, but it galloped on, its leg only bruised by the clash.

William could no longer see the flights of arrows. Brothers Argento and Paolo were lost in the turbulence of galloping horses and Bedouins, and there was no sight of Peruzo and the rest of the company.

Another Arab fell at William's side and rolled away, before the charging pack opened up and William hauled back on his horse's reins, almost going over the animal's neck. Now the course of the battle was appallingly clear. William turned his steed about and watched as wave after wave of Bedouins were hacked down by the blue ghosts that fell upon them, striking with lightning-quick blades. William saw five Bedouins charge, their swords held high; one of the Rassis was trampled instantly, but the others sidestepped and leapt from the ground, cutting great arcs across the riders. One by one, the Bedouins toppled from their mounts, suffering gushing wounds and severed limbs. Resolutely, the ghost warriors advanced and attacked another wave of the Ayaida, slashing and carving, *effortlessly*.

William jumped from his horse, realizing that elevation brought no advantage against the Cult. He pulled a long knife from his belt and held it with the blade pointing to the rear. Then he charged into the melee with Engrin's sword extended.

At once he faced a dark blue warrior, his movement a blur, his blue cloak billowing behind him. As the cultist closed on him, William saw armour about his torso, covering shoulders and waist. The cultist's dragon mask leered at him as the Rassis danced over bodies sprawled face-down in the sand. He skipped over one more corpse before he landed and then lunged with a long sword.

As the point darted towards him, William drew up his long knife from the left, parrying the thrust. The blade's momentum swerved it to William's right, and then William leapt, swinging Engrin's steel from over his head down towards the mask. The blade split the mask in two and then drew a spray of blood as it cleaved through the skull. The warrior slumped and William stumbled, losing his grip on his sword.

As he pushed himself up, another Rassis lunged. The long sword came at William and he parried again with the knife, only to be punched in the face by a gloved fist. He reeled back seeing nothing but stars, feeling the cutting of air as a sword came down. He rolled, but the blade sank into his left hand. He screamed and kept on rolling, clutching the wound with his right hand, feeling the gush of blood between his palms.

The warrior swung down again at William, but two combatants staggered between them. The cultist's blade cut into a Bedouin who was wrestling with another Rassis, and both men fell into the mire of sand and blood.

In the chaos, William reached for a sword, *any* sword, as the cultist recovered and attacked again. His bloodied and numbed hand found a Tarabin sword and he pulled it over his body, parrying the first attack. William kicked out and his boot struck something hard: the attacker's knee. It took out the cultist's leg and the warrior stumbled, falling with a thud that dazed him. William swung the Tarabin sword at the bared neck. A crunch, and it severed head from shoulders.

Dazed and in nauseating pain, William slipped to his knees, letting go of the sword. Blood poured from the injured hand. He propped himself against a dying horse and examined the wound.

The Rassis weapon had taken the whole of his little finger and the first two joints of the next. He was bleeding profusely and felt faint. Battle was raging around him, the bodies spilling across the sand. Though there were occasional dark blue robes amongst the fallen, most of the dead were Bedouins.

William's nausea grew. He could see that they were losing.

△ IV △

Peruzo traded blows with a cultist. The man was shorter than Peruzo by half a foot, yet he was quick, and already Peruzo sported a wound to his right shoulder; a glancing blow but enough to sap his strength. His opponent was superior in skill and speed. Yet what Peruzo lacked in youth and agility, he made up for in experience. As he feinted with the sword in his left hand, he felt the adrenalin flood down his numbed right arm. The dark blue warrior – his armour wet with Bedouin blood – went for what he took to be Peruzo's weaker side. He swung for the bloodied shoulder, but Peruzo swapped hands and parried with his right, unsettling his opponent. Peruzo's left fist stuck the man hard in the wind-pipe and he fell back choking, before Peruzo swivelled his shortsword and thrust it just above the chest armour, once, then twice, and a final time, each thrust a death blow.

The lieutenant stood up and rallied Brothers Cristiano and Garibaldi to him. Garibaldi was lurching to the left, a hand pressed to his ribs. He was bleeding badly, and it was sheer determination that kept him standing.

'Once more!' Peruzo half yelled, half gasped, and all three charged into the melee, their feet churning through the blood-soaked sand.

△ V △

William bandaged his hand with a strip from a Bedouin robe, his grey jacket now a rusty colour. The bleeding had halted, but the hand throbbed. Amongst the corpses he had found Engrin's sword again, and not too soon. A cultist appeared from the fray, his armour cloven, blood pouring from his wounds, yet still he staggered on. It seemed across that vast expanse of carnage that the warrior wanted to fight William, and William only. He marched towards him, ducking strikes from Bedouins and dodging grappling bodies that were resorting to wrestling as the ground grew boggy with bloodshed. William rose to meet him and they traded blows in quick succession. Weak himself, William eventually managed to hack through the man's wrist before ramming the tip of the sword into the assailant's breast-bone. Still the warrior fought on, and William jerked his sword loose, swinging it wildly as dexterity deserted him. With a lucky strike that glanced up off the armour an inch or two below the mask, he sliced through the Rassis's neck.

Once more, William fell to his knees, exhausted. But this time he didn't think he had the strength to rise again. It took much to destroy these dervishes of death, these ghosts of the valley. William did not know how many they still faced, but the peak of the carnage had passed. How much time had elapsed? Again, he did not know. He did not know if any of the brothers were still alive, or whether Peruzo still lived. Or the sheikhs.

William resisted the temptation to look to the rear where he hoped his nephew waited. Victory or defeat had still to be decided. Putting his head down, he lifted himself from the ground, urging his legs to work again.

Standing, he swayed for a moment, bent double to cough harshly, tasting sand and blood on his lips. Through flailing arms and legs he forged on; past horses lying on their backs, struggling with their wounds, their flanks struck with arrow shafts; blood on every square yard of ground . . . Staggering through it all, lacking the strength to strike at anyone, William went in search of his men.

△ VI △

It was Marco who saw them first. He pointed to the right of the battle and shouted.

'There! Over there! Do you see them?'

Brother Ettore trotted his horse forward, his eyes not as young as Marco's. Squinting under the shade of his hand, he could see the shapes now, sallying from what first appeared to be a jagged edge of rock, but on longer inspection turned out to be an opening, maybe even a concealed stairway.

'The boy is right!' Brother Ettore exclaimed, turning his horse about. 'There are men down there!'

Brother Jericho watched intently, holding his breath as he saw several shapes emerge from the cleft, followed by more.

Brother Ettore galloped up to Jericho. 'You see them as well as I,' he growled.

'I see figures, that's all,' Jericho replied, but felt Ettore's impatience. 'You wish to break our orders?'

'You wish to see our men massacred?'

'Our orders are to stay here and look after the boy,' Jericho said, looking past Ettore to where Marco fidgeted in the saddle. 'My eyes are young, Marco. But yours are younger. What colour are they?'

Marco stood up in his saddle and frowned. 'They're blue, I think,' he replied, and urged his horse forward. 'We must help my uncle!'

'Marco!' Jericho shouted back. 'You are to stay here! Those are your uncle's orders!'

'They're no good if he dies!' Marco cried and spurred his horse.

The monks watched in horror as Marco galloped off to the right, the momentum of the horse almost jolting him from the saddle.

'I think our decision is made,' Jericho groaned. He drew his sword and glanced at Brother Ettore. 'Are you with me?'

Brother Ettore grinned. 'Of course!' he said, and dug his boots in, launching into a gallop. The remaining monks of the Order gunned their mounts across the valley floor behind Marco, who continued to ride hard, the dust of the battle hiding them until they broke right behind the melee, and drove straight at the unsuspecting Rassis.

Marco drove headlong towards the first, unable to draw his sword as his horse bolted like a wild animal, not the tame beast he had ridden since Rashid. It ran down a scurrying warrior, trampled him flat with a crack of bone beneath his armour. The cultists behind him dived to the side, but one was hit as the horse stampeded by, flinging his body against a rock with a lethal crunch. A third Rassis swung low, bending to his knees, to cut the horse's legs from under Marco. He lost hold of the reins as he was dispatched from the saddle, flying over the beast's neck, head over heels, the world turning brilliant white in a flash of pain.

Marco felt and heard little for an uncertain while. There was nothing apart from the sensation of rolling across soft ground before resting against something hard. He opened his eyes, and tried to focus on someone who was moving in front of him, raising something, breathing hard and fast . . . And then a broader shadow fell across Marco, followed by the swish of sundered air. With a wet cracking noise, warm blood jetted onto Marco's chest, splattering his chin and cheeks.

'Marco! Marco!' someone said. 'Get up! *Get up, Marco!*'

Marco wiped the blood from his eyes and looked up, focusing on the shadow. He got to his feet, his legs wobbling.

'Find your senses!' demanded the voice.

'*Jericho?*'

'Your sword! Get your . . .' Jericho said from astride his horse before one of the Rassis leapt into the air to strike the horse. The monk defended the beast's flank with two swift parries, before pulling the horse about to kick the Rassis in the ribcage. The iron-shod hoof shattered the warrior's armour and staved in his ribs, crimson spraying finely from the mask. The cultist stumbled about, choking on his own blood, before falling in a heap next to the dead body of Brother Ettore.

'*Marco!*' Jericho screamed again as the boy searched heedlessly for his sword on the saddle of his dying horse. He had not seen a Rassis by the rocks raising his bow. Jericho pulled out a throwing dagger. The hurled blade sank into the cultist's wrist, sending the arrow wide. Marco found his sword, but never knew how close he had come to death again.

Pulling his horse around to act as a temporary shield for the boy, Jericho leapt from the animal and slapped its hind quarters, sending it out of battle. 'Someone has to keep you out of trouble!' he half shouted, half laughed hysterically, dragging Marco away from where Brother Michael was locked in battle with another cultist.

'What do I do?' Marco cried as the battle intensified around them, another monk falling under a Rassis sword. It was Brother Michael.

'Just follow me and kill any that come your way!' Jericho shouted back at him, and they ran full-tilt into the nearest fray.

△ VII △

Sheikh Fahd saw Anwar fall. He saw Sheikh Galal dragging his bloodied corpse to the edge of the battle where the struggle was less intense, a wall of Aquila fighters protecting them as Galal tended to the boy sheikh. Sheikh Fahd himself was bleeding from his brow and there was blood on his clothes, his men's blood as well as the enemy's. His sword had slain five of the Rassis. He wanted more.

Weary, his arms like lead and his heavy sword almost a hindrance, he stumbled into the thick of battle, seeing several Tarabin drop in moments against two of the cultists. These armoured fighters seemed to simply dance from man to man, dealing death with their long swords. Each Bedouin fell with chest cleaved open, head severed or limbs detached. It was carnage on a scale Sheikh Fahd had never imagined. The valley was a charnel house, but most of the dead were Ayaida, Aquila and Tarabin. The Rassis dogs had hardly been touched.

The inkling that he might be denied his brother's revenge enraged Sheikh Fahd and he charged onwards, straight at two of the enemy, swinging his scimitar up above his head. The first of the cultists leapt back, and the second might have escaped, but a reeling Bedouin knocked into him from behind. The collision disrupted his fluency; his sword rose late as Sheikh Fahd's descended, cleaving the Rassis through the shoulder.

The other lunged fast at Sheikh Fahd, and only the sheikh's

loss of balance saved him from being skewered in the heart. The blade sank in just over an inch under the ribs. He cried out, and tumbled over. The Rassis threw the long sword aside, pulling out a dagger from his belt. He leapt over his dying colleague to thrust it into Sheikh Fahd as he lay prostrate on the ground. The sheikh looked up, knowing his life was finished – but as the Rassis's blade arced down towards his heart, it was dashed aside. A white-robed figure grabbed hold of the masked cultist and drew a knife across his throat. The Rassis held on to his assailant, and they struggled, blood flowing down both of them. At last the cultist weakened, his struggles grew less, and he sank to the ground, still in the grip of his assailant.

Sheikh Fahd looked on, willing his eyes to stay open and his consciousness to remain, staring at the man who had saved his life. His rescuer was small, covered in blood, and his face bedraggled; he was staring at his own knife that had done the work, his hands trembling. He looked up into the eyes of the sheikh, who simply gasped.

'*Hammid?*' he choked.

Hammid nodded. 'You are wounded,' he said and looked down at the sheikh.

Sheikh Fahd groaned as he tried to move. Hammid knelt beside him, still with the dagger in his hand, and despite all that had happened, the sheikh feared that Hammid would plunge it into his chest and finish the Rassis's work.

But when Hammid didn't, when he laid it on the bloody sand, Sheikh Fahd felt ashamed that he had distrusted this man. That he might even have executed him if Captain Saxon had not intervened.

This man, *his saviour.*

Hammid looked up fearfully at the clamour about them. He made to leave, but Sheikh Fahd held his arm. 'I will not go,' Hammid said reluctantly, but smiled with compassion, and both men stayed where they were for the remainder of the battle.

△ VIII △

William found Peruzo fighting for his life beside some out-matched Bedouins. He arrived at the blind side of the attacking Rassis, focused on their prey. It seemed they too were tiring from the fighting.

William mustered his strength and dragged up his sword. His run took the blade through the back of one Rassis.

'Captain!' Peruzo cheered and fought his opponent with renewed hope, punching the man in the mask twice, before kicking him between the legs and then cutting his jugular with a swift stroke of his shortsword. The cultist fell, and then Peruzo yelled out in delirium as he went for the next, his fury stoking the courage of the Bedouins around him.

The Rassis began to fall back.

Their numbers were depleted, their strength waning. All along the line they began to retreat, disengaging from their enemies, who were mostly too tired to follow. Those few who did – those Arabs still on fire with battle – made it to the foot of the rocks before a hail of arrows drove them back.

William was panting like a sick dog when Peruzo staggered over to him.

William looked up, his face awash with blood. 'You live, my friend?' he gasped.

Peruzo grinned. 'I am no ghost,' he said, but slumped a little. 'They're retreating . . . I don't believe it . . . We've beaten them . . .'

William nodded, but it was scant relief he felt. They had driven the Rassis back, but for how long? The sounds of fighting dwindled, and as William closed his eyes to gather his composure he wondered how many of these fiercest of foes were left.

The battlefield lay quiet. Those left standing bowed breathlessly or shook with fatigue, not even daring to count the dead. Through the murk came two figures, both looking dishevelled in their grey uniforms, dusted with sand and blood. William was sure these were monks, but as they approached he saw that one was tall and the other slight. Almost like a boy.

'Marco?' William said.

Marco stumbled towards him and straight into William's arms. William held him tight on waves of relief. *The boy was safe.*

Marco held him harder, and for a moment William thought he heard him sob. But when the boy stood back, William noted a dramatic change in him. Whether by the blood that crusted his brow, or by those eyes, dark and serious, he saw that this was no longer a boy before him. It was a man.

William was stunned by the transformation. Stunned and angered. 'I ordered you to stay,' he said, and looked up at Jericho reproachfully. At first Jericho said nothing, regarding Marco proudly.

'Your nephew saw them outflanking us, Captain. He saved your life. He saved everyone's,' Jericho told William, and recounted the charge that led them into battle. It was hard to hear, especially with the loss of the brothers, but William was grudgingly thankful. They had survived the encounter with the Rassis Cult . . .

But the battle was not over.

CHAPTER TWENTY

The Cult's Last Stand

△ I △

Peruzo deployed the survivors behind the largest boulders scattered at the foot of the mountain. The shadows about them grew thick as the sun dipped behind the hills. Almost an hour had passed since the battle had ended, yet the Rassis were as diligent as ever. Another flight of arrows rained down, killing a further dozen Bedouins who were tending to the wounded. It was a warning to all that the Rassis were far from defeated.

'What are our losses?' William asked.

'Fifteen dead, seven survivors,' Peruzo said bleakly. 'With the casualties suffered by our allies, any assault on this mountain would be catastrophic. We could not hope to win.'

If William agreed, he kept it to himself. Of the sheikhs, Galal was unscathed, Anwar was dead, and Sheikh Fahd unfit for battle. Only a third of the Bedouin army were in any condition to fight. The Tarabin had suffered devastating losses, while the Ayaida and Aquila were at less than half strength.

'We cannot turn back now. We must assault the mountain before night falls. By morning, we will be dead in any case,' William said.

'We have but six hundred Bedouins and only one sheikh who can lead them. Will he follow us?' Peruzo said.

William had not considered this. Sheikh Galal was largely unknown to him. The leader of the Aquila had said little throughout the journey from the camp of the Ayaida to the Valley of Fire, yet Sheikh Fahd had never once questioned his courage as he had Mazin's. Would Galal turn and leave? Or would he stand and fight?

Of the company of monks William knew five: Brothers Jericho, Filippo and Vincent were with him, Brothers Neil and Orlando had been sent out across the field of the dead to recover the company's rifles, while the other surviving monks, Rocco and Mattia, were the last of Vittore's Spanish company.

And then there was Marco. William would have baulked at taking the boy on a mission akin to suicide, but Marco had shown courage and resilience, and his youthful high spirits heartened the other men. He had proved himself as much as any of them. And if the past battle had taught William anything, it was that a Marco unsupervised would only get himself into further trouble.

'Captain?' Brother Jericho addressed him as he cleaned his sword on the hem of a Rassis robe. The monk looked worn and battered, with his jacket in shreds and one cheek gashed to the bone. Yet under the blood and fatigue, Jericho was alert. 'Marco and I noticed a hidden track up the mountain fifty yards to our right.'

William looked at Marco, who nodded.

'A *hidden* path?' Peruzo chimed in.

'We only noticed it when the Rassis tried to outflank you,' Jericho explained. 'If it's a secret stairway, we could scale the mountain quicker, couldn't we?'

William nodded. 'Find out for me, Jericho. And keep your head down.'

Jericho nodded and grinned, and then he was gone.

'The rest of you, make ready,' William commanded. 'We must assault the mountain and take that temple at the peak. I am certain the Hoard of Mhorrer lies above us. Should we turn back now, we fail our mission, and all of our fallen friends have died for nothing.

'So do we turn and flee? Or do we take what is ours?'

The response was unanimous and rapturous.

'I will speak to Sheikh Fahd. Perhaps he can rally the tribes for us,' William said aside to Peruzo, leaving them to prepare.

△ II △

Grief was most prominent within Sheikh Anwar's tribe. The surviving Tarabin sobbed quietly, staring out at their hundreds of corpses and fatally wounded. The cries of the dying wailed across the valley, swirling upon the wind. William wanted an end to that lamentation as he made his way past clusters of resting Arabs, so many of them bloodied and dejected, their thoughts on the friends and relatives who lay where they had fallen in the sand.

William found Sheikh Fahd leaning against a rock, with a heap of blankets for a seat. His white robes were now stained rusty red where a tear revealed the bandage wrapped around him. He looked pale, but the colour had returned to his cheeks over the last half-hour. And with it his humour.

'I think I'll fight on, Captain Saxon,' he chuckled.

'Indeed,' William replied. 'You could wrestle a young bull in that state, sir.'

Sheikh Fahd chuckled again, and then began coughing. 'Perhaps not,' he said, and groaned as he held his side. 'Where is Hammid?'

William shrugged.

'Find him, Captain,' the sheikh requested.

'Why? Did Hammid do this to you, sir?' William asked uneasily.

Sheikh Fahd shook his head. 'He saved my life, Captain.'

William was astounded.

'Find him. Keep him safe. He has earned my gratitude.'

'I will try. It is hard to find anyone at present. He may have been killed,' William said, gazing at the Bedouins strung out along the line of nearby rocks, out of sight of the archers above.

'I will pray to Allah that he was not,' Sheikh Fahd declared. He shifted about and looked up the slopes of the mountain. 'What are your plans?'

'Would you have us leave, sir?' William asked him. 'We have suffered heavy losses, and your allies seem demoralized.'

Sheikh Fahd looked angry. 'They will stand and fight, or I will declare them cowards!'

'And what of Sheikh Galal? He is the only one who can lead. What will he do?' William asked.

'Galal will do what is in the best interests of the Aquila. If he agrees, you will still attack?'

William nodded. 'We face only half our enemy and we may yet prevail. But we must strike soon.'

Sheikh Fahd nodded. 'My men will follow you. As will the Aquila and what is left of the Tarabin, I promise. I only wish I was fighting by your side.' He reached up a hand to William.

William took the hand with his right, his left now bound with rags over severed stumps. They shook and William smiled. 'If we succeed, I will have you carried to our victory.'

Sheikh Fahd grinned. 'Very well, Captain. May Allah's blessing fall upon you and your men, and keep you safe.'

William parted company and turned back to the monks. Brothers Neil and Orlando had returned from searching the battlefield for the discarded rifles, and were already handing them over as William arrived. Brother Neil passed William a rifle. Methodically, he cleaned and checked the firearm, removing the sand and ensuring that the flintlock was intact. He tied two small ammunition pouches around his waist as the company waited on their captain.

Brother Jericho came back looking more dishevelled than before and caked with rock dust, but his smile was broader than ever. 'Our guess was correct, Captain. There's a narrow stairway carved inside a fissure about forty yards down to the right. It runs up the mountain to that flight of steps to the left. But I cannot tell if the Rassis are lying in wait.'

'You've done well, Jericho,' William told him.

'Are we going to fight?' Brother Jericho asked.

'We are,' William said calmly, handing him another of the company's rifles. He slung his own over his shoulder and gestured behind them. 'We wait on Sheikh Galal, and then we shall storm your stairway.'

△ III △

Sheikh Galal returned from his meeting with Sheikh Fahd. The battle had sapped both his wits and his courage, yet Sheikh Fahd's words struck him like a blow: 'If we turn back now, all those who have died will have perished for nothing.'

Sheikh Galal had asked the sheikh what they were fighting for. To which Sheikh Fahd replied: 'Because this honest man of Allah has told us of a great catastrophe. Because this prophet of doom is ready to sacrifice himself and his men to stop a great death falling over *our* lands. And if we do nothing, these "ghosts" of the Sinai will destroy our tribes. We men of the Sinai are not cowards!'

The speech was bold, and yet Galal knew it was also flawed. Most of their army had perished, and the strength they had once commanded was all but shattered. As for these men of Allah, they were almost utterly destroyed, and yet . . .

. . . *And yet* it had been the sight of them in action that caused Galal to reconsider retreating from the valley. He had seen several of these Europeans fighting alongside the Aquila. They had charged in with their grey uniforms and strange weapons, full of a matchless bravery. They leapt into the thick of battle, slaying and being slain in return. And regardless of their suffering, they would keep fighting until their lives were utterly spent. And when death came they did not sink to their knees and beg for mercy. They did not cower in the face of a sharp blade.

Sheikh Galal stood at the foot of the mountain and stared long and hard towards where this man called Saxon waited with his much-depleted company. He nodded thoughtfully, then he addressed the Bedouins to his left and right.

'Warriors of Aquila, of Ayaida and Tarabin! Draw swords with me and remember Fahd and Anwar. We follow the man in grey,' he said. 'And we will follow him with Allah in our hearts. Remember: mercy will not be offered by our enemies. And by Allah, they will not receive it. This battle is to the death!'

The message flew like the wind along both flanks, and a tide of energy with it. William saw it happen and looked bewildered. 'What do you think that means?' Peruzo asked.

William was about to shake his head, but found the Bedouins drawing their weapons with one hand, the other placed on the rock face in front of them as they prepared to climb.

William turned to Peruzo with a broad grin. '*It means we fight.*'

'Good,' Peruzo said gruffly. 'I didn't travel through a waste-land for nothing.'

'Are we prepared?' William asked his company. They nodded. 'Marco?' he asked, more nervous for his nephew's life than for his own.

Marco smiled. He didn't look afraid, and he held his sword like an old friend. 'Stick close to Peruzo,' William said to the boy, and winked, 'and you'll be fine.'

A cry went down the lines of the Bedouins and William took a deep breath. 'Good luck, gentlemen,' he said, and headed for the hidden stairway.

△ IV △

For a while it was a leisurely ascent. Half an hour when not a Rassis could be seen, nor did a single arrow fly. The steps Jericho had discovered took them to the right of the main assault, and while it was a steady and daunting climb – believing at any time they would happen upon a pocket of Rassis warriors – they were halfway up the mountain before there was any sign of the enemy. The mood was queer, the quiet broken only by the Bedouins below them, their voices rising in optimism that the enemy had fled and the mountain was deserted.

As the company rested for several minutes, William watched from the steps high above as several Ayaida began to break cover very slowly, some pausing for breath to sit on rocks in the open, growing nonchalant about the assault. Some were even openly congratulating each other.

William's monks were too wary to take such a lull for an omen, and they kept their heads well down. 'Lower, Marco . . .' Peruzo hissed, prodding him in the back with the hilt of his sword until the boy ducked under cover.

'Where are they?' Marco hissed back. 'Why don't they fire at us?'

'They're just waiting,' Peruzo assured him. 'Don't raise your head for anything, understand?'

The sky above was bright enough, but with the late afternoon sun already hidden behind the hills of the valley, the air turned quickly cold. Below them, the first Bedouins appeared on a long slope of scree that ran up at a gentle angle to a line of boulders that screened the staircase. Persuaded by the easy appearance of these stone steps, two dozen of the Arabs began to clamber towards the slope, laughing to each other as they sank up to the ankles in shingle, pulling each other up as they joked in the eerie quiet.

As the first three Bedouins came within a few feet of the steps there was a sudden shift of air, like a whistling . . . and then sounds that went 'Thwack! Thwack! Thwack!' broke the silence. The three men stopped, foundered in the soft scree, then rolled down the slope with arrows in their chests.

More whistling came, more impacts, and several more Bedouins fell. Their deaths froze the other Ayaida for a moment, time enough for another volley to strike the remaining Arabs caught in the open, cutting them down at once.

William watched hopelessly as another wave of arrows fell from the air amongst the unshielded Bedouins and screams and

cries mingled with the clatter of metal on stone. 'Keep down!'
he warned the monks. He urged them forward to where the
steps narrowed along a fracture in the rocks, the occasional
arrow skipping off a boulder nearby. Soon they were on their
knees and Marco crawled on blindly, his heart racing; when an
arrow ricocheted a foot from his head, he gave a yelp and almost
collided with his uncle's back.

William guided them to where the stairway broke into the
open. The steps dropped away to a ledge which wound its way
up to where the stairs went on uninterrupted.

'Be ready,' he began, 'and run after me . . . Flatten yourself
against the far rock. Peruzo, take the right and watch our rear . . .
The others . . . Follow tight and quick . . .'

And then William ran, springing to the rock face at the far
side of the open ledge. Peruzo dashed to the right as instructed.
Then came Marco, followed by the monks, Brother Filippo
leaping just before arrows whistled along the fissure. Below
them, the Bedouins were pinned down.

'We have to reach those archers,' Jericho said.

'They're above us,' Peruzo replied. 'Even with our rifles, we
couldn't hope to shoot them. They have a higher elevation and
better cover.'

'Nevertheless, Jericho is right: we must try,' William said. That
very moment there was a rush of feet behind them near where
Peruzo stood. A Rassis flung himself at Peruzo seemingly from
nowhere, but the older man's ears were fine-tuned and he heard
the swish of steel cutting air. He ducked, and the long sword
clanged on the stone behind him, before he swung the butt of
his rifle up between the cultist's legs. The warrior groaned in
agony and fell to his knees.

As the warrior squirmed helpless on the floor, William saw
an opportunity. He stopped Peruzo from slitting the cultist's
throat, and instead dragged the man to the edge of the outcrop
and launched him over it to sail down the mountainside and
land with the snap of breaking bones close to where the
Bedouins were pinned down by the Rassis archers.

It had the desired effect. The Bedouins cheered at once, rais-ing their swords defiantly to renew their attack up the slope with fresh hope, while others ran to the prostrate cultist and repeat-edly stabbed the body with their swords.

Pleased with the effect, and with the sound of the Bedouins starting upwards again, William signalled to move up the staircase. Gusts of arrows continued to fall, impaling climbing men where they stood, tearing through flesh and bone. It was bloody, and at times it was a slaughter, but the Bedouins struggled up to the ledge as William and his monks made their way up the stone steps.

Ahead, the stairs wound their way through another fracture in the rock face, and then snaked off to the left, before rising once more. After another quick ascent, the steps broke out of cover again, flanked by a steep drop on one side and a gradual slope on the other that lay in view of the Rassis positions high above. William sprinted across the yards of open space, the monks close behind. The Rassis fired too late, the arrows impotent as they clattered harmlessly off the steps.

'We can't hope to use our rifles, so be ready to fight at close quarters,' William ordered. 'Make sure you engage with your back against the rock face. Do not be turned. And fight as one. Double up, make them tire, and go for the groin, the arms, and the neck.'

His advice was timely, as from the steps ahead dashed three Rassis, running in silence towards them, their dragon masks glar-ing. William held his ground where others might panic. Peruzo stood just off to his side, and as the first Rassis lunged for him, the captain feinted to the left and struck the assailant's long sword upwards, while Peruzo closed in with his shortsword to skewer the warrior. As the lieutenant withdrew the blade, he ducked the blow from the second Rassis, just as one of the brothers ran his sword through the cultist's belly. William drove his sword down on the wounded Rassis, cleaving him from the crown to the chin. After Jericho and Neil hacked down the third cultist, William waved the monks on.

Marco was careful not to run into his uncle again with each abrupt stop as the company dodged arrows or paused to view the progress of their allies now far below them. He observed Peruzo and Jericho, especially their determination, and it grew upon Marco: he had to be as resolute as they were if he was to survive this, and he concentrated grimly.

Another Rassis leapt from a niche in the cliffs above. Jericho ducked the assassin in blue, but one of the brothers was not so lucky. The cultist drove his sword through Brother Vincent's chest, but the monk embraced his killer and pulled him off the staircase. Both men cartwheeled to certain death below.

William glanced down into the deepening shadows, following Vincent's outline until it disappeared from sight. Night was falling. There was no time to mourn, or even to pause, and he dragged his company further up the stairs. As the steps rounded a corner, two waiting Rassis sprang. Peruzo dropped to his knees and fired point-blank at the first. The shot tore a hole in his armour and the warrior dropped.

The second Rassis swung wildly at William, who deflected the sword with his rifle, spinning to club the warrior over the head. Jericho yelled as he thrust his sword through the cultist's belly, and then Orlando and Neil dived in and stabbed the cultist until he moved no more.

William loaded his rifle carefully and looked to each man. 'We're near the heart of the Rassis' defence,' he said. 'Load your guns and shoot cleanly as the lieutenant did. Aim for the heads if you can.'

At the top of the steps came the tread of running feet, the sounds of alarm. The Rassis knew the men in grey were coming.

△ V △

The sun was beginning to set as Peruzo appeared, the first to reach the top. Several attackers came at him, but with the glare of the setting sun directly behind him, the Rassis ran blindly, not even seeing the rifle. Once the barrel was level with the first dragon mask, he squeezed the trigger and the wearer's head exploded.

The others continued charging, but Peruzo stood at his shoulder and brought his own rifle to bear. Instead of shooting the next Rassis in the head, he aimed for the legs. The bullet blew a kneecap apart and the warrior fell down hard in front of his brethren. Two fell over him, while another leapt over the writhing figure just as William dashed forward. The cultist ran onto his sword and the momentum knocked William to the ground.

That was a stroke of fortune, for another wave came running across the long landing at the top of the steps. Waiting behind William were Brothers Neil, Mattia and Orlando, who now fired a simultaneous volley that cut down three more of the Rassis. By now both Peruzo and Jericho had loaded again. At this range it was slaughter, and a further two enemies fell. One of the wounded tried to rise, but Brother Rocco bent forward and broke his neck.

With the dark orange sun at their backs, William positioned the monks in a line at the top of the stairs, and they swiftly reloaded as they scanned the scene before them. The stairs stopped abruptly at a wide outcropping that was a dozen yards wide and a hundred in length, so that it formed a long lip of sandstone against the mountain, its gradient undulating upward. Along this rising slope were cave entrances and lean-tos where the Rassis now streamed out, their swords drawn, but looking disorganized. They had not counted on anyone reaching so far up the mountain so quickly.

Between them and William's men were the enemy archers. While they'd been perfectly sited to pick off the Bedouins below using the parapet of boulders as cover, they were wide open to enfilading fire from their right flank – which the brothers now began, raking volleys across the Rassis from out of the sunset glare.

As the monks aimed and fired, and archers died, William

gestured to Marco to keep his head down. Despite the crack of gunfire and the torrent of smoke that rolled before them, Marco was chafing to join in. He weighed his sword in his hand and watched eagerly as the Rassis charged towards the monks in desperation. When they got within ten yards of the brothers, William ordered the company to fire again. Each shot found its mark and another eight Rassis were dead. In a matter of minutes, a score of Rassis were either killed or wounded.

As the monks reloaded, Marco wriggled past his uncle and hunkered down next to the wall of rock immediately on the left. Above it was a slope and a narrow stairway that ran to the top of the mountain and the temple. The setting sun made it sparkle like a dull jewel, and William was impatient to reach the end of their mission.

The Hoard of Mhorrer was *so* close.

Amid the mayhem and the smoke of gunfire, the Rassis repositioned some archers at the tight stairway to the temple. There they could shoot, and a volley sailed down at the monks.

'To your knees!' William cried out.

The brothers ducked, but Brother Rocco was too slow. Two arrows struck him in the belly and he fell to the ground, screaming out in agony.

As they rose to fire back, a second volley streaked towards them, and the company scattered for safety. Peruzo pulled three of the brothers down the steps just as arrows hit the ground where they'd been kneeling, while Mattia, Jericho and William flung themselves against the wall of rock to the left where Marco was crouching.

Using the steps as cover, Peruzo raised his rifle and returned fire. The shot whined harmlessly off the wall of the stairway, and he reloaded as Brother Rocco continued to squirm in the dirt before them, twin shafts protruding from his stomach. Brother Filippo dared to reach for him, only for Peruzo to pull the field surgeon back from danger.

'Hang on, brother!' Filippo cried out. He loaded his gun

desperately, raised it and fired towards the archers above them, but in his haste he only hit rock.

William took Marco by the collar and hauled him upright just as a lone cultist charged down the wall to where they stood. With his left hand still grasping Marco's jacket, he tried to parry the strikes that rained down on him, but the warrior disarmed him in seconds. Jericho reacted by reflex: he drove his sword with all his might through the cultist's belly to lodge in his spine. As the warrior stumbled back, the sword went with him. Jericho might have reached to retrieve it, but William hauled him away with Marco, back to the steps, to a measure of safety.

Brother Mattia defended their rear against several charging Rassis and paid the price; after cleaving three Rassis, he was run through by the fourth. Crying out in fury, Brother Orlando fired his Baker rifle at Mattia's killer. But another volley of arrows soared their way, and William and his nephew barely reached safety as several struck the top step. A couple of arrows sailed inches past Brother Neil's crown, but one tore into the chest of the prone Brother Rocco, and his cries of pain were silenced.

'We're pinned down,' Peruzo shouted, 'and we're fast running out of ammunition, Captain.'

The Rassis began to return fire at will, single arrows cutting through the air about them, disrupting the aim of their Baker rifles. Brother Filippo yelled out suddenly and stumbled back as an arrow struck him through the cheek. He flailed his arms in the air and stepped blindly over the side of the steps. William threw out his hands to stop the monk from falling. 'Filippo!' he cried, but fell silent as the field surgeon tumbled into oblivion.

William felt beaten. Victory had been in their hands. He had tasted the elation, if only briefly – had marvelled at their fight against the odds. But surely now the Hoard was beyond them. Their numbers were too few, the Bedouins had been all but massacred at the foot of the mountain, and now his company were being killed off one by one as the Rassis gained the upper hand.

If the Dar'uka had aided them, it would have been so easy.

But they hadn't. Unlike their last-ditch intervention during the battle on the *Iberian* and at Aosta, they had not come, and it angered William. He felt betrayed by them, betrayed by his best friend. And now they would all die, because of him. The brothers, Peruzo . . . And Marco.

'Damn you, Kieran,' William murmured, as another flurry of arrows fell among them.

△ VI △

While the archers loosed another volley at the enemy (those soldiers in grey who had come so miraculously far up the mountain), at the other end of the landing the Rassis began to chant: 'Egori ratsa Ifer! Egori ratsa Ifer!' The words were in an ancient language, and the Cult used it now to boost their courage.

Translated, the words were: 'The Champion of the Traitor steps forth! The Champion of the Traitor steps forth!' And so the Champion did. He was taller than the other Rassis, almost seven feet in height. His shoulders were broad, and hung about them was armour of leather and iron that covered his chest and waist. Over this armour was a dark blue gown trimmed in gold that reached to the ankles. The warrior did not wear a mask like his brethren but a band of cloth around the forehead, where a single eye wreathed in fire was embroidered. His skin was darker than the rusty sand, his hair jet-black, and his eyes narrow and fierce.

As the chanting rose, the Champion of the Traitor stepped out of the cave and into the copper sunlight, lifting his weapon of choice: a staff of iron that would have taken two of his fellows to hold. He turned to the Rassis massed about him and brandished the staff in the air. The Rassis' chant rose to a cheer that echoed from the mountaintop; behind the champion, they surged forward.

The enemy at the steps were weakening – it was time for the Rassis to conquer once and for all.

The monks loaded again and fired. Above the reports of the rifles, the company could hear the Rassis' mantra. It was a dreadful sound, eerie and vengeful. Its wailing menace threatened their resolve, and William fought to master his trepidation as marching feet trod closer in the background.

Marco cowered and shrank against the steps.

After another volley of arrows sailed inches above their heads, William shouted up to Peruzo: 'What is happening up there?'

Peruzo rested his rifle for a few moments and peered through the gun smoke. The Rassis were emerging again, but they were behind something, or some*one*, that dwarfed them all.

'*Peruzo?*' William shouted again.

'I swear to God . . .' Peruzo gasped and stared back at William. '*We have to retreat.*'

William looked staggered. 'What are you talking about?'

Peruzo reached down and pulled William up to his position. It was crowded at the top of the steps, but already Orlando and Neil were moving away, as awestruck as Peruzo. William peered through the dissipating smoke and saw why. There were dozens and dozens of Rassis marching towards the steps, their swords held above their heads. But even the massed ranks of warriors in dragon masks did not compare in terror with the giant who led them. He was enormous, and the weapon in his hands was a pendulum of death.

'I'm out of ammunition, sir,' Orlando said to William.

'Get back,' William said reluctantly. 'All of you . . . *Back now.*'

The monks retreated and Peruzo loaded his rifle to cover their escape. With their ammunition all but spent, the giant's appearance was the final spur that William needed to abandon their assault. Marco and Jericho led the way while he stood with his lieutenant and covered the slow retreat down the stairway.

The first of the Rassis appeared at the top of the stairs and they both fired; two cultists collapsed and tumbled down the steps.

William loaded again. 'Fall back! Fall back!' he cried as he descended another step. A cultist appeared and flew towards them, and only Peruzo's glancing blow from the Baker rifle stopped him from harming either man. But the rifle broke, and Peruzo threw it to the floor, drawing his sword in desperation as William fired his last shot, taking out another blue-clad warrior who lurched down the stairs, clutching at the wound in his chest.

Following Peruzo's example, William threw the rifle down and drew Engrin's sword. His left hand was cold and numb, his right hand trembling as he watched the Rassis hesitate at the top steps. Both he and Peruzo had dispatched the first attackers swiftly, enough to deter the others from succeeding them. But they wouldn't wait long, and no doubt archers or even the giant must soon appear. William did not wait to see which came first; he practically drove his survivors around the corner. As the last man jumped for his life, arrows ricocheted against the stairs and wall.

'We cannot defeat them like this,' William conceded. 'There is no other choice. We must fall back to where the Bedouins are . . . Maybe together we can stop the Rassis. Maybe we'll have another chance at . . .' He paused at the look on his men's faces.

Even in the fading light, Peruzo could see despair in William's eyes. 'We did our best, Captain,' he said. William made no reply, but waved them further down the steps.

As Jericho led the way again, he stopped short with a shout of alarm. There was warning, consternation and then urgency as more voices entered the fray. *Bedouin voices*.

William pushed past Orlando and Neil, and stepped around Marco, who had backed up the stairs, sandwiched between the Rassis at the top and the tide of men flooding up from below. He found Jericho with his arms in the air, several swords hovering in front of him. Their owners looked up as William approached. Several dark faces stared at him.

'*You*,' William said and pointed to the youngest of the warriors. 'You are Mazin's son.'

At the mention of the name, the young Bedouin nodded and smiled. 'Mazin,' he replied and patted his chest. He lowered his sword and strode forward to shake William's hand.

'How did you get here?' William said, all but forgetting the Rassis further up the stairs. Mazin's son just kept smiling, not understanding a word William was saying. He grinned and pointed to the valley below.

'Mazin,' he said again.

William narrowed his eyes as he peered through the waning light. He noticed dark shapes there, more than there had been before. *With wagons and something else . . .*

'The cannon?' William said. It appeared as though Mazin's son understood this word at least and his smile grew.

'Captain, they're coming!' Peruzo warned as the Rassis charged down the steps under cover of their archers.

The Suwarka pushed past the beleaguered monks with their swords and clubs. As the Rassis rounded the corner, the Suwarka attacked. What they lacked in skill they made up for in freshness and numbers. The Rassis killed several Suwarka, but the Bedouins piled forward and simply pushed the Rassis from the steps. The cultists fell into the chasm below or retreated to the cheers of the monks.

As the first wave of Rassis were struck down, the archers loosed a volley of arrows that fell upon the elated Bedouin. William watched as the brave Arabs tumbled down the side of the mountain or fell to their knees impaled by thick arrow shafts, their cries resounding about the ledge, shocking the Suwarka and piling on the misery for the company. With the Rassis archers holding the top step, their position was little improved.

Mazin's son spoke quickly to one of the Bedouin warriors, who leapt to the edge of the steps pulling two great flags, one orange and one yellow, from his cloak. He waved them down to the valley below while the Suwarka huddled back against the rock face.

William had only seconds to realize what was happening, Sheikh Fahd's warning about Sheikh Mazin's cannon ringing in his ears. 'Bloody hell!' he yelled at his men. 'All of you . . . Get down!'

Flame gushed from each of the guns on the valley floor. A whistling noise ripped through the air, and William closed his eyes. There wasn't even time enough to pray . . .

The first shot landed below them, a dozen feet away. It exploded harmlessly on the mountainside, shaking the stairs where they knelt. The second fell off-target to the left, not far from the steps that wound their way up to the landing, and its closeness alone would have given William cause for alarm if the third shot hadn't landed several yards above them. The noise was shattering, shaking them to the bone and pelting them with broken rock and dust. William had his hands over his ears, and feared that he would open his eyes to many casualties about him. To his relief, everyone was stunned but unharmed. Marco looked terrified.

'The bloody fools will kill us, Captain!' Peruzo shouted.

William could only agree, yet their views on the salvo's accuracy were ignored as the Bedouin warrior got to his feet and drew up the flags again. He swept his arms upward three times, and shifted the yellow flag to the left. Then he dropped the flags to the floor and returned to the scant cover of the rock face again.

'Keep down,' William shouted. 'Here comes another salvo . . .'

The cannons spoke again, and three more shots came whistling their way. William heard Brother Neil behind him muttering a prayer, but the monk did not finish it before the stairs shook. This time the cannonade struck the landing above them. The boulders at the lip were blown asunder, tearing apart the enemy archers who hid there. Some were thrown across the landing, their bodies broken. Others lost arms and legs, tossed

417

into the air to fall down the side of the mountain. A body even fell among the Suwarka.

As the dust and smoke cleared, the Bedouin gathered the flags. As he began to signal, an arrow took him in the back and he slumped to the ground. Mazin's son rushed over, and pulled the flags from his grasp. He waved them above his head, in a direct line, and then ran from the edge, throwing himself down near William.

William covered his head with his hands as a third cannonade rained down on the Rassis above them. Marco screamed out in despair, believing that each explosion would be his last, while Jericho simply laughed hysterically as the ground was littered with rock, pieces of Rassis armour, and lumps of flesh.

And then the bombardment ceased.

Coughing and cheering, the Suwarka rose and charged up the stairway. William had no need to urge his men forward: despite being utterly exhausted, they followed their allies into battle.

△ VIII △

The Suwarka streamed over the top steps and were greeted by several archers. In the chaos that followed the last cannonade, their arrows were not as accurate and only three Suwarka fell. The others rushed over the debris and the dying cultists, and straight into battle.

The Champion of the Traitor was largely unharmed, though his armour had been torn away by one of the explosions, and he sported a wound to his cheek. Yet his strength was no less, and he met the Suwarka with his iron staff, swung in a sweeping arc. The first blow struck two of the Bedouins, staving their skulls and hurling them over the edge. The staff swung back again and caught another, crushing his ribcage. In the confusion the Bedouins had not appreciated this formidable warrior, and without any caution they flung themselves upon him. The giant swung the staff again, crushing skulls, breaking arms and legs, punishing any Suwarka who came near him.

Mazin's son was among the first to attack. He saw the staff crash down on his men, and rushed out to strike the giant across the arm. The champion saw the sword slash towards him, and the iron rod twirled in his hands to smash Mazin's son in the face. The blow crushed the front of his skull and the young warrior tottered back to fall into the arms of his tribesmen.

William saw him die, and saw now that the Suwarka assault had faltered as theirs had. Desperately, he urged Brother Jericho and Brother Neil forward with their rifles. They aimed through the gloom and fired. Brother Jericho missed the giant by inches, but Neil's shot struck him in the belly. The champion staggered back, one hand going to his stomach. He lost his grip on the staff, and one end crashed noisily against the floor. Brother Neil reloaded, aimed . . . but a warrior leapt in and stabbed him through the heart. As Jericho fumbled with his last cartridge, William battled the Rassis away, cutting down one and then another, giving the monk a clear path to the giant, who had since recovered and was raising his staff once more. Jericho fired and the shot tore through the giant's chest, yet still he advanced.

Several Suwarka retreating in the face of the champion could not escape and the iron staff swung out again, a little less deftly than before, yet still with devastating force as Bedouins were crushed and smashed in a flurry of screams. As the carnage thundered closer, William reached down and pulled Brother Neil's rifle from under his body. He looked up as several Rassis descended on him and William was thrown to the ground. Everything went black and he felt bodies clawing on top of him, expecting a dagger to pierce him at any moment.

When their weight was lifted and William was turned over, Peruzo stood above him, clutching his bloodied sword. 'Shoot, Captain!' he shouted desperately.

William pulled the rifle to his shoulder and looked up as the giant lumbered towards them. The iron staff swept round at William's head, and he fell back, blindly firing the rifle. At hardly a yard, the bullet could not miss, but the shot was fortunate: it flew dead-centre between the blazing eyes. The sash around his forehead exploded in tatters along with the back of the giant's head. The lumbering warrior tottered, but before he could fall full-length and crush William, he sagged to the ground and lay still, amid Bedouin cheers.

The Suwarka swarmed forward again in a quest of vengeance. And behind them came the Ayaida, the Aquila and the remnants of the Tarabin. The Rassis' organized ranks fell apart under the onslaught. The sheer weight and momentum of the Bedouins storming the ledge forced the Rassis to fight against the walls or simply brushed them off the mountainside to tumble head over heels down the slopes. Some retreated up the steps, but were pounced upon by blood-hungry Suwarka, who looked to revenge the death of their leader's son and of all those the Rassis had killed before – generations of terror, centuries of death.

In the melee were the remnants of the company, their spirits renewed, clambering to the steps to cut off the Rassis' only means of escape. When at last they made the second flight of stairs, Peruzo, Jericho and Orlando fought back to back with the Suwarka, using the height to their advantage. William struck down several opponents, lunging with Engrin's sword at each dragon mask that came his way. The Rassis were desperate now, their defeat inevitable as they fell to the swords of the Bedouins. They forgot their courage, forgot their supremacy, and more importantly their charge: the Hoard of Mhorrer.

Yet despite their disarray, they did not forget to fight for their lives: as the last of the Rassis battled on, they struggled savagely with their enemy. They came again at William and his monks, and many of the Suwarka were killed, Brother Orlando lost a hand, and each man bore a wound. Even Marco.

William's nephew had rushed in at the last moment as William lost his grip on Engrin's sword, his severed fingers oiling the handle with fresh blood. It was Marco's intervention that stopped a cultist from wounding William further. Marco lunged and his sword sank just below the armpit of the frantic warrior. With the sword through his lungs, the cultist swung out and punched Marco in the face, flooring the boy. William recovered and pulled Marco back with his bloodied hand, while with the other he swung his blade and cleaved open the cultist's skull.

With their opponent slain, William helped up his dazed nephew. Blood leaked from Marco's broken nose and he could only grunt in pain. William led him over to the steps behind them and out of the battle.

'My nose hurts,' he groaned.

'It'll mend,' William promised, trying to contain himself. He was so proud of him it was all he could do to stop himself holding Marco close and laughing deliriously. 'You've done enough. Stay out of sight until the battle ends.'

Marco didn't argue but kept touching his damaged nose. He looked up for a moment and met his uncle's eyes.

'You saved my life,' William said.

Marco smiled and tears stung his eyes proudly. William slapped a hand on his shoulder, biting down on emotions that had seesawed all over the place, from fear to horror, from murder now to pure love and joy.

Yet the battle was still in progress, and William rejoined it. Before them the ledge was thronged with Bedouin warriors until very few Rassis could be seen, and the final dragon mask was overwhelmed.

'It's over,' William said and felt his arms sag. He looked up at Peruzo, who was splattered in gore. 'We did it, Peruzo. By God, we won.'

Peruzo looked too exhausted to be pleased, but he simply nodded and slid onto the steps beside Orlando, who was pale with loss of blood. Jericho slumped nearby, falling onto one knee, before subsiding completely. He closed his eyes and uttered a small prayer to whoever might be listening, thanking them for their victory.

The battle was over. The Rassis were destroyed.

Sheikh Mazin's cries could be heard across the valley. They shrilled through the smoky silence of the battlefield, with not one other matching their despair.

Sheikh Fahd listened in sadness. 'Whatever chiding he gave Abdullah, he loved his son very dearly,' he said to William, who thought of Marco.

'He died very bravely,' William replied.

'That will bring little comfort to Mazin,' Sheikh Fahd said. 'His last words to him were no doubt scornful.'

William looked across the valley. 'We all lost someone today,' he said distantly.

Sheikh Fahd nodded. Now, as promised, William had the sheikh carried up the mountain to where their victory had finally been sealed. The litter was carried by the Suwarka and Ayaida, and William supervised it. It was exhausting work, especially through the dark, but a promise was a promise. They would return the sheikh soon after, but not before Fahd saw the site of the Rassis' last stand.

'How many of your brave men survived?' Sheikh Fahd asked.

'Three,' William replied. 'And my nephew.'

'A grave loss, Captain Saxon,' Sheikh Fahd remarked. 'I myself lost over five hundred men.'

'I am so sorry,' William murmured. 'I wish . . .'

'Wishing will not bring them back, Captain,' Sheikh Fahd said gently. 'But like Mazin's son, they died bravely. Songs will be sung, and stories told.'

Lieutenant Peruzo came over to them. 'Sir,' he greeted William and half bowed to Sheikh Fahd.

'Speak, Lieutenant.'

'Brother Orlando is in a bad way. The bleeding has stopped, but he is very weak and the journey back to the Ayaida's camp is long. He might not survive it.'

'Make sure he is comfortable, and we'll see what the morning brings,' William replied. 'What about Fahd's doctor?'

'He is no Filippo, but he is competent. I thank the sheikh for that.' The lieutenant left the two men to talk alone, and as he walked away Sheikh Mazin's cries faded.

'Mazin has come to terms with his grief,' Sheikh Fahd said. 'But only for his son's death. There will be more to grieve for at dawn.'

'How many were killed, do you think?' William asked.

'No one knows, Captain,' Sheikh Fahd replied. 'The Tarabin were almost all killed. Galal survived, but who knows how many of the Aquila perished. And there are many Suwarka dead on this mountain.'

William blew out his cheeks. He sighed and tried to take in what had happened. Yesterday, they had suffered grievous casualties. Today, the army was all but in ruins.

'Was it worth it?' William asked himself, but out loud.

'My brother is avenged, Captain,' Fahd said and shrugged. His smile was lost in the darkness, but William saw his eyes sparkle. 'The reputation of the Ayaida will become legend. It might even rally the tribes to face Ali.'

'I am glad,' William murmured, but it was scant consolation.

'What of you? Was the sacrifice worth it, Captain Saxon? Did you get what you came for?' Fahd asked.

William looked over his head towards the shadow of the temple at the peak. 'Not yet,' he replied. 'But I will.'

CHAPTER TWENTY-ONE

The Hoard of Mhorrer

△ I △

They climbed the steps, steep and narrow, as the sun left the sky. Daylight was falling behind the turning world as the captain and the lieutenant reached the top. From the summit William looked out across the Sinai, at the hills and mountains in the distance, smeared by the red fire of dusk. It was a miraculous sight, yet both men were too exhausted to truly absorb it.

'I'm glad you didn't send me back down there for the gunpowder,' Peruzo said, breathing out heavily. 'You would have had to carry me, like Sheikh Fahd.'

'You look old,' William teased him.

'It's not the years that age a man, Captain, it is *experience*,' Peruzo replied, and laughed. 'How is the hand?'

'It hurts when I walk,' William replied and then began laughing too. 'Adriana will scold me, Peruzo. This was my *best hand*.'

Peruzo started laughing harder, and for those short minutes the rank, the Order and the mission did not matter. They had made the temple at last – against all hope, they had arrived at the storehouse of the Hoard of Mhorrer, achieving something the vampyres had not; that Count Ordrane had not. Nor even the Dar'uka. And it came as a blessed relief to think about something other than the death of most of their friends and colleagues, and the slaughter that lay below.

As their levity declined, both stared up at the temple before them. From the valley floor the building had appeared like a squat lump of rock with a large doorway carved on its face, but on closer inspection it was more intricate. The large double door that William had seen from afar was supported by four massive and equally imposing columns of rock, obelisks many feet thick and made of granite. They were covered by a smoky-grey dust, yet the swirls of the colouring made William think the dust had been applied on purpose.

The doors too were carved in granite, and smeared with the grey dust, and he wondered why the Rassis had gone to such lengths. In the dim light, and with the sun no longer glaring on its surface, the marbled black seemed in shadow, almost like a night's sky.

'A façade,' he said, and placed his hands on the cool stone, 'so no one can see what this is.'

'Can we get inside?'

'You know, I really haven't thought about that,' William admitted. He looked for a lever or a handle, but there was none. The fading light was making it hard to see. William's hands touched something engraved against the hinge, and he bent closer.

'Have a look here.'

Peruzo too peered close. 'A lock?'

'It doesn't feel like one,' William replied. 'A symbol? I cannot tell in this light.'

'If Brother Jericho has any sense, he'll bring a torch from down there,' Peruzo said.

'I do hope so, Lieutenant. In a short hour we'll be completely blind on this mountain.'

'How long will they be, do you think?' Peruzo asked as he wandered wearily over to the edge of the landing. He stood with the tips of his boots over the rim and looked down at the Bedouins far below. Already looting had begun of the Rassis fortress, and torches had been lit along the stairways as they sought survivors and friends who had fallen.

'Depending on whether those camels of Sheikh Fahd can

climb the stairs, it could be a good hour or two,' William replied. 'Maybe more.'

Peruzo grunted and walked away from the edge. He sat down near the entrance and looked up at William.

'What's on your mind, Lieutenant?'

'If you'll forgive me, I was only wondering how you must feel now that you're victorious,' Peruzo said.

'I will feel quite pleased if we can get inside this damned temple,' William said, and sighed as he pushed at the door again.

'And what about your future in the Order?' Peruzo was almost pleading.

'My future?'

'You once spoke of wanting to leave,' Peruzo reminded him. 'Is that still true, now that we've climbed this mountain? Now that we have beaten the Rassis?'

William wandered over and sat down near the lieutenant. 'I've given it no more thought, if I'm honest.'

'May I be candid with you?' Peruzo asked.

William nodded.

'Thomas Richmond put those thoughts in your head for a reason, William. He thrived on deception. He set out to poison you with words. You are the Order's greatest soldier. If you leave, then the Order is no more. Richmond knew this. He wanted to undermine you and your belief. He lied to us. He used us. Forget what he told you,' Peruzo said.

William sighed. 'If only I could, but it isn't just Thomas who put those thoughts there. Adriana dreads every departure. And I'm tired of fighting, Peruzo, aren't you?'

Peruzo laughed. 'Of course I am, but then I'm older than you are.'

'Have you ever thought of leaving the Order? Retiring to a nice cabin in Villeda?'

'Yes,' Peruzo admitted. 'But what would I do? I'm a soldier. I always have been. I would make a terrible farmer. I am no husband. I have no children to look after me.'

426

'I'm sure you could find a pretty widow or someone to run their fingers through your beard,' William joked.

Peruzo laughed with him. 'Ah, that sounds quite blissful, Captain . . . But I cannot see it being so,' he added and looked saddened. 'I've given my life to this cause. I expect that cause will take it soon enough.'

'Not if you retire after this mission,' William said. 'You could train initiates at the monastery. Teach them to be better soldiers.'

Peruzo seemed interested. 'You think the Secretariat would let me?'

'For a hero from the Valley of Fire, why not?' William replied.

△ II △

Someone gave Peruzo a prod with his toe. The lieutenant started to awake and looked around, bleary-eyed. Around him it was oddly bright, and his eyes stung. 'Was I sleeping?' he slurred and then adjusted his eyes to find Brother Jericho grinning down at him with a torch in his hand. Marco too carried a torch and was standing by a pair of mules. 'You took your time,' Peruzo added and pushed himself up from the floor.

Jericho looked aggrieved. 'Have you ever tried carrying four heavy kegs of gunpowder up a mountain before?'

'Fahd gave us donkeys, Uncle,' Marco explained to William as Jericho helped the lieutenant to his feet. 'I don't think those strange creatures with paws for hoofs would make it up the steps.'

'Camels, Marco, they're called camels, and I agree, they're too gangly to climb such steps,' William said as they untied the kegs. 'I hope you thanked the sheikh for me.'

'We did, though I don't think he understood us,' Jericho said.

'I'm sure he understood you *perfectly*,' William said, laying the kegs on the floor. 'What about Brother Orlando?'

'He's still in a bad way, Captain,' Jericho replied. 'Fahd's physician cauterized his wrist but now he has a fever. We should never have left him in the hands of these Arabs.'

'The only man left who is even close to the calibre of a field surgeon is Fahd's physician, Jericho,' William chided. 'I realize he is no Filippo, but he has followed the proper course. If the wound is left to fester, then Orlando will most certainly die.'

'He might die anyway, Uncle,' Marco said. 'He looked *ill*.'

The news of Orlando was desperate, and it was all William could do to stop himself displaying despair. But then they had lost so many men this day that Orlando's condition was simply numbing. Putting his head down, he lifted a keg to his shoulder and walked between them to the door. 'Leave Brother Orlando to Fahd's people – we have a mission to complete,' he said to them. 'And we need to find a way to open this door.'

He rested the keg at the entrance and pressed his palms against the rock.

'You wish to blow it open?' Peruzo said, taking the torch from Marco. He stood a few feet back from the keg, as if out of respect for what it might do if ignited.

'It's an idea,' William admitted. 'We do not have a key.'

'That symbol could be the lock,' Peruzo suggested.

'Symbol?' Jericho asked and walked over. William gestured over to the right near the hinges of the door and Jericho lifted his torch to view the engraving. As he placed the flame near to the rock, the symbol started to glow. Jericho murmured in surprise and brought the torch closer; the movement caused the symbol to burn brighter. 'Captain, look at this . . .' he whispered.

They gathered around Jericho as he shone the torch over the lustrous mark: it was the symbol of the Rassis Cult, and it was glowing like iron in a smithy.

'*Incredible*,' Peruzo murmured.

'Indeed,' William agreed, but he was not blinded by the miracle. 'This is the Valley of Fire, and this sect is the Eye of Fire. Maybe it takes fire to unlock the temple . . .' He took the torch from Jericho's hand and thrust the tip of it into the symbol. It was an assumption, a wild one at that, but to William it made sense that fire would open the doors.

The engraving was made by a conductive element that quickly grew hot, expanding in the metal lock embedded in the stone. As it expanded, the grooves around the eye ground and pushed against the mechanism, and the stone doors began to groan open.

'It's working! It's working!' Marco shouted, his voice carrying over the mountain.

They all staggered back, apart from William, who kept the tip of the torch pressed against the lock, the flames licking around it, the heat growing until the rock was now red-hot and the torch was only smouldering.

The doors groaned and creaked, they shifted against the stone ledge, and a low rumble sounded as the edges ground against the floor, scraping stone upon stone. Sparks flew, to scatter across the floor like darting fireflies. The doors tipped over the keg of gunpowder William had propped against them, and Jericho ran over, dragging the keg back in case it got crushed or one of the sparks ignited it.

Still holding the torch, William waited for the doors to open fully. Looking at the awed expressions of the three men facing the doorway, he wondered what they could see.

The doors rumbled to a stop and the groan of hinges ceased. William dropped the spent torch and rounded the door to stand near his friends. 'The temple . . .' Peruzo whispered, his hand pointing inside.

William adjusted his gaze and fell silent. The chamber beyond had no windows, no lamps and no torches. It would have been a complete void if it were not for the splintered blue light scattering over the ceiling, the walls, and the steps inside. The light never stayed in one place and flickered about like a full moon trapped on the surface of an agitated pond.

And there was something else: a sound like insects, or maybe a choir of voices in the distance. A humming that rose in anticipation as William took steps towards the entrance. Peruzo put a hand on his shoulder.

'That sound . . .' he said, and shook his head. 'I've heard it before.'

William nodded.

'What's making it?' Marco asked, his voice as hushed as the others'.

'Scarimadaen,' Peruzo replied and his hand slipped from William's shoulder. '*Many* Scarimadaen.'

'It's what we came here for,' William reminded them and stepped forward into the temple, taking their remaining torch from Marco. Jericho followed, and then Marco, while Peruzo glanced about and entered last, the sound of the fearful chorus rising and rising.

△ III △

Sheikh Fahd looked down at the bodies. 'When?' he asked.

The two Ayaida shrugged and then looked apologetic. 'Not long ago. Within the last hour,' one of them replied.

Sheikh Fahd examined their wounds, the gashes across their chests and the cuts to their faces. 'You are certain they weren't killed in battle?'

The Ayaida nodded unanimously. 'Bassam and Iqbal were part of Sheikh Mazin's guard,' they explained. 'They were here at the cannon during the battle. We think they were sent up the mountain to retrieve his son. They never got there.'

'They fell?' Sheikh Fahd said and looked up at the shadow of the peak against the stars. There were torches lining the stairs up there, and for a moment there had been a light at the peak, but that had soon disappeared.

'No,' one of the Ayaida disputed. 'I think' – he was quickly nudged by his brother – '*we* think, they were murdered.'

'*The Rassis!*' Sheikh Fahd growled and spat on the ground. 'They should *all* be dead. Yet if any have escaped . . .' He looked up at the peak again. 'Where are my guard? Call them at once! And send them to the top of the mountain, or else Captain Saxon and his friends will be massacred!'

△ IV △

The inside of the temple was quite broad and long: forty yards in width and the same in length – a square chamber supported by great stone pillars at each corner. The roof rose inwards from the pillars and tapered to a point high above, matching the geometry of the mountain peak. Below it ranks of steps descended from each of the four walls, like a square amphitheatre. These steps fell down for about twenty rows and halted abruptly at an abyss that was twenty yards square.

Suspended over the abyss was the source of the light. It sat on a platform supported by a great pillar of rock that fell and fell and fell into the darkness below. Leading across to the pillar was a timber bridge weighted with black rock at each end.

And on the platform lay the two hundred and fifty Scarimadaen: the Hoard of Mhorrer. Each one was different. Each was formed from some special element, unique in its shaping, unique in its material. There were stone Scarimadaen, made of marble, granite, basalt; Scarimadaen of diamond, gold, platinum, and lead ... They saw Scarimadaen of oak, of sand, of glass ... And impossible as it was, they saw pyramids made of coloured smoke that seemed to lose composure for only a few heartbeats before remoulding themselves. There was a pyramid of water that sat at the top, rippling like the surface of a pond, shimmering with light. There was even a pyramid that beat like a heart, seemingly made of flesh stretched over bone ...

The sound of voices intensified, as if an army was clambering up the sides of the abyss. Peruzo would have put a hand to his ears, if the light from the two hundred and fifty Scarimadaen had not been so blinding that he had to shield his eyes.

'*Oh my God,*' Jericho murmured, trembling.

William too was struck dumb with awe and a measure of horror. He stood at the top of the steps and willed himself to stand closer, but he was too afraid. The light of the Scarimadaen flashed and flickered, animating shadows in the temple so that it seemed that ghosts were leaping up the walls and against the ceiling.

He recoiled and looked to the others, who were just as troubled. The voices from below seemed to fracture and converge again, rising and circling the platform as the infernal light flickered and crackled over the pyramids.

'*What now?*' Jericho whispered, his mouth dry.

William looked about them and saw torches at each corner. 'They're just Scarimadaen, gentlemen,' he assured them. 'The voices you listen to are nothing but the fear in your own hearts. We will not submit to them, *do you hear?*'

They murmured in agreement, though not too convincingly. 'This is but a parlour trick,' William added, and walked over to the first corner of the room where a hollow length of wood was propped, stuffed with oil-soaked grass. He raised the torch and lit the grass, which burst into flame, then he marched to the second, igniting this in its turn. When at last he returned to their side, four torches were aflame and the azure light no longer played on their fears. The temple room was completely lit.

They relaxed and concentrated on the task at hand. 'We need to destroy the whole room and the Hoard,' William told them. 'That hole in the centre . . . How deep do you think it is?'

Jericho took a deep breath and walked gingerly down the steps, concentrating on where he was treading in the torchlight while blocking out the clamour nearby. He ignored the Hoard for a fraught few moments and stared down into the gaping pit. There was no bottom to it and it seemed to fall away for ever, causing his spine to tingle, his balance to teeter. He stepped back and laughed nervously. 'Very deep, Captain,' he called. 'Deep enough to lose the Hoard in.'

William was relieved. 'Jericho can lash a keg of powder to the platform support down there, and run a fuse under the bridge. And then you and I will lay some powder around the pillars here and put the rest of the two kegs at opposite corners. That should destroy the Hoard and bring down the temple,' he said to his lieutenant.

'Only if the explosive is strong enough,' Peruzo said quietly to him.

'Engrin has never let me down,' William replied. 'Jericho, make sure you tie up that wound. Don't let a drop of your blood touch a Scarimadaen.'

Jericho nodded and looked to the cuts on his arm and cheek.

'What about me?' Marco asked.

'You can help Jericho. But keep away from the Scarimadaen, understood?'

The stars of worlds trillions of miles away began to shine brighter in the sky above the mountain, yet during those passing minutes nothing in the whole universe seemed as important as the process now at work inside the temple. The men within laboured wearily, yet spurred on by the sacrifices already made that day. They summoned up new strength, and carried out the tasks William assigned them.

Peruzo opened the first keg and filled the grooves of the flagstones around the pillars of the temple, laying a trail to a length of fuse that William had fixed to run out of the temple entrance. It would burn for ten minutes only, and William hoped he had the strength in his legs to run down the steps before the temple exploded.

While Peruzo worked on the pillars, William joined two lengths of fuse together and then trailed another down the steps to the platform. He handed Marco the end of the fuse and showed him how to tie it to the length that Jericho carried as he made his way carefully across the bridge.

With one length of rope tied about his waist and a second looped over his shoulder, Jericho stepped bravely off the bridge and onto the platform. Under his left arm was a keg of powder and in his right hand was a fuse that he let drop over the side as

433

he crossed the end of the bridge. The keg was heavy and the way around the Hoard was precarious, yet he closed his eyes until he could barely see and ripped up his shirt to tie rags about his ears to dampen the chorus of the Scarimadaen. He would not look at the pyramids; *he would not listen*. He would only follow his captain's orders.

As he navigated around the Scarimadaen, he looped the first rope around the Hoard. Then he gave a short, firm tug to see if it would hold the rope in place. The first tug was fine. As was the second, and he squinted back along the bridge to where Marco was standing holding the other end of the rope. Marco nodded at him nervously, sweat dripping from his brow.

Jericho nodded back and began to abseil over the edge of the platform, the keg still under his left arm. From the far edge of the chasm he had spotted a small natural ledge six feet below the platform. He aimed for this now. He swung precariously for a while as he let himself slowly drop, his feet seeking out purchase on the rock. When his feet reached the outcrop, he edged himself closer in and let go of the rope with his right hand to find a hand-hold on the column.

Marco felt the rope give and breathed sharply. Beads of sweat dripped off his chin and down his arms, as he anticipated disaster. Yet Jericho did not swing away, but stayed fixed to the column as if his hand was glued to it.

About two feet to Jericho's right, in the irregular surface of the column, was a broad schism in the rock. It was a vertical cleft, shallow at top and bottom, but wide and deep in the centre. Jericho turned round so his back was against the column. He inched sideways and then leaned over to the cleft and slowly pushed the keg into it. He then lashed the second rope from his shoulder around the keg and the opposing sides of limestone. Using the rope which Marco held, he swung around the column in a full circle until the second rope was taut around the keg and the column, pressing it further inside the cleft.

Trying to ignore both the vertiginous drop below and the unholy chorus of the Hoard above, Jericho climbed up the rope and reached for the trailing fuse that he'd thrown over the edge of the bridge. After two attempts he snatched the end and drew it to him, then dropped gradually down the rope again to the ledge. Once there, he slipped the fuse into the keg and made it secure.

Throughout he kept glancing back at Marco to make sure the boy was concentrating. Even with all the hard work done – the keg secured and the fuse running from it to the other side of the chasm – Jericho could see the Scarimadaen were working on Marco's attention. Despite his best efforts to watch Jericho, his eyes were straying, looking up at the prize.

And what a prize . . .

. . . The Scarimadaen were piled up, almost bleeding into each other. The humming that had been so constant when they first entered grew into something else, a song, a wailing of tortured voices and broken whispers.

Marco.

His jaw grew slack. His mind began to waver and break open, his thoughts to spin and churn into a tempest.

Marco. Marco. Marco. Marco . . .

He shook his head and rubbed his eyes. They were talking to him. These strange, small pyramids of metal, of stone, of vapour and blood and shit and water and sand . . .

Marco. Marco. Marco. Marco. Come to us . . .

Marco stepped forward once more, the rope in his hands slipping away, the song drowning his ears, pouring into them, down his throat, drinking the morose wailing as though it were honey. Before him, the Scarimadaen reflected his face, his heroism, his desires. He took more steps forward until he could see himself clearly in the pyramid of water, rippling and cascading down itself. The rope slipped further through his fingers.

Jericho grabbed hold of the rope as he saw Marco falter. Panicking, he climbed the rope as fast as he could, drawing deep breaths in his haste as Marco wobbled.

Marco. Come . . .

Marco reached out his hand and the rope fell from his grasp.

Jericho reached the side of the platform just as the rope fell slack and he dangled from the edge. The end of the rope fell from the bridge into the chasm below. Cursing, he swung his leg over the edge and the tip of his boot scraped the side of the Scarimadaen. At once blue light writhed out and struck the leather, recoiling from the touch of dead skin. Jericho pushed himself up as the choir grew louder, the voices screeching through the cloth about his ears.

William heard them too and looked down from the steps to see his nephew moving across the bridge towards the light. The voices were striking out at Marco in unison as though a horde of castrati were trapped inside the pyramids. Hypnotized, Marco could do nothing more than reach out to the nearest Scarimadaen – the one composed of smoke.

'Stop!' Jericho warned and leapt forward. He was unbalanced and almost fell from the bridge as he pulled Marco away. 'Gods, boy! What the hell are you doing?'

Marco looked back at him blankly. 'The voices . . .'

'Don't listen to them, Marco. Don't make that mistake,' Jericho said and led him away.

Marco felt the urge to pull from him, to go forward and be with these strange singing pyramids that shone so beautifully, but as they got further away, he grew sick, his head reeling, his stomach rebelling until he arrived back at the steps above and vomited in the corner.

'Are you all right?' Jericho whispered to him.

'They promised me . . .' he said, and shook his head.

'They promised you the world, I am sure,' Jericho said and snorted. But he too felt terrified, unnerved by the power of the Hoard. They had promised him much when he first neared them. A kingdom of eternity, power unimaginable. To sit at the right hand of the Traitor. Of the Prince of Hell himself.

Jericho looked over to William. 'It is done, sir,' he said, a little relieved. 'The keg is secure under the platform and the fuse runs directly under the bridge. When it goes up, it should take the platform with it.'

'Good,' William replied, and then looked over to Marco. 'What happened to him? Was he hurt?'

'Just overcome. It is a persuasive treasure, Captain.'

'A *deadly* one,' William replied. 'Take him outside. Let him get some fresh air . . . and then the two of you can return down the mountain. Make sure the Bedouins leave here as quickly as possible.'

Jericho nodded and took another look at the Hoard, for the last time. 'Must we destroy them?' he heard himself say. 'Can't we take just one to Rome?'

'Not one,' William said resolutely, remembering the remaining vampyre. 'Go now. Warn our allies they must leave. I will not wait long.'

Jericho helped Marco to his feet, who resisted long enough to look to his uncle. 'I understand now,' he said to him. 'I understand why they must be destroyed, Uncle.'

William smiled and patted him on the shoulder. 'Then you are learning,' he said. 'There is no greater evil in this world than what lies here. Wait for me at the foot of the mountain.'

Marco nodded and allowed himself to be led away.

△ V △

Peruzo patted the side of the keg. It was half full and he rested it near the temple entrance. He sat on it, the wood resisting his weight with a low creaking sound, as William walked up the steps after inspecting the fuse. He was sweating heavily despite the chill in the air; the intensity of the Scarimadaen was oppressive.

'What happened to Marco?' Peruzo asked.

'It was a scare, little more,' William replied.

'The Scarimadaen seduced him?'

'For a moment only,' William said. 'I cannot blame him. His first encounter with a Scarimadaen, and there are hundreds of them.'

Peruzo got up from the keg and stretched. 'Not for much longer. I . . .' he faltered and quickly put his hand on his sword. '*Did you hear that?*'

'It's probably Jericho,' William said as he glanced over his shoulder.

'No . . .' Peruzo whispered. 'Someone else is out there. Skulking . . .'

William turned about and felt the hairs rise up on the back of his neck as he heard another footstep; a cautious one. His right hand went to Engrin's sword as Peruzo quietly stepped over to the wall by the entrance. William flanked him to the opposite side.

Peruzo saw a shadow, ever so slight, sliding towards them, and he rushed forward. He grabbed at a handful of robes, pulling them desperately. There was a yelp as he dragged them into view, unbalancing Peruzo; both he and the person he caught tumbled into the temple.

William drew his sword and pulled the fellow off his lieutenant. Levelling his sword to the assailant's face, he towed him into the light.

'Hammid?' William gasped.

The Arab was terrified.

'What the hell are you doing here?' William asked, even though it would elicit little response.

Peruzo got to his feet, furiously. 'Treacherous, sneaking . . .!' he began, placing the tip of his sword against the back of the Arab's neck.

William was too tired to gainsay Peruzo, and too tired and bewildered by Hammid's sudden appearance.

'He followed us, Captain,' Peruzo said as Hammid whimpered. 'I told you he couldn't be trusted!'

William stepped outside into the cold night air beyond the temple, Peruzo hauling Hammid after him. 'What should we do with him?' William asked.

'I'd like to throw him off this mountain,' Peruzo said angrily.

'There might be an innocent explanation,' William replied. 'He did save Sheikh Fahd's life.'

Peruzo seemed to back down slightly, but kept his sword close to Hammid, who began to keen like a baby. 'This scum is a traitor and a liar, Captain. Can we really tru—' Peruzo stopped abruptly. He seemed to lose his grip on Hammid's shirt, and then dropped his sword. He looked at William in despair and then began to fall forward.

'Peruzo!' William cried and caught him before he could hit the ground.

Behind the lieutenant, and behind Hammid, a figure emerged from the shadows, outlined by the half-moon. It pushed Hammid gently aside and looked down at William.

The figure was a man, tall, yet slouched slightly and favouring an arm that was held in a makeshift sling. His hair was matted with blood and his face was covered in the same grime of sand and rock dust. His clothes were torn, one sleeve missing completely, yet the man standing over William was unmistakable.

'*Thomas*,' William gasped.

'Captain Saxon,' Thomas Richmond greeted, bowing slightly.

William looked down to his lieutenant and felt a wound at Peruzo's back, wet and bloody. He didn't need to guess how it had been done, or who had done it: Thomas was twirling a sword in his good hand, the tip wet with Peruzo's blood. 'You bastard . . .' William hissed.

'I owed him that, Captain,' Thomas replied, and touched the scar at his cheek.

'How did you survive?' William said, trying to stall him.

'There was more than one loose bar in that pathetic cage of yours. I took a risk and tried to grab hold of the roots that held the wagon before it tore free. It *almost* worked,' Thomas replied and looked down at his own appearance. 'Apart from my arm, I was lucky. I landed in a patch of soil below, not the rock that obliterated my prison.'

William could feel the lieutenant's breath on his hand.

Peruzo was still alive, but that didn't mean he could fight. 'What are your intentions, Thomas?' William demanded.

'To take the Hoard for myself,' Thomas replied.

William laughed out loud, though his throat was dry and it came out as a fragile cackle. 'With an army of Bedouins below, not to mention my own men on this mountain? Surely your arrogance does not extend to the impossible?'

Thomas smiled. 'No, Captain. It doesn't. But as you have already demonstrated by getting here, *nothing* is impossible.'

Hammid crept away, hiding by the entrance. His eyes darted fearfully about, to Thomas, to William and then to Peruzo.

'As long as you die, Captain, that will be enough,' Thomas continued.

William grimaced. 'So this is revenge? For what? Why kill me now? You could have let the militia do it at Bastet.'

'I could have,' Thomas replied. There was hesitation there.

'You don't want to kill me, do you?'

'If I had the choice, I wouldn't,' Thomas replied, and then smiled viciously. 'But then I don't have that choice. You have orders, as do I. Mine were to ensure that *you* destroyed the Rassis and took the Hoard. Then *I* had to kill you and the lieutenant. With you both dead, your men will proceed with the mission as ordered and attempt to return the prize to Rome. Leaderless, the remains of your poor, poor company will be no match for Baron Horia. An army of one hundred kafalas have landed in Dumyat, Captain Saxon. They will move south to intercept any camel train carrying the Hoard of Mhorrer to Rashid. Against them, your leaderless company will be no match. Horia will spare no one.'

William coughed, his throat sore and clogged. 'And what do you get for this service, Thomas?' he croaked. 'Immortality?'

'Of course,' Thomas smiled.

'And Hammid? Will he be given the same?'

Thomas smiled over to the Arab who waited in the shadows. 'Alas, he will die of the black poison in his belly. He is being eaten from the inside, yet this cancer is nothing compared with his own cowardice. He was easy to turn back to my side, Captain. *Quite easy.*'

William dragged Peruzo into the temple, over to one of the pillars, and drew his sword. 'I won't be so easy, Thomas,' he said. 'You know I'll fight to the death.'

'Yes,' Thomas recognized, 'I know you will. I won't enjoy this, Captain Saxon. I quite liked you. But all friendships must end,' he said as he came towards him.

△ VI △

Jericho found it hard to convince the Bedouins they were in danger. He gestured as clearly as he could to the Arabs who were plundering the Rassis quarters, that the temple was about to explode, but made little impression on them. Even Marco could do nothing but shout until he was reduced to murmurs and hopeless shrugs.

'I know,' Jericho conceded. 'They won't listen to me. What is Arabic for a big bang?'

Several Suwarka were stealing glances at the two Europeans, one even laughing and pointing to Jericho's poor state. His shirt was in ribbons, and the rags he had tied about his ears were still hanging by his shoulders.

As Marco tried again to motion them to go, like trying to shoo a flock of geese about a farm, there was a commotion around the first flight of stairs and several Ayaida appeared, more urgent than the pillaging Suwarka. They had swords drawn and they were coming in Jericho's direction. Jericho, who was unarmed, froze. For one terrible moment it crossed his mind that the alliance with the Bedouins had been terminated and they had come to claim the Hoard for themselves. But as they approached they lowered their weapons and the foremost warrior handed Jericho a note. He looked over it and shook his head. It was in a language he did not understand, save for the name at the top, 'William Saxon', and the signature at the bottom, 'Sheikh Fahd'.

'What is this?' he said aloud and handed it to Marco.

'It's my uncle's language. English,' he replied.

'You can read this?'

Marco shook his head.

Jericho looked frustrated. 'Why can't everyone speak Latin?' he said and cursed. 'What shall I do? I cannot urge these men off the mountain, and I cannot read what the sheikh wants!'

He looked at the warriors before him, still with their swords drawn. 'I fear something has happened for these men to come to me like this. We must warn the captain.'

'He told us to stay here,' Marco said. 'What about the explosion?'

'We must delay it,' Jericho said gravely. 'If this sheikh has written so urgently to the Captain, it must be important.'

△ VII △

'I hoped this would not happen,' Thomas said as he swung the sword about and struck at William.

William raised Engrin's weapon and the blade rebounded off its edge, the momentum tipping him back until he was against the black walls of the temple. 'I can see the murder in your eyes,' William replied hoarsely. 'You've *always* wanted me dead.'

'Not true,' Thomas replied, stepping back breathlessly. They had been duelling for the past fifteen minutes, yet neither man was in much shape to fight. 'I had hoped one of the vampyres would have killed you. Or perhaps the Rassis. I didn't wish to be your executioner.'

'*You are lost!*' William shouted back at him. 'You will trade every ounce of humanity for something that is nothing. Neither daemon nor human! That is what it is to be vampyre, Thomas. A bastard offspring of neither. Cursed. Repugnant. Reviled. And hated by both sides. Didn't your master tell you?'

'Tell me what?' Thomas asked, sounding indifferent.

'That Hell has turned its back on Count Ordrane of Draak,' William said. 'Ordrane does not fight for the Devil. He fights only for himself. That is why the Rassis destroyed the vampyres, because they are more of an abomination than the daemons are. Is that what you crave, Thomas? To be something despised by both good and evil?'

Thomas laughed and raised his sword. 'I only want immortality, William. Nothing more,' he said and slashed forward towards William's left. William pulled up his hand quickly and swung his sword about to clatter along the back of Thomas's weapon. He then shoved him into the wall of rock and punched him in the kidneys with his left hand. He forgot his own wound and screamed out just as Thomas groaned. Blood spurted from the stumps of his fingers and William hopped back in agony, barely able to grip Engrin's sword. Thomas in turn staggered around, reaching in vain for his back with his damaged arm. Furiously, he lunged at William and shoulder-barged him, but the contact was light and William was only pushed across the temple towards the steps. He almost fell, and recovered, raising his sword in his right hand, trying to ignore the terrible pain in his left as he dripped blood over the temple floor.

Thomas leant against a pillar and breathed heavily. 'We're in such a state, you and I,' he said, and looked to William's hand. 'Though I fear you're in poorer shape than I am.'

'You deceive yourself, Thomas,' William growled back. 'I am the better swordsman.'

'We shall see,' Thomas murmured and smiled. Charging again, he brought the sword about, feinted to the left and then dashed right, swinging the blade towards William's collarbone. William reacted fast, but couldn't stop the tip of the sword from opening up his cheek, which split and bled profusely down his chin and neck.

'First blood to me, I think,' Thomas announced as William staggered back to where Peruzo lay. The lieutenant had not moved since Thomas had wounded him. If ever he needed

Peruzo's intervention it was now, but his trusted officer was either out cold or . . .

'He is dead, William,' Thomas called over. 'It was a mortal wound I gave Peruzo. Another death for *your* cause. Doesn't it feel like a hopeless one?'

William roared out defiantly and marched forward, furious that Thomas should ruin everything they had made sacrifices for. 'You. Will. Not. *Succeed!*' William shouted and rained down blow after blow on Thomas's sword. The attacks were unrelenting and drove Richmond to his knees. Brushing aside Thomas's weapon, William hacked through the makeshift sling and the blade cut through his forearm.

'Damn you, Saxon!' he cried out in agony.

'*Not I, Thomas. Not I,*' William hissed. '*You damn yourself.*'

Thomas looked up through red eyes, hatred blazing from them. 'You will not deny me my victory!' he declared and then kicked William. His boot connected with William's knee and he too uttered a groan of pain, falling to his side. Thomas dived after him, bleeding from the arm, but still clutching his sword. They grappled at the top of the steps, and traded punches with the hilts of their weapons. Thomas punched William on the cheek, splitting it further, and William swung his sword about in desperation, but the blow was too wild and he lost his grip on Engrin's sword once again. It flew across the temple and clattered against the wall near the entrance.

Elated, Thomas shifted his grip on his sword and leapt on William, pinning him to the floor, trying to use the weapon as a long dagger. William grabbed Thomas's arm as he strove with all his weight to drive the sword through William's chest. William felt his hold weakening, and he thrust his knee up between Thomas's legs, knocking the wind out of him. He seized Thomas's throat and they tumbled down the steps to the platform, each roll as painful as the last.

Thomas's sword fell from his hands and slid past them, clattering across the stone until it came to rest close by the bridge to the Hoard.

William struggled free and punched Thomas again. The traitor went down hard, but kicked out again and this time struck William's shin. A shooting pain burned through his knee, and he fell back hard, raking his spine on one of the steps. The pain grew nauseous.

Thomas crawled away and sat at the other side of the steps, nursing his bleeding arm. He looked over at William with contempt.

William could only feel sorrow and loss. 'Why, Thomas?' he murmured. 'Why did it come to this?'

'Because the Hoard is mine,' Thomas replied as he pulled himself from the steps. 'You cannot prevent that.'

'I can, and I will,' William replied doggedly and managed to stand, nursing the mangled mess of his left hand, and retching with nausea. His head swam and his eyes blurred as the light of the Scarimadaen fractured the shadows. *The Scarimadaen*, he thought suddenly, feeling blood dripping from his chin. The Hoard was a matter of feet from both men, who were shedding blood freely. It was only a miracle that not one drop had reached the side of a pyramid, releasing the daemon within.

He crawled away from the platform and up the steps, hoping that Thomas would do the same. *Does he know the danger?* William asked himself. If he did, he chose not to fear it. Instead Thomas looked ready to fight on, grinning stupidly through the dirt and blood that smeared his face.

William raised his right fist and stood threateningly. He needed a weapon, but his lay up the steps and out of reach.

As for Thomas's sword . . . William looked about and found it lying precariously at the edge of the chasm. He glanced over at Thomas, and he too had seen it, resting between them. William might have rushed for the sword as soon as he saw it, but the pain in his hand was too great and the threat of the Scarimadaen far too real. He stared at Thomas, waiting for him to make the first move as the chorus of the Hoard grew louder: it could sense a victor. It could sense blood.

'So . . .' Thomas slurred, '. . . it comes down to this.'

'Take it,' William goaded him. 'Go for the sword, Thomas. I won't stop you.'

Thomas looked at William long and hard. 'Why so eager to face your death, William?'

'I've faced death more times than you'll ever know,' William replied, ready to charge at Thomas the moment he went for the weapon. Just a quick shoulder-barge while the bastard bent down to retrieve his sword; a quick push into the chasm to the right and it would all be over.

As both men faced each other, neither ready to expose himself with the first move, they didn't notice another man enter until he calmly walked between them, bent down and picked up Thomas's sword.

'*Hammid?*' William gasped.

'Hammid!' Thomas repeated joyfully.

'Give me the sword, Hammid,' William called to him.

'Why would he?' Thomas chuckled. 'I have promised him much. More than you ever could. You can't compete with me, William.'

Hammid looked over to the captain of the Order. 'Hammid . . . Don't do it . . . He's lied to you. He's lied to all of us . . .' William pleaded, shaking his head.

Weighing Thomas's sword in his hand, Hammid stared at William and began to back away.

'Hammid *please!*' William said hopelessly as the Arab stepped closer to Thomas.

'He can't understand you, William,' Thomas mocked as he opened his arms to Hammid. 'Admit it, you have lost! There are some causes that are worth fighting for. Was yours worth *dying* for, Captain William Saxon?'

William sagged as Hammid took the sword to Thomas, who laughed triumphantly as he reached out to take the weapon. Hammid offered it up . . . then turned it about and drove it through Thomas's chest. He choked as the cold steel pierced through rib and lung and emerged on the other side.

'Ha . . . *mmid* . . .'

446

'LIAR!' Hammid yelled in Arabic as he held on to the hilt of the sword, driving it deeper.

Blood frothed over Thomas Richmond's lips, seeping down each corner, and he tottered for a moment, staring blankly into the Arab's eyes. Then he grabbed Hammid by the throat, and with laboured and struggling movements he shoved him backward. Hammid lost his footing and the Arab's look of victory turned into horror as he stumbled and clawed the air, falling over the side of the chasm. William could do nothing but watch Hammid tumble away, his cries echoing up from the dark abyss below.

As Hammid's screams faded into oblivion, Thomas stood swaying on his feet, ready to follow Hammid into the darkness. More blood poured over his lips, and he staggered down the last steps, but at the final one he managed to stumble away and began to lurch over the bridge to the Hoard of Mhorrer. In turn the Scarimadaen's voices grew terrible and discordant. A babble of shrieks and pleading burst from every one of the two hundred and fifty pyramids. Light flickered over their surfaces in their longing for a host.

'No, Thomas!' William implored, realizing his intentions.

Peruzo opened his eyes a fraction. He vaguely heard the tumult of struggle about him, vaguely heard the goading and the torment. He even heard the death cries of one, but could not tell who it had been.

And now there were more sounds, of voices calling him, not from the Scarimadaen, but from outside. Raised voices calling his and William's names. He parted his bloodied lips, but the weak breath from his punctured lung could barely make a sound. He groaned, moved his head and looked to the entrance, just as William shouted out below.

'There's another way, Thomas!' William shouted out to him.

Thomas Richmond looked over his shoulder, and shook his head. He stood mere feet from the Scarimadaen, which now seemed to shriek in approval, a wave of excited voices that rocked the temple with anticipation as Thomas took hold of the sword jammed into his chest. He knew there was no victory for him, but nor would he let William win the day. With a look of triumphant defiance, Thomas drew out the sword. His blood sprayed over the Scarimadaen before him.

William turned away and flung himself doggedly up the steps, driven by the dreadful shriek behind and the fear of what was to come. William had seen enough possessions before to know that a Scarimadaen would reach for its victim and incinerate his soul as it invaded him, but with the multitude of pyramids before Thomas, William could only guess at the effect of so many released Scarimadaen.

He got to the top step and lurched over to Peruzo. As he reached his side, the entrance to the temple was suddenly alive with Bedouins, led by Jericho and Marco.

'Uncle!' Marco shouted out and ran into William's arms.

Jericho looked over to the screams and bursts of lightning that came from the centre of the temple, and the colour drained from his face. He saw a nest of viperous filaments of azure light writhing above the form of Thomas Richmond. Where his blood had sprayed upon the Hoard, the light of the Scarimadaen drank deep on those warm beads, and hungrily dozens of tendrils sought out more of it. Thomas appeared to fall sideways, his body almost drained of life, but the strands of light coiled themselves about the torso and held him on the bridge, searing through his flesh. Thomas's clothes caught fire and he ignited as the nest of light writhed again, one strand more vibrant than the rest licking the air and stretching from the gathering tentacles of incandescence. It swung about, dipped and thrust itself down Thomas's throat to the joyous chorus of the Scarimadaen.

Jericho turned away in disgust, while William was comfortable only to hear Thomas's screams cut short as his soul was burnt to ash. He had no love for Thomas Richmond now, but once there had been a friendship there – an affinity that William could not discard as easily as Thomas had. It was this that forced

William to turn away from the terrible torture and the rending of flesh and bone that suddenly occurred. It stopped him from looking on as Thomas's body was rent apart, stretched and cauterized out of all recognition, bloated and deformed into a horror twice as tall, and infinitely more terrifying.

Peruzo reached up through the din and whispered to William: '*The fuse* . . .'

William got to his feet and took Marco's sword from him. He staggered down the steps and hacked the fuse through, tossing one end over the side and down into the abyss before the flames from the burning body could light it prematurely. As he did so, he looked up and the remaining colour drained from his face as he saw the abomination that had been Thomas Richmond.

It was erect and gigantic, a beast nearly twelve feet in height. The warping of the host's body had ripped open vein and sinew, knitting them back in a weave of blackened and smouldering flesh and muscle, so that the legs were like poles of matted cartilage, twice as long as before; the arms were thin and fine, fused into a knotwork of bone and tissue. The head had suffered disfigurement as great and appalling as the rest of the body. The skull was split open, stretched on a distended collar so that it hung behind the column of twisted neck, the weight of its swollen face and jaw keeping it from lolling backwards completely. The chops were loose, flapping wildly amid huge rolls of smoke and sparks of blue light. Fire flashed across what once had been teeth, licking up the side of the mouth over the smoking remains of Thomas's beard. The light continued to flare down through the torn nasal cavities, while above the nose, teardrops of flame leaked from the haemorrhaged eye-sockets, each the size of a fist. The fire burned itself out before it hit the ground and turned into balls of smoke that scattered before it.

Looking away, William drew on his fading strength to trudge back up the steps. 'We must leave,' he said, and pointed down at Peruzo. 'Help me carry him.'

Peruzo shook his head and beckoned William close. He put

his ear to Peruzo's lips and struggled to hear him above the shriek of appalling torture from the pit below.

'I have to stay . . .' the lieutenant murmured.

'We can carry you,' William protested.

'There's a daemon here . . .'

'Yes, this is why we must go.'

'The powder around the pillars, William . . . We can still destroy it – all of them. Give me a torch . . .'

'There's no time, my friend. The temple would be destroyed with you inside it.'

'But so would . . . the daemon . . .'

William turned his head to look Peruzo in the eyes. There was little sparkle left in them, but the lieutenant's grey face had formed a contented smile. It was fragile enough, but he was already resigned to dying.

'I must . . . I must . . .'

William swallowed down his sadness, and tears began to roll down his cheeks. 'I know,' he replied.

'I'll give you . . . enough time . . . You must go . . . *Now*.'

William nodded and took hold of Peruzo's hand. He looked up at the others. 'Jericho, get them out of here.'

Jericho hardly heard William but was staring down at the abomination that had been Thomas Richmond. The daemon opened its mouth wider than it could conceivably manage until the bottom jaw hung down its belly, spewing out smoke and cinders.

And then it spoke: '*DOOMDARRRR* . . .'

The syllables were nonsense, but the sheer shock of hearing the daemon address them at all shook Jericho to the marrow. Never in the history of the War had a daemon talked through its host. This was not just a devil conjured by a box of tricks, but something greater. Something more powerful than any of them had seen before.

'Jericho!' William shouted again, this time furiously. Marco pulled on Jericho's arm, too afraid to look at the daemon himself. 'Get them out of here!' his uncle ordered.

Jericho half staggered and was half pulled away by Marco, who was eager to escape the horror growing from the pit. The Ayaida who hadn't fled from those infernal cries now shook off their paralysis, throwing down their swords and torches in their desperate flight from the daemon climbing from below. Jericho and Marco followed after them.

William reached over and took one of the discarded torches from the floor. He handed it to his lieutenant, regarding him proudly. 'I'll say a prayer for you, my friend.'

'Say several, William Saxon,' Peruzo replied and smiled weakly. 'It was a pleasure to . . .'

'The pleasure was mine.' William pulled himself to his feet and stepped away, taking a last glance at the daemon, the warped horror of what had once been Thomas Richmond.

Thomas's body could not cope with the daemon's essence. At any moment it seemed the unholy merging of mortal flesh and immortal spirit would split asunder in a geyser of ash and light, yet the daemon stepped elegantly forward, rolls of smoke billowing before it. It raised its blackened, sinewy arms to William and shouted again: '*DOOMDARRRR . . .*'

William backed away. He paused to retrieve Engrin's sword from where it had landed, and then fled the temple.

△ VIII △

The procession of fleeing Bedouins was infectious. The panic that spilled from the first Ayaida to take flight spread to the other Bedouins scavenging the Rassis dead; very soon these too began to flee. But while some of the tired Aquila and Tarabin followed at a slower and more uncertain pace, the fresher Suwarka were more wary and some even scoffed at their warnings: 'The Devil is coming! The Devil is coming!'

That is until Marco and Jericho and the remaining Ayaida appeared at the temple doorway and rushed down the stairs towards them. This time the Suwarka *were* concerned and the terrible howling roaring from above gave them cause to panic. Fearing that the Devil would descend upon them, they turned tail and fled with their trophies, some dropping Rassis masks or swords in their haste.

In the chaos, Marco halted abruptly and stared back up the steps.

'Marco!' Jericho called to him as he dashed to the next flight of steps after the fleeing Bedouins.

'I won't leave without him!' Marco shouted back.

'Blast you!' Jericho cursed and grabbed hold of the boy's arm. He wouldn't budge, and only when William appeared, hobbling and puffing down the stairway, did Marco relent and the three of them try to escape.

△ IX △

Peruzo battled to stay conscious. He could feel little except for the warmth of the torch flame near his cheek. The light of it was blinding, but he could still see a shadow shuddering up the stone steps inside the temple; crashing closer with the stench of sulphur growing.

Peruzo opened his eyes as much as he was able, the better to view this abomination. He was eager to face his last enemy.

The daemon appeared above the top step before its feet were halfway up the rise. It glowered down at Peruzo and at the flame in his hand, its burning eyes triumphant in their warped sockets. As it rose higher and higher with each step, the daemon opened its mouth and belched a flurry of seething sparks over the landing that only missed the trailing end of cut fuse by mere feet. It was followed by a belch of sulphuric smoke that made Peruzo cough.

He smiled, quite pleased with the creature before him. He had never met a foe so challenging, and doubted that anyone else had.

'The stuff of legends . . .' Peruzo murmured as his vision

452

began to tunnel. His hand seemed to droop a little and then the torch fell out of his fingers as he died. It landed to the side, near the thin line of gunpowder poured through the cracks of the flagstones around the pillar. The flames writhed about for a moment and then the gunpowder ignited.

△ X △

They had just started down the second flight of steps when the first explosion came. It rumbled above them like a distant earthquake, preceded by a brilliant flash of light. William paused momentarily to see it happen, but then urged Jericho and Marco on down the steps, their path uncertain in the dark of night.

The next two explosions moments later shook the stairs and William fell. Marco heard him drop and turned back, rushing up the steps to take his arm. They reeled along the quaking stairway, pieces of the temple falling in a hail of stone. Larger pieces fell at their feet, and it was pure luck that neither of them was struck on the head: the chunks would have staved in their skulls.

A fourth explosion followed fast after the second and third. It appeared to be closer than the last, had that been possible, and there was a bright flash that lit up all the steps for a moment. The sound was colossal and Jericho stumbled forward, falling against the side of the stairway. He put his hands over his head as more rock and dust rained over them, William too dazed to move, while Marco hung on.

The last detonations were the worst. The remains of the temple blazed with white light, stronger than the rising sun, and the world about the peak turned to day for the briefest of moments. Then the ground trembled, heaving about as though an unseen titanic hand was moving beneath it. The stairway split apart. Huge fissures tore through the quaking rock, and blindly again they retreated, lost in the storm of rock dust and pelting scree. At one point William believed he might simply stumble

453

sightlessly over the edge. He had no idea where he was going, and yet Jericho guided them forward.

Too weak to go on, and with the fissures along the stairs widening, now they collapsed on the steps where they stood and simply huddled by the wall of rock, hoping to ride out the worst of it. Jericho held on as best he could, and William sat back, his arm around Marco, who clung to his uncle and huddled against the stairs as they bucked about. William closed his eyes and waited for the world to open up and swallow them whole.

Soon after that, the temple above them collapsed. It fell inwards, the pillars no longer standing to support it. The Hoard of Mhorrer and the remaining keg of gunpowder tied to the platform were sucked into the abyss below.

They were followed in their descent by the shattered torso of the daemonic prince, blown apart by the first of the blasts. Its flaming body overtook the Scarimadaen and debris and collided with the keg of powder. At once the keg exploded, and then the mountain's peak did the same with a catastrophic roar.

Chapter Twenty-two

Graves of Stone

△ I △

Next morning there were stories of heroism. Tales of sons and fathers helping each other to escape the avalanche of rock. Stories of men carrying the wounded, even stories of sacrifice. But some stories were more incredible than others.

The Ayaida who had witnessed the daemon gave the most vivid accounts. It was the daemon, they said, that brought down the mountain. Sheikh Fahd had other ideas, yet they were only confirmed when three men were carried before him; three white ghosts plastered in the rock dust that covered them from head to toe.

'You did this?' he asked William, who was supported by both Marco and Jericho. William had sprained his ankle during the flight from the temple and it was still quite sore – that and the other wounds to his cheek and his hand.

William smiled slightly. 'It wasn't entirely my fault.'

'My people believe the Devil caused the collapse of the mountain,' Fahd said.

'That is closer to the facts, sir,' William replied.

Sheikh Fahd crossed his arms a little sceptically, but his previous experience of the vampyre and the Rassis was enough to convince him that maybe it *was* true. 'What about your prize?'

'Destroyed,' William said wearily. Jericho lowered him to the ground and William sat, his aching leg stretched out in front of him. He rubbed gently at the ankle and looked up at Fahd. 'Thank you for trying to warn me.'

'Ah . . . The letter,' Fahd replied.

'It was a little late,' William admitted. 'But I thank you anyway.'

'I thought it was the Rassis who had killed Mazin's men. Was I right?'

'No. It was Thomas Richmond,' William replied.

'But Richmond was killed . . .'

'He wasn't. But he is now. So is Hammid,' William said sadly, remembering Hammid's brave act. 'And so is my lieutenant.'

'You have lost your prize, and your men,' Sheikh Fahd remarked. 'I am sorry for that.'

'Don't be,' William murmured and looked over his shoulder. 'The mission was a success. The Hoard is no more.' But as he looked to the mountain, nothing more now than a hill that resembled a dormant volcano, William felt the loss of Peruzo keenly. He had not expected to leave the lieutenant on that mountain. That had been one sacrifice too many.

'At least you live, Captain Saxon,' Sheikh Fahd said, appearing to read William's thoughts, 'as do your nephew and some of your men.'

William regarded Marco and Jericho in turn as they sat by their captain. He felt immensely proud of both of them. Against all odds, they had survived the mission.

△ II △

The army that was – the army of the Ayaida, Tarabin, Aquila and Suwarka, and the grey-clad Europeans – did not leave the Valley of Fire until two days later. They spent that time digging a mass grave for their dead, and much sombre and sorrowful prayer was conducted for their passing.

William cleaned himself up as best he could and attended the funerals of the Bedouins, specifically of Sheikh Anwar and

Mazin's son. They were given honoured cremations away from the mass pyres of the hundreds of other Bedouins who had lost their lives in the battles.

Finally, William returned to the grave of the monks of the Order, a grave gratefully dug by Fahd's people. It was a long trench, where the men of the Order lay side by side as they had fought. Jericho had provided markers, a weapon of the Order thrust into the ground beside each brother. As with the tribesmen, oil was poured over each man, and Sheikh Fahd handed William a torch which burned brightly even in the afternoon sun. Prayers were spoken, and William was struck by overwhelming sadness as he listened to the song of a lone Bedouin who attended the funeral.

Then William tossed the torch into the pit and the bodies were aflame.

Afterwards, Jericho stood apart with Marco, his expression likewise numbed by sadness. He had grown to know each of the monks during their journey from Rashid. They had bonded like true brothers and Jericho had learned much. Each face was one he would never forget, from the joking Ettore to the gallant Donato.

There had been bodies that could not be found, among them Brothers Filippo and Vincent, and of course Lieutenant Peruzo. Marco and Jericho had dug anonymous graves themselves and placed something by them to mark the three lost men.

William looked across the grave in silence. He could not think of a fitting prayer, nor a psalm, and part of him was too angry to say any hymn. He felt betrayed, betrayed by God's guardians: the Dar'uka. They had forgotten them, and forgotten their mission. William and his company had sacrificed their lives for something the Dar'uka should have willingly taken part in. There was no excuse for their betrayal and this enraged William further.

He clamped his teeth together against his emotions and lifted his face to the sun. 'There is little a survivor can say on occasions such as this,' he began. His voice roused Marco and Jericho and they stood upright, only moving when they noticed Sheikh Fahd, Galal and Mazin appearing behind William. Quietly, the leaders of the Bedouin tribes stood by as William continued with the service.

'A warrior goes into battle knowing that he may die. A captain goes into battle knowing that those he commands may die. And yet, when your brothers fall, there is no victory on this earth that can justify their deaths,' William said, his voice breaking. 'Our mission may have been the most vital mission for any warrior on this earth, but I would not count a thousand Scarimadaen worth the life of any of you who have died under my command. You were the best soldiers . . . The best *men* I have had the privilege to lead. And you had the best lieutenant there has been. A man of infinite courage, honour and friendship. And I will miss greatly Lieutenant Carlo Peruzo, as I miss all of you.

'May God grant you peace . . .'

Marco wiped his eyes and was comforted by Jericho. Marco had known Peruzo almost as long as his uncle, and now there would be no more secret fencing lessons, or discussions about tactics. He would no longer hear about his uncle's exploits through that silver-haired lieutenant of the Order.

William lowered his head in quiet prayer and turned from the grave. He was surprised to find the three sheikhs standing behind him and bowing humbly. William bowed back to them, solemnly.

'It is done, Captain Saxon,' Sheikh Fahd said.

'It is,' William conceded. He walked from the grave and Sheikh Fahd joined him away from the others. 'I understand Brother Orlando is making a fine recovery.'

'Are you so surprised my physician could take good care of your man?'

'Just grateful,' William lied. From all accounts he had expected Orlando to die from his wound, yet the monk had spoken to William that very morning and was taking in water following the fever. 'There could be another battle ahead of us. I need every man who can stand.'

'You speak of this vampyre?' Sheikh Fahd said. William nodded. 'You can count on the Ayaida, William Saxon, for help.'

'Your people have done enough, sir. I cannot ask anything more of them,' William replied.

'After yesterday, I am sure they would follow you, as I would. And perhaps even the Aquila and Tarabin. Maybe even Mazin's people. You are a legend in their eyes, and they'll tell stories about you for generations to come,' Sheikh Fahd said. '*The man who conquered an army of ghosts and destroyed a mountain.* There has never been such a story before. They would die to keep that legend alive. You may call it an obligation, if you wish.'

William thought about this and then turned around quickly. He paced a few steps, stopped and then shook his head. 'They don't have to,' he said distantly. 'Maybe there *is* one thing you can do for me.'

'Ask what you will,' Sheikh Fahd offered.

'I need to write two letters . . . Would your fastest rider deliver them for me?'

Fahd nodded.

'The first letter will be for a man called Andreas, who is staying at the British consulate in Alexandria. He is our only point of contact in Egypt and must be apprised of our situation.'

'And the other?'

'The other letter will be trickier, I think, for it must go to your enemy – the commander in chief of the Rashid militia: a man known as Khalifa. And I will need your help to write it, for he will not understand Latin or English.'

'If he can read at all . . .' Fahd mocked. 'Why Khalifa?'

'He made a similar promise to yours, yet he has not suffered as much as the Ayaida, and I think this obligation would rather suit him. If he agrees, then the vampyre and his army of kafalas will no longer be a problem.'

'And if he doesn't?'

'I'll need more than luck to get back to Rome,' William laughed bleakly.

'Once you have written your letters, we will leave this place,' Sheikh Fahd announced.

'I can write them on the way to your camp,' William said. He looked out at the ruined mountain and the burning graves at its foot. 'We should not stay in the valley much longer.'

'But there is no danger, Captain Saxon,' Fahd remarked cheerfully. 'The ghosts are defeated.'

'No, Sheikh Fahd,' William disagreed. 'There are more ghosts here than ever before.'

Epilogue

Marco watched patiently as the monks packed up the camp. The remnants of the company – those brothers who had stayed with the Ayaida to recuperate – struggled against old and healing wounds, but they were as efficient as usual. They would leave little for the morning, except for their tents, blankets and what they would eat from. Apart from their rifles, which they would carry with them, the weapons were all stowed away. It was the last of a long list of actions that marked their final days in the Sinai, and despite having blended into the Bedouin culture quite easily over the past weeks, they all seemed glad to be going home. Including the man who stood with Marco, looking past the monks to the horizon.

He could have passed for any Bedouin. He was dressed in their dark robes and wore a white keffiyeh head-dress that was tied about his head with an agal. His face was tanned but paler than most Arabs, and he was smooth-shaven. His demeanour was serious, yet calm.

As a gentle breeze fluttered the ends of his keffiyeh, William Saxon closed his eyes against the sun and sighed. He had enjoyed staying with the Ayaida. Their hospitality was equalled only by the people of Villeda, and he had quickly become firm friends with Sheikh Fahd. Often they would go hunting together, or riding along the desert passes. At night William sat in Fahd's company and they talked about matters such as the British empire or life in Rome. Not once did they speak about the Valley of Fire. This was left to the storytellers of the tribe, who spun tales and songs about their exploits.

(It was Jericho who regaled the remaining monks with the full story of the battle, having experienced it from the point of the first assault to the rise of the daemonic prince and the explosions that followed. He embellished Peruzo's death, imagining what their lieutenant had done in his final moments: his brave defiance and sense of victory. It was a story that would live on beyond the cloth walls of the Bedouin tents, across the waters to Rome and in the cobbled streets of Villeda.)

But there came a time for them to leave, and after staying with the Ayaida for over a week, William announced to Sheikh Fahd they were to head home. The sheikh was disappointed but understood. He felt he would be losing a friend, but William promised otherwise.

Marco was also sad to be leaving. He was quite the centre of attention since their return from the Valley of Fire. Jamillah had recovered from her wound and they spent much time together – with a chaperone of course. William had teased Marco about this, saying they would be married in no time.

'No, no!' Marco had protested. 'I couldn't possibly marry her!'

'I thought you loved her,' William had remarked.

'I do,' said Marco, '. . . But I want to return home with you.'

'To Villeda?' William said wistfully and sighed, remembering that a vampyre and an army of kafalas still lay between them. 'As do I.'

'If I marry Jamillah, I cannot return home. If I marry Jamillah, I cannot join the Order,' Marco added cheekily.

William had eyed him then and crossed his arms. 'After everything we have been through, you still wish to become an initiate?'

Marco nodded cheerfully.

'I see,' William conceded.

'I have learnt so much,' Marco explained. 'And you promised.'

'I may have,' William replied.

'With more training, I can be a better monk,' Marco said. 'I won't fail you.'

William smiled sadly. 'You never have,' he admitted, and embraced his nephew. 'You proved yourself time and time again, Marco. If this is what you really want, I will not stand in your way.'

'Then I can join?'

'The Order would be poorer without you.'

Marco hugged his uncle back, then stood to attention. 'You will not regret this, Captain.'

That evening, as the brothers continued to pack and William watched nearby, Sheikh Fahd emerged from the cluster of Bedouin tents. Marco bowed to him, as was the custom, and the sheikh dismissed it with a playful wave. 'Please, Marco, don't be so humble,' he said in English, and Marco frowned, not understanding a word he said. As usual, this caused Sheikh Fahd to laugh heartily. 'Your nephew needs to learn another tongue, William.'

'He will be learning plenty in Villeda, my friend,' William replied, patting Marco on the shoulder.

'So still I cannot persuade you to stay?' the sheikh grumbled.

'Alas, no,' William replied.

'That makes me sad,' Fahd said, and he shrugged. 'The very least we can do is celebrate your time here. Tonight we will hold a great feast.'

'For us?'

'Of course,' Sheikh Fahd said, delighted. 'Song, dance and more stories. And good food, of course.'

'It will be our pleasure,' William said politely, but judging from the revelry that had occurred when they returned from the Valley of Fire several days ago, he doubted the term 'celebration' would do any of the festivities full justice.

'And I have some other news which may interest you,' Fahd said. 'A short while ago, a rider returned from south of Dumyat.

There was a battle there between a foreign army and the militias of Rashid and Dumyat.'

'A foreign army?' William said hopefully. 'Who were they?'

'I do not know. Only that the infidels landed illegally near Dumyat and were crossing the desert during the night. The militias ambushed them in the passes. Many were killed.'

'Was a vampyre mentioned?'

Fahd shook his head.

'I can think of no other foreign invader who would land so near to the Sinai,' William explained, '*and* I'm also eminently optimistic.'

'A vampyre was not mentioned in the report,' Fahd said sadly. 'But then fate has been good to you so far, it might be again. If it were these kafalas you have told me about, then your way back to Rashid will be a safe one. I will pray to Allah it is so. And Allah has not ignored my prayers of late, William Saxon.' He put his hands on his hips benevolently and grinned. 'I will leave you now. I have a great feast to prepare for, and must dress for the occasion. Your uniforms are clean, I believe. Will you wear the regalia of your Order for dinner?'

'If it pleases you, I will continue wearing the robes you have given me, Your Highness,' William replied light-heartedly.

'Splendid, old boy,' Sheikh Fahd joked; the English expression sounded odd coming from the Bedouin, yet he carried it well – a testament to his teachers in Rashid, and to William, who chuckled a little as he watched the burly Arab march back to his tent.

'You can wear my jacket if you wish,' William said to Marco. He nodded eagerly. 'You should go and ready yourself. Dress smartly for Jamillah. This will be the last night you see each other.'

Marco was suddenly forlorn, remembering that tonight would be one of goodbyes. He walked away with a heavy step, and William tried to remember what it was like to love at that age. Then he remembered Adriana and realized that young love was probably nothing compared with his feelings for her.

William spent the next ten minutes thinking about Adriana and what she would be doing right now: sitting on the porch, making bread, riding through the fields, or lying calmly in bed. Seeing her in his mind, he pined for her company, her embrace, her touch. And he knew it was time to go home.

'Uncle?'

William turned from his thoughts. 'I thought you were going back to dress?'

Marco looked scared. He shot a nervous glance over his shoulder to the desert outside the camp.

'What is it?' William said.

'There's someone out there who wants to speak with you.' Marco pointed out into the desert, the sands a blur in the sunset glare. It took a while, but by cupping his hand over his eyes, William discerned a shadow against the light.

'Who is that?'

Marco shook his head.

'Stay with the brothers.'

William set out across the sands, his right hand brushing the hilt of Engrin's sword. The touch was as comforting as ever, even if his left hand was shorn of a couple of fingers. He would have to retrain with the sword and discover his balance again, either that or hope that the artisans in Villeda could fashion false fingers to replace those the Rassis had taken.

As he passed the last of the Ayaida tents, William paused and looked out again to the shadow more than fifty yards away. The figure had retreated a little, but stayed close to the camp. William blew out his cheeks and wondered who or what it might be. If it was the vampyre, the move would be impudent, not to mention suicidal. But vampyres usually burned up in daylight.

William strolled out to the desert, squinting into the light. It was only as he got closer that he sighted a brilliance other than the sun. Blue light flickered about the shadow, shimmered around the shoulders, arms and legs, the sweep of the figure's black cloak. William now recognized the shadow, and he strode on with purpose, relaxing his grip on Engrin's sword, even though his heartbeat increased. As did his anger.

When he stopped a few feet short of the silent figure, William spoke.

'Where were you, Kieran?' he growled. 'As omniscient beings, you must know how many times I have cursed you and the Dar'uka. I'm surprised you found the courage to face me.'

Kieran stared at William, impassive as usual. 'It was always our intention to aid you against the Rassis, William,' he replied in those many tongues. The myriad voices were not as loud or capricious as before. They were far from united, and strangely subdued.

'Your *intention?*' William mocked, and uttered a bitter laugh. 'Do you know how many men I lost in the Valley of Fire? Your intentions have done nothing for our cause, Kieran. *Nothing.* The Hoard is destroyed because *we* destroyed it, not the Dar'uka. We needed you, and you forsook your duty to protect mankind. Damn you, Kieran. We are allies, yet you treat us as strangers.'

William paced about for a few moments, seeking calm. He stopped at last, and looked over his shoulder. 'I thought I could count on you and our friendship. I was wrong, and the cost was dear: Lieutenant Peruzo, many monks of the Order, a host of brave Bedouins. The brothers believed you would save them, even when I did not. Do you not see? Your betrayal cuts deeper than just our friendship.'

This comment brought no retort from Kieran, who simply stood and listened to William rage on. 'Why *are* you here, anyway? To apologize? To say sorry for missing the most important battle in the War?'

Kieran's eyes flashed, the azure light crackling across his face. 'I'm here to warn you.'

'*Warn me?*' William bristled. 'Is that a threat? What do you mean?'

'Marresca has betrayed the Dar'uka,' Kieran said coldly.

William could hardly believe his ears. Was this some ruse to escape a chiding, to explain away a flaw in their judgement? All he could do was mutter: '*Impossible.*'

'We once believed so, but we were wrong,' Kieran said firmly.

'But how could this happen?' William said in disbelief.

'We cannot say,' Kieran said. 'When he became Dar'uka we thought we could perceive his true thoughts. He hid them from us. He hid the truth.'

'But I was his captain. He destroyed vampyres with me. *He even destroyed daemons,*' William remarked incredulously. 'I cannot believe he would be disloyal.'

'He has deceived all of us, William. Including you.'

William shook his head in a daze. 'This can't be right . . .'

'Do not doubt it,' Kieran insisted. 'He betrayed the Dar'uka at Hell's Gate on Gran-Terra. There is no doubting his allegiance now.' Kieran fell quiet again and William noted the disquiet on his usually emotionless face. 'There are only three of us now. We do not know where or when Marresca may strike again. We are sure he was not acting alone.'

'You suspect another?'

'Yes. A traitor in the Vatican,' Kieran said.

'Cardinal Issias was killed seven years ago,' William reminded him. 'That traitor is dead.'

'There is another. That is why I have come to you. Not to warn you about Marresca, but about the traitor in Rome. With Marresca revealed, this traitor will certainly move against you and the Secretariat.'

William couldn't comprehend what this meant. He was too stunned by the revelation of Marresca's treachery to accept this hidden enemy in Rome.

'The Hoard is destroyed, but the War has not finished,' Kieran told William. 'There are other battles to fight. And should we lose them, then we will lose this War. Be vigilant, William, and remember what Engrin told you.'

'Trust no one,' William murmured.

Kieran nodded and turned away to walk back into the desert.

'Wait!' William shouted to him. The Dar'uka halted and looked round. 'Can I . . . Can I *at least* trust you?'

To William's pure amazement, Kieran smiled. It was unheard of to see the ice-cold warrior do so, and the transformation raised William's spirits. The Dar'uka walked back to William, keeping that smile, if a little awkwardly. 'Yes, you can trust me,' he said. 'You and I have always been friends . . . and always will be.'

William nodded, choking down his emotions. The Kieran he remembered had returned, if only for this moment.

'Look after yourself, William. Watch those around you,' Kieran added as he turned away.

'I will. Goodbye, Kieran,' William said and watched the Dar'uka leave for a second and final time.

He said little about the meeting to Marco, and nothing to the brothers. As Marco dressed, William stared into darkness. He felt no joy about their accomplishments now. The destruction of the Hoard of Mhorrer hardly seemed to matter now that Marresca stood revealed as a traitor. The War with Hell had taken an unexpected and terrible turn.

William felt deflated, wearied by the secret ambitions of those around him. He had been betrayed by Thomas, and now by Marresca. The one man he believed *had* betrayed him was still his friend, but William felt more vulnerable. The Dar'uka would be concentrating on finding Marresca, wherever he was. They would not be fighting the daemons on Earth.

And there was another matter, something just as serious, which William had so far ignored. What would happen when he returned to Rome? He had disobeyed Cardinal Devirus's orders. He had destroyed the Hoard instead, and while there had been nothing else to do at the time, he doubted the cardinal would see it that way, especially as William had involved the Bedouins in a legendary battle. He had been taken prisoner by the militia, and had broken so many rules of the Order that William would not be too surprised if he was excommunicated altogether. Given that the Father at the monastery of St Catherine was also likely to stir up a hornet's nest, William felt his chances back home were precarious.

With the prospect of another traitor working within the Vatican, only the thought of Adriana made him want to leave Sheikh Fahd's hospitality.

'What are you thinking about?' Marco said.

'What's that? Oh, nothing.'

'You are, you know. You've been miles away for the last quarter of an hour.'

'It's nothing, really. Are you ready?'

Marco nodded proudly, looking down at the grey jacket and shirt. As before, they were too big for him, but Marco had grown a lot over the past month or so, and he would soon fill out the uniform.

Outside the tent came sounds of celebration. They could hear music and chatter, and already the smell of cooking food and burning fires was enticing. Marco led William into the cold night air and William breathed in long and hard. Above them the stars wheeled majestically, yet William felt scant comfort. He had once imagined Kieran and the Dar'uka flying among them, fighting for the salvation of every man, woman and child on this world. Yet now these angels were fighting for their own survival.

And mankind? William realized they had to look after themselves for a while. As long as the Order remained, they would fight the War, fight on the Dar'uka's behalf, with William leading the struggle – he could not contemplate retiring from the Order now.

As Marco led him to the festivities, he realized that Lieutenant Peruzo had been right all along: there was no escape for Captain William Saxon from this secret war . . .

Special thanks from the author

This book and *The Secret War* would not have been possible if it weren't for the following people:

Will Atkins, Mike Barnard, Julie Crisp, Sophie Portas, and all the folks at Macmillan New Writing and Pan Macmillan. Louise Curran and Lee Harris for their help on the penultimate drafts of this book. Mel Hudson for *MFWCurran.com*. Family Curran, Family Hind, and the Macmillan New Writers community (*macmillannewwriters.blogspot.com*) for their unwavering enthusiasm and support. And friends of the past and the present who have always said I could make it, even when I thought I might not – your voices have helped silence my inner critic.

And finally to Sarah L. Curran – my muse, my inspiration and my greatest friend.

M.F.W. Curran
Sheffield, 7 April 2008